dying

by the hour

Kory M. Shrum

TIMBERLANE
PRESS

ISBN-10:   0-9912158-3-4

ISBN-13:   978-0-9912158-3-6

Praise for the Jesse Sullivan Novels

"Kory Shrum's writing is smart, imaginative, and insanely addictive! I have begun to think of her books as my Kory Krack. I beg of you to pick them up. You will NOT regret it!" -Darynda Jones, NY Times Bestselling Author of the Charley Davidson Series

"Sexy, Snarky, and supernaturally fantastic! This one has it all!" – Angela Roquet, acclaimed author of the *Lana Harvey, Reapers Inc. series*

"Twists, turns, and surprising endings–Jesse Sullivan marks a new era in urban fantasy."–Monica La Porta, Author of *The Ginecean Chronicles* and *The Immortal series*

"This book is filled with a cast of interesting characters … and a fat pug named Winston – all helping to solve the mystery around {Jesse Sullivan's} attack—and you have a fast-paced story, and a great start to the series!" -- LG O'Conner, author of the *The Angelorum Twelve Chronicles*

"Jesse makes a living by dying in other people's place because she's a Necronite and comes back to life. The whole Necronite condition was both interesting and creepy. The author did a great job of explaining it and making it real for the reader." –*Urban Fantasy Investigations*

"{Kory M. Shrum} writes Urban Fantasy which I truly believe will become the next BITTEN on TV… a series and an author whom we have special dedicated shelves too."—*Cabin Goddess Reviews*

William,

this one is for you

The Dying for a Living Series

Dying for a Living

Dying by the Hour

Dying for Her: A Companion Novel

Dying Light

Worth Dying For

dying by the hour

Jesse

When they describe female special agents in the movies, or in books, it's always like this: a sleek, cat-like body that slithers in tight clothing, gorgeous exotic face and a sultry voice that can lure any target into submission.

While I am a female agent, double agent even, I'm *not* sultry, exotic, cat-like, sleek or even remotely alluring. I'm an idiot wearing a clown suit. And I don't mean clown suit figuratively.

I am wearing a clown suit at a birthday party.

I have the red nose, the floppy shoes and this horn around my neck that honks obnoxiously every time a grubby kid with sticky fingers runs up and gives it a squeeze.

The *double* part is more complicated. Neither my official job nor my unofficial off-the-books job requires I wear a clown suit. Yet, here I am dressed as a clown because my current client Regina Lovett begged me to.

She apparently believes a clown is less terrifying to her daughter, the person she's hired me to protect, than just being a regular old death replacement agent. Death replacement agent is my "respectable" job—though that depends upon whom you ask. The double agent part of me is here to gather intel. This is the *only* reason I'm willing to jump through Regina's obnoxious hoops in order to keep her business. Usually I hold all the cards in a death replacement because without me, they *die*.

I'm not even sure Julia, turning four, will agree with her mother anyway. She's done a good job of keeping her distance from me, the red-nosed wonder, backing away slowly every time I offer her a balloon.

My floppy shoes squish against the ground saturated with six days of September rain. I rock on my heels and watch Julia twirl in her party dress, a good twenty feet away. It's a pretty lavender color, complete with lacey ankle socks and Mary-Janes. A tiny gray peacoat protects her from the elements. She looks like any other privileged upper-class kid, standing in a big, beautiful yard, her thick brown locks pulled up into curling pigtails that graze the top of each shoulder and the lacy white collar of her dress. A white fence establishes the boundaries around the property and along the edge of the fence stands a few large saggy trees that have seen better, dryer days.

The pool has recently been drained, a military-green tarp stretching from one end to the other. I can't help but look at it and wonder if Julia will fall through and crack her head open on that poured cement or something. Or maybe the birthday candles will ignite and catch her hair on fire.

Occupational hazard, I'm afraid. I spend lots of time pondering death.

A little boy, maybe a year older than the birthday girl, tugs one of her curly pigtails. She stops twirling, squeals, and takes off chasing him through the yard. It is a shame the kid will die today being as cute as she is and on her birthday even.

Unless I can change it, of course, and that's what Regina Lovett is paying me to do—without her husband Gerard Lovett's knowledge, I might add. Given my real reason for being here, I am perfectly fine with this arrangement. Gerard doesn't need to know about me. But what his wife said to him to keep him away from Julia's birthday, I have no idea. When I suggested she pick another day for the birthday party, since she knew this would be Julia's death day, she said: *but I've already sent the invitations. I can't just cancel now.*

The woman has strange priorities, but it's really her husband I have to watch out for.

Gerard Lovett, the religious freak that he is, would have never allowed me—*especially* me—to be his daughter's death replacement agent. The Unified Church has a particular view on people like me. It doesn't matter that I have the ability to sense death coming, the ability to see its sneaky blue fire and put the kabosh on all that. Taking help from a death replacement agent would be a sign that they didn't have faith in God. All high-ranking church officials like Gerard Lovett have to demonstrate the solidity of their faith at all times. I often wonder if they'd refuse blood transfusions too, having faith God would just add a few pints when he got a chance.

Or maybe it's because I don't go anywhere when I die that I can't be trusted.

I turn at the sound of a sliding glass door and see Regina appear cake in hand. My personal assistant Ally is with her. She holds open the door for Regina, and then slides it closed behind them both.

"Time for cake!" Regina exclaims. The smile she'd given me when entering my office with Julia's death report two months ago had been forced, practiced, the smile of a woman married to an important man.

Her smile is softer now and Julia abandons the boy she's been chasing for it. She runs toward her mother with renewed laughter.

I look away, focusing on something mundane—Regina's clothes. They're some kind of modern business casual, classy and feminine. Her mousey hair is side swept and elegant, curling at the ends naturally. She's attractive, not *gorgeous* like Ally, but she knows how to do herself up, glossing up her plainness enough without screaming *I AM TRYING, OKAY?*

I notice all of this instead of looking at her and Julia together. For me, it hurts to look at mothers loving their daughters. My mother is dead and we weren't speaking for years before that.

Ally leaves Regina's trail, escaping the children gathering like rats around the Pied Piper, and comes to stand beside me. She pulls her red A-line coat tighter against the chilly air icing our cheeks and gathers her straight blond hair, the color of honey butter. I'd have helped her free it from the collar, but before I could she'd already done it, and with a single toss her locks had spilled down her back. Her nose stud looks silver in the dull overcast sky, instead of sparkling like the tiny diamond that it is. Her brown eyes are equally muted from their usual vibrant amber to an unremarkable brown. Dull light aside, she seems radiant against all this lush, landscaped green, moist with rain. The light flush in her otherwise pale cheeks suits her.

"Are you cold?" she asks, nodding at my colorful polka-dot jumper.

The answer is yes. Cold air has collected in my thighs and stomach, where the fabric of my polka-dotted jumper feels thinnest.

"I'm wearing layers," I insist. Ally can be quite the mother hen, and I know myself well enough to admit I can't be alert and babied at the same time.

"Are we good?" she asks.

Do I sense Julia's death coming? Not yet. "For now."

We watch Regina arrange the cake table, and launch the birthday song. It isn't until I start singing that Ally nudges me.

"Quit that," she says.

"What?" I play coy.

"I hear what you're saying," she accuses. "You're replacing *birth*day with *death*day."

"It *is* her death day."

"You are so morbid," she murmurs, but she's smiling. *Happy Death Day, Little Julia.*

"What does morbid mean?" a kid asks. This kid is pudgy, as tall as he is round and apparently uninterested in singing to the birthday girl. Also, his face is an unnatural green color from eating something made mostly of food coloring.

"Weird," Ally says. I am not sure if she is defining morbid or if she is as surprised by the ninja appearance of this kid as I am.

"Clowns are weird," the kid says, sucking on his sticky fingers.

"*You're* weird," I say. Ally nudges me with an elbow, but it's unneeded. This kid is too young to recognize an insult or he is just impervious beneath all that fat.

"I want a balloon," he demands.

I offer the big black trash bag to him, filled with animal balloons of every shape and color. When I took this job, I knew better than to improvise a skill I didn't have. So *voilà!*—a big bag of balloon animals.

"I want to see you make one," the kid groans.

"I want to see you leave," I say and stick the bag in his face.

Ally intervenes. "She can't make them because she has a bad wrist."

"Really?" the kid asks. He warms to her the way everyone warms to Ally.

I tell the kid, my cover story. "Yeah, carpel tunnel from all that juggling, camel riding, and whatever the hell clowns do."

"You said a bad word."

"I'm going to call you a bad word if you don't go away."

Ally is doing a decent job of keeping a straight face. She is also doing a great job of being pretty and convinces the little fatty to take a yellow "lion" and go get some cake. The words *before it's all gone* seem to work.

"You promised not to make the children cry," Ally says. She's not kidding.

"Sorry," I grumble. "I'm in a piss poor mood today."

"It's the first kid since Nessa."

And that's why Ally is my best friend. She knows

what bothers me before I do. I let out a big exhale and the breathing hole in my red nose whistles, dramatizing my despair.

Nessa.

I've thought a lot about Nessa this past year, especially in the past month leading up to Julia's replacement. It was this time last year that I'd failed to save her. Granted, I hadn't been her death replacement agent, so technically my perfect record is still intact. But she'd also been just a little girl and I'd promised her mother I would save her from some bad people. When you have this ability to save people, and a perfect track record of doing so—when you screw up—

Yeah, I'm a sore loser.

"Nessa Hildebrand. Our first casualty of war," I whisper. An ache fills my chest and I look away from the kids.

"Are we calling it war now?" Ally asks. She let her own breath out slow, weary.

"Two sides. Good versus evil. Only one can win. That's war, isn't it?"

"Evil hasn't made a move in over a year," Ally whispers. "Openly anyway."

"Oh they've made moves, I'm sure," I say. "Just not that we can see."

"That's a good sign though, right?"

Oh Ally, my ever optimistic companion. Just

because someone hasn't stabbed her in a year, she thinks we're safe. I know better. I can feel them sliding through the dark around us, large and scaly, looking for the right moment to spit acid venom in our faces.

"Sure. That's a great sign," I say. I don't believe what I'm saying and she knows I don't believe it. But sometimes you say things to be kind to the people you love. It wouldn't comfort her to hear *We're all going to die, Ally. They came for us once and they'll come again. Harder and harder until they win, and God help us, I can't imagine anything worse than what we've already been through*—No.

Some things you don't say to people you love.

Besides the word *war* suggests a fighting chance. War means a prolonged battle where either side could come out on top. This isn't war. This is a death sentence.

Ally gives my hand a quick squeeze, bringing me back to the present moment, to a moment when I am just a clown at a little girl's birthday party.

"Go on," she says. "Get what you came for."

I cast a last look at Regina, Julia, and the others, then hand Ally the balloon bag.

"If they ask, I went to pee."

She gives a cute salute and I slip away. I take my huge floppy shoes off by the back door and creep inside, careful to slide the door closed behind me.

The kitchen welcomes me. A large island with a granite countertop sits off to the left, and behind that, mahogany cabinets and a stainless steel fridge. The place looks like an ad in *Better Homes*, with only a few stray coats from guests and the occasional toy forgotten in a corner. Otherwise, it is pristine.

I turn on the bathroom light and shut the door, hoping to give the *occupado* impression should someone wonder where I am. Cover story secure, I creep up the stairs and down the hallway. My ears strain for any people noises—voices, footsteps, maniacal whistling, for anyone who might wonder why a girl wearing a rainbow wig is sneaking around up here.

But I hear nothing and see no one.

I place my hand on the door handle of Mr. Lovett's office and find it locked. Then I do what I've been taught to do. I pull two pins from my thick rainbow wig and slip them into the lock. I push against the bearing—turn, and *pop*.

It sounds easy, sure, but I've practiced a *million* times on a variety of locks purchased from hardware stores. A box of locks in the corner of a living room is a great conversation starter, by the way, and a lovely way to spend a Friday night alone.

Gerard Lovett's office is large. The desk lay in the middle of the room, directly opposite the door. The desk itself is immaculate, *nothing* like mine, which has piles of paperwork, junk mail, and bills needing attention. Behind his neat desk is a regal black chair, with a high back and wheels. The desk and chair itself are perched on top of a red and gold rug matching the red and gold drapes on either side of the fireplace behind the desk. One side of the room has a massive book case. The spines look unbroken, unread, and I'm not surprised to think of Mr. Lovett as a man who likes the appearance of being erudite rather than the actual reading. The remaining side of the room has a wooden chess set on a table between two more regal chairs, this time made of red leather.

Before entering the room I look around. I'm glad I do. Because up above me, sitting on a ledge above the chess set, is a camera. It isn't trained on the whole room, just the desk and the wall behind it, so if I'm lucky, I'm still invisible.

I admit I'm pretty freaked about the camera. I'm staring at its little black eye, trying to determine my next move when—*POP*.

I jump. My heart explodes in my chest, taking off like a rabbit fleeing a fox and I am about to run like hellfire back down the stairs and out the door. Then I hear a child crying. I swear, steady myself against the door frame, breath caught in my throat like a cotton ball and cross to the window to see what made the sound.

A balloon had popped and a child, devastated, is

crying against Ally's leg while she searches the bag for one in a similar shape and color. She finds one and the girl brings her weeping to a raggedy, shuddering stop. Her face brightens. The smile still tight, turns into a half-hearted, lopsided grin and the sobs become a kind of gleeful hiccup.

"Je*sus*," I mutter. I swear I can feel my ovaries die.

When I turn back to the room I realize something is wrong. Not just that I'd run into the room without thinking and was surely caught on camera, but the room is suspiciously quiet. The hum and click of electronics I'd noted upon first entering the room is gone. The clocks have stopped ticking. Latent electricity in lamp wires, phone outlets, an answering machine and internet modem have all stopped. The camera too, of course. Everything still, everything quiet—the way a house is quiet after a power outage.

"Shit."

This time last year, when my life started to get out of control, and homicidal maniacs tried to kill me and whatnot, I started to develop this new—I can't believe I'm going to say this—power. Unfortunately, there just isn't another word for it. It's not part of my weird death-replacement thing, but something that can't be explained scientifically by my NRD—my Necronitic Regenerative Disorder, a neurological disorder that allows me to die but not stay dead.

No, this is something else entirely.

It would seem I have some strange connection to electricity. It's not like I can control it. When it started last year, it was just a shocky thing—a static sort of electricity managing to blow light bulbs at the flip of a switch, or shock people quite a bit stronger than the usual I-shuffled-my-feet-and-now-*zap*.

It's evolved.

Lately, I can do this surge thing. When I'm startled, or scared, I send a shock out and *BAM*, electronics fail. So far I've only managed to blow up my own shit—bye, bye the possibility of morning toast or midnight margaritas, which is fine except now I'm blowing up other people's shit.

This is a serious problem.

I can't fall apart over fried electronics. I have to do what I came up here to do. I relax against the side of Mr. Lovett's desk and steady my breath. Once I feel somewhat together, I pull out a small Phillips-head screwdriver from my rainbow wig. I hold my hand above Mr. Lovett's computer listening for any kind of electric static crackling around my skin. When I feel none, I start to dismantle his computer.

Three of the six tiny screws are out of the computer, the ones that would release the hard drive from its little plastic nest, when all hell breaks loose.

A wave hits me. I rock back on my heels, topple, and hit the wall. My shoulder brushes something and I hear a crash. I quit moving, knowing because I can't see, I'll only knock more shit over if I continue flailing blindly.

"No, no, *no*," I whine as if that will make Julia's death turn on its heels and leave. Because that is what I feel—Death come calling.

I work faster.

First I reach out for the desk, find its edge and pull myself back to the computer. In my hurried panic, I start dropping the little screws on the office rug.

I have the last screw loose, but not completely out, when my vision changes.

The world dissolves from its usual solid self into a shifting world of color. The only equivalent I can think of is heat sensory, like the way they show it on TV or in the movies where someone puts on special goggles and then the world turns into an orange-yellow-red blob. This isn't exactly right, what I see in the moments before a death. I see more color and nuances, but it's close enough that you get the idea.

The problem with it happening *now* is two-fold. Problem one—I can't see the last freaking screw anymore. I can't clearly define *anything*, now that the world has reduced itself to something less substantial than an acid trip.

Problem two, Julia Lovett is about to die and I'm not close enough to save her. I can feel her out there, moving around in the yard, feel the pull surrounding her, centering and drawing close. If she dies and I am not near her, she can't be saved. Proximity is required for a death replacement.

The only thing I can do now is force myself to focus.

Even after my best effort, the colors are still there, making it hard to see. I have to rely on my fingers, the feel of grooves against the tips just to figure out what I'm doing, really hoping that it *is* the hard drive I'm removing.

I'm not a computer expert. I only know how to do this because Brinkley, my ex-handler, showed me on an old garage sale computer making me practice until I practically wept for a break.

Finally, it falls free of its case. Clutching the stolen hard drive in one hand, I rush back toward the stairs. I can't afford to be casual. I can't afford to take my time or even stop to turn off the bathroom light or open the door. In fact, I'm forced to crawl down the stairs the way a baby would, butt first so I don't fall. I make slow progress, but I can't save Julia's life if I break my own neck before even getting to her.

Somehow I manage to make it back to the sliding kitchen door and see Ally on the other side. Sure, she is a blur of color like everything else, but I *know* Ally. I know what she looks like even in this form. Maybe it's because I've saved her life once, or because she's been on a *bagillion* replacements with me, or even because she's my best friend. I don't know or care as I pry open the glass and croak her name.

Nothing.

Louder: "*Ally.*"

She turns around and it must be the way I look because she comes running.

"Are you—"

"Here," I say. I shove what I hope is the hard drive at her and step fully into the backyard.

"Jesse, your shoes," she says.

"No time." I'm already walking to the edge of the brick patio stretching like a giant doormat away from the kitchen entrance. I'm searching the yard for Julia.

I find her colorful blur twirling again and I know it is her, because something isn't quite right with her "thermal" reading. A menacing black blur mars her color. She's out by the fence and I can't see anything around her that's of danger, but I know better than to let that assumption stop me. Something can fall from the sky at any second. Some insane driver could crash through that white fence. Hell, little Julia could be having a heart attack from all that twirling.

I run through the soggy grass, my socks soaking up the cold rainwater. My toes curl. I run and Ally follows, but not too close, yelling, "Everyone back up, please!" She knows to do crowd control and create as much distance between me and the others as possible.

I have no idea if it works. I can't afford to focus on anything but Julia.

I run across the yard, arms out to grab her. Julia must see me coming and stops twirling for long enough to scream and run in the other direction. It isn't until I hear her screaming "Mommy the clown! Mommy!" that I realize *I* am the one terrifying her, a clown with a manically determined expression, rushing her at full speed.

"Come here!" I yell, unable to pretend like this was anything but urgent. "We don't have time for this."

And of course I'm right.

I hear Ally yelling. Something unclear, directed at Regina. People always want to rush in and save their loved ones from dying, but it only gets in the way and causes more causalities. After all, I can only replace one person at a time.

Death is different for everyone and I see it differently for everyone.

Sometimes I see death as a tiny black hole created inside a person, an empty swirling vortex sucking all the warm, living colors out of a person, leaving nothing behind that can survive.

Sometimes a hot-cold chill settles into the muscles in my back and coils around my navel before yanking me down into oblivion.

Then there are deaths like Julia Lovett's.

A death where I just have to throw myself out there and hope it works out. No vision guidance. No conscious effort on my part. Just faith that being who I am, *what* I am, the exchange will happen.

Julia has almost reached the fence when I grab ahold of her. I hold her against my scratchy polka-dotted jumper while she screams and flails. I try to say soothing things: "I'm not going to hurt you. Gee-*zus*. Calm down!" My best efforts fall short as I look up and see my worst nightmare.

A tall, stupidly beautiful man, dressed in a three-piece suit, strides across Julia's yard toward us. With determined, dedicated steps, he unfurls his black wings on either side of him as he closes the distance between us. I haven't seen that shaggy dark hair or those animalistic green eyes in a year. Now here he is, walking straight toward me in all his angelic splendor.

"*Shit*," I say.

Julia quits squirming in my arms and turns her wide eyes up to mine. Her mouth is open in horror as if my profanity is the worst thing that's ever happened to her.

Before I can apologize or even comprehend what's happening, what Gabriel's reappearance might mean, something hard and heavy slams us from behind.

The entire world goes dark.

Ally

Jesse's legs protrude from under the tree as if pantomiming a bizarre Wicked Witch of the West scene. It's the shrill cry piercing my ears that sharpens my focus and it breaks the spell of the polka-dotted legs lying so still in the mud.

I whirl to find several mothers clutching their children. Regina is closest to me. She stares at the tree in horror. Her hands are cupped over her mouth and her eyes are rimmed with tears.

"Regina," I say, softly. I get very close to her so she is forced to look away from the tree. "Will you help me?"

She doesn't respond.

"Regina," I say, sharply. "What is my name?"

"Alice Gilligan."

Close enough. "And why am I here?"

"To assist—"

"Exactly," I cut her off. "I am here to assist. So will you *assist* me? We need to move everyone inside. Will you help me get everyone inside?"

"Is she—is—"

"Jesse is very good at her job." I'm calm. I tuck my hair behind my ears. "Julia will be fine. Regina, *look* at *me*."

She does.

I have to be firm with her. "Take everyone inside and stay there until I tell you otherwise."

When I worry she won't respond again, I clap my hands in front of her face a couple of times. It does the trick. Her eyes focus and turn toward her daughter's guests for the first time. I help her with the words.

"We need everyone to go inside, please," I say. "We need to make room for the emergency crews. Go inside. Go on."

Everyone is slow, sluggish with shock but they begin to move. The children and many of the mothers are still crying, but at least they're moving. As they funnel through the sliding glass doors, I pull out my phone and call 911. Julia, though probably alive, will still need medical care. Jesse only has the ability to heal herself, not others. Then I call the fire department so they can come and cut up the tree. The firefighter asks me to repeat myself twice before accepting that a tree fell *on* a person.

Then I'm alone.

Waiting. I look at my clock: 3:58 P.M. I move closer to Jesse and Julia. I look at those legs sticking out from under the tree and say my silent prayers to myself—my reassurances. *She is not dead. She will wake up. It's okay, it's okay. She is safe.*

I've seen her dead so many times you would think I have no fear of her dying.

You'd be wrong.

I crouch beside her as a piercing siren cuts the day in half. It's very close and the wail forces me to cover my ears. Once it falls quiet again, I place one hand on Jesse's calf and find it damp and cold.

A small terror rises inside me and I say my silent prayers again. And again.

Firefighters erupt from the side fence. They flood the yard in their yellow jumpsuits. One is carrying a chainsaw. Another carries something that looks like a jack. I give a little wave to draw them over. They come at a run.

"This is authorized replacement #60432," I tell them. "There is a little girl under there with the agent."

"Stand back, please," the one carrying the chainsaw says. He's young with a scruffy jaw. I oblige.

I'm relieved that he starts farther down on the tree. The sound of the saw eating wood, its high-pitched whine of hunger, still makes me nervous, but at least I know they will not miss and cut flesh.

The heavy trunk falls away and only a considerably smaller piece of wood lies on top of Jesse and Julia.

The firefighters shout orders to each other over the noise. They say *the bodies. The bodies.*

I keep my anger under control.

The paramedics arrive while the firefighters are still removing the tree. I wave them over and they come running. It's a man and a woman. The man carries a large bag, the woman a stretcher.

"This is authorized replacement #60432," I repeat. "There is a death replacement agent and a little girl, four years old."

"Do you suspect head trauma?" the man asks.

My heart swells with gratitude. He's considering Jesse's health as much as Julia's. Unfortunately, you'd be surprised how often Jesse's well-being is overlooked. People equate NRD with invincibility. But Jesse is not invincible—despite what she might think. Her NRD has its limits.

For people with NRD, once they die, their brain starts sending a bombardment of electro-impulses through the body to wake them up, not unlike a hypnic jerk some people feel when falling asleep.

When they wake up they get a metabolic boost which allows them to heal the damage accrued in a death. Neurologists aren't sure why this happens, or how a person develops NRD. There appears to be a heredity link because it runs in families. However, it is unclear if the disorder is always active, or dormant until a person's first death.

Because it is neurological and controlled by the brain, Jesse needs her brain in order to wake up from a death replacement. No brain equals no pulsing. Hence why the paramedic is inquiring about head trauma.

"It is possible," I admit. I let my gratitude for his concern show. "They were hit from behind. I think spinal trauma is more likely, but the trunk could have clipped the back of her skull."

"I'll get a second stretcher," the female paramedic says. She jogs back to the side gate and disappears.

"Free," a firefighter calls and I turn to see them lift the trunk off of Jess.

I see something.

It's quick. So quick that I'm not sure I saw it at all.

Jesse lies on her stomach. She is propped over the little girl, shielding her from much of the tree. Julia has a large scratch across her cheek, presumably from bark, but for the most part she looks unharmed. Jesse's back doesn't look quite right, but I don't know what's wrong with it. That is the extent of my medical knowledge.

It isn't the injuries that bother me. It is what I see for the briefest of moments.

Covering Jesse and Julia is a thin layer of—what is that?

Light?

A purple shade of light is pulsing an inch or so

around them. If the firefighters see it through their face shields, they show no sign of recognition. By the time the paramedic kneels beside her to inspect the damage, the light has faded away.

"No spinal trauma," the male paramedic says. "In fact there doesn't seem to be much damage at all. Her shoulder might be dislocated."

Clearly, he didn't see the odd purple light.

"Is she dead?" I ask.

The paramedic humors me with a soft frown. "Yes, unfortunately."

But why would she die if there is no damage, no trauma? I don't have an answer.

Julia cries. It is the slow, growing sort of cry. The kind sleepy children are prone to. The paramedic inspects her enough to determine it's safe to move her and then lifts her free from Jesse's embrace.

"Mommy!" she sobs more loudly. She is quite pitiful in her muddy and torn party dress. Her cute wool coat askew on her shoulders and her little fists pressed against her closed eyes. "Mommy!"

"Is she okay?" I ask the paramedic as the woman appears with the second stretcher.

"Not a scratch on her," he says. His amazement is apparent. "You know direct force replacements are very difficult to pull off."

So he knows something about death replacing.

"Jesse is very good," I say. I text Kirk and tell him

to meet me at the hospital.

"She must be," the paramedic agrees.

He puts something on a clean cotton ball and dabs at Julia's cheek while cooing sweet words. I motion to the glass door where Regina stands watching. I mouth the words *Come on out* to accompany my wave.

She doesn't have to be told twice.

When Julia sees her mother she cries louder.

Regina can't wait. She is running across the yard crying, her arms out to scoop up her little girl. The paramedic doesn't want to release her, but Julia's upstretched arms cannot be denied. Regina pulls her up, then sinks to her knees still clutching the child close.

They sob with abandon as Regina rocks her daughter back and forth.

The paramedics unceremoniously inspect Jesse's head for damage and when none is found, pronounce that she will survive. They load Jesse onto the stretcher and I follow them through the backyard to the ambulance.

I cast one last look over my shoulder at the mother holding her daughter and crying. I wish that Jesse could see this part—what it was all for.

Once we arrive at the hospital and the female paramedic helps me from the back of the ambulance, I watch them carry Jesse inside. She's taken to a hospital room in the general wing, where all nonemergencies go.

Now I have no choice but to wait.

Sitting in one of the uncomfortable hospital chairs, I use my phone to check the database for an estimate of her "death-time" or DT. There is a database online constructed by death replacement agents, handlers, and assistants like me. Each death is logged, as well as recovery time. Overall, it gives a good sense of what sort of time will be needed for recovery. For example, a fire typically takes three days. It's one of the worst replacements. A strangling, or suffocation, is only a couple of hours.

I'm having a hard time finding an entry for *death by fallen tree*. I try a couple of others: blunt force trauma, eighteen hours. Spinal damage, nine hours. Crushing, twelve hours. I'll make an entry myself once this is over, but being the first to log a death doesn't help me with timing her post-replacement care.

Dr. York, her primary care physician, enters the room and takes her away. It is protocol to make sure some significant damage hasn't occurred during the replacement. He's gone for almost an hour when he brings her back.

Dr. Stanley York is a good guy. He is completely bald on top, with his small patch of snow-white hair covering his ears and the back of his head. The white serves to dramatize his bright blue eyes and thin smile.

Jesse has been cut out of her clown suit and is wearing a hospital gown. Someone cleaned the mud from her face and fingers.

"I don't see anything," he says. "No tree limbs to remove or anything of the sort." He pulls a piece of butterscotch from his pocket and pushes it into my hand. "I will have to look again once she *reboots*."

"She isn't a cyborg, Dr. York," I say. I put the butterscotch in my mouth because to not do so would be an insult.

"How are you, Alice?" he asks. "Are you getting enough sleep? Fluids? Are you eating well?"

I smile. "Yes, thank you for your concern."

"She isn't working you too hard, is she?" he grins.

"No," I say. "You?"

He casts a look at Jesse and smiles. "Not this week."

He is about to say something more when my phone rings. The number is blocked.

"I need to take this." Saying no more, Dr. York exits with a little wave.

I take Jesse's cold hand into mine before answering the call. "Hello."

"We need to meet," a deep male voice says.

I trace the edge of her cold, soft finger with my warm one. "I'm at the hospital right now."

"I know. I saw you come in. Can you meet me in the cafeteria?"

I look at Jesse's placid face. I feel her cold stiff hand in mine and the terror is still there. *This isn't real,* I tell myself. *It isn't like before.*

Eight years ago, Jesse died for the first time.

It was a barn fire and her step-father died with her. I didn't know about Jesse's NRD and had no idea she'd survived. Her mother never told me and for years—*years*—I thought she was really dead. I thought I'd lost my best friend and first love in a pyre of ash.

I can't describe the emptiness of those years. Countless months of moving as if I were programmed. There wasn't a day I didn't think about her. I suffered the kind of grief that someone can't possibly understand unless they've lost someone they love. The way the mind keeps remembering and grieving again and again. It isn't a brush with death, painful panic that can be relieved with a phone call or an embrace. It was the kind of grief that stayed with me, day and night. The kind that has no remedy, coloring everything. *Consuming*, everything.

Then I found out she was alive. She was *alive*. It took me almost a year to find her, but when I did, oh my God— when I walked into her office and saw her alive and smiling—

It took everything I had not to kiss her, slap her, s*hake* her, or cry like a crazy person. All I wanted was to squeeze her to death again and again.

Now that I know the truth of her condition, I am

supposed to be able to let go of this fear—that she will never wake up. The fear that she died at seventeen and everything that has happened since has just been a mad illusion of my grieving mind.

But I can't. God help me, I can't. Every death replacement, every threat, tastes like the grief I carried around for those long years.

"I'll be right there." I tell him, and he hangs up without saying goodbye.

I press my warm hand to Jesse's cold forehead. I kiss her cheek and tell her I'll be back before she wakes up. Because she will wake up. She will.

The nurse at the station takes down my message for Dr. York: *I have to run an errand. If I'm not back call me when she wakes up.*

I am still deep in thought as I cross to the elevator and punch the *up* button. I step off on the sixth floor, and walk into the bustle of the cafeteria. Thankfully, it smells like food and not the antiseptic mixture usually clogging the hospital corridors.

I scan the cafeteria for him, but he isn't here yet. The lighting is lower, a soft orange sunset. It's comforting compared to the fluorescent brilliance of the rest of the hospital. This little nook is also several degrees warmer than the bleached hallways. Few people are here in the post-lunch hours. A couple of doctors and nurses have come to eat on their break. An older man reading a book sits alone at a table, his plate showing signs of a meal long since devoured, little brown napkins crumpled on top. At another table, two women talk solemnly over steaming cups. A row of televisions on the far wall play a collection of news, talk shows, and a soap opera.

I go to the build-it-yourself taco bar. I've only eaten cake today and the smell of real food is unbearable. I don't go easy on the hot sauce or the water. I choose a booth that is highly visible from the elevator. I'm on my third taco when he arrives.

"May I join you?"

Because my mouth is full, I can only gesture. He slides into the booth. Jeremiah is wearing dark clothes again today—the only thing I've ever seen him wear—dark sweaters with a dark dress shirt collar protruding, dark dress pants. If I look under the table, I'm sure I'll see the same dark shoes.

"You look tired," he says. "Are you on duty?"

"That's a terrible thing to say to a woman." I swallow. "You look tired."

He doesn't smile. "I apologize if I've offended you."

His coolness unnerves me, those unwavering eyes behind silver-rimmed glasses, the meticulously trimmed beard covering his jaw and the skin above his lip. He is too polished. It isn't normal.

"Why are you here? In the hospital?" I ask.

"I brought Nikki to get a few stitches. She's fine."

He watches my face but I think I do a pretty good job of remaining unreadable. Not that I have anything to hide or be ashamed of. Only that I'm a little embarrassed by my attraction to Nikki. And it isn't exactly something that I want her boss to know—that I'm attracted to her.

"What did you want to talk about?" I ask.

"What did Jesse say?"

"I haven't asked her," I admit.

"I don't understand your reluctance to include her."

"She doesn't want to fight," I say. I don't want her to fight. "She gets enough danger in her day job, don't you think?"

Jeremiah's eyes flick up to the row of televisions above our heads and I follow his gaze.

It's Caldwell, North American Leader of the Unified Church. Plastic surgery or not, he still looks like Jesse to me. Jeremiah doesn't know the man on TV is Jesse's father. Almost no one does.

Because the volume is turned down, I must read the black and white closed captioning.

Announcer: As leader of the Unified Church, what is your position regarding North Carolina's latest amendment?

Caldwell: I respect every State's right to amend their constitutions as they see fit, to best serve its resident citizens.

Announcer: You do?

Caldwell: Yes, oh yes. I understand why they might favor

this bill.

Announcer: If you have NRD and you die, you are not allowed to reclaim any property, voting or marriage rights.

Caldwell: Yes the loss of rights is unfortunate. However, I can understand their attempts to make everyone equal.

"It's on the ballot for November," Jeremiah says. His ears have turned red and his mouth has tightened. "They may pass the same laws in Tennessee. Then what will you do?"

"Then we will sell Jesse's house and move," I say. "I hear Portland is nice and they love NRD."

I give up on the third taco.

"We would be so much stronger with her help," Jeremiah urges. "I'm sure she would want to fight, if she knew it was by your side."

That is what I'm most afraid of. I will give anything to keep Jesse out of danger. Anything to know I will never feel that empty sense of loss again.

"I'll ask her if I feel like the time is right," I say, knowing I never will.

"I've been respectful of your relationship." Jeremiah meets my eyes through those silver-rimmed glasses, waiting. "But if you do not bring her into the fold soon, I'm afraid that I will."

Jesse

I wake up in the typical zombie fashion: stiff and starved. The first thing I see is a super tall, black man with his back to me. Kirk, my mortician, wears a nice dark green suit, white shirt and red tie. He's busy packing little cosmetic bottles and jars back into a small carrying case.

The second thing I notice is the white walls and gray comforter of my spare bedroom. A bland room, I admit, because I never have guests stay in my second, let alone third bedroom and because I am pretty unmotivated when it comes to décor. I've never even hung curtains. The rest of my house looks livable and inviting purely by Ally's design.

"Why are we here?" I ask. Kirk owns Mt. Olivet, a funeral home and cemetery in Nashville. Usually after Dr. York makes sure I'm healing okay, Kirk takes me there and fixes me up. Not in the cemetery, of course. He has a little room for me in the back of the funeral home. I've gotten so used to waking up in the softly lit, rose-colored room that finding myself anywhere else always means something is wrong.

"Oh my God, did she die?" I ask.

"Nothing like that," he says. His voice has the faint drawl of New Orleans, where he lived before a hurricane laid waste to the levees, and the city was lost. He turns toward me, palms out in surrender. "It's only that we are doing renovations at Mt. Olivet. I thought you'd be more comfortable here at home."

I watch him make a big show of arranging his little black case, his zombie-care case as I like to call it. He's more used to working with stiff bodies than living ones, so I can trust him to fix me up at any stage of decomposition, no matter the damage my body took in a replacement. It is Dr. York's job to put everything back in place—like my bones and stuff. It's up to Kirk to do the cosmetic stuff. I have no objection to letting him put a little makeup on my unconscious body because even though I have a really fast metabolism and some regeneration-healing skills, pretty isn't in my post-replacement vocabulary.

"So Julia is okay?" I ask again because he still hasn't answered me.

Kirk snaps the lid on the case closed but doesn't turn around. "She's fine, just fine. I heard she didn't have a scratch on her. You were hit by a tree."

"A tree? That's a first. They usually don't move much."

Kirk laughs and the robust sound of it relaxes me. But again I notice his tight shoulders and turned back, Kirk with his bag poised and ready to flee the bedroom.

I want to ask what's wrong because something *is* wrong, but stop myself. I don't want to be that girl. *Are you mad at me? Is everything okay? Is it something I did? Said?* I tell myself not everything has to do with me. Maybe Kirk has something else going on. Something that is probably none of my business.

"Thank you," I say. "For destiffing my corpse."

He finally faces me and places a hand on the top of my head, a very grandfatherly gesture. Then he opens his mouth as if to say something. Only his mouth closes, jaw flexes, and he is gone.

I listen to his heavy steps on the stairs outside my darkening bedroom. My eyes are on the desk in the corner beneath the windows, but I'm not really seeing it. I'm listening to Kirk leave. His soft voice calls out to someone who makes some reply, followed by footsteps on the stairs.

Winston, my fawn-colored ball of fluff with a cute black face, looks up at me from the end of the bed and snorts. I sit up and scratch his velvety ears. He is adorable with his smushed face and perked ears as he tries to bite my wiggling toes through the comforter. A crisp breeze from the open window has a sharp, sobering effect on me. I pull the blanket and the dog tighter just before the bedroom door opens again.

Lane comes to the side of the bed and kneels, a lovely wave of intoxicating cologne coming with him. "Hi, beautiful."

His chilly hands slip under the covers looking for mine. I reach out for him.

"Hey," I reply and my shoulder blades soften against the pillows. I try not to look sad. For a moment I expected it to be Ally, but I don't know why. She used to be the first face I saw whenever I woke up, but Ally has been distant for the last few months. As Lane and I grow closer, she seems to slip deeper into the shadows of my life.

Lane leans in to kiss me, a soft brush of the lips. He smells musky, a sweet but boyish cologne making me think of the smell oozing from certain clothing stores in the mall. His dark hair, tousled, falls forward into his Mediterranean blue eyes.

Our mouths make a soft, wet sound as he pulls back. "How do you feel?"

"Sore," I say, truthfully. "But I'll live. For a few more days anyway."

Last year Lane found out about his own NRD and is now privy to the pain of a replacement. The benefit of this is *now* he's much more considerate of my post-replacement needs. He's always been considerate, but nothing like experiencing rigor mortis firsthand to promote post-death sensitivity.

"Are you hungry?" he asks, kissing the back of my hand. "I want you to see something, but if you need to rest, I can show you another day."

"Are the seeing something and the eating something connected? Or are you just being random?"

"Connected." He's being cautious, but his eyes are all excitement.

"Well then." I let him pull me from the warm bed and help me into my clothes.

Our first stop is Lane's place. I don't go up to his apartment, the top half of an old house he shares with his tenants below. The house belonged to Lane's dad but when he died, he inherited the house and the commercial building housing his comic book store. Lane doesn't want the whole house to himself, so he's sectioned it and rents the lower half out. Because it is close enough to Vanderbilt University, it's usually empty in the summer and taken during the fall and spring semesters.

A couple of cute college girls who love to give me dirty looks are his current tenants. I admit, I am a little concerned about big-boobed Vandy girls parading around in their panties in the communal kitchen, but I can't say anything without sounding crazy. I try very hard not to let anyone know I'm crazy—which of course makes me think of Gabriel.

It isn't uncommon for death-replacement agents

to lose their minds and hallucinate. All that dying deprives the brain of oxygen and it has its consequences. I had full blown hallucinations of Gabriel last year, which lasted for weeks and *weeks*, but I assumed it was the stress. Yet here I am now, hoping the brief glimpse of Gabriel just before Julia's replacement was a harmless flashback and nothing more.

Lane goes upstairs for the keys to his black Kawasaki Ninja. I know this brief reprieve from the rain will be one of our last chances to ride this year. And being the sweetheart he is, he brought me down some black knit gloves and a hat for my ears.

It's a good time to go riding. The sun is melting into the horizon, dissolving into an iridescent puddle of melted gold. After Lane backs the bike out of the gravel driveway, I climb on. I keep my eyes open for Gabriel or anything weird, but I see nothing long enough that the worrisome knot in my stomach starts to relax.

The Nashville skyline is fifteen minutes behind us when he pulls off the interstate and leans the bike onto back roads crowded with imposing trees turning bright with hints of candy apple red and pumpkin orange. The tires against the pavement make a slick-rubber sound as we cut deeper and deeper into the countryside, the engine whining with each acceleration. It's getting dark and the air whizzes past my iced cheeks almost to the point of real pain, but it feels good. I feel alive and maybe you'd have to die as much as I do, to appreciate this rare feeling.

I hug him tighter, soaking up the heat of him and letting the vibration of his bike make the muscles in my legs tremble and tense. I use his back as a windbreaker and I get comfortable there, warming one cheek before turning my face to warm the other against the soft fabric of his jacket.

Then I feel the bike slow and light hits my closed eyelids. I open my eyes to see a beautiful cliffside and water. The sunset is gorgeous and casts us both in bronze shades as he pulls over to one side of the road. He lets me climb from the bike first before parking it. I pull off my helmet, adjust my little hat over my ears, and set it beside his on a low stone wall.

"Is this what you wanted to show me?" I ask. I gesture wide to the sight of the sunset stretching over pale-gray water as far as I can see, distant stretches of land encroaching on the little waves.

"Yes," he says.

"It's beau-tee-ful. Did you make it yourself?" I move to kiss his cheek, but he turns to claim my mouth, pulling my jacket collar so I have to come up on my toes or be choked. The gesture might be possessive, but his lips are soft and after a handful of heartbeats, he releases me.

"I sure did," he says. "Took me awhile to get it just right."

As he pulls back I see how beautiful he is in this late afternoon light. I can even see sunlight collecting on his lashes as I come in for another kiss.

"Who knew you were so talented?"

He frowns and clamps his hands on my shoulders. "You're shaking."

I'm about to say it's from the kiss, when he pulls off his green canvas jacket and offers it to me. He bounces it impatiently until I slip one gloved hand through the sleeve and then the other. He reaches under and pulls my hair free. Then he makes me a place to sit on the stone wall beside him.

The towel he used to wipe water from our seats becomes my seat cushion, draped over the deteriorating rock face. Then he surprises me.

Lane opens his backpack that I'd been wearing on the drive up, and pulls out our dinner: General Tso chicken for him, fried rice and egg rolls for me.

"I thought I smelled Chinese!" I say. I open one of the boxes. "I thought maybe one of my brain nerves got smushed and I was just going to smell rangoons for the rest of my life—which actually wasn't a bad prospect."

"I picked it up just before I picked you up," he says.

"Sneaky," I say. "You knew I'd come with you."

"Or we'd have eaten it in your bed."

"But then we'd miss your magical landscape," I say and I snuggle as close as our elbows allow. "How long did it take you to make this again?"

"It took me six days to pull it all together," he replies, with a wink.

We sit on the wall, watching the day die and eating Chinese food. Me warm in his coat, wrapped in the smell of him. Him sitting close, thigh-to-thigh, smiling at me as much as the sunset.

And this is why I love Lane.

Because loving Lane feels—safe.

His world is safe. Little girls don't die here. People aren't trying to hunt and kill me. No one leaves hateful messages in soap marker or eggs my house. No one calls me the Devil's whore or soulless. I don't spend my days in hospitals, or funeral homes, or in several pieces for that matter. With Lane, I am just a girl who likes Chinese food, who has the cutest dog ever, who likes to watch bad TV and read sleazy tabloids and eats too much ice cream and doesn't give a shit about the condition of her nails and yet—

Lane looks at me like I am this sunset. Beautiful. He makes me feel beautiful.

It's why I chose Lane when I could have chosen Ally.

It isn't that I don't love her. It isn't that I am not attracted to her—I am. But with her, it's duty and responsibility. With Ally, it is fear, concern, and worry. It's all about *them* and what we need to do to stop them. Little girls die in Ally's world. Hell, Ally died. If I hadn't been there to replace her—

God, I can't imagine it.

So when I reach out to hold Lane's hand in the fading sunlight, I tell myself that this is the world I live in. I can have my life any way I want it, and I want this. Chinese food and silly boyfriends.

No fighting.

No death.

If only I could make Ally understand that, then maybe she wouldn't pull away from me.

Ally

What am I doing here?

Nothing good can come of this. Best case scenario, I'm about to suffer through the most awkward dating encounter I've endured in years. Why am I even trying to date? Why now? I mean, I guess I could argue why *not* now? After all, Jesse isn't going to leave Lane any time soon. They've been together for a whole year, much longer than I anticipated that lasting, actually. I've been single for—longer than I care to admit, but she isn't going to dump him for me.

That has been made clear.

Maybe that is why I'm here, trying to date someone Jesse doesn't even know about. The word *date* suggests I want to get to know someone better. You don't go on a date with someone just to tell them this will never work—you don't drive to the *date* compiling a list of reasons why *not* to be with them. Just because I'd finally agreed to having coffee with Nikki after months of her insistence didn't mean this was a real date, did it?

I wedge my Smart car between two massive SUVs and spot Nikki immediately standing outside the coffee shop. She's looking my way and probably saw me park. With every moment I wait in the car, her smile falters a little. Though I'm dreading telling her what I'm here to tell her, I'm not cruel. I take a breath and yank open the door.

She recovers most of her smile before I can cross the parking lot, dodging strollers, unruly dogs and a couple of cars cluttering the busy shopping complex.

"I thought you might change your mind," she says. She stands taller than me, even in her flat sneakers. It's a change considering I am used to looking down at Jess. Nikki's eyes are gray today, but that could simply be the lighting. Nikki has those eyes, the kind that conforms to what she is wearing or the light around her. The slant of her eyes make me think of a cat. It could be the roundness of her cheeks and nose, or the way she does her makeup to exaggerate the kittenish look. Or it could be the one thick strand of hot pink in her hair despite the platinum blond.

"I didn't change my mind." I try to hold her gaze, but I can't.

"Good," she says. She slips her hand in the pocket of her jeans and uses the other to brush her bangs back away from her face. "Because I've only been trying for a year. If you had said *yes*, only to say *no* again, it would've crushed me."

"You exaggerate."

She puts a hand against her chest and mimics shock with an open mouth and wide eyes. "I'm devastated just *thinking* about it."

She thinks she's funny, but it's practiced. She isn't the kind of natural hilarious that Jesse is just by pure dramatics and a gift for hyperbole.

"I'm certain," I say, humoring her. "But you've only shown your interest a few weeks ago."

"It feels like years," she says. There is her amused smile again. A little quirk in the corner that is more smirk than smile. It isn't that vulnerable look Jesse gives—the one that says she's only having fun, if you are. Nikki is far too confident to need my reassurance.

"Can we go inside or do you want to hold the dangerous ground between people and their coffee?" she asks.

We go through the motions of ordering coffee. I pretend to look at the noticeboard while the barista makes our drinks. I *pretend* to be interested in all the information tacked to the wall—lost dogs, offers for tutoring, other services, work from home flyers, and meditation classes. The warmth of the café is slowly melting the chill of the afternoon away, but it isn't enough to make me sit down.

I don't know why she makes me so nervous—or why I can't just sit down and talk to her. We've been working together for a year. Not as intimately as I work with Jesse, but she is hardly a stranger. We have common interests, similar aspirations—for the time being anyway. From what I can tell, she is intelligent and compassionate. She is certainly attractive and takes good care of her body. I should want this.

From a few feet away, jiggling a bundle of sugar packets between pinched fingers, she watches me silently debate all of this but pretends not to. Is this her attempt to give me space? After adding sugar to the black coffee, she becomes impatient with her long hair and pulls it up in a high, twisted ponytail, securing it with the elastic tie she keeps around her wrist.

The barista calls my name and I go to the counter as if I'm a robot, relying purely on my programming. I choose the table beside the window so I can pretend to look out of it, and we both finally sit down.

"Relax," she says, settling into the squeaking chair. "I'm not going to throw you down and have my way with you." She nods in the direction of an empty sofa beneath a large splatter painting at least half as big as the wall itself.

I smile. It's genuine enough. Perhaps the words *have my way with you* did it. "I haven't dated since, Jesse. I'm sorry if I'm being—weird."

"Did you date Jesse?" she asks. She arches an eyebrow. "I thought you just spent a lot of time in her bed."

I still spend time in her bed, I think, but it is probably best not to mention that. "You know what I mean. Since we've been *together* then, however you want to put it."

Nikki blows the steam rising from her ceramic cup, then sips. "How is she?"

"In bed?" I blush.

She grins and presses her lips together against a laugh. "Uh, *no*. I was referring to work."

"She's fine," I say, feeling stupid. "83 replacements and going strong."

Why did she look away when she asked me about Jesse? Does she want me to change the subject? Or is she trying to not sound too interested? Or maybe she only asked to be polite and doesn't even want to talk about her at all. I'm probably overthinking this.

There. Her smile does tighten. I'm not imagining it.

"Institutionalization of death replacement agents is becoming more common. We've recorded a significant rise in the past few months," Nikki says as if I'm not haunted by the statistics already. "She needs to be careful."

The federal policy of being interviewed by a therapist after a few replacements hasn't changed. If Jesse were to lose her mind, I think that would hurt almost as much as losing her completely—to see her live out the rest of her life broken, lost.

"Jesse's old mentor Rachel was institutionalized," I say, I think I do a decent job of sounding casual.

Nikki nods like she already knows about Rachel, and I want to ask what else she knows. I'm sure Jeremiah has checked up on Jesse's past as thoroughly as he investigates everything else. And Nikki appears, for all intents and purposes, to be Jeremiah's second-in-command. It would make sense he would tell her everything. About me. About Jesse and her NRD—or even Caldwell—if he's even made the connection between Jesse and Caldwell yet.

Or maybe they're learning everything from me. Jesse uses the word *expressive* to describe my face. Perhaps I am being too expressive now.

Nikki smirks. "You can ask."

"What?"

"Whatever it is you want to ask," she says. "You've got this look on your face like you want to ask me something. Just ask. You don't know much about me.The way we met was—interesting, but not conducive to building a friendship."

I grin. "You weren't wearing pants and you were drunk."

"Exactly," she grins. "You must have questions."

I look out the window as the first drops of rain begin to fall. It's a slow, sleepy drizzle. People cover their heads with newspapers, briefcases or bags. Very few manage to have an umbrella on hand.

I ask her the only question that matters. "How did you meet Jeremiah? How long have you known him?"

"Shop talk? I say you can ask anything and you choose shop talk?" She crosses her legs and leans back in her chair. "Has anyone told you you're a workaholic?"

"You don't know me well enough to make that judgment."

She senses my irritation and backs off.

"Fair enough. I met Jeremiah same way I met you."

"Pantless?" I ask.

"Through our common interests," she says, twirling the cup between her hands.

"Why do you care?" and for clarity because I worry my words are too sharp, I add, "About all of this."

She cocks her head to one side as if listening. "Why do *you* care?"

I hesitate. Is it too soon to bring Jesse up again? It has been so long since I've dated—high school probably—that it is all I can do just to sit here, pretending to drink coffee and obsess over my ex-girlfriend. Oh my God, am I one of those sad, *sad* people?

"I know you're worried about Jesse and you think

she'll be attacked again. So I can only assume you joined up with Jeremiah in hopes of making sure that doesn't happen. He told me he found you online, all cavalier, spreading the "be safe" anti-victim rhetoric to anyone who would listen. Then when he realized you were in Nashville, asked if you wanted to get a little more physical in your campaign. Is that about right?"

"*We* were attacked." I want to draw attention away from Jesse.

Nikki isn't fooled. "Yes, but I've seen you working enough to know you're a bit selfless. You might be doing this for the both of you, but it is *mostly* for her."

"We haven't worked together *that* much. You barely know me," I say. Again I'm irritated. Pissy even. Wow, I am really terrible at dating.

"Okay, so you are doing this for yourself," Nikki relents. "I suppose being stabbed in the spleen is decent motivation for joining a rebel cause. I can hardly blame you. I'm rather attached to *my* spleen."

"And what was your reason?" I ask. *And Jeremiah's?* Maybe I could grow to trust them and tell them more about Jesse if I understood why they're doing this. I've known them for almost a year but I've only worked a handful of jobs with them. So I guess it is natural that I feel like I don't know nearly enough. "Or are you just a general do-gooder who would take up arms against any unjust cause?"

Nikki looks out the window at the rain splattering the glass. One bead connects with another, doubles in size and begins to glide. Those collide with another and another until it becomes one unstoppable droplet funneling down, like a thick silvery trail left by a snail.

When she doesn't answer, I take the first real drink of my coffee because I don't know what to say. I'm not sure I want her to talk about it. Every day I ask myself what I would do if Jesse died—if I had, by some cruel fate, been the only one to survive that basement horror scene. Would I still fight? *Could* I after losing her again?

I take another sip of my coffee and a smooth taste of bitter chocolate warms my lips, tongue and throat. "Do you like bowling?"

She laughs. A genuine cackle that isn't as adorable as Jesse's, but it is infectious nonetheless.

"Do *you* bowl?" She asks. I can't imagine you in those hideous shoes."

I'm shocked. "You think I'm prissy?"

"You seem a *tad* more girlie than me," she says. When I fall back against the back of the chair, she asks. "Does that offend you?"

"I don't think I'm girlie." I turn the cup in my hand. "I'm feminine, okay—but *so* girlie you can't see me bowling? That's just wrong."

"Your nose ring is pretty hardcore," she says. She leans forward as if to inspect it. The look in her upturned eyes makes my stomach quiver. "But you take an obvious nonviolent approach to our work. Jeremiah and I go in with guns and you're all Band-Aids and water."

"There's quite the distance between bowling and violence," I say. The café is comfortable and I get the sense that there is more to her. I don't know if it's attraction, but there is something there. An allure. "But that depends on how you'll play, I guess."

"Is that an invitation?" she asks. "To go bowling with you?"

My confidence falters. The banter train just stops and she is smart enough to see this for herself.

She puts her ceramic mug down and it clanks against the saucer. "Listen."

I look at her. Note the furrowed brow, but her mouth is soft, not hard in agitation.

"You still have feelings for her."

The honesty almost incites me to protest on principle alone. She doesn't give me a chance for such a knee jerk reaction.

"That's fine," she says with a dismissive wave. "Really it is."

"Is it?" I ask. I keep positioning my cup in its little saucer.

"It doesn't change the fact that I like you," she says. "You're gorgeous, smart, kind, and brave."

The heat rises in my face as if someone is holding a match under my chin and my heart is doing something strange. It's her voice. I realize for the first time that I really like her voice.

"I've known these things about you ever since Chattanooga."

Chattanooga. Jeremiah received a tip from his network that six people with NRD were being held captive by one of Caldwell's cells—the smaller tactical groups he relies on to do his dirty work and keep his hands and image clean—like the group that got Jesse, Lane, Brinkley and I last year. This group had the hostages chained up in a suburban house, torturing them for days.

"I watched you talk down a gunman," she continues. Her admiration is apparent in her beaming face. "You reasoned with that guy like a pro. I bet professional negotiators aren't half that good. And like I said, all you brought were Band-Aids and bottled water."

"You're exaggerating again." My face is on fire. "I would never bring a plastic bottle to a gun fight. Plastic is so bad for the environment."

She reaches across the table and takes my hand. It isn't just that we are in a public place, in the South, in a generally homophobic region of the United States. It's that I feel like I've done something wrong. By touching her, or letting her touch me—and for *liking* the feel of it.

Jesse isn't your girlfriend. I remind myself. *She chose Lane. Get over it. You have to get over it.*

I manage to keep ahold of Nikki's hand despite the clenching in my abdomen.

"I just want to get to know you," she says, still beaming. "This beautiful girl who does amazing things."

"OK," I say, but it feels like a mistake. Like a betrayal. "What do you want to know?"

Nikki grins and it's triumphant. Even as she settles into her seat like a victor ready to relish her first prize, I can already feel myself pulling back, curling around Jesse's secrets protectively as if they are my own.

"Start from the beginning," Nikki says. "I want to know everything."

And that is what I'm afraid of.

Jesse

I wake up to an empty bed. First, I spread my arms wide, seeing how much of the mattress I can take up by myself. Then a sort of panic settles in. I'm so used to sharing my bed with Lane, or Ally, that so much space feels weird.

I hear a *plop* against my window on the opposite side of the room, like something has smacked against the glass, and I jolt upright in my bed. A dart, one of those soft ones with a suction cup on one end, is stuck and wiggling there. The sucker looks like one of those bottom feeder fish slurping away at the glass of an aquarium. At the end of the suction cup, something dangles.

I open the window and work the dart back and forth until it releases with a loud *POP* into my hand. The attached note says:

Bring you know what to you know where

Is this the best code he could manage? Brinkley is supposed to be a high-class secret agent. Or maybe that says more about his confidence in my decryption skills. I guess I'm not the one who managed to evade the law, fake my own death, and uncover a huge operation. So I'll give the man his due.

I yank on jeans and pull a T-shirt over my head. As I grab a black hoodie from my closet, I spot another note on the nightstand.

I love the way you look when you're sleeping in my arms

I grin. I take a step toward the stairs and my thighs clench, a deep sore ache that only makes me smile bigger. For a moment, I'm lost in the memory of Lane. His hands on my bare back, his lips starting on my neck and ears before working their way down to the soft inner part of my thighs. Lane holding me up, his arms strong around me as I straddle his lap, legs pinned wide.

Winston gets a bowl of kibble for breakfast, which he inhales without chewing. Then, with the harddrive jutting from the back pocket of my jeans, I grab a banana from the counter and trot out the back door. It's a sliding door like the Lovetts', but mine connects with a deck, not a patio, and my yard is smaller, unfenced, and less impressive. At least I don't have any killer trees. None that I know of anyway.

All the houses in my subdivision are two stories high, with an attached garage. Lots of trees, flowerbeds and running trails weave themselves in and out of the woods, forming a two-mile loop around Greenbrook. Each house has an acre or more of grass, and trees are plentiful, which I like. Mine particularly has Japanese maples that Ally planted two years ago. In their dark purple and burgundy hues, they match my house's white-gray brick exterior and black shutters.

I love my house. It's nice and comfortable and far enough from the city that I can get some decent sleep every night, without listening to horns blaring, loud music or ambulance sirens. It was Ally who found this house, Ally who put all the furniture inside, and Ally who makes it feel like home. She insists on having her own apartment, but she practically lives here.

For some stupid reason, my throat gets all tight at the thought of this and how little I've seen her lately. How long before I lose her completely?

I try not to look suspicious, chomping on my banana as I cut through my backyard to the part of the trail closest to my house. I push past the trees marking the edge of my yard, and it is only a few feet until the dirt trail begins.

"Right here," a voice says from the trees.

If I wasn't paying attention, I would have thought the large maple in front of me had sprung to life. But then a man-shaped shadow detaches from the tree and moves forward.

At first, I barely recognize Brinkley. It's only been a month or so since I've seen him, when he rolled into town just long enough to insist I do the Lovett replacement. He looked worn then, but now he looks like *hell*. His last bit of a beer gut is completely gone.

His face used to be a full macho man, but now it's more like emaciated supermodel. The right side of his face is a purple color, the hint of an old bruise. His favorite leather jacket hangs off of him.

"What the hell happened to you?" I ask. "Are you sick?"

He makes no reply. In one hand, he still has the dart gun, something you'd find in the toy section of a store. He points it at me playfully and shoots me in the cheek with a dart that bounces off and falls into the mud.

I pick up the dart and hand it to him. "Oh so it's fine if you know what I've been up to, but not the other way around?"

"I have my reasons," he replies.

"*What* reasons?"

He points the gun again.

"Never mind. Forget I asked." I reach out and push the plastic barrel down. "Put that away before you take my eye out or something. As far as I know I can't regrow those."

Brinkley faked his death so he could investigate his own organization, the FBRD—the Federal Bureau of Regenerative Deaths—and my employer. A couple of other agents double-crossed him and tried to kill us, so we knew something was up.

The bureau licenses me but I've been sans handler for almost two weeks since my temporary handler

Garrison was reassigned. In my mind, I'm still taking orders from Brinkley, so it doesn't matter.

"So I guess I'm not supposed to ask about your face?"

Brinkley shrugs but he doesn't raise the gun. "You should have seen the other guy."

"Why do men always say that?" I ask.

"Not all of us heal in a heartbeat." He rubs a calloused thumb over his bruised cheek, scraping a jagged nail over his scruff.

"I don't heal in a *heartbeat*. I have to be dead for at least a few hours." I notice his tan. "Where have you been?"

"Arizona," he says. "At the old base where Eric Sullivan was last seen."

My heart begins its vicious climb up the back of my throat, the way a cat crawls up the drapes to get away from a yappy dog. *Eric Sullivan.*

"Not much to connect him to Caldwell," he continues.

Because that's the latest theory—Caldwell and Eric Sullivan are the same man.

Eric Sullivan, with his newly discovered NRD was swept up in protective custody. For over 17 years, the protocol was to detain those with NRD and those detainees suffered unknown tortures at the hands of their military captors. Eric was unfortunate enough to discover his NRD nine months before the public forced the military to release their prisoners. Brinkley thought the reason Eric managed to stay hidden so well after his release was because he'd taken on a new identity, emerging eight years to the day of his death as Caldwell—North American Leader of the Unified Church—a social climb I can't even imagine. If Caldwell and Eric Sullivan are the same person, then what he did in the years after his release remain a mystery.

"I got this," Brinkley says. He opens his jacket enough to pull out a folded piece of paper.

I trade him the hard drive and my mush of a banana peel for it. "Gerard's going to know it's gone."

Brinkley drops the peel in disgust. "Of course he'll notice. A computer won't work without a hard drive."

"Oh he'll notice *long* before that," I say.

"Jesse—" My name is a growl in the back of Brinkley's throat.

"It was the best I could do just to get the drive into Ally's hand and jump in front of that tree."

Brinkley raises an eyebrow. "Tree attacks child. That must have made headlines."

"We might still be in the dark," I say pointing at the hard drive. "Lovett might not have anything on there."

"Even things people think they've deleted can be

pulled off their hard drives. Maybe we'll get lucky," he says. I hope so. We've been keeping our eyes on all the higher Church officials for over a year. About time something works out in our favor.

I open the sheet of paper Brinkley has given me and swear under my breath. "Is this a medical record?"

"For Eric Sullivan," Brinkley says. He has a small device in his hands which he is attaching to the hard drive. Oh Brinkley with his gadgets. It is impressive actually, seeing as he comes across as very old school. He's all pen, paper, and *cell phone, what's a cell phone?*

"Eric Sullivan, 34," I say. "But he's got to be at least 50."

"This is from his file in Arizona, back when he was still in custody."

"Caldwell could pass for much younger," I argue.

"So he's been dying like you," Brinkley says, referring to the fact that I don't look a day over seventeen, despite my 25th birthday last month. It's true that death-replacing or dying in general, helps us not age. When we die, we get that metabolic boost as our bodies heal the damage. It just so happens this boost doesn't discriminate between normal cell deterioration and that caused by trauma. Death-replacing is certainly the only explanation I have for Caldwell's preservation, yet the Church believes we are soulless and they use the fact that we don't *go* anywhere when we die as proof. I can't believe they'd follow a leader who openly revealed his NRD. It must be his dirty little secret.

The machine in Brinkley's hand whirls and clicks as we stand in the shade of the maple tree, just far enough off the trail that should someone approach, they can't see us immediately.

"I just don't understand why he would infiltrate the Church and secure a high position. And how would he do death replacements without media attention? He's watched constantly."

"He could be working off the radar and they might not be replacements, just dying for other reasons."

Enough deaths are happening off the radar already. Almost *thousands* in the last few years combined. Not just death-replacement agents are being cornered and killed, or even those living openly with their NRD in mainstream society. Many of the victims had not yet made their condition public when they were attacked.

This meant someone with power and authority is able to discover who has NRD and is turning that information over to the wrong people.

But who is doing it: the FBRD, the Church, or the military? That's what I'm trying to help Brinkley figure out. He pulled me out of the barn fire that killed me eight years ago. He gave me a new life and purpose. The least I can do is help him.

"Did   you compare this to a picture of Caldwell?" I ask. This is the first picture I've seen of Eric.

Brinkley nods. "It's close, but not exact. My consultant agrees with our theory that Caldwell has had slight facial reconstruction. Just enough that his body wouldn't reject the alterations."

"Then Caldwell is my father."

"Jesse—"

"No." I stop him from patronizing me. "I need to accept the fact that the guy who wants to kill me is also my dad. If I don't get it through my head he's going to catch me off guard again."

"A *father* and a *dad* is not the same thing," Brinkley argues, looking up from the whirl and click of his device to warn me with fiery eyes.

I remember being little and lying under a car with him—Eric—Caldwell—my *father*. He was telling me what different parts of the car were. He had a great smile and his laughter was the laughter of a good-natured rogue in one of those swash-buckling movies. I also remember blaming him for dying and leaving me at the mercy of Eddie, my mother's pervert of a second husband. I remember crying myself to sleep, wearing his old mechanic shirts for years. Begging him to come back. *Begging.*

All I want to know now is what happened.

What happened to him when he died? What happened in that internment camp in the desert? What happened when he escaped? Why didn't he ever come back for me? If he loved me, he would have come back to his daughter, back to his wife—wouldn't he? He wouldn't have run to the Church, run to the monsters and then *become* one. I want answers, but—

"This is encrypted," Brinkley says, breaking into my thoughts. "I'll need to see a guy before we figure out what's on it."

"Suckfest," I say.

"In the meantime, I want you to go see Gloria, all right?" he says. "She knows what our next move should be. I'll check back with you once I get the hard drive open."

When I don't move, he adds: "Go on."

Some things never change. We almost die together and he still treats me like that seventeen-year-old kid he rescued.

Maybe *I've* changed.

Because instead of arguing, I give a little salute, turn on my heels, and head home.

Ally

This particular apartment is only a small unit inside a massive complex. From what I can tell, there are no other businesses in this building and even this space has an artificial name on the bills. Jeremiah opens the back door for us with his key.

In the apartment's main room, a large wall of monitors is responsible for recording all of the various angles surrounding the building. It's Parish who works security today. He's a round guy, more round than muscle. He has a McDonald's soda cup in one fist and a crumpled sandwich wrapper in the other. A section of his belly is exposed between his pants and shirt as he stretches back in the swivel chair. He has little flecks of food in his beard. I make a motion with my hand to indicate they're there.

"I'm saving those for later," he says, but then he shakes himself like a dog.

"Eyes on the screen," Jeremiah says to him. He's wearing the same dark clothes and appears as the antithesis to Parish's sloppiness.

Jeremiah leads us in a staccato step toward the back of the apartment. Nikki and I follow past a room with walls covered in corkboard with pictures and strings connecting the images. We call it the storyboard room where we map out our search and rescue strategies.

I want everyone to come into the digital age but Jeremiah insists we keep everything hard—actual files and photos, written notes and all that. He says these can be controlled and destroyed while digital files can be hacked and accessed from anywhere. It's why he only allows the computer monitors in one room, if they're hacked all they will see is Parish lounging.

The office is completely devoid of any kind of interior design: no rugs, curtains, pictures or certificates to indicate what kind of office this is supposed to be. The hallway is dark except for a single bulb hanging overhead.

He stops and looks through a glass window. It takes me a second to realize what I'm looking at. I don't hide my astonishment. "What the hell happened to her?"

First of all, I didn't realize we even had a room at the end of this hallway, let alone with one with a large pane of glass allowing us to see the woman inside.

Her face is swollen, especially blue and puffy on one side. Blood has dried all down her shirt front, and is crusting at the collarbone.

I grab the door handle intending to go inside and help her. Jeremiah grabs my upper arm in a way that instantly angers me. I shrug hard and he's forced to let go of me and to regain a step he lost. Nikki, for the briefest of moments, places a hand lightly on my back as if to steady me.

"She is not a victim," he says, calmly. "We are interrogating her."

I look at her again, at the swollen face, the soft heaving of her chest and the red mangled skin of her wrists, irritated by the cuffs chaining her to the metal chair bolted to the floor.

"How long has she been like this?" I ask.

"We brought her in last night," he answers.

Just after you spoke to me at the hospital, I think.

"You've been hurting her?" I ask. Because I can't imagine Parish doing so.

Jeremiah doesn't answer.

The rage inside me blisters. I shove past both Jeremiah and Nikki and storm toward the front of the building. I have to get out of here before I hurt someone myself.

Someone grabs my wrist. I yank it away. She is hardly deterred. Nikki grabs me again and pulls me into the storyboard room.

"Just wait!" Nikki yells in growing desperation as I resist. She puts herself between me and the door. "Wait, *wait*! You don't know the situation. *I* don't know the situation. We have to at least find out what's happening."

I shrug her off again and she gives me the distance. "She's a woman, Nick. A woman tied to a goddam chair with her face bashed in. In no world is that right."

"Women strap bombs to their chests and blow up marketplaces full of children," she counters.

I blink. My mouth opens and closes. "What is your point?"

"I'm saying it doesn't matter that she is a woman. You don't know what she did."

"What did she do?" I ask. I'm clutching the side of my head with my fists to keep them from hurting her. I might just end up tearing my own hair out.

"I don't know," Nikki admits.

"Then why are you defending him?" I ask.

"Because I trust him," she says. "I think we should at least *ask* him what is going on."

"She is responsible for several kidnappings," a deep voice says. Jeremiah stands in the doorway. He leans heavily against the frame and I see his hands for the first time. They are red across the bone.

"So that makes it okay?" I ask, choking on my anger.

"You happen to know one of the children," Jeremiah says. He doesn't waver, his voice or gaze. "Her name was Nessa Hildebrand."

Nessa.

"I believe her mother attacked Jesse because the Church told her if she didn't, then she would never see her daughter again. Is that right?" he asks.

Eve almost completely decapitated Jesse. I'd never seen so much blood in my life.

"And she never did see her daughter again, did she?" he continues, when I fail to say anything. "Because this woman you're so quick to protect, never returned what she took."

The world is rushing back. I lean against the nearest piece of furniture. A desk, chair, cabinet—whatever it is, it's cold, even through the wool fabric of my coat.

"I am not proud of what I am doing," Jeremiah says. He removes his glasses and cleans them with the end of his shirt before replacing them on his nose. "But that woman is part of this. She receives her orders from *somewhere*. She takes the people, the *children* somewhere. We need to know so we can get them back."

I look at Nikki. Her face is stricken with grief. Tears threaten to spill from the corners of her eyes and the bridge of her nose and cheeks are flushed red.

"I wouldn't have joined if I thought this was how you gathered your information," I say.

"Our methods escalate as the threat escalates," he says.

He's watching me over the rim of his glasses. He looks like an English professor, not an interrogator.

"That is why war is so devastating, because no one knows when to quit," I say. I'm dizzy with anger. I try to think of my breath, hoping to slow all of this down, but I can't focus.

"If she knew where Jesse had been taken, wouldn't you do anything to find out?" he asks.

"Don't bring Jesse into this," I say.

"She is already in this."

Jesse—*Jesse*, it always comes back to her. Jesse dying. Jesse dead. My years of walking in a death-like dream myself. Would I do anything to that woman if it meant saving Jesse?

"We are supposed to be saving people," I say. *I just want to end this so she'll be safe.* "Is that what we are doing?"

"Follow me." He doesn't wait for me to follow or to refuse.

When I step out of the room, he's already looking through the window at the woman.

One breath turns into another, then three, stretching in a long silence. It feels like we're waiting for something, so I don't speak.

"It was my sister," he says, finally. "She wasn't a death-replacement agent like Jesse. She was just a kid. Thirteen years old."

My heart sinks. I don't like where this is going.

"When the drunk driver hit us the summer before, she died on impact. My parents and I had multiple injuries, but nothing fatal. We were completely devastated to lose Ruth. Then we discovered her NRD. She was returned to us and even though my parents were God-fearing folk, we considered this a blessing. By some miracle, God had restored her. Like Lazarus, she was alive."

I look at the woman in the chair. Her swollen face, her sobs. I look at the floor again and brace myself for what I know is coming.

"One day she was riding her bike home from school and a group of boys surrounded her. They were classmates, five boys she'd known her whole life. It wasn't a big town, you see, and somehow word had gotten around from parent to parent back to the children about her condition."

"These boys, probably because their parents spouted their own condemnation at the dinner table, saw fit to punish Ruth just for being what she was."

"Stop," I whisper. The ache in my chest threatens to collapse my chest.

"They beat her first," he says in the same slow and even tone as if I had never spoken. "One of the boys cut her hair. They carved the word *whore* on her forehead, as if they even knew what the word meant."

"Stop." I am crying. I'm holding my chest and trying to breathe. Nikki comes toward me, but I wave her back.

"They hung her from the tree at the edge of our property with her own jump rope. My father was the one to find her that way when he came home from work. She died from strangulation and a broken neck."

"That wouldn't have killed her," Nikki says. Her voice is far away. The world under me tilts and vibrates. I press my palms against the wall for strength.

"No," Jeremiah admits. "It was my father's shotgun that eventually did it. But when she awoke that second time, she wasn't the same. And it only got worse with the torment at school, at church, the threat they might find her again and do worse things to her. She shot herself in the head before she turned fourteen, but not before enduring months of threats, isolation and condemnation from people who'd known and loved her all her life—people who no longer welcomed her into their homes, at their dinner tables, or into their yards to play with their own children."

Putting one arm on the glass, I use it to brace myself against the world whirling around me. I try to slow my breath again and again. To focus and breathe the way my therapist taught me to breathe through my anxiety. It begins to work, but Jeremiah isn't finished saying what he needs to say.

"My father died of a heart attack at sixty-three. Only he didn't die," Jeremiah says. "Once he realized he was the one who had NRD—who had given Ruth her condition—he used the shotgun on himself."

My chest is so tight I can't catch my breath. "What about the law?"

The first real hint of anger tinges his words. "The law sided with the boys. The *good* boys from *good* families. The attention my family drew from their demands for justice incited more threats of violence. My father lost his job. My mother's closest friends quit speaking to her. You think there is a right way to do this, Alice, but there isn't. The corruptors take the *right* way and twist it. What do you think Caldwell is doing with all his law-making? All of his propaganda and media attention. Don't tell me he's building a better world."

I turn away from the wall because I can't bear to see the woman, but I leave one hand to steady myself as I face Jeremiah. "It doesn't mean we should become like them. If that is what I have to become just to win, it isn't worth it."

Jeremiah turns to me, taking his eyes off the woman for the first time since beginning his story. "She has told me the location of two children. Jo and Hector have already found one child and took her to a safe house. I need you and Nicole to pick up the other."

"From where?" I ask. But I am not paying complete attention to him.

"I'll go," Nikki says. "Ally needs sleep."

"She's twelve," Jeremiah says. "She'd been on the run for almost seven months before they caught up to her. When her mother discovered her NRD, she turned her out. You would be surprised how many of the homeless children are homeless simply because they were thrown out."

"40%," Nikki says. "It's the same for LBGT youth."

I turn to leave but Jeremiah grabs ahold of me.

"No one is looking out for them," Jeremiah says, releasing me gently. "But I am." He raps his fist against his chest. "I am but I need you with me, Alice. We need Jesse."

"She's been through enough," I say, thinking of Jesse's own horribly dark past. The molestation, the rape, the suicide—all of that on top of the prejudice against her condition. "I can't ask anything more of her. No one should."

Jeremiah's face softens for the first time. He nods and turns back toward the glass. I'm almost at the end of the hallway, at the edge of his sight when he stops me one last time.

"Unfortunately," he says and his expression is soft and sad. "Jesse may not have a choice."

Jesse

I'm really dragging ass on the way home. I can't quit thinking about Caldwell, especially when he was still Eric. Back when he was just some mechanic, married to my mom, Danica, with a chatterbox kid following him everywhere. Back when he was my dad.

No—*He isn't Eric Sullivan anymore.*

Your dad is dead.

But—his smile, his face as he opened his arms and bent low to scoop me up. The smell of him: cedar, oil and aftershave.

He ordered his men to kill you. He considers that life as over as you do. You are not his kid anymore.

It's definitely true that my old life seems a million miles away. So why can't I stop thinking about him?

When I open the back door to my house Winston comes running. It's something that never happens unless it's dinner time. I think that much fat just makes it hard to run.

He is solid enough to knock me back a step as he throws himself against my legs and whines. His tail is tucked and ears up and alert.

"It's okay, baby," I say. I coo in the pug's ears and

rub the soft velvet between my fingers. "What's wrong?"

He whines more desperately, staring toward the front of the house. He wants me to pick him up, but he's too fat for that and I need my hands anyway because something is obviously wrong.

The hair on the back of my neck is at attention. I see knives in the block on the counter and think about grabbing one, but that feels dumb. I'd probably just stab myself like some stupid horror movie girl.

I creep, pug close at my heels still whining to be lifted like a baby. I want to soothe him, but I am trying to pay attention. One room at a time, I strain to hear anything despite the racket my panicked heart makes.

The kitchen is empty. The space between my counters and island are clear. Nothing is hiding under the dining table nor is anything lurking in the high archway leading into the living room. The office is clear and so is the living room, unless they are crouching down between the couch and coffee table, on the other side out of sight—which is a possibility.

I take a few tentative steps to the left so I can check the front door before moving toward the stairs that will take me to the bedrooms.

Then I see it.

A spray of glass in the foyer glitters, and in the mess, a small wrapped bundle waits. I order Winston to stay. He doesn't listen, taking a step forward as I do, his nails clicking on the wood.

"*Stay*," I say. Fear and anger fills my voice. Feeling guilty that I've scared him more, I try to explain. "The glass, baby. You'll get it in your paws."

I take another step closer as I cast a nervous glance into the living room. No one is crouched beside the couch. I strain again to hear anything over the silence: a floorboard shifting under someone's weight. A stair creaking. Breath or a rustling of clothes. Movement of any kind.

I hear nothing except the cool air wafting through the shattered pane.

Rib cage sore from the still constant flapping of my heart, I carefully take the cloth wrapped bundle in my hands.

It is an odd shape, and heavy. I unroll the wound cloth and take a good look.

It's one of my T-shirts—bloody and torn and one of my shoes, smushed flat, both wrapped around a brick which I'm assuming is what broke the window. The shirt and shoe I recognize. They came from two different jobs, but they were both lost during replacements. On the shirt, written in blood—and this is when I start praying it isn't *my* blood—someone has written a short, but clear message:

"Closer than you think," I read aloud.

Close enough to snatch the clothes off my dead body.

"Yeah, that's not creepy."

Crash.

I scream and jump back, tripping over my stupid dog. I reach out to catch my fall and let go of the brick at the same time. The dog yells as I step on him and I hit the floor hard just after he scampers out of range. Then the brick comes down. I slide my forearm on shattered glass when I yank away from the explosion of pain as the brick connects with my knee.

My arm burns. An angry red welt rises to the surface as a tuff of torn flesh fills up with blood. My knee burns too where the brick fell on it, but my jeans have protected the skin, so what I feel instead is the dull throb of impact.

Winston is okay. He's trying to climb on top of me as I lean on my uninjured elbow and inspect myself. I say more than a few words that are as ladylike as a sailor's whore.

I am even more pissed when I realize it was just a piece of glass that had fallen from the shattered pane that made the noise in the first place. But it freaking terrified me.

Winston is jumping up and down trying to lick my face.

"I'm okay," I say, pushing him away but he just won't give up. "Gee-*zus*. Fine. *Fine*. Come here."

I pick up the dog like he wants, but God, he's heavy.

And there is something else wrong. It isn't until my heart slows from a jack rabbit pace to something like mild cardio that I recognize the silence in my house. *Pure* silence. I manage to pull myself onto my feet and shuffle into the living room. I check a couple of light switches and my suspicions prove true.

I've blasted it—every single light in the house is blown—and everything else probably.

With no lights and threats written in blood, it's time to get the hell out. I decide not to check upstairs but instead I put Winston in the car and drive to Gloria's. Brinkley wants me to pay her a visit anyway and there's no time like the present. I'm almost to Gloria's when I realize I should've left a note, in case Ally or Lane came by.

Whoops. If they do I'll certainly get a call.

Gloria lives in Nashville proper, in a little neighborhood of one-story houses. Her house looks like a face. Two front windows for eyes and a door for a nose-mouth. It's brick with peeling shutters. It has some wrought iron for a nice touch, but the paint on the wrought iron is peeling too, revealing rust beneath.

Her grass is uncut and probably houses a million-strong rabbit colony.

Still shaking, I knock and knock but no answer, so I use my spare key to let myself in.

In the creepy basement is where I find her. She's sitting at a long desk, a massive beast that stretches from one corner all the way to the water heater. It looks like a cafeteria table, with its fake wooden top and metal corners. Her back is to the rickety stairs, creaking as I make my descent clutching the pug. A light swings over my head, swaying a little with the unsettled house. All over the concrete walls are pictures, fixed with chunks of duct tape to the painted cinder blocks behind them.

By the time protective custody was started, the military had just finished conducting ESP research to see if they could develop psychic warfare. This research was discontinued, but what came out of it was remote-viewing. I'm not making this shit up. Google it: *remote-viewing*.

The military tried to recreate NRD, by injecting magnetite into the brains of volunteer soldiers. Few survived the procedure. If they weren't brain damaged to the point of death they became discharged outcasts with little to no benefits. The only option most of them had was to become Analysts of necromagnetic phenomenon—A.M.P.s—and only if they were good at remote viewing, particularly death prediction, did they even have this option. Otherwise it's food stamps, unemployment, or homelessness.

It's my understanding remote-viewing is like clairvoyance because viewers see pictures of stuff in their heads, but remote-viewers can do more than just see something. Somehow they can keep "entering" into a vision differently to get several pictures. Then they piece these pictures together for a more accurate assessment of the situation.

As I search the walls, I realize she is definitely looking for someone now.

The sound of her pencil scratching furiously over the paper fills the basement. I put Winston on the cold concrete floor. He still doesn't stray far, but he's feeling better, or at least brave enough to search the basement's corners for stray crumbs.

I want Gloria's attention, but I know better than to interrupt. Though Winston's snorts don't seem to bother her. I search the pictures for clues as to what's going on.

It's the same girl in every single one of the pictures, from different angles. Sometimes she's smiling. Sometimes she's looking at the viewer. In others, it's her profile. Despite these differences, some things are the same. In every one, she is young—fifteen or sixteen—with thick dark hair, a big nose and thin lips. She stands in protective postures, like someone who isn't comfortable with herself, cradling skinny limbs across her small chest. Most of the time her wild hair covers half her face.

Gloria finally stops, and puts her pencil down.

"Who is she?" I ask.

"Liza Miller."

"She looks young," I say. What I really wonder is what would Liza think if she knew an African-American woman in her late 40s she'd never even met was sitting in her basement drawing pictures of her.

I tell Gloria about the brick.

At the end of my story she says, "Call Dr. York. Ask him where the clothes were. *Who* had access? Get it tested to see if it is your blood."

"You didn't see this coming?" I ask.

"I can't see everything," she reminds me. Even if she could, it doesn't mean she can stop it. In fact, trying to save me proved to only put me in danger last year when we got trapped in the church basement. "You still need to report it."

"And say what?" I laugh. "I can't tell them who it is. Most people would at least have an idea, but not me. Is it a religious freak? Someone with a zombie fetish? Or it could be—"

Gloria intercepts my escalating voice. "I think we have established that Caldwell isn't the type to get his own hands dirty."

"He has minions," I say. "It could be another

Martin-drone."

"What happened to your arm?" Gloria asks softly. She sounds as tired as I feel.

"I tripped and the brick fell on me and there was glass."

"You tripped over a brick and fell on it?"

I let out a long exhausted breath. "No. I tripped, holding a brick and then dropped it—on myself." A long stretch of silence expands between us with the exception of the low click of Gloria's water heater and Winston's investigative snorts. "And I think I broke my house."

"You broke your house?" She asks, flatly.

"Yeah, like all the electrical stuff."

She pushes away from her desk and starts to ascend the stairs. "A headache is coming. I need a drink."

I scoop up Winston, happy for an excuse to get out of that dark dank basement. By the time we reach the top of the stairs, Gloria is chugging a 2-liter of soda like a beer at a frat party.

I remember why I came. "Brinkley said you'd know what was next."

"Liza Miller is next."

"Is she a zombie?"

Gloria gives me a warning glare. No one but Lane appreciates the z-word.

"I don't know what she is," Gloria admits. The

plastic soda bottle, which partially deflated in her ravenous sucking, pops back into place. Winston lets out a startled grunt from the floor and I give him a reassuring nudge with my foot.

Her cheeks redden. "Brinkley should have planned this better. The three of us are not enough."

"Don't Black Ops operate in small tactical units?"

"You, Brinkley and I do not make a tactical unit. I'm surprised Lane and Ally aren't doing more."

"Lane would help but he's trying to get his certification and Ally—" I say. "I think she needs a vacation, not more work."

Gloria's gaze narrows. "She still loves you."

I shrug and force a tight laugh. "Yeah, she's just tired of my shit."

"She just has her own way of doing things," Gloria says, twisting open a new 2-liter.

Yeah, without me, I think. Then, *it's your own damn fault. Did you think she'd be happy you got all monogamous with Lane? Would you be happy?*

"No," I murmur to myself because Gloria has stopped listening to my girl problems. Something else has darkened her features.

"Any signs of the other player?" I ask, taking a guess.

The other player is what we've taken to calling the mystery A.M.P. up Caldwell's sleeve. He—or she— has already managed to outsmart Gloria a couple of times. That can't be easy on the ego.

"I want to be sure," she says.

"You're the *best* at what you do, G," I say. "You were just caught off guard. We all were. How they hell were we supposed to know someone was viewing *you*? We couldn't have."

I try to reassure her, but she still looks so defeated, standing in her yellow kitchen with its aged yellow countertops and yellow-brown floor. Even the fridge is the color of spicy mustard and the cabinets—you guessed it—yellow metal matching her card table turned dining set. Only the white sheer curtain covering the small window above the kitchen sink looks like it's been bought in this decade.

My phone goes off and Lane's picture appears in the screen. It hits me like a thump in the chest that Ally hasn't called me all day. She used to call multiple times a day to check on me, and that was only when she wasn't with me.

Maybe she really is, slowly and painfully, untangling herself from my life.

Ally

I'm exhausted. My limbs are little more than wet bags of sand.

The stairwell to my apartment building is dim and quiet as I trudge my grocery bags up the stairs and then down the narrow hallway to my door. My keys are impossibly loud as they jingle and clank against the wooden frame and metal lock.

As soon as I close the door behind me, I fall against it. *Home*.

I feel like I haven't seen it for years.

Immediately, I dig through the bags for the chocolate and cleave a giant truffle in half with my teeth. I put on the kettle for a cup of tea and while it builds steam, I put away my groceries.

Only then do I settle into my fluffy chaise by the balcony. The heat of the tea warms the cup and my hands. There are no windows because my apartment is an interior room, but the balcony lets in the light of orange streetlamps framing the parking lot and the high half-moon above.

Jesse may not have a choice.

I remember the night of her suicide. I've played it over and over in my head many times. I said *go to sleep*.

We'll talk at school. Because it was in the middle of the night and my mom had yelled at me because she'd called so late. I should have known something was wrong. I should have known that slur in her voice wasn't sleepiness. I should have known she was calling to tell me goodbye.

Then there's the dreams. Jesse is always in this white night gown. The blaze of the pole barn her father built before we met lit up the whole night. In the dream, she is always walking toward it, slowly, deliberately, as if entranced.

I'm always behind her, screaming and *screaming* her name. I beg her to stop, beg her not to go into the fire, but she does anyway.

Every time.

I can only watch her nightgown catch first and burn.

I wake up to the sound of a ringing phone. I've slept the whole night away in the chaise, the tea cup long empty and cold on the side table. I rub at my sticky eyes again as the phone trills urgently. I fumble for it with groggy hands and cradle it against my ear. "Hello?"

"Is this Alice Gallagher?" a man asks.

"This is she."

"This is Davis, a meter inspector with the state department. Are you still the contact person for 1321 Greenbrook Drive?"

I cough and clear my throat, trying to sound more professional than unconscious. "Yes, I'm Ms. Sullivan's assistant. How can I help you?"

"We received reports of an electrical disturbance in the neighborhood, so they sent me out to check. It appears a power line is down outside the residence. Were you aware of this?"

"No."

"The damage to the outside box suggests a power surge. I just checked the meter and it has stopped completely. There's no reading whatsoever coming from the residence but you have not reported a power outage."

"The house has no electricity?" I ask. *What happened?* "Is Jesse home now?"

"I knocked on the door but there was no answer. Also, there's a pane of broken glass by the front door."

"I'm on my way," I say. I am already pushing myself out of the deep armchair and falling into my shoes and coat. "Can you wait there for me? It'll be ten minutes tops."

"Sure," he says.

I try to call Jesse's house phone but no one answers. Nor does she pick up her cell or answer the office phone. I remind myself Jesse is really bad about answering her phone, or remembering to bring it at all. That it doesn't mean she's been kidnapped and decapitated.

I don't feel any better by the time I pull into the driveway behind the *Concept Energy* truck. A tall man with a yellow hat and thick gloves gets out of his truck as I do.

"Ms. Gallagher?" he asks coming toward me, a utility belt jolting against his hips as he walks.

"Yes," I say. "I'll let you in." I don't know what else to say so I just focus on the problem at hand. My heart beats harder when I see the broken glass beside the door. It's been covered with a small piece of cardboard from the inside. I try not to stare at it too obviously as I let him into the house. I tell him the fuse box is downstairs and he disappears through the door leading to the unfinished basement.

When another attempt to reach Jesse fails, I call Gloria.

"Jesse's window is busted out and she has no power," I say.

"She's fine," Gloria says.

I suck air, unaware I'd been holding my breath at all. My relief turns to anger. "What happened?"

"Someone threw a brick through the window. It just scared her."

"Why didn't she call me?" I ask.

Gloria says nothing as if waiting for me to say more, but the technician reappears.

"I have to go," I say.

Gloria hangs up without saying goodbye. Then again, she's not known for her phone etiquette.

"A power surge destroyed the wiring. We can repair the conduit to the home and the busted wire outside, but the house itself may have to be rewired by a good electrician. Many of the components have been damaged."

"What would it cost to replace it?" I ask. When he looks hesitant I ask. "What is your best estimate?"

"15-20 grand, depending on the cause and the extent of the damage. Your house insurance may cover it."

I try not to look crestfallen. "Thank you."

The technician taps his hat and leaves. He pauses just before getting into his truck and gives the house one more look. I sigh and feel the last of the adrenaline leave me.

It's like uncurling a fist that's been clenched for a long time—painful and slow—I keep repeating it. *You can't be everywhere at once. You can't do everything.*

"Watch me try," I say.

Someone pounds on the front door and I can see through the glass it isn't the electricity guy having forgotten something.

Regina Lovett, mother of the little girl Jesse saved, pushes past me and enters the darkening house without permission. It's a wonder why she even bothered to knock.

"Where *is* she? Jessica Sullivan! Come here right this minute."

It's the voice a mother uses.

"It's just Jesse actually. With an "e" and she isn't here," I manage to say. Regina's wild movements shake the last bit of calm from me and despite the fact that we're past the part in the day when lamps are no longer needed, the house comes into sharp focus. The white light of the damp overcast day stretching the shadows around Regina.

Her skirt is torn and muddy and she's only wearing one shoe. Her hair is wild, tangled and the cut on her right cheek, a tiny thing, has bled quite a bit.

"Jesse!" Regina screams.

"I told you she isn't here," I say again. I'm looking for weapons stashed under the remains of her clothes. That'd be my luck. "What happened?"

"What *happened*? Don't you know what they did?"

I shake my head no. I realize she can't hide a gun or knife under the tattered remains of her clothes. That doesn't mean she won't try to harm me using her bare hands. I keep a distance from her, enough that I can move if she lunges.

"They came to my house. They called him into his office for a *chat*." She pauses for exaggerated air quotes. "I thought it was important Church business.

Then he calls me into the office. He starts screaming at me for the replacement, saying I betrayed him. How did they even know about the replacement?"

I shake my head again. "I don't know, Regina."

"He threw me out! My own husband!" She laughs. It's manic and frightening. "I was furious but fine. He was angry but he would forgive me. He covered up the theft, whatever Jesse took. He said it would be best just to pretend it didn't happen rather than report it. But when I tried to take our baby and leave, he wouldn't let me go. He told me she was dead. He told me she was dead!"

She screams this at me and the hair on my arms rises. Spit flies from her mouth like a rabid dog. Her eyes are wide, dark and crazed. I take another step back.

"She isn't dead," I say, disbelieving. Unless he hurt her. "Did he hurt her?"

"I don't know," she answers. "I managed to get her into the car, but they followed us and hit us. They *hit* us. They pulled my baby from the car and took her. All because that *thing* came into my home and stole something."

"You need to go to the police, Regina, if someone has your daughter."

"No. No, Gerard doesn't want me go to the police."

"Who cares what your husband wants. Your little girl—"

"They'll kill her," Regina says. She comes toward me and grabs my coat. Her blood-caked fingers bunch the red felt into her fists. "They'll kill her for being an abomination."

All over again, I'm looking in Eve Hildebrand's eyes through the plexiglass of the Davidson county jail. The same glossy crazed look of a mother begging for her child's life.

They'll kill Nessa. Please. Please.

"Regina," I say. I can't pull away from her even if I want to. She has a death grip.

"I just wanted her to live," she says. Her eyes well up with tears and her lip quivers. The first ream of sobs rakes her body. Her back bows with the pain of it and she pulls me down into the floor with her, sobbing. "I just want my baby to live."

"I know," I say and put one hand on her head. Something sharp rubs against my fingers and I realize it's little shards of glass. Regina's hair is full of little bits of glass as if she'd pulled herself from the wreckage of her car and walked to Jesse's.

Once her sobs begin to quiet, her grip loosening, I dare to speak. "Listen, Regina. Listen, okay? We can find your daughter, but we need help. We need to call someone."

"We cannot ask for help without him knowing,"

she says, softly.

I ignore her fears. Fear never accomplished anything. I see the image of the woman tied to the chair in Jeremiah's safe house. If I tell him a child is missing, I know what it will mean for that woman in his custody.

"Have you spoken to your husband? He might know something."

"He won't speak to me. He's furious about what I did."

I try to keep my anger to myself. How could he be anything but grateful that his daughter survived? How can he believe in a God that would approve of a child's premature death? Why do so many idiots assume that we are supposed to stand back and let God's will be done? What if it was God's will that Regina's daughter be saved by replacement? He helps those who help themselves right?

"We need to talk to him," I say.

"He won't speak to us and he leaves tomorrow afternoon for Chicago."

"We'll have to try," I say. "We want to get her back, right? We can't give up."

She's quiet and I think she won't answer me. She pulls back, her face a mask of smeared mascara.

"Thank you," she says.

Regina stares at me through the mess of her face. I speak her name twice before her eyes focus on mine. "How did you get here?"

"I drove," she answers.

I inspect the driveway. A heap of car sits behind mine. It looks like it's been driven through hell and back.

"How did you know where Jesse lives?"

"We all know," she whispers. "The whole congregation."

That explains the hate mail Jesse gets. The TP in the trees or the pile of dog shit on the porch. Once there were several windows blotted out with slurs written in soap marker. And now the brick.

I let out all my frustration in one long breath. "Okay. I can get a tow truck for your car. Is there somewhere I can take you?"

"What about Julia?"

"We'll get her back," I say. "But not tonight. We'll speak to your husband tomorrow morning before he leaves, okay?"

She falls to her knees and begins to inch toward catatonia again.

I kneel in front of her and take her hands. "Regina, where can I take you?"

"No one will have me," she says. "Gerard is such an important man."

"Is there someone else? Family maybe? Someone who will shelter you just for tonight?"

Because I need tonight to think. I have to decide if I'm really going to take this to Jeremiah. If I do, I'm all in. I can't ask for his help and then bail on him later. But this isn't my problem, not really. I shouldn't keep trying to save everyone. If I really want to get Jesse out of this hell, I have to quit getting involved. I have to walk away and let someone else deal with it.

"My sister," she answers finally. "She lives in Brentwood. In River Oaks."

I want to get her out of here before Jesse comes home. "Is there anything you need from your car before I drive you there?"

Somehow I manage to get her out of the house and into the car. She wants to grab a couple of things from her front seat and I let her while I call the tow truck and pay with my credit card over the phone.

"One more thing," I say to the silent Regina as I fasten my seatbelt and pull forward enough to edge around the demolished car blocking me in. "Promise me you'll never come to this house again."

Jesse

I'm in the back of a big white van, being driven to an unknown destination by a stranger.

It's every girl's worst nightmare.

Except most big creepy van nightmares don't have the following animals involved: three ferrets, two rabbits, a cage of gerbils, and another cage of rats running those multi-colored plastic tubes. Beneath them is a larger cage with two half-squirrel, half-rabbit creatures called chinchillas. Across from me sits Lane and beside him are three aquariums full of snakes and spiders—also known as the reason I won't sit on that side of the van.

"You owe me," I say, watching a spider with furry legs press itself against the glass longingly, like it wants to come over and suckle my *face*.

"I have to have someone licensed by the FBRD to observe my last replacement."

"Your last probationary replacement." I grin and jiggle the dog tags around my neck identifying my NRD—the official *don't cut me open* tag—required by all death-replacement agents. "Soon you'll get your very own pair of these."

Lane flashes a brilliant smile: half-eager boy and half-mischievous guy trying to get into your pants. I *really* like that smile.

"You love this, don't you?" I ask.

"I never knew I'd love doing anything more than comics," he says.

I lean forward and run my fingers through his hair, ruffling it. I am going to tell him how adorable he is when he's excited, but my stomach cramps. The nausea rolls me like a surprise wave, pulling me down with it.

"What's wrong?" he asks. "Are you getting car sick?"

"Don't you feel it?" I groan, reach out, and grab ahold of the wire mesh of the rabbit cage. The rabbit inside sniffs my fingers. *Please don't mistake me for a carrot, Bugs.*

"Feel what?" he asks.

I don't have time to explain it to him. I don't have time to say maybe he is different. Maybe he won't get the pre-death sickness like I do. Maybe he won't get the funky vision either. Or if he's *real* lucky, he definitely won't hallucinate.

However, I don't have time to do anything except squeeze his hand and say, "Get ready." Besides maybe it's a blessing Lane isn't a freak like me. Maybe he'll stay off Caldwell's radar that way. Though I'm not sure how much that has helped other agents.

Lane realizes what I am saying and starts to crawl to the front of the vehicle, toward John Jones owner of Petsapalooza and driver of this large white delivery van. One second Lane is poking his head through the little window separating us and the animals from John, the next, we are rolling.

I fly forward and my face slams against one of the snake aquariums. It shatters and I don't feel the glass as much as hear it. It isn't until the van stops rolling that I realize I'm lying in a pile of snakes and something is running down the side of my face. My first thought is *spiders*. Then more realistically *blood*.

Near hysterical, I kick open the back door of the van and climb out. I do a funky dance in the street to make sure no tarantulas or snakes have slipped under my clothes.

The cars around us stop moving and begin to clot up the road. The sounds of squealing tires and horns echo off the close-knit buildings of West End. A few people are climbing from their cars and taking fucking pictures with their phones. Others sit behind the wheel with their mouths open as something warm spills into my eyes. I wipe at it and my hand comes away red.

Limping from the van, I go to the closest car. It's a burgundy sedan holding a plump woman with teased blond hair behind the wheel. Her mouth is completely open, giving the impression of a round black speaker for the soft country music seeping from the car. Her daughter, or whoever the pudgy blond kid in the passenger seat is, screams bloody murder. It splits my eardrums.

"Gee-zus, shut up," I beg and press my palm against the glass. "I just need your help."

The child keeps screaming. My words taste metallic, like I've been sucking on spare change. Then I find the raw piece of my cheek flapping against my tongue. Damn. Unless I die—and it is Lane's gig not mine—I'll have to heal this cheek the old-fashioned way, with stitches and shit. Just wonderful.

I yell through the window. "Do you have a cell phone?"

At least the driver nods yes, but her child hasn't stopped screaming at full decibels.

"Call 911 and tell them there's been an accident at—" I look up to check the street signs but I can't see through the blood in my eyes. "At wherever the hell we are right now."

Then I feel something on my left shoulder, see the shadow of huge furry legs in my peripheral. I scream like a banshee and tear my clothes off. Just the first two layers, my black hoodie and T-shirt until I'm standing in the street with just my bra and jeans on. Then I shake my shirt like it's on fire. It isn't until I watch the spider hit the pavement that I can stop screaming. The kid falls into giggles. The little shit.

But then the child has stopped laughing too and now simply stares at me the way her mother does.

Until I realize why.

In those few seconds when my shirt is off and my chest and stomach are bare, they've seen my scar. Everyone has. In fact, some of the assholes taking pictures of the accident have turned their cameras my way. My Y-shaped scar cuts just below my collar bone from one side to the other. Then a longer line stretches between my breasts down to my navel. It's my autopsy scar, the one scar that embarrasses the hell out of me and that I am completely powerless to heal.

In my very first death, I was dead for two days. Everyone's first death is the longest. In my case, by the time the coroner diagnosed my cause of death as smoke inhalation, he realized something was different. My incisions were healing in front of his eyes and my heart started beating while the cavity was still open. Instead of sewing me up, he panicked and made a phone call.

Because my skin was held open, peeled like a freaking banana instead of sealed in a position to grow back together, the healing wasn't clean. Even the partial decapitation I suffered last fall had healed clean, thanks to Dr. York and Kirk.

"What are you looking at fat ass?" I yell. I yank my

shirt over my head, tears mixing with the blood. Then I slam my hand against the hood of her car. "Go feed your kid another Ding-dong!"

Not my finest moment. I already feel like shit before I even make it back to the van. As sorry as I am another part of me doesn't give a shit. That part is just mad. Mad that people stare. Mad the people standing around take pictures instead of coming to see if I'm okay. I'm bleeding from my head. Surely that's a clue I need assistance, not a photoshoot.

The point is I am not one of *them*.

I never will be.

Seething, I return to the van. It's still on its side, a redneck truck with ridiculously large wheels, pushes up against its belly. I climb up the side and peek into the van first. There's John's body, unmoving, Lane beside it. He's crawled through the broken windows separating the seats from the back into the front cabin with John. Lane has a deep cut down one arm, which he seems oblivious to. He has straightened John out the best he can and is giving him CPR.

"You're doing it wrong," I say and regret it.

"I know!" Lane snaps at me. His eyes are saucers, white, angry, terrified. "But it isn't working."

"What do you mean?"

"I can't do it!"

My vision changes. It slips from the normal *sky is blue, grass is green,* vision to the thermal temperature reading. Lane is a blue flame, the way I am a blue flame and anyone else with NRD. But John Jones isn't the red-orange-yellow of the living. He's fading from green to gray.

"Shit." I pull myself into the window, falling into the cab rather clumsily and landing on poor John Jones.

"What are you doing?" Lane asks.

"Move back."

Lane, though clearly angry, does move back. "Be my guest."

I ignore his tone. He's as unhappy about rolling around in a van as I am, and he's just spent the last few minutes trying to save someone without being able to. I try to be compassionate but the best I can manage is indifference to his attitude.

I open John's bloody shirt and the image of my own destroyed clothes thrown back in my face is clear—*closer than you think.*

I push the thoughts back and focus. *Here, Jess. Be here now.*

I put my hands on his chest, rubbing the skin as if the friction could warm him.

A hot-cold chill settles into my muscles and coils around my navel and spine as I push my own flame deeper into Jones. I try to focus despite the raucous of the overturned animals. Something is getting eaten back there, or trying not to be. I block that out too.

John Jones warms to my touch as I push that electric part of me through him with urgency, aware I'm running out of time. *There*—a spark where our flames dance around each other. Against the line showing the division, I push hard. That electric part of me, the one that destroys electronics and makes owning Williams-Sonoma kitchen stuff impossible, is there. I call on it.

Jones' chest jerks as if I've placed a paddle on his chest. It isn't enough. I try harder. I think about the little girl's look of disgust again. Of the mother's horror. Of the brick through the window, and my pug shaking with bristled fur against my legs.

I pulse again.

I think of Ally, trying to leave me for some new girl. Ally, my best friend in the whole world, who stays up late with me to watch bad television. Ally who makes the best grilled cheese sandwiches ever and can't tell a good joke to save her life because she over explains *everything* and starts laughing so hard she can't finish it anyway. Ally who instinctively knows if I need coffee, ice cream, or chocolate just by looking at me.

Pulse.

Jesse. I hear my name spoken softly as if carried on a breeze.

Pulse.

Jesse. He says again but I'm terrified to look up. I

know exactly what—*who*—I'll see.

Tears sting the corner of my eyes and Jones' chest rises. He gasps for air like gasoline thrown on the blaze. That green-grey flame inside him burns bright orange, tinged with red. Lane's voice can barely be heard over the stridency of the animal screams. "Are you crying?"

I shrug off what I assume is his soft hand on my shoulder. I want to remind him emergency crews must be called, hospital arrangements made. The other driver has to be checked on, the crowd controlled. I have a moment to miss Ally and how she handles these situations so thoroughly. She makes it so easy for me to just fall because I know she will catch me.

I feel *him*. Terribly close.

I look up.

There outside the car, in all his black-winged glory is Gabriel. I swear I can feel him wrap those wings around me as I fall back into the darkness of Jones' death.

Ally

I'm running through the hospital. It's hard to do in the traffic of wheelchairs, nurses escorting patients and the slow shuffle of the ill. But I keep moving deeper and deeper into the building until I reach the intensive care ward.

Lane texted me *room 203* and I'm counting down. *211, 209, 207, 205* on each square plate beside the dark doors.

203. I screech to a halt, my wet boots squeal against the tile. I rush into the room and Lane's head snaps up. He's sitting beside the bed, holding her hand. Someone has already cleaned Jesse up and put her into a hospital gown.

"Ally," he says. If I didn't know better, I'd say he's relieved to see me. "Thank you for coming. I didn't know what—"

"Has Kirk been called?" I ask.

"No," he admits. The appreciation in his smile dims. "I didn't think to call him."

I call the funeral home immediately and tell Kirk what's happened. I ask him to come as soon as he can. But I am not done with Lane.

"What the hell happened?"

"She was just supervising my replacement," he says. "I tried but—."

"So, it should be you in the bed?"

His jaw clenches. "I tried, I really did. He wouldn't—accept me or whatever."

"Accept you? It isn't a dinner invitation."

He closes his mouth and again I see the line of his jaw tense.

My voice rises. "You couldn't do it yourself, so she's just supposed to come in and fix everything? She's just supposed to wave her magic wand and make it all better?"

The room blurs with my anger. I feel I am yelling at Jeremiah who isn't even here. Lane stands from the chair and walks past me.

"Hey," I call after him. "*Hey!*"

He turns slowly back and for the first time I get a good look at him. Tall, hair even darker than Jesse's and really blue eyes.

His anger is apparent in the deep crease of his brow. "You won't let me tell you what happened and you aren't a death-replacement agent. Don't act like you understand."

"I've accompanied her to every replacement for the last three years and you can count on one hand how many times *you've* watched her die."

His ears are bright red. "I wouldn't have asked her to come if I thought she'd get hurt."

I see blood on his shirt. "Is that hers or yours?" I'm losing control again. Breathe Ally. *Breathe.*

Lane opens his mouth to say something only to close his mouth again. The jaw clenches, unclenches, clenches. Then he turns and walks out of the room altogether.

A moment passes. Then another. And another, but he doesn't come back.

I flop into the chair and try my breathing techniques again. I've been using them a lot today.

When I open my eyes I see the dark purple bruise on the side of Jesse's head. It's puffy around a deep cut that's healing.

I close my eyes and try to calm down. I haven't felt this out of control in a while. What is wrong with me? I even forgot to ask Lane how the death occurred so I could look up her D.T.

A soft knock comes at the door.

I tense instantly until I realize it isn't Lane. Kirk bends just enough to clear the doorway and enters, carrying his black case. He doesn't look too happy himself. Maybe this is just a terrible day for everyone.

"As soon as the doctor gives the OK, you can take her to Mt. Olivet's," I say. I sound tired, my voice thick as if I just woke up.

Kirk stops just short of the bed. He looks like he has something in his mouth.

"What?" I ask.

"I can't take her back with me," he says. His voice is deep, booming over the silence of the room. Even the monitors are silent because Jesse has no vitals to record yet.

"Why?"

He shifts his weight uncomfortably and rests his black bag at the end of the bed in the space between Jesse's cold feet and the footboard.

"I don't think she's safe there," he says.

"Why?" God, I sound like a broken record. I'm shaken. I wasn't expecting this replacement and yet here I am. I need to be at home thinking, figuring out what I'm going to do about Jeremiah, Regina and Julia—if anything. I can't think when Jesse is in danger.

"First it was a shoe," he says. "I wasn't even sure it was stolen, you know how she is with shoes. But then her shirt went missing too and I distinctly remembered putting it aside."

"Do you have an idea who it might be?" I ask.

"No," he says. The halo of fluorescent light overhead gives him the appearance of a repentant saint. "And that is why I can't bring her to Olivet's anymore."

I can't say I blame him. The vandalism to Jesse's house has increased this year, ever since her identity was released during last year's attack. If he thinks his funeral home isn't safe anymore, it probably isn't.

"Please don't tell her," he says. He sits beside me, dwarfing the little chair. "I don't want her to know I've let this happen."

"It isn't your fault," I tell him. I put a hand on his. It makes me look so small and pale in comparison.

"I just want her to feel safe," Kirk says. He's watching Jesse, waiting for her to come back as if we could will it ourselves.

"I know," I say. "Me too."

Regina is clean and presentable when I pick her up outside her sister's house in Brentwood. The remnants of blood have been washed from her hair and face and only a small Band-Aid appears on her left cheek. She wears her hair down to cover the purple-black bruise just above her temple.

She clutches her camisole over her flowery dress with a clasped hand as we slip through the gate protecting her home from the street. Her arms are little more than pale little sticks extending from her shoulder.

"Are you okay?" I ask as I press the doorbell. A prim chime can be heard resonating inside.

She nods.

"Are you sure?" I ask. I haven't agreed to bring Jeremiah in on this yet. I stayed up all night analyzing the hell out of my problems but I didn't come to any conclusion that would allow me or Jesse to get out of this unscathed.

She gives me a small smile and it surprises me. "I got a call this morning. Julia says she is fine. That she's having fun with Uncle Cal."

She clutches herself harder as if it hurts to mention Caldwell. Maybe we are not the only ones afraid of him.

"At least we know where she is," I say, trying to comfort her. I touch her shoulder blades through her pink camisole for the briefest of moments. "We have that much to go off of."

When no one comes to the door, I knock harder.

"Maybe he's already left," she says sheepishly.

I try the handle and the door opens. Regina starts to protest about entering her own home but I walk in before she can formulate an argument. Gerard is on the first floor, sitting behind maplewood desk, pen in hand. I can see the kitchen beyond him and behind that the sliding glass door leading to the yard where the birthday party took place.

"Who are you?" he asks. His gaze fixes on me without so much as a cursory glance at his wife. When I don't answer he turns on her. "Who the hell did you bring into my house?"

The "my" irks me. "Alice Gallagher. I'm Jesse Sullivan's personal assistant. I'm responding to a complaint that you were not satisfied with the services rendered here."

His face burns bright red. The red that is common only in men with histories of high blood pressure. A *flustered* red. "Get out of my house."

Instead I come closer. "If you are unhappy with our services, we are required by law to offer compensation. Can you please describe the nature of your dissatisfaction?" and here is where I let my professional tone slip. "Perhaps you are dissatisfied by the outcome?"

His attempt at imaginary bill pay isn't working. His fat fingers bulge around a thick gold wedding band and a pinkie ring bearing a crest I don't recognize. He looks up.

Regina breaks in before her husband can answer. Her voice is too high, hysterical and I wished I'd made her stay in the car. A shrill voice like that is bound to torment even the most cooperative of ears. "That tree would have killed her!"

"There wasn't a scratch on her," his voice rising to match hers. He stands and the chair scrapes back.

I try to redirect the conversation. That's easier than pulling them apart if they decide to go at it. "Ms. Sullivan is responsible for your daughter's condition. You can thank her personally, if you like."

"If I ever see her, *thanking* her will be the last thing I do," he growls and now he turns those dark eyes on me. He comes around the desk but I'd rather have his attention on me than Regina. I'm not sure what I can or would do if this devolves into a domestic dispute. "She put everything I spent my entire life working for in jeopardy. I've proved my loyalty to this organization over and over, and now because of what you did—" He jabs a dramatic finger at Regina. "And she did. I'm being called in for questions."

I fight to keep a clear head despite his aggressive posturing and tone. The exhaustion from the last few days of chaos is heavy on my shoulders and having a man yell in my face is not helping. When I told Jess I needed a few days to get my head together, I wasn't lying. So what was I doing here? Maybe Nikki was right. Maybe I really am a workaholic.

"You did nothing wrong, Mr. Lovett." I try to say it with genuine feeling and concern despite what I think of him. "Your wife only wanted to save your daughter's life."

"He doesn't believe we have faith," he says. His voice drops but his eyes are wide and feral. I don't want to be so close to him but I don't take a step back either.

"Will you still have your faith when he kills your daughter?" I make my voice a low warning growl much like his own. I can play the body language game too.

Regina lets out a shriek of terror but covers it.

"Get out of my house," he hisses.

I don't move. "Eve Hildebrand had a daughter. Surely you saw that on the news. You know what happened to the little girl?"

I wait for him to defend Caldwell, to defend his honor but he doesn't.

"You're lying," he finally says but no heat returns to his voice.

"This is public knowledge. You can find Eve's testimony and charges in public records. Do the research yourself." When he seems to consider this I add. "I believe Caldwell is going to use your daughter to manipulate you like he manipulated Eve. And he will kill her anyway once he gets what he wants."

"That's preposterous," he says. "If I can just talk to him—"

"He'll be too busy punishing you for imaginary crimes to listen," I argue, and for the first time Gerard's face pales.

"Please," Regina whispers and she reaches hands out toward her husband. He lets her take his hands into hers. "Please, Gerry."

"I will go to Chicago as he has asked. I will talk to him and bring Julia home."

"What makes you think he'll let you?"

"I'll only say this once more, get out of my house," Gerard says. He pushes me back and I'm forced to take a step or fall.

"Gerry, stop this!"

He pushes me again closer to the door. "You've done enough."

I think about hurting him. I think about the aikido I've learned and know I could hurt him, but I don't. I won't stoop to his level.

Frustrated I storm out of the house and go back to my car. If they don't want help I can't force it on them. And maybe Jesse will be better off without us getting involved in anything else. What I really wanted to confirm here was that there would be no repercussions for Jesse's theft. No authorities. But it seems Gerard wants to keep it as much a secret as Jesse does. This is a relief and a lucky strike for Brinkley, who's next in line to get a piece of my mind.

I don't even make it to my car before the sound of Regina's heels click after me down the driveway. I turn to see her clutching the cardigan.

"Wait, wait," she pleads. Her bone-thin hands clutch mine. "Please help us. You must know people, doing the kind of work you do."

"Your husband doesn't want my help," I say.

"I do," she says in her thick drawl. Her grip tightens and her red-rimmed eyes clamp on mine. "*I* do."

And here it is. My choice. Do I help her? I can't find anything out on my own. I simply don't have enough information or even access to information. I could ask Jesse directly, but I want her out of danger, not in it. And anything with Caldwell is bad news. I can't ask Gloria because she is overworked and I don't have contact information for Brinkley.

That leaves Jeremiah and Nikki.

"I know someone," I say and pull my hands free of hers. "But I don't know if he can help you."

"Thank you," she says. Tears well in the corners of her eyes and it's almost too much for me to bear. "Thank you so much, Alice. Please call me the moment you hear something. Day or night."

"Don't thank me yet," I say, chest burning. I failed to save the little girl last time.

Jesse

As soon as I stiffly climb the stairs to my bedroom and push open the door, I find another small yellow and orange suction dart stuck to the window. I wiggle the bugger free and unfold the message.

Diner at midnight.

Midnight is only 3 hours away. I think about sleeping but change my mind. My bed seems impossibly large and cold without a cuddle partner. And it isn't like I have someone to call. Ally's jumped ship and Lane is probably still mad at me.

And my house is too damn quiet. I keep going into rooms and hitting light switches only to have nothing happen. I should have told Ally about this electrical problem before she took a vacation. Maybe I can get Lane to do it. And the window. I can't forget about the window. What good is a lock with a big damn hole by my door? I should also consider an alarm.

But I'll think about all that later, after I talk to

Lane.

My downtown office isn't that exciting. There's a parking lot in the back, connected to Broadway by a short, narrow alley. I park in the lot, then walk around to the storefront of Full Bleed, Lane's comic book store. It's how we met actually. He owns the building and I rent one of the offices. Brinkley chose the location, so it isn't like I chose my office space for the hottie landlord.

Though it is totally something I would do.

I find Lane standing by a glass case talking action figures with a kid that's probably sixteen years old. The kid wears black jeans and wide shoes matching the red skateboard leaning against his thigh. The kid points at something in the case and gestures wildly. I know this for the geekspeak it is and don't interrupt.

The place is tidy and well-lit. Lane takes good care of it. Some comic book stores feel cluttered and dark to me, like a mother's basement inhabited by a troll. But Lane's store feels like what it is, a store. The center tables have comic books alphabetized like CDs and you can flip through each of the plastic-coated volumes. In the glass case, the cash register sits on is where the role-playing dice, collectables and anything Lane is nervous about getting stolen are kept. Along the walls are other action figures and paraphernalia for this or that series or show. In the corner, are two kids playing the newest version of *Call of Duty: Ghosts*.

That is the extent of Lane's generosity, the option to preview most games before purchasing them.

After the skater leaves without buying anything, I approach Lane.

"Hey." I think this is an acceptable greeting. Obviously not.

"I'm working." His snotty tone is hard to overlook. Because Lane is usually incredibly sweet, it makes his tantrums more obvious.

"O-*kay*." I know waiting it out will just cause a bigger fight later. "What did I do?"

Lane plops onto the high stool behind the cabinet. "Nothing. You just did *your* job. I'm doing *my* job. Everything is fine."

At least it's something to go on. "So you're mad about Jones."

"You saved a man's life," Lane says, but his jaw is working on an invisible strap of leather.

"Yet here we are," I tell him.

"I'm not mad," he spits.

"Oh really?" I ask. I touch my forehead with my index finger. "That's not what this vein in your forehead here says."

"Just drop it, okay? You don't understand."

I shift my weight, leaning against the counter to try and alleviate the pain in my hip. Freaking rigor mortis.

"I get it. You didn't complete the replacement.

You're disappointed and you hate that your license will be postponed. But you will get it, I promise."

"You've replaced 100 people—"

"84," I correct. "Jones was 84."

"*84*," Lane hisses, venomous. "None of them died."

"And you've only replaced like 8 or 9," I say.

"11," he counters.

"I lost Nessa to the same man who'd stabbed you," I say. "And I almost lost *you*."

He gives me a look. A look I have never seen before.

"What?" I ask.

"Nothing."

"Look, I'm just saying I think Nessa would disagree," I say. "Just because you got lucky and sprouted your NRD wings doesn't mean everyone walked out of that church alive."

"And what if I hadn't?" Lane asks. He looks me dead in the eye and it's almost a challenge.

I don't understand. "What if you hadn't what?"

"What if I hadn't sprouted my NRD wings?"

I lean my weight against him. "Then I'd be a really sad girl."

Lane makes a show of cleaning the fingerprints off the glass. I keep touching a corner, leaving a big thumbprint for him to wipe off until annoyed he looks up at me. When he opens his mouth to argue, I stick my tongue in it. What starts off as another attempt to annoy him, turns into a good long kiss, until the last bit of fight is gone from him and I feel his arms finally wrap around my waist.

"Wooo," a chorus rings out from behind us. The boys playing the video game, a boy and a *girl* actually, have the game on pause, watching us. "Go, Mr. Lane."

Lane grins, caught off guard. "Are you going to buy that game or what? I've let you play it for hours."

The boy looking worried that he is about to lose his video game privileges turns back to the TV immediately. The girl is more reluctant, grinning at us for several heartbeats longer.

Lane pulls me into his arms. It's rough and possessive but it feels good. "I'm sorry. I shouldn't be mad that you saved him."

"I still like you. And don't be so hard on yourself. We can't all be as awesome as *moi*."

His grin falls at the corners, and bit by bit draws itself up into a pout.

"Oh come on," I say. Man, I'm just saying the wrong thing left and right today. "I was joking."

"But that's it, isn't it? Death-replacing is your thing," he says.

"I've been doing it for years!" I say. "You've been doing it for months."

"But even from the beginning," he says. "You've

been good. When I found out about my NRD I thought 'Awesome'. This is *it*. This is my *something*."

"I thought comics were your something." He talks about being on the other side of the page a lot, being the artist, not the seller, but he isn't sure how to launch himself in that direction. He's the type to want more, the next thing, no matter what it is.

"Yeah, maybe. It's becoming clear that I'm not meant to be an agent," he says.

"Why can't you be both?" I say.

"I'm not like you," he says. "I wish you could see yourself in action."

"What does that mean?"

"It means," he says. "You can tell the difference between an Olympian running for the gold and Joe Schmoe out for a jog."

"Who else have you seen death-replace?" I ask.

"No one, but—" he begins. I don't intend to let him get farther.

"Exactly, no one. The girl who trained me, Rachel, she did like 200 something replacements. She makes us all look like amateurs."

"You elec-tro-cute people," he says, emphasizing each syllable. "You are different."

I drop my voice low. "You're not supposed to mention that."

Lane glances at the kids playing the video game before murmuring. "They can't hear me."

But I know better. Someone is always listening. And I am a little different, aren't I? A little freaking *weird*. I have the crazy vision, thermo-whatever. I have the gut twinge cramps that come just before the death itself. And my hallucinations—

"About that," I say. "Do you know anything about electricity? Wirings and stuff?"

"Why?"

"My house," I begin, but I'm distracted—by the big black crow that has landed on a light post outside the store, as the remains of the day bleed out. The last time I saw a crow, it appeared heralding Gabriel's appearance in my life before everything went to shit.

And though this crow doesn't look supernatural in anyway, and I'm almost certain that it's just a bird on a light post, not some messenger that the worst is yet to come, I curl deeper into Lane's embrace. It's the way the black feathers shimmer the suggestion of cascading light, like seeing the world in thermal. Like seeing the shadow of something approaching around the corner, before the something is actually there.

Gabriel. I don't know how I know but Gabriel is back, circling somewhere just beneath the surface and I don't know how long I can hold him back. Because I realize that's what I've been doing. Holding him back, pretending I'm okay and normal-*ish* again. But it isn't working anymore.

"Your house?" Lane asks, frowning down at me.

"You were saying something about your house?"

But his voice is so far away.

Ally

I pull up outside the safe house and see Nikki's car parked by the dumpster. Seeing the deep blue trim makes my heart lurch and I stay in the car a tad too long before deciding to go up.

Thighs burning from the climb, I rap twice on the outer door and it opens. Parish gives a little salute without looking away from the monitors. It's a Burger King spread today, not McDonald's, covering the work station. I try not to stare too hard at the crumpled orange wrappers, French fry boxes or seeping soda cups. But I admit I'm a little horrified by the way he eats.

"Where's Jeremiah?" I ask.

Parish is particularly fixated on a camera in the upper left corner. It's a small dark woman and a man conversing in black and white pixels like an old movie. White words appear across the bottom as their mouths move.

"What is that?" I ask. I point at the monitor in question.

"Closed Caption," he says. "I don't speak Spanish. Delaney is translating remotely."

I recognize the name, but I can't recall the face or

where he's located. Chicago? Portland?

"Where is that coming from?" I ask.

"Arizona," he asks. Then as if he remembered my first question. He waves toward the back. "They're with the bitch."

"Don't call her a bitch," I say.

Parish huffs. "She spit on me when I offered her my last burger. She's a bitch."

"Maybe she's vegetarian," I offer, already moving away toward the dim hallway.

"Vegetarian? That shit's for the birds."

I pat his shoulder in friendly way. "Birds eat insects actually, and sometimes smaller birds. They aren't vegetarian at all. And Jesse is vegetarian. I'm going to tell her you said that."

He grumbles through a half smile, then leans closer to the monitors as if trying to read something unclear. His mouth moves slightly but no sound comes out.

I inch toward the torture room, musing on my own ignorance, how just days before I hadn't even known this room existed, believing it nothing more than a glorified mop closet. And now—it's amazing what the presence of a woman and a couple of chairs can do to change the purpose of a room.

Jeremiah has her hair wrapped up in his hand as he knocks her hard across the jaw. The cheek blooms immediately, flowers purple and the long stretch of her exposed neck and the jaw bone that protrudes blushes deeply.

My hand goes over my mouth and a small sound escapes my lips. The hallway is suddenly cold as my skin ices. The blood in the corner of her mouth catches the overhead light and could be mistaken for smeared lipstick, if not for the thick moist appearance.

I look away from Jeremiah and the woman to Nikki.

She's stoic, almost casual, in the corner as she watches the two of them. It is strange to see her that way—so cold and hard—when she is so warm with me. She says something to Jeremiah and he lets go of her hair and straightens. I can't hear her words through the glass and realize the room must be sound proofed. Jeremiah regains his composure and pulls at the bottom of his thin sweater. The woman says something and Jeremiah tenses but doesn't say anything.

Instead he turns his back on her toward a tray on the low table behind them. It's a fold out dinner tray more than anything. The horror digs its claws into my spine as he lifts a silver scalpel from the tray.

I'm rapping hard against the glass before I realize what I'm doing. Both Jeremiah and Nikki look up, then at each other. The woman looks alarmed and I can't bear it. The wide whites of her eyes in fearful anticipation. Her hair has grown greasy and damp in the warm room. I could only imagine how sore her body is from sitting in that chair for days. Her chaffed wrists, red, swollen, and peeling, are hard to look at, but easier than her bruised face. And I have to look. It's the least I can do.

Jeremiah and Nikki both come through the door. Jeremiah's face tightens in anger when he sees me. At least Nikki still looks concerned, if a little worried.

"What is it?" Jeremiah says.

"I have news," I begin. I realize I'm shaking and my voice trembles with the rest of me. "I know of a child Caldwell took. It's a little girl that Jesse replaced recently."

Jeremiah's anger recedes and his questions begin. I answer what I can but I don't know any more than what Regina told me.

"The father is uncooperative," I add.

"No surprise," Nikki says.

I'm doing my best not to look through the glass back at the woman. But it's harder to look into Jeremiah's eyes than I thought it'd be. "I'm hoping we can make arrangements for the mother and the child, if we find her. Is there somewhere we can send them?"

I already know the answer is yes. We'd send them away like we've sent away dozens of others. But I need Jeremiah to share his rationale. I need him to act human before I run out of this building and never return.

"If she was taken yesterday then it wasn't like the other children."

"No, it wasn't," I say, and I tell him about the men who collided with Regina before taking her daughter away. None of us marvel over the audacity to run over a woman and take a child in broad daylight, the lack of police involvement and so forth. Caldwell has deep pockets and we've known that for a long time.

"Either Julia is a special circumstance," Jeremiah says. "or this woman isn't as integral to his plan as we thought."

My heart leaps at the opportunity. "Let me take over."

"Excuse me?" Jeremiah shifts his weight from one leg to the other.

"Beating her to death isn't getting anywhere. Let me investigate this Lovett lead and see if we can find the children that way. Just put her on ice for now."

Please, please, please. Let me show you this isn't the right way.

"I'll help her," Nikki says. "We'll go through the intel we already have and try to pinpoint a better connection. We can collaborate with the mother, get descriptions, run them through and follow the leads. A traffic camera might have gotten the plate."

Jeremiah opens and closes his hand. I wonder if it's his boredom with torture more than my well-timed request that works in my favor.

"Fine, but you only have a few days. After that we either need to transport her or kill her."

He pushes past me toward the large front room where Parish sits at the monitors. I turn and watch the two men exchange words. Soft fingers brush my abdomen, making me turn back.

"I know you're trying to save this woman," Nikki says. She leans against the wall with the door and watches me with careful eyes. "Let me help you."

"I'm trying to save a lot of people," I say. I sound bitchy even to myself. But I know Jeremiah would have never let me take the case if she hadn't spoken up for me. I squeeze her hand for just the briefest of moments.

"You can't save them all," Nikki warns.

"It doesn't mean I won't try," I say, but I'm terrified that she is right.

Jesse

It's 12:30 at night and I'm gobbling my stack of pancakes while Brinkley catches me up on the status of the Lovett hard drive. He managed to decipher most of it and it has given him two pertinent pieces of information. But it's hard to take him seriously in his current disguise, a ridiculous disguise if you ask me: long strawberry-blond beard and mustache, dark shades, and Rasta beanie hat. He's kept the leather jacket, but he's changed the collared dress shirt for a Bob Marley T-shirt and jeans full of holes. His boots are the same black combat boots as always.

"I have reason to believe this is the list of potential targets," he says, the beard bobbing.

I cut one more bite of my pancake stack and shovel it in. "This is a million pages long."

"Look up the word hyperbole," he says. "It's only 44 pages."

I roll my eyes. "Yeah but look at how tiny the font is. It must be 100 names per page."

He shrugs. "Roughly. Your name is on the first page."

I was about to add more ketchup to my hashbrowns but shove my plate aside instead. "Let me see."

I am on the first page, *second* name.

"Why am I the second name?" I ask.

"I think it's ranked in order of importance," he says. "I would consider anyone on the first couple of pages top priority."

"Is Lane—"

"Page 44," he says, stroking his fake beard.

Brinkley has to wear a disguise whenever in public for a couple of reasons. The most important is that he's supposed to be *dead*. According to the FBRD's record, he died in the line of duty, protecting his charge—me. He even has a grave marker and everything at Mt. Olivet.

"At least he isn't a priority," I say. I exhale a breath I've been holding and my shoulder blades slide away from my ears.

"He isn't the only one we know," he says.

It's hard to read Brinkley's face in this getup of his. But I know the bad news voice.

"Who?"

I scan the pages again, more closely. I sweep my eyes down the column and don't see it. Then I look again and rely on the point of my finger to separate the names out of one big alphabet soup blob into individual lines.

Name: Alice Gallagher. Last Known Location: USA/Nashville. Priority 8

"She's number 8," I say. How could I miss that? "If I'm number 2, how the hell is she number 8? She's not even a zombie!"

"Keep your voice down." Brinkley's cheeks reddened ever so slightly at the z-word.

"But they only know about Ally because of me and I'm not even the most important person," I say. I look at the names again. "Liza Miller is number one. Wait, I know that name—"

Brinkley stops me from saying more. "Gloria's trail is hot. Not that I'm surprised."

Nor am I. Gloria is damn good.

"Cindy is on page 2," he says. "Gloria is number 23. Rachel is on page 14 and I couldn't find my name anywhere."

"Because you're dead," I say. My heart knocks hard against my ribs. "How is Ally on this list?" Maybe if I just keep repeating it, it will make sense.

Rastafarian Brinkley comes forward on his forearms, clasping his hands together in front of him.

"Unfortunately they didn't post a detailed explanation of their ranking system," he says. "They aren't working strictly in order anyway. Look at the names I've highlighted."

There are eleven highlighted names on the first two pages. "Who are they?"

"They're victims with NRD that have been killed since this list was last updated."

"Gee-*zus*," I say. "Why rank them if they're just killing them at random?"

Brinkley sits back in his seat again, and tries to look relaxed. We both know we're on camera. Everyone and their maids have cameras these days. "Maybe this is a prize system. Higher rank, better prize."

"Gruesome," I say. "So you still think they're working in small groups?"

"Yes."

"Then maybe some groups are just better than others," I say.

"I'm not sure of anything," he says. "But I want you to take a good long look at your name. Number *two* Jesse."

I stare at my name on the page. *Jesse Sullivan. Location: USA/Nashville. Priority 2.*

"That word priority is my only clue. I've tried to see if it's alphabetical, geographical, financial, and a bunch of other ways, but priority is the system that makes most sense."

As I stare at my name on the sheet my eyes gravitate downward. It isn't my name that worries me on the page. I've known for a whole year my own damn father wants me dead. But why Ally? Ally has never hurt anyone in her whole life. And Ally is normal, perfectly human. Worse—I've replaced her already. I had to in order to save her life after she was stabbed, which means I can't ever save her again. Something about replacing a person reverses that person's magnetic charge. A second replacement is impossible—for anyone. It simply doesn't work. So I can't even beg my boyfriend to save her if she dies a second time.

"I can't save her twice," I tell Brinkley. I feel sick. "If they try again—"

Brinkley stares at me through the dark shades, unmoving.

"If they take her. Maybe torture her—" I begin.

"We won't let them get that far," Brinkley says. If those words are meant to reassure me, they don't. The more I think about it the more I'm certain I will puke.

"Jesse?" he asks. "You're losing color. Look at me."

"Tell me about Liza or something," I say. "And get this freaking plate out of my face before I barf on it."

"She used to be a death-replacement agent in Philadelphia," he says. "Then she was attacked a few months ago like you. She disappeared. Her handler's body was found in the Delaware Bay. Probably dropped into the river outside Philly and washed down. And they found another body too, Liza's boyfriend who also had NRD."

That sounds familiar. "Wasn't there a huge earthquake there recently?"

He nods, stroking that damn beard again. "It's one of the reasons they were reluctant to claim foul play on the body. There were a couple other deaths in the quake."

"So she's missing and her handler and boyfriend are dead," I say. "Déjà vu."

"We need to know what she knows. Maybe she saw something or maybe she knows things about Caldwell," he says.

"If I were her," I say. "I'd keep running and never look back."

"Gloria has found moving targets before." His voice is steady. "I don't doubt her."

I tap Ally's name one last time. "This really freaks me out. Why her? Just to hurt me?"

"There are others on the list connected to you, but they aren't high priority. She must be doing something more than picking up your dry cleaning."

Secrets. Ally is keeping secrets.

Brinkley is speaking again, pulling me out of my thoughts. "When Gloria finds Liza, I need you—"

"I know." I cut him off. I just need some time alone to think about all this—about Ally. "Liza is more likely to trust me if she knows what I am. And we need her to trust us and tell us what she knows."

"Exactly," he says and throws a twenty on the table to cover our meal.

And who else would be willing to go anyway? We're our own small tactical group. Sometimes I hate Brinkley for taking on half the freaking world and asking me to go down with him when really all I want to do is spend a Saturday night on the couch with my boyfriend and best friend—as if they could ever be in the same room together—eating junk and thinking about stupid shit like when is the next time I'm going to get laid.

Then other times, I know better. Even if Brinkley hadn't gone rogue, even if I hadn't been attacked by Eve and the hate mongers hadn't rolled in like the tide, I'd still be in this shit sooner or later.

Because Caldwell is my father and he wants me dead.

But why Ally?

Why?

Ally

Nikki and I crouch around my low coffee table littered with papers, photographs and notes. I've also taken the trouble to place a plate of cheese, crackers, and fruit, along with steaming cups of tea on the low table. It is the best I could do as hostess, failing to recall the last time I'd had someone here for any reason at all. I've spent the last year—since I stopped staying over at Jesse's— just getting used to sleeping in my own bed.

Part of me wanted to stay at the safehouse and not come back to my place at all, just to make sure Jeremiah honored his promise not to hurt the woman. However, Nikki assured me Jeremiah is a man who values his word, which means it is safe to work somewhere more peaceful and familiar.

"This is the missing person's list?" I hold up a print-out that's been highlighted.

Nikki lowers the cup of tea carefully to the coaster and looks up from the photograph she's been examining. "Yes. The yellow ones are the children."

"Why is Jeremiah only focusing on the children?"

"Women and children first?" Nikki shrugs. Her hair falls forward over her shoulder and the lamp lights make her eyes shine. "Maybe he just has a soft spot for children."

"Who doesn't," I say. *Jesse.* I look at the list again and notice a few of the names also have a small star beside it. "What about the stars?"

"Confirmed or possible NRD," she says. She plucks a slice of cheese from the plate and pops it into her mouth.

"How do they determine possibility?" I ask.

"Family history."

It's true that most NRD-positive people have the same AB- blood type and it's common for parents to pass on more than their blood type. Like Jeremiah's poor sister.

"Does Jeremiah have NRD?" I ask.

"He doesn't know," she answers. "It's never been put to the test. But he doesn't have AB- blood so it seems unlikely. Less that 1% of NRD-positives have a non-AB- blood-type. And most of the outliers are AB+. Jeremiah is B-."

I'm surprised she's volunteered such personal information about him. I start to wonder what else I could ask, but I don't press my luck.

"Not everyone from this list has NRD," I say. The list of nearly fifty people has no more than ten stars.

"In fact, most of them don't."

"Let me see." She comes around the edge of the table and sits beside me. The side of her thigh brushes the side of mine and my heart responds with a funny little leap. I'm hyperaware of her scent, clean with a hint of vanilla. I like it a great deal as she takes the missing persons' sheet from me and our fingers brush. I pay a good deal of attention to the pale green rim of my tea cup.

"You're right," she says. "Maybe we've been reading it wrong."

"Who did the highlights and stars?" I ask. I try to keep my voice level.

"I did. I was looking for connections," she says.

Her hot breath warms my cheek as she turns toward me. I keep looking at the list without really seeing it. God, how long has it been since I've had sex? Not since Jesse—ages ago.

"Jeremiah told me to make the children a priority so I highlighted them and then I marked the family history or confirmed NRD. I figured this was a missing persons or presumed dead list for NRD-positives, all of them Caldwell's targets."

"This time last year, we had no idea if it was the military, FBRD, or Caldwell calling the shots," I say. "And now look at us."

"He's the puppeteer," Nikki says. "He can't do it all on his own." Yeah but at least we know who the bad guy is," I say.

Nikki frowns at her list. "Julia changes everything. She was replaced, so there's no possibility that she has NRD."

"Maybe she's an exception," I offer. Because Jesse is an exception and my guts tell me that Caldwell's interest in Julia is also somehow connected to his interest in Jesse.

"Maybe not," she argues. "Maybe she was the missing piece to the puzzle."

"I'm not following you," I say and I turn to look at her. Her face is dangerously close. So close her eyes are big and beautiful with darker blue around the edge.

"What if they are all like Julia?" she says.

I look at the list she presses flat on the table. "Children who've been replaced?"

"Children have a high replacement rate." She sits up straighter, bringing her knees under her. "Parents are always screening them, right? So perhaps the reason why this list has so many children is simply because they have been replaced more often."

I tuck my hair behind my ears and look away from the soft petals of her lips. I also try to ignore the growing burn in my groin. God, how long has it been?

I try to distract myself by saying something. Anything useful. "But if everyone on this list has been replaced, what about the ones with confirmed or possible NRD? If you have NRD, you can't be replaced."

If Jesse tried to replace someone with NRD it wouldn't work. Something about the condition prevents it from working. Gloria says it's because the magnetic charge can't be reversed and that's the same reason why someone who's already been replaced can't be replaced again.

"There aren't that many with confirmed or potential NRD," Nikki argues. "It's possible they really are missing or dead. They may not be part of the roundup at all."

I count nine who are probably dead—if Nikki's theory is right.

"So we need to find out if these others have been replaced by an agent," Nikki says. "Do you recognize any names?"

"Maybe a couple," I admit, but I can't possibly remember everyone Jesse has replaced. "But I can run them through the database to see if they've been replaced by others. There's a program to make sure no one lies to an agent trying to get a second replacement. I can run the names through and see if any of them turn up with a history."

"Perfect," Nikki says. She turns and smiles at me and I'm forced to look away. My God, what is wrong with me? *It's just a girl. You've been around girls before.*

Pretty ones.

"But if that's the case, what does he want with people who've been replaced?" I whisper. My body leans into hers of its own will.

"I don't know, but at least we'll know what we're looking for."

I turn to say something and she catches my eye. *So close.* I can feel the heat of her face near mine. And a static charge seems to build on my skin and bristle. A feverish wave warms me as her hair brushes my cheek. It's as if someone has picked up the other end of the rope and is gently tugging me toward her. A solid, slow tug. Inescapable.

Her lips brush mine like a question. *Is this alright?* And because it takes all I have just to keep breathing, let alone give an answer, she kisses me.

Oh my God is this happening?

It is soft and tentative. It stops and because I say nothing—can *say* nothing—resumes again this time with more force, more excitement.

Is she kissing me? Is Nikki really kissing me?

Her hand comes up and clasps the side of my neck. Her fingers in the back of my hair remove all possibility of escape.

I haven't been kissed since—

My guilt supersedes the desires of my body and I manage to get one hand on her chest.

I feel her breast swell and I push harder to send a

different message. Her teeth come together in a kind of grit as she pulls herself back. Her face presses against the side of mine.

Don't be stupid, Ally. It's just a kiss. Enjoy it. You're not cheating on anyone for God's sake.

"I'm sorry," Nikki says. Her eyes open and that glaze of pleasure recedes.

It's harder to find my voice than I thought. "W-what are you apologizing for?"

"You look upset," she says.

My hand stops pushing and slips up around her neck. I give her a soft reassuring kiss on the cheek. "It isn't that."

"You didn't like it?" she asks.

I blush. "I *liked* it."

She grins and runs her fingers through my hair. I shiver and resist the urge to press the full length of myself against her. A very docile and feminine inclination that I haven't felt in a long time, or that clenching ache between my legs.

"Then what is it?" She kisses my cheeks.

I don't know seems false. And *I'm in love with someone else* seems like the wrong thing to say in a moment like this.

I turn back toward the sheets of paper on the table. "We should solve this first."

"It can wait," she says, playfully.

"Can it?" I ask. "I'm not sure the mothers or the

missing children will agree."

She pulls back from me and takes her tea cup to the kitchen. I listen to her refill her cup and sit the kettle back on the stove with a *clank*.

God, why am I so awkward? I haven't hurt anyone. I haven't cheated on anyone. I'm not destroying any homes unless—

"Are you married?"

"What?" Nikki looks taken aback. "No."

"Engaged?"

"No."

"Committed in any way?"

"*No*," she says and smiles. "Why?"

Because I'm a crazy person who can't handle a little tongue.

My explanation never fully forms before someone bangs on my door. I jump up and knock papers off the table. Nikki makes it to the door first.

"Are you expecting someone?" she asks, on alert. "Faux-blond. Uh—glossy."

"Glossy?" I nudge her out of the way and come up onto my tiptoes to look out the peep hole.

"Do you know who it is?" she asks, her breath warm on my ear.

"I do," I say and open the door.

Jesse

Sunday seminars are nice and small which is a plus. I'll admit I don't have the best track record with seminars. Though they were created by state departments to foster "sensitivity" amongst employees in certain civic roles, I find many of the people aren't "sensitive" at all. I'm no longer required to do these seminars, but I know Dr. York personally and he's the Death-Replacement liaison for this hospital. And Dr. York is also the kind soul who usually puts me back together after a bus, or only-god-knows-what tears me apart, arranging me enough so I don't have another ugly scar and so Kirk can do the cosmetic corrections. I think it's only fair to show my appreciation once in a while.

And I'm overdue for a psych evaluation anyway. Two birds.

All my lanterns arranged at the ready and with a flashlight by the door in case I come home after dark, I leave. Today is considerably sunnier than the last few dreary days of rain and gloom, so I roll down my window, turn up the music and enjoy the twenty minute drive to the hospital. The air is crisp and smells like leaves. A vanilla air freshener dangles from my rearview, mixing with the smell of the wind. I tap my fingers lightly against the steering wheel to the tune of the song.

I manage to hold onto this feeling even after entering the hospital.

Because the seminar is held in the same room every time, a spacious, conference room on the main floor, I can find it just fine.

Dr. York smiles as I slip in and take a seat at one of the smaller, moveable tables.

He stands up front, hands in his lab coat pockets and says the exact thing he says every time he begins one of these things. "I want to welcome everyone. I know most of you are here because your employer requires it. Regardless, I hope you find the information interesting and helpful. Our program is divided into two parts: a short orientation video about twenty minutes long, followed by a Q&A with two death-replacement agents."

I look around the room to see twenty, give or take, diverse faces. Cindy, a fellow death-replacement agent, slips in beside me and gives me a short acknowledging smile.

Her hair is cut near her chin and her big blue eyes are like glass marbles. Cindy has a little mole on her cheek and pretty white teeth to match her pretty French-tipped nails. Her Texas drawl adds to her good southern girl persona. She usually wears knee-high boots, thigh length coat and overlapping necklaces, which is to say she looks like she just walked right out of a fashion magazine. We are quite the contrast, compared to my torn jeans, a zippered black hoodie and my dirty, mismatched sneakers. Clearly, we have different priorities.

Most of these people are morticians, social workers, police officers, firefighters or EMTs.

There are other occupations of course, doctors, nurses, etc. Anyone who comes into contact with our dead bodies, and also happens to be a state employee of some kind, is required to take this training.

Many of these people come into contact with zombies like myself either because they're part of the cleanup crew, or because they play some other part in the death replacement industry. For example, insurance workers encourage their clients to screen for death replacements once a year for lower insurance rates, so sometimes underwriters turn up at the seminars.

Dr. York finally turns off the lights, throwing us into darkness.

The video flashes an opening montage of healthcare professionals, law enforcement and school teachers before moving into the testimonies.

"Death-replacement is the greatest scientific discovery of the twenty-first century," a doctor says. A general intellectual type, probably chosen for his sense of authority. "But not all those with NRD choose to be death-replacement agents. Most fear announcing their condition to their communities because of discrimination, possible violence…"

Must be nice to have options.

When Brinkley turned up offering me a job it was a dream come true because I was seventeen with no family or money. I'd even died before finishing high school so college wasn't an option unless I got my GED, but considering I was homeless and *starving*, it wasn't high on my to-do list. My only choice was to let Brinkley take me in. Of course, he made me get my GED anyway.

One of my favorite clips in this video is of a pretty blond schoolteacher moving with the shuffle-step most death replacers have before a good rub down and steam.

"I know this might be frightening," the schoolteacher says. Her neck is twisted oddly to the side, looking pale and bloody like a zombie in the traditional sense. "But I only look this way because I saved someone's life."

I giggle. It gets me *every* time.

I don't know why but that teacher always cracks me up. Maybe it's the bizarre angle of her face? Her squeaky voice? I don't know but it just tickles me.

Cindy's blue-glow face flashes me a quizzical look, but she doesn't say anything before turning back to the screen. Ally would've shot me an elbow at least.

A social worker speaks now as a child stands beside him. "Sometimes the children must be removed from the home for safety reasons or they are abandoned. And placing these children can be especially challenging. A child who can be tortured to death, and then resurrected, attracts the wrong kind of foster parent."

The video gives a parting shot of a mother who's discovered her six-year-old daughter, thought dead after drowning in a river had NRD. "I'm just so happy she's alive," she cries. "It's a miracle."

Maybe my mother would've felt that way if I hadn't killed her husband in addition to myself.

The lights come on as the film's credits roll on the black screen. A few people clap. I don't because Ally isn't here to force me.

Dr. York reclaims the room. "Before we turn it over to our guests, does anyone have any questions?"

"Is it true they're beginning to test children for NRD? Like genetic testing?"

Dr. York gives a curt nod. "They are developing tests that can register the elevated concentration of magnetite in the cerebral cortex. This is one of the defining characteristics of NRD. But a person will not know for certain they have NRD until they die."

"No other questions?" He pauses. "Then allow me to introduce Ms. Jesse Sullivan and Ms. Cindy St. Claire." Dr. York gestures for us to join him at the front of the room.

"Ms. Sullivan and Ms. St. Claire are both residents here in Nashville and two of the three death-replacement agents serving the Davidson County area."

I say the line Dr. York has taught me to say, robotic as usual. "We are here to answer any questions you might have about NRD and the death-replacement process."

It's hard for me to fake enthusiasm.

Cindy and I spend almost an hour covering the usual topics of death replacement: no we don't decide who lives or dies. No we can't save people who are terminally ill. We prevent death, we aren't magical healers. And of course we have to explain what the hell A.M.P.s are and how they were made. Of course, no amount of explaining ever covers it.

"But how do you make a person?"

"The only way to make a person is the way your mommy and daddy made you," I say. A couple of people laugh while I huff at the bald bulky guy in the front row, who looks like a large gorilla in that tiny plastic chair. Cop probably. "The military just tried to change them. The military was not successful in recreating NRD, but they did make something else: Analysts of necro-Magnetic Phenomenon, A.M.P.s. The acronym is supposed to reiterate the whole electrical current and magnets thing—it doesn't matter. But basically the military isn't allowed to make A.M.P.s anymore since it's basically torture."

"What is magnetite?" someone asks. A petite woman in back. Nurse, if I had to guess.

Cindy answers. "It's a ferrimagnetic mineral that some animals have in their bodies. It helps them sense magnetic fields. Birds have it in their beaks and they use it to fly between the north and south magnetic poles in the winter."

She is so perky. I don't know how she does it. Every new question grates on my nerves.

"Any more questions?" Dr. York asks the class. A final tentative hand goes up, from a small red-headed girl in the back of the room. I have no idea what she could be. Nurse? Mortician? Reporter?

Dr. York motions for her to speak. "Yes?"

"Ms. Sullivan?" she bumbles. Ok. Not a reporter. Way too shy.

"Yes?" I ask.

"Were…were you scared?"

"Nah, I die all the time," I shrug.

She wets her lips. "No, I mean…I mean last year. About what happened—about what was in the news?"

Cindy and Dr. York give me apprehensive looks like they're worried about what I'll say. "You mean when I was trapped in a basement with a few psychos and I had to watch one stab my friends while they made me choose who I'd save?"

"Jesse," Dr. York says.

"Or do you mean when the prostitute—"

"Sex worker," Cindy corrects.

"—tried to cut off my head with a machete?"

The girl is blood red in the face making her hair seem even more enflamed. "I...I...both."

My own face has gotten pretty red. The burning heat in my cheeks tells me so. "Because you know that's the only way to kill us. So if anyone in this room wants to kill me, you've got to chop off my head and destroy my brains, all right?"

Cindy's lips are pressed together so hard they're white as she stares at the floor. Dr. York's mouth is slightly open, gawking, as is true for most of the people in the room.

"I...I'm sorry," the girl blurts. Oh God, she's going to cry. Seeing her red-cheeked and bleary eyed makes me soften. I feel my bulldog response pull back, the leash relaxing around my throat.

"Yes, I was scared," I say. Then I add something I know Dr. York would heavily approve of. "And I hope that by doing these seminars, people will be a little more compassionate towards people like me." I look at Cindy. "Like us."

And on cue, Dr. York beams. Of course, I ruin it by taking it one step too far.

"I only wish a freaking blood bath wasn't necessary to foster compassion, you know?"

The girl nods. Apparently, she's lost her capacity to speak. Dr. York seizes this momentary silence as a chance to close the session. He gives everyone, including Cindy and me, a piece of butterscotch candy. Like we are *five years old.*

We smile and shake hands with people as they file out of the room. I watch them go, wondering if even one of them would bother to stand up for me if Caldwell came for me again.

After the seminar Dr. York gets paged and leaves in a hurry. I grab Cindy and pull her aside before she gets a chance to run off too.

She looks startled to be seized by the arm and held back. Maybe she doesn't want to be alone with me in the conference room.

I don't let her wonder what's going on for long. "When is the last time you saw Raphael?"

Cindy's eyes double in size as she searches the room around us for eavesdroppers but it's sterile white and empty. "Jesse! Someone could hear you!"

"I need to know," I tell her. "When did you last see him? Or when is the last time you hallucinated at all?"

She squeezes my arm so hard I know it would leave a bruise. "Why does it matter? It's over."

"I know right?" I say. "I thought I was like, back to normal and shit. But now I'm not so sure."

Her eyes widen. "No, no. We got scans. We stopped seeing the you-know-whats. We got *better.*"

"I've seen him twice," I say and I know it sounds dumb, but if I can't talk to Cindy about it, the only person I know who might be as crazy as I am, then I can't talk to anyone. "And I can *feel* him."

Her eyes couldn't be more round. "It's just PTSD or something. It's not real."

"Or I'm losing my shit."

"Stop," she says. "Sweet Jesus, just stop talking." Her gaze snaps right at the sound of feet approaching us and someone yanks the door wide.

It's the girl who I mistook for a reporter with the crazy red hair. She's no older than twenty, and she's short like me. Her hair is cut straight across, and because it's thick, it poofs out at the sides, flaring at the ends. I want to tell her layers are the secret. Layers make thick hair manageable. But I have a strong feeling she didn't come back to talk to me about hair.

With her arms folded over her chest, Cindy and I stare at her waiting for something to happen. But she doesn't speak. It's like she's under a spell until Cindy smiles.

"Hey honey," Cindy says, saccharin sweet. You'd

have never guessed that thirty seconds ago we were discussing how on the verge of sanity we are.

"Hi." Her smile is more of a reflexive reaction than a genuine smile. "Ms. Sullivan?"

"Just Jesse," I say. "Ms. Sullivan is my mother and she's dead."

I laugh but the girl just looks horrified. Ok, so I'm not as good at faking it as Cindy.

"So what's up?" I ask her. I hope by getting to the point, we'll get past this cup of awkward.

Cindy has a sweeter voice than I do, with that soft Texas twang and she really works it now.

"Are you okay, honey?"

Arms wrap around me. One second this girl is standing before us, clutching herself. Then she has her arms around me like a damn barnacle.

"What the—" I am about to use the strong explicative term when Cindy gives me a look, that would translate to something like *it's a hug. Deal with it.*

I reach one arm up and pat her on the back. Then I realize she is talking, her voice muffled against Lane's canvas coat.

"I can't hear you," I say.

She lifts her head. Wiping her nose with the back of her hand. Great. She probably snotted all over this jacket and there's no way to check without making her cry more.

"Thank you," she says. "For saving him."

"Who?"

"My dad," she says. "You replaced my dad last year."

"Who's your dad?" I ask.

She gives me a name which conjures a vague picture of a robust man and beer gut. "Construction worker?" I ask.

She nods. "If you hadn't saved him, I...I don't know what we'd do. We all love him to death."

I'd caught Mr. Frank Johnson falling off a beam. His fat ass broke my spine in three places and almost bashed my brains out of my skull. Had I not been wearing the required hard hat when we went down, I probably wouldn't have made it.

"He'd just healed up when we saw you on the TV." She goes on. "He was like 'Sadie, that's the young lady that saved my life. Now someone done went and hurt her. That's just shameful.'"

She hadn't quite imitated Frank's robust, good ol' boy tone, but it's close enough.

My throat is real tight all of a sudden and my eyes burn with tears. What the hell is wrong with me? "I'm glad your dad is okay," I say.

Then she starts to cry. *Cry.*

"Oh Lord," Cindy says and wraps the girl up in her arms. "Darlin', what's wrong?"

"He's missing," she sobs. "My dad is missing."

"Why are you telling me?" I ask. I can't do

anything. Not that you'd know by the dirty look Cindy gives me. "You should call the police or something."

The girl steps away from Cindy's embrace. "I'm sorry. I know that isn't your problem. I'm sorry. Really I just wanted to say thank you and to say I was real sorry for what happened to you."

Sadie turns and hurries away.

The second she's out of earshot, Cindy jumps me. "What's wrong with you? We could've helped her. Taken her to the police or something."

"I don't know," I say because a strange feeling overtakes me as I watch Sadie disappear around the far corner of the corridor. Am I being watched?

Closer than you think.

I turn a full circle in the hospital hallway, searching for the eyes I know must be fixed on me.

But I see no one.

Ally

Cindy enters the apartment with all the air of a Duchess. Her white-blond hair doesn't have a strand out of place and her heels click in sharp, strident steps across the brief stretch of linoleum between the front door and the living room carpet. Her lashes are ridiculously long as she blinks dramatically in surprise.

"Am I interrupting?" Cindy asks.

I know Cindy mostly through Jesse. We've lived in this same apartment building since I took the position as Jesse's assistant, long before Jesse even remembered who I was, but I don't know her very well. When I moved to Nashville and started working with Jesse, she was the one who suggested this place, having liked it herself. But she is on the 4th floor and I'm on the 3rd. She might as well live in South Dakota as I've never seen her here.

"What's wrong?" I ask. Nikki tenses beside me.

"I just wanted to talk to you about Jesse," she says. "Is your—friend—going to stay?"

"I was about to run to the store actually," Nikki

says. She gathers up the papers on the coffee table and turns the pile face down, placing her tea cup on top. "We need real food."

"Sure," I say and try not to sound surprised she's leaving or disappointed that she is apparently dissatisfied with my attempts at a fancy cheese spread. "Chipotle is down the road."

Nikki smiles. "Sure. Do you want anything—?"

"Cindy," she says, flashing her perfectly white teeth and extending her hand toward Nikki. "Cindy St. Clair."

Nikki must recognize the name of one of the few death replacement agents in the area but she does a good job of not reacting to the name. "Are you hungry?"

"No, thank you, darlin'," Cindy continues. "I just ate."

Nikki grabs her coat off the back of the chair and slips through the front door. The rush of it all makes it hard to adjust. A couple of minutes ago I was kissing Nikki and now Cindy is standing in my apartment.

"Do you want tea or something?" I try to hedge my confusion by giving myself something to do. "I believe I have coffee too."

"I can't stay long," she says. She crosses to the corner and sits on the edge of the big arm chair, as if the only way to avoid being swallowed by the thick arms is to perch precariously on the edge of the seat.

"I assume this is work related." *Jesse embarrassed me in seminar today. Jesse said this. Jesse did that.* Most of the time when people want to discuss Jesse, it's to complain. "So what did she do?"

"Oh, nothing. It's not like that." Cindy presses her palm against her chest. "I'm just *so* worried about her."

"Why? What's happened?" I sink into the couch, and pull a pillow into my lap.

"Has she ever talked to you about—" Cindy stops and exhales. I've never seen her look so uncomfortable. She's bouncing her leg in place and her back is bowed forward protectively. "I mean, you and her, you're best friends, right? Of course she'd tell you."

"*What?*" I demand. She's killing me. "Just tell me."

She pulls at the end of her bob then proceeds with a doubtful look. "Does she ever talk to you about Gabriel?"

"Who's Gabriel?" I ask.

Cindy's lips pursed. "Never mind. I'm sorry I bothered you."

Cindy stands and moves toward the door but I stop her and push her back into the chair. I'm confused and almost angry at the idea Cindy knows something about Jesse that I don't. Jesse, who I practically wait on hand and foot, can't possibly have secrets I don't know about.

"No, tell me," I demand. "You said you're worried and I'm sure I would be too. And who else can help her?"

"I shouldn't have come," she says.

"Just tell me," I say and tuck my hair behind my ears. "Whatever it is, I'll deal with it."

She considers me for a long time and I begin to worry Nikki will come back before this conversation is over and now I'm not sure I want Nikki here at all.

Cindy nods as if agreeing with someone I can't hear. "Okay, yeah. Of course, you probably are the best person."

"Exactly," I say. "Now what's going on?"

"Just remember you asked for this, darlin'."

"I know," I say. "So start from the beginning."

She exhales long and slow before speaking. "Do you remember last year, the whole *church* thing—and what am I saying! Of course you remember—you were there, weren't you? Well about that time, this whole Gabriel-Raphael problem started up too."

I don't fixate on this new name Raphael because I want her to keep talking. "This problem began a year ago, around the time I was kidnapped and we were all attacked in the Church basement."

"And I can't believe they still let that place stay open!" Cindy exclaims.

"They pleaded ignorance of course and the

evidence just disappeared," I say. "But please, continue. Something about Gabriel and Raphael a year ago?"

Cindy arches her eyebrows and tilts her head. "I started seeing angels. Sweet Jesus, I'm not kidding. I can tell by your face you don't believe me, but you'd better. I saw honest-to-God angels. Well, one angel anyway, with wings proclaiming the word of God."

My mouth slides open. I could feel my mind hollowing out, opening up from the unexpected turn.

Cindy goes on, gesturing as if this is her point. "I saw Raphael and Jesse saw Gabriel."

"Last year?" I ask. "She saw an angel last year? And she just found you and told you about it?"

But not me. Why not me? Oh god, if she's hallucinating— if she's sick—

"No, no—okay. Let me back up. I saw angels. I might have been a little upset about it and I went to Gloria because that woman sees the strangest things, *bless* her heart. I thought she'd be able to help me get a handle on this, you know? Instead, she takes me to Jesse, gets us to admit to each other that we've been talking to imaginary men. Gorgeous men, mind you, at least Raphael is—*was*—but invisible nonetheless. And we go to get brain scans and find out there is nothing physically wrong with us, but yet here we are, talking to them anyway."

"Gabriel?" I ask. "And Raphael."

"Exactly," Cindy looks relieved.

"Wait, back up," I say. "Why did Gloria bring you to Jesse?"

Cindy shrugs. "She must've known that Jesse was hallucinating."

My head is swimming with this information. How could Jesse be having hallucinations and not tell me? *Why* wouldn't she tell me? "Go back to the part about why you're worried now, if this was a year ago."

"I think she's still having hallucinations," Cindy says.

"But you aren't?" I ask.

"No," Cindy says. "It all just went away. Now I can use the toilet just fine and I haven't seen a single thing in months and months."

"Were you afraid to use the bathroom with Raphael watching?" I ask. I'm having a hard time trying to figure out what is important in this conversation and what I should focus on. One problem is simply Cindy talks too fast.

"Oh goodness, no, but that would be terrible. No, my problem was toilets would sort of explode," she whispers as if someone can hear us. "I wouldn't even have to be in the bathroom. But if I did need to use the restroom, I had to be sure I was nice and *calm* first."

Too much information. "So why do you think Jesse is still hallucinating?"

"She asked me some questions at the seminar today and she was—" she says. "I don't know, it was just an impression I got. She seems on edge, you know? I'm not saying we need to commit her. I'm just saying someone needs to help her. If she lets it go too far, well, *you* know."

I do know. If someone were to find out Jesse was hallucinating, then only one thing will happen. She would be given a one-way ticket to the asylum, just like her mentor Rachel. I don't blame Jesse for keeping this quiet and I'm really glad she didn't bring it up in front of Nikki.

But why wouldn't she tell me? Doesn't she know she can tell me anything?

The buzzer on the building sounds and I know it's Nikki needing to be let back in. Cindy stands as if a fire has been lit under her ass and rushes toward the door. I push the button on the intercom unlocking the front entrance.

"I better get going anyway," Cindy says. "I'm meeting Momma for dinner. She's staying with me 'til Tuesday."

"Thank you," I say. *Even though you told us you just ate.* "For coming to me with this. You could have gone to Gloria again."

"I tried but she wasn't home," Cindy says. *Or she didn't come to the door for you*, I thought.

Cindy proceeds down the hallway toward the

stairwell. She passes Nikki, laden with a food bag. She flashes a grin as she passes. "Nice to meet you, honey. See you around."

"Good night," Nikki says to the passing whirlwind of glamour and shine.

"Everything okay?" Nikki asks. She's watching me, clearly curious.

I force a smile despite the pounding in my ears. "I hope so."

Jesse

$\mathbf{P}$art of my FBRD-certification requires that I be psychiatrically evaluated every few deaths because of the high risk of going totally batshit crazy.

"How are you today, Jesse?" Herwin, my therapist asks. He invites me into his office, moving stacks of paper out of a desk chair so I can take a seat.

"Stiff," I reply, coming into the dimly lit room. "Do you have time to do my eval?"

Herwin is wearing his usual brown tweed suit. I think it's his work uniform or something. Maybe someone should tell him to mix it up every once in a while. After all, all this brown tweed—his outfit and the 70s era furniture—packed between four white cinder block walls is just too oppressive.

I stretch myself long on the couch, but it is lumpy and I can feel the springs through scratchy upholstery. Once I settle in, Herwin moves his chair closer and pulls out the pointer light. The lights in the warm room soften, making the pointer light look like a searchlight pouring into my skull.

"Just try to relax and listen to the sound of my voice. Okay?"

I grumble some kind of agreement.

The longer I stare at the light the more relaxed I become. I drift off and before I know it, Herwin is out of his chair, exchanging the pointer light for the soft glow of the lamps. He offers me a tissue and I have to sit up to wipe the water out of my eyes.

"How do you feel now?" he asks.

"Still tired. Still sore." I pinch my eyes shut beneath the tissue. "What's the prognosis?"

"So far so good," he says, taking just a moment to adjust his bowtie.

As I toss the damp tissue in the direction of the wastebasket and miss, the temperature changes.

I know this feeling—

The way a room warms suddenly, the feel of a person standing near me.

I'm terrified to look up, to turn my eyes in the direction of the large white wall with a hint of shadow on it. Whatever Herwin was saying has been completely obliterated by the pounding of my heart in my ears.

Finally I dare to sneak a glance.

Gabriel stands on the very same spot where I first saw him a year ago, a black smudge against the white cinderblock wall. That time he'd been casual, almost bored, with his black wings folded over each dark sleeve of his suit jacket. His impossibly green eyes merely curious and watchful. Now he reaches toward me in panic, stretching his arm out as if to catch me from falling. His black wings wide and glorious cast menacing shadows on the wall behind him, before he fades into the darkness entirely.

"Oh shit."

"Excuse me?" Herwin asks and looks up from his legal pad.

"Uhhhh," I start, scrambling for something normal to say. "Want me to put a quarter in a jar or something?"

Herwin laces his fingers. "That is not necessary. You're an adult and can express your feelings in whatever language you feel is most appropriate. However, I must ask, what has garnered such a strong reaction?"

Eyes still fixed on the wall behind him, I try to think of how to tell the truth without giving myself away. "I think some things are just coming up again. From last year, I mean."

"You were kidnapped. Your loved ones were physically assaulted in front of you and you yourself were attacked," Herwin says with a sympathetic and grave face. "It is only natural that those experiences should resurface and upset you from time to time."

"But I was doing so well."

"Try not to think of it as a competition, Jesse," he

says, steepling his fingers. "There is no prize for most well-adjusted person."

There is when you do what I do for a living. The prize is staying out of the nuthouse.

"I find the best way to deal with traumatic events such as these is to face them head on," he says. "Look at them without turning away and recognize how strong you are for surviving such a horrible ordeal. By acknowledging your own strength, it's easier to remove the fear."

"Sure," I say. "I'll try that." But I don't mean it. And I can tell by the totally bummed look on Herwin's face he knows I'm just telling him what he wants to hear. But what are my options? There's no freaking way I'm just going to embrace Gabriel. How the hell will that remove the fear? Because I'll be too crazy to fear anything, I guess.

When Gabriel came last time my whole life fell apart. There's no way in hell I'm just going to invite that back in. I need a clear head. I need to be ready for whatever Caldwell will throw at me next.

Ally

Gloria's house is dark when I pull up. Her yard looks dreadful. I'm surprised she hasn't had the city called on her for codes, what with the overgrown grass and random collectibles in the yard. A tire here. A barrel drum there. God knows where it came from.

I pull up the short gravel drive and park in the back. The single wood step, bent and warped with time threatens to snap altogether as I climb up to the door and open the back screen. I knock once but no one answers. When no one comes I use my spare key to let myself in.

"Gloria?" I call out.

No answer.

I squeeze into the tiny space between the door and the wall and shut it behind me. The house smells like dust and dank water. I move through the dark across fading tiles into the kitchen. This room is brighter with the front facing window. I always marvel at the grotesque décor of the kitchen, everything a hideous yellow color from the 70s.

Because the bedrooms are all dark, there is only one place left to check.

I slip down the basement stairs carefully and sure

enough there she is, scribbling away at her desk. She has several pictures of a girl taped to the wall in a circular pattern.

There are three pictures in the middle that aren't pictures at all. Only dark angry black holes have been scrawled onto the page, as if in a fit of rage Gloria has wasted all her lead just to carve out these hungry mouths.

When she stops long enough I put my hand gently on top of hers to let her know I'm here. Tactile perception is best to break the spell. And it's better than all that damn caffeine she drinks.

I keep my voice low and gentle. "You've been working overtime. You know what will happen if you don't take good care of yourself." I point at the black scribbles. "What are these?"

"I can't see it yet," she says.

I don't ask her to explain more. "Are you working a missing person case? She looks young."

"I can't decide if she is missing or doesn't want to be found."

She turns to face me more fully in the overhead light. It looks like I'm about to interrogate her and for just a second I think of Jeremiah's captive. But without doubt, Gloria is a good woman. And I wish she'd take better care of herself. She deserves it, all that she does for everyone else.

I lean against her work table as if bracing myself

for the worst. "I came to ask about Gabriel."

"Jesse didn't tell you about him." It isn't a question.

"No," I say. "Should I be worried? Hallucinations are a sign that the brain has been too damaged."

"There is nothing wrong with Jesse," Gloria says.

"With all respect, you aren't a medical professional."

"They went to Dr. York and received cerebral scans. They're fine."

"Seeing something that isn't there isn't okay," I say.

Gloria's eyes narrow.

"I didn't mean you," I add. "Jesse isn't supposed to be seeing anything."

"But she does." And I don't like the way she says it. Her voice implies she sees more than angels.

"This is about everything else. The electrical problems, the shocky thing she did to the bad guys last year—" That strange purple shimmer comes to mind, the one I saw enveloping her and Julia during the replacement, protecting them from the tree.

"The angels aren't hallucinations," Gloria says. "Her mind is trying to comprehend something she is experiencing but has no word for."

"I didn't think you believed in God," I say.

"I don't," she says. "I'm not saying it's God. I'm saying her mind is trying to process something. And her mind has given her a face and an idea to help her understand it."

I don't bother to hide my confusion. One of the benefits of our friendship, Gloria and I are past all that.

Gloria points at the three black pictures on the wall. "I didn't actually see black spots. But my mind senses something and gave me a shape to try to understand what I was looking at—a void, confusion, interference. They aren't angels. Jesse is experiencing something and her mind gives her the image of an angel in order understand what she is looking at. Divinity, power, protection—or whatever it means to her. It is a message."

"It," I repeat. "You think *it* is communicating with her."

"I don't know if it's conscious. Energy isn't conscious," Gloria says. She looks to her sketches and casts a long dark shadow across the page. "I see my visions but they aren't conscious. They aren't *speaking* to me."

"Why didn't she tell me?"

"She knows how you'll react," Gloria says.

I cross my arms. "Is that why you're not telling me why Jesse is in this picture?"

Gloria doesn't want to answer. I can tell by her pinched brow. "Brinkley wants us to retrieve this girl and bring her back."

"Why the rush to find the girl?" I ask. I'm thinking of Nikki's list and Jeremiah's search and rescue.

"Caldwell is looking for her too." Gloria looks truly pained. "We have to find her before he does."

Anger tears through my body. Afraid of what I may say to Gloria, I turn and leave. She lets me go without a single question.

On the way home I try desperately to let all my questions go. Why Jesse? Why does everyone insist on bringing her into this? What do they expect her to do? Confront Caldwell? Kill him? Do they realize how insane that sounds? How incredibly and stupidly unfair it is to ask her for anything after all she's been through?

I fall into my bed exhausted. It isn't physical exhaustion, not like running a few miles or an afternoon of errands. It is purely mental. The pillow sinks around my face and the cool sheets are like a mother's comforting hand. I curl into the softness and pull the comforter close.

I'm so tired of worrying about Jesse. For every *one* thing I do to protect her, to keep her out of harm's way, three more threats crop up.

I became her assistant so I could keep an eye on her, keep her close. I make the situation as comfortable and as low risk as possible, but then the threats start, both at her house and now Kirk's mortuary. Add that to her bumbling boyfriend's incompetence and we've got complications galore.

I joined up with Jeremiah, hoping to protect her. I thought it would keep us informed, active, and connected but all it has done is bring Jesse to his attention. The way he talks about her I can tell he is assessing her usefulness. He wants her *in* the fight, which is the exact opposite of what I want.

And Brinkley. Don't get me started on Brinkley.

The point is, I keep trying to put more and more obstacles between Jesse and danger and yet no matter what I do it finds her again.

My fingers slip under my shirt and trace the ragged scar where I was stabbed, the point of entry where my skin grew back dimpled. It cost me my spleen but at least it had bought Jesse time. For *once* I was actually where I was supposed to be—between her and the danger.

Jesse tried to tell me what her stepdad Eddie was doing. She tried to get me to save her then and I didn't—I was too afraid to give up my own life and face the situation. I'm still afraid. Some nights when I wake up from nightmaring about the barn in a cold sweat, I'm more terrified than I've ever been in my life. Not of her dying. Her job has rid me of that fear. I'm terrified of becoming that empty shelled person again, that ghostly wraith of a woman who wandered for years believing Jesse was dead.

It might be selfish of me—to look at it this way. But I'm being honest. I can't bear that level of pain, not *again*. But God knows how we're going to come out of this alive when Caldwell's marked us all for death.

A rock hits my bedroom window and I jolt upright. My heart jumps like a monkey screaming and rattling its cage and my fingernails bite into the scar. When the rock comes again, I slowly ease toward the window. My big bed is placed firmly against the wall, so I have enough room to get in and out of my closet. The mattress sinks under my knees, as I peer out the window to the parking lot below.

Nikki smiles when she sees me. Her hair is a fluorescent halo around her head in the orange streetlight. She stands in the center beneath it so I can see her clearly, the pavement black beyond the orange ring. I slide my window open and call down. It isn't that long after dusk, so no one will call the cops on me.

"A rose by any other name," I say, laughing. "What are you doing down there?"

"Yeah, I was going for romantic. Can I come in?" she asks.

I look out the window to either side. "How did you know this was my window?"

She points to the right of me at my balcony. "That's your fern and your bistro table."

"What if someone else has a fern and a bistro table?" I ask.

"They don't. I checked."

"Creeper," I say. And I wave her toward the entrance.

I hold the buzzer long after I hear her clamoring up the stairs. Then I unlock the door and let her in. She has a small blue bag slung over one shoulder and a few droplets of rain on her face.

"Was it raining?" I ask surprised. I hadn't noticed even hanging out the window.

"It's starting to," she says.

"I should give you back your coat," I say. I point to the back of my kitchen chair where her coat hangs to dry. "There. Take it with you when you leave."

"That's not what I'm here for. I brought more work. I thought we could finish up our theory before presenting our plan to Jeremiah. Parish says he's getting restless."

"Our plan?" I ask closing the door behind her.

"I don't want the woman to be tortured either," she says. "I don't think we should be like them."

"No," I agree but my chest tightens. "But maybe I'm an idiot for thinking we can come out of this any other way."

"Don't say that." Nikki stops shuffling papers in the bag and looks up at me from where she crouches on the floor. She stands suddenly and takes both my hands in hers. It's an incredibly sweet and incredibly commanding gesture. My body warms to her touch. I only look away to her mouth once her lips start to move. "Listen to me. You are a good person. You are a good person now and you'll be a good person when this is over."

When this is over— I used to spend a lot of time thinking about *when this is over*. I mostly picture me and Jesse happy and free of all the horrible things that haunt us. But since she met Lane my *when this is over* picture has been blurry.

"What are you thinking so hard about?" Nikki asks. She hasn't released my hands and I'm very aware of how close our mouths are.

"When this is over," I say. "What does it look like to you?"

Nikki smiles. "It looks pretty good."

She grins again. I don't know what I did, if it was my body language or if Nikki really just doesn't have any self-control, but she kisses me. She slides in and plants one on my lips.

"Doesn't your future look good?" she asks, breaking the kiss.

My future. I want a future with Jesse in it. I want a future *with* Jesse. But what if that never happens? What if we survive but we are horrible people? Or what if we survive and we've seen each other do so many terrible things that we can't bear to look at each other anymore? What if Jesse loses her mind completely with all this? What if she is too far gone to even recognize me, let alone love me? As it stands half the time, I don't even know if Jesse is human.

"Hey are you okay?" Nikki says. She has me by the shoulders.

"Can I just lie down in my bed?" I ask. My knees feel weak and the room is spinning.

Nikki leads me to my bedroom and tucks me into the big fluffy covers. She is careful to stay out of the bed, only kneeling down beside it and taking my hand like I'm dying of something serious, like cholera rather than just having an emotional crisis.

"Are you coming down with something? Everyone and their mother has the flu," she says.

"No," I say. "I'm just tired and stressed."

"Then you should rest. I shouldn't have come without calling. I'm sorry."

"It's okay," I say. "We're running out of time. But I'm just so tired of it all."

"Can I get you anything?" she asks.

"No," I say. "Just give me a minute to clear my head."

"I'll take off," she says and stands. "We can meet up tomorrow after you've slept. I don't have to be at work until 4, so we have all day."

"No," I grab her hand as she turns to go. I don't want to be alone. I'm so tired of fighting all on my own. I need someone to stand by me for once.

She looks down at my hand holding hers. "I can stay."

"Thank you," I whisper.

She smiles, slips off her shoes and climbs into the bed beside me.

Jesse

Gabriel, Gabriel—what the hell to do about Gabriel?

Even after I make it home, I don't have an answer. I am so exhausted either from the usual energy dip of an afternoon or from the emotional rollercoaster of the day. As I tumble into my bed sheets, my elbow connects with something hard.

"Ow!" Yelping and cradling my funny bone, I peel back the covers to find a book. *A Tale of Two Cites,* the hardback edition. "Gee-*zus*. What the hell is this?"

It's not my book. As if I could bear to read something so thick or so depressing. I saw that little Oliver boy on TV. I know how Dickens rolls. No thank you. So what the hell is this doing in my bed?

I open the front cover. "It was the best of times, it was the worst of times, it was the age of wisdom, it was the age of foolishness, it was the epoch of belief, it was the epoch of incredulity, it was the season of Light, it was the season of Darkness, it was the spring of hope, it was the winter of despair…" I fall back onto my pillows and yawn. "So, basically, a lot is going on?"

I toss the book away and it bounces off the mattress before tumbling onto the floor. On impact, a strange sound escapes the book, like the sound of the air whistling. Curious, I lean over the edge of the bed and lift the book again. I turn it over in my hands but I don't see anything. The back cover, the inside, is different. Puffy. The edge of the glued-down flap is up and I use a fingernail to wedge it apart further and find a torn bit of note card inside.

"Pack a bag. G's tonight."

So Brinkley has graduated from foam darts to book messages.

"Message received," I grumble and start to pack a bag. So much for a nap.

And I want to see Ally. Not just because I need her to watch Winston, but because I want to see her. So after I pack a bag and load up Winston, his stuffed skunk toy and food, I drive over to Ally's apartment. By the time I get there, it is raining really hard. I'm holding a forty pound pug and punching the speaker on Ally's apartment for a full two minutes before she answers.

"It's me!" I beg. "And it's raining."

I hear a click and the outside door unlocks. I haul the fat pug up three flights of stairs and stumble, wet and huffing, down the dim hallway to the door marked A7. Ally left the door cracked for me and I push it wide with a knee, my hands stuffed full of pug.

She stands naked. *Completely.* We've seen each other naked so it isn't a big deal, but the sight of her, all that bare skin and I suck air and look away. The fact that she is towel drying her hair tells me I'd caught the tail end of her shower, otherwise I'd have thought this was a different kind of hello.

Unsure of what else I should do, I plop the pug on the floor. I don't dare leave the little square of linoleum that makes up her entryway and step onto her clean carpet. Not when I am all wet and muddy.

"I need you to watch Winston," I say.

"For how long?"

"I don't know," I say.

Ally makes a face that I can't quite read. And she goes still. "Where are you going?"

"I'm not sure," I say. "Brinkley is sending me somewhere to pick up some girl."

"Alone?"

I shrug my shoulders again.

"So you brought me Winston?"

"It was dark," I say, pouting. "I can't leave him in the dark all by himself."

She's watching me again, pulling the towel down from her hair and wrapping it around her body. "You can look at me."

I look up from my shoes, a blue chuck and black chuck with the plastic white caps across the toes. "I was just trying to be polite. You having a girlfriend and all."

"I don't have a girlfriend," she says.

But you have something. Something you're running to, to get away from me.

When I meet her eyes she is closer to me, the towel clutched in one hand.

I kiss her.

I don't know what I am thinking. I know I have a boyfriend. I know it's stupid to kiss someone. It's not like I expected the kiss to change anything. Or that she would suddenly confess everything.

Her lips are soft, yielding and at the last moment they part, offering the softest brush of tongue. My heart races and I press more of myself against her, our bodies connecting, mouth to mouth, hip to hip. And I feel it. I really do feel something in my chest and stomach when I kiss her. And not just horniness either.

"Do you still feel anything?" I ask. *Like what I'm feeling. Or are you totally over me?*

She smells like shampoo and soap. Her skin is still warm from the hot shower. I forget about keeping my muddy feet on the linoleum as I back her up to the arm of the couch, ready to fall into the cushions and take that damn towel away from her if she tries to stop me. She is up on her toes, pressed against the couch arm, but she won't let herself be pushed down onto her back.

It's a gentle stop. No slapping or yelling. No words. But she's turned her cheek so I'm kissing her neck instead, strands of her wet hair sticking to my cheek.

"Jess—" she whispers. Her voice is throaty, breathless, and I can feel the quick pulse in her neck throbbing against my lips. "You have to stop."

I tug at the corner of her towel, pulling it down enough to see the full spread of her cleavage. Her hold tightens and her knuckles go white.

"Just tell me what's bothering you," she says. "You only act a fool when something's wrong."

"I'm sorry," I say, meeting her eyes for the first time. Those pretty brown eyes, the opposite shade of Lane's. She isn't wearing her nose ring and a little dimple blemishes the side just above the flare of the nostril. "I shouldn't have done that."

"If you need to tell me something," she says, tentatively. "You know you can."

"What about you? Can you tell me everything?" I ask, thinking about that horrible hit list. "There's only six people between us."

As soon as I say it, I regret it. Her brow pinches together. "What are you talking about?"

"Just," I start. But God, what to say? "Whatever

you're doing, just stop."

She shifts her weight. Her mouth forms a question but no words come out. She still can't tell me. I'm standing here letting her know I know, but she won't *tell* me. She probably didn't feel anything either, which is why she stopped me. Wow, it hurts more than I thought it would—knowing that Ally and I might not ever be close again. Good friends, maybe—but not best friends—and not like before I gave her up for Lane. And part of me thinks *God you should drop Lane and you're an idiot if you don't before it's too late*. Another voice says, *it's already too late*.

"I'm sorry that—" I take her hand and kiss the back of it. It's hard to do, considering I feel like I can't breathe. "—that you couldn't tell me. Just please be more careful."

And then I leave before I make a real fool of myself.

Ally

I stare at the back of the door for a long time after Jesse leaves. I can still smell her, sweeter than my salty ocean-scented soap. Honey, maybe. Or vanilla. And her lips, so soft when they—*stop it, Ally. Don't be an idiot.*

Why didn't she mention Gabriel? *Why didn't you mention Jeremiah?* Fair enough. Because it is clear Jesse knows something about it. From Brinkley? Gloria? I cannot keep up anymore. Is this how people wake up one day and find they are strangers to each other— one secret builds upon another until no one knows what to believe anymore?

Winston waddles to his spot, where Jesse threw down his sleep pillow in a corner and curls himself into a ball. His curly tail wags when I kneel beside him, a few appreciative *thumps.* I scratch the back of his soft velvety ears and he snorts, inclining his head into my hand and rolling those big eyes up to meet mine.

"What are we going to do with her?" I ask. He

snorts again. "I *know*."

I tiptoe down the dark hallway and open the door to the bedroom. Nikki is beneath the tangle of sheets, still wearing all her clothes. Her face is framed by the thin strand of hallway light, her skin against my dark sheets looks pale and perfect. Her hair covers most of her face except the full lips, in a slightly open part, chest rising with each slow inhale and exhale.

What would I have done if she had awoken when Jesse came? Introduced them? That would have been a riot. Jesse would have been herself times 100, I'm sure. Why had I lied to Jesse? And how long do I think I can keep these two parts of my life separate: Jeremiah and Nikki, and Jesse. Why do I even feel like I need to?

I don't know.

I know why I let Jess kiss me. Of course I still love her, but I want more than that. I miss her. I miss her now, thinking of her standing there in Lane's jacket, those dark curls falling down her back and hiding one eye. The same hazel eyes catching the living room lamplight and sparkling. The way her mouth quirks to one side when she's being mean. Her smooth soft hands in mine, or clasping the back of my neck. With her close, I could smell Lane in that jacket. And Nikki is asleep in the other room.

Why didn't I tell her Nikki was here? Was I ashamed? I haven't done anything wrong. Having another girl sleep in my bed is hardly a crime. I reconsider all my actions and replay over and over the few minutes Jesse stood in my apartment until my mind grows tired of this obsession.

They are leaving tonight, heading off to somewhere to get this girl Caldwell is after.

Gloria must be watching the situation for any sign of Caldwell but surely they know they might run into him. They're chasing the same person after all. Chances are high.

I sink into the couch with a cup of hot tea and turn on my computer. If I'm awake at this ungodly hour, I might as well get work done. I take the papers from Nikki's bag and sort through them until I find the sheet with the highlighted names and interspersed stars.

I log into the database using my FBRD access code—those given to all agents—and begin to plug in a few names from the sheet: Stephanie Mason. Charles DuMonte, George Payton.

Three hits. All three of them have had death replacements. Not from Jesse though. Mason and Payton are from the East Coast and Mason is from Atlanta, but replacements nonetheless. Then I choose a name that looks familiar: Frank Johnson. Match. He was replaced by Jesse February of last year. Now I remember. A construction worker who fell from the beam with Jesse under him. She complained about that replacement for nearly a month, but I'd liked Frank. He had the kind of laugh that turned heads. You couldn't not laugh when you heard it. And he loved his kids. He must've showed me a dozen photos of his two girls.

I keep checking the names and realize they all match except for eight. Everyone but the eight have been replaced by an agent in the last year or so. But these eight are still connected. They are the agents that did the replacements.

"So why would Caldwell kidnap agents *and* the people they replaced?" I ask Winston. He snores loudly. "What could he possibly want with them?"

Exhaustion settles back in, and I close my computer. I check the locks, give Winston a kiss on his upturned nose, and turn out the lights. I slip into bed and lay beside Nikki.

"You smell like soap," she says.

I'm glad that's all I smell like and not like a great big Jesse kiss. My lips were getting lots of action these days. For over a year, nada and now, it's like rush hour traffic.

"Showers will do that," I say.

She surveys me for a moment longer then sits up on her elbows. "Time for me to go?"

"You can stay."

"Really?" she asks and I can't help but smile at her big goofy grin.

"But I need to say some things."

Her smile stiffens a little.

"But there is no point if you don't really like me," I say. I look up to meet her eyes. "So you can save yourself from this disclaimer speech if you want to."

Her brow furrows. "But I *really* like you."

"Okay, then, yes. I need to say some things."

She puts her head in her hand. "I'm listening."

"I'm still in love with Jesse," I say. I just throw it out there like slinging a clay pot into the air to be shot. If I hit her with the worst first, surely she can handle the rest.

She barely bats an eyelash. "I know you are."

"I don't expect you to understand but I feel a lot of responsibility for her, for—" I search for a word but don't find it. "For reasons, I'm not sure I can explain."

"You feel guilty," she says.

The word stings like a slap.

"Oh come on," Nikki says in the dark confidence of my bedroom. "I might not know what you did or what you *think* you did, but guilt is an easy read. And it's all over your face."

"It doesn't matter what I feel," I push on. "I only need to you understand that I can't change the way I feel about her."

"So why am I in your bed? What do you want me *for*?" she asks. "Just sex? Because I won't say no."

I blush. "It has been awhile."

"Was Jesse the last person?" she asks. And I find myself nodding before I have a chance to consider what a bad idea it might be to tell Nikki this.

"But it's been like 18 months."

Nikki grins. "That is *like* a very specific number. Have you been counting?"

"No."

"So just sex then?" she asks. "Because I've worked with less."

And for some reason I start laughing. And then she is laughing.

"No really," she says. "Getting you to want me back is half the battle."

I'm still laughing. "I find it hard to believe that Ms. Nicole Tamsin wouldn't be able to bed any conquest she likes."

"Oh you'd be surprised," she says. "And did you just use the word 'bed' as a verb? Are we in a Jane Austen novel?"

"Maybe."

"Too bad." She sighs.

"Why?"

"Because we can't do this in an Austen novel."

She leans in and kisses me. I shouldn't be surprised considering the context. We're in my bed. I'm in my night clothes. We're laughing and talking about sex. But when she touches me something hardens. A part of me steps back.

Nikki knows it instantly. "What else do you need from me?"

I don't like her tone and I start to pull away.

"Don't get mad," she says, gently turning my chin toward her. "Explain it to me."

I take a moment to think about where to begin—what needs to be said first.

"I don't feel like I've been working *with* anyone," I say. My cheeks are hot with anger. "I feel like I've been working against everyone. Everyone keeps putting Jesse in danger rather than protecting her. Take Jeremiah. He wants to storm her to the front lines, for Christ's sake."

She wets her lips before speaking. "So you want someone to help you look out for Jesse?"

"No," I groan. *Yes.* "I just feel like I can't be lying around having sex when everyone is trying to kill my best friend."

"Aren't you insulting Jesse just a bit?" she asks. "She isn't an invalid."

"I *know*," I say, defensive. I come up on my arms and face her. "But she isn't invincible either."

Before she can say more I snatch her hand and put it under my shirt. The shock registers on her face for a second before I press her fingers against the indent beneath my left breast. The deep scar of the knife wound.

"I only survived because Jesse died for me, so I know she isn't an invalid. That doesn't mean she's safe. No one is safe if they are being attacked on all sides. And that's her problem. She's got trouble coming from every angle."

Nikki rolls me on my back in such a simple gesture my breath catches in my throat. I don't realize she's stronger than me until she has me pinned under her. She lifts my shirt slowly and inspects the scar more carefully in the orange street light from outside. Then she bends her head and kisses it once. Then again. My body shivers. All the red hot anger in my head and chest simmers down, spreads through my arms and legs and pools in a very different place entirely.

"You'll do anything to protect her," she says.

"Yes."

"I need to be okay with that," she begins, her eyes flicking up from my stomach to my face. It's almost a predatory look. Almost. "And stand by you while you face whatever comes at her."

"I'm tired of feeling like the only one who cares more about her safety than winning," I say. "That's not true though. Gloria cares and she helps. But Gloria is even more of a mess than Jesse in a lot of ways."

"Do you really trust me enough for all that?" she asks. Her hands still on my stomach but she isn't looking down anymore. She's looking into my eyes, watching me carefully for some sign.

Not yet, I think. But I want to. God help me, I *want* to trust someone. "I'm not stupid. I know she'll never be with me. I'm not trying to keep her alive so I can whisk her off into the sunset or something but if she died—Jesus, if she died *again*—" I can't finish my sentence and thankfully I don't need to.

Nikki's face softens. "I understand, Alice."

My body shivers to hear my full name on her lips.

"I lost—someone and it changed me. Losing her cleaved my life in two. *Before* and *After.* If you lost Jesse it would change you."

"I did lose her," I say. I don't ask who *her* is. She'll either tell me or she won't. It isn't my business—not yet anyway. "I thought she was dead for years before I found out she was alive."

Nikki's face alights with recognition. "That's why it scares you so much. You know how much it would hurt. It isn't just a vague idea for you."

I feel my back muscles relax and my stomach softens under her hand.

"I don't want you to change," she says. "I don't need another reason to support you other than that."

"It's that easy for you?" I ask, suspiciously. But even as I say it a wave of relief washes over me. *Please God, don't let me regret this. Though I'm not even sure what this is.* "I'm surprised you can handle my honesty so well."

She grins. "I prefer honesty."

"Is that *all* you want from me?" I ask. Because it's only fair that I ask her what she wants from this too.

"Not exactly," she says. She places her other warm hand on my belly. "I'm in this for a little more."

My cheeks flush. Muscles low in my body warms and tighten. We've moved from "sleepover-confessing-our-dark-secrets" territory to "I'm kind of-horny-and-you're-clearly-making-an-offer" territory.

She kisses me and my body responds to her touch. A shiver arches my spine and I have my arms around her before I know what I'm doing. Her fingers tug at the waist band of my pajama pants, yanking them down so I feel the bare sheets against my skin. She lifts me up just long enough to pull my shirt over my head so that I'm left with only my underwear.

"Wow," I say. "That was fast."

She laughs, low in her throat and shamelessly looks me over. "I got a little excited, sorry. But damn you're beautiful."

She presses the full length of her body to mine and slips one knee between my legs to ease them apart. I can feel the pressure of her quad against me, and the small movements are making me crazy.

"Can we make this a little more fair?" I reach up and pull off her shirt and unbutton the top of her pants to reveal boxers. Because I'm beneath her she has to take off her own pants—leaving her topless in those cute shorts with some pattern I can't see clearly in the dark.

"You're not so bad yourself," I say, which is a gross understatement. The muscle definition in her arms makes me feel a tad ashamed of my own softness, but I feel like this is probably a really inappropriate time to compare weightlifting notes.

"Thanks," she says as her pants hit the floor and she climbs back on top of me. "Is this good enough?"

"You can keep your boxers *for now*," I say but it's hard to keep up my playful tone. All kinds of feelings are mixing together in my head.

I don't love Nikki. She heard that part right?

"Are you sure you can do this?" I ask her.

Her kisses fan out, slide across my cheek and nestle into my neck and ear. Her breath behind my ear just makes the throbbing between my legs worse.

She laughs low in her throat. "I have no doubt."

"I'm not talking about the sex," I say.

"I know," she says. "The answer is still yes. I'm a big girl. I can handle this."

"Even though I'm in love with her," I say again. I want her to be sure—even if I'm not.

"You love her now," she whispers in my ear and her fingers hook into the side of my underwear, pulling them off in one long motion. "But feelings change."

Jesse

I sneak into Gloria's house, moving quietly and carefully like a creeper. Coming into the moonlit kitchen, I see my first hint of light. Beneath the closed door leading to the basement is a sliver of gold and the soft sound of hushed voices.

I open the door a crack. "Hello?"

"Get down here," Brinkley calls up. He's standing in the spotlight of the swinging overhead bulb. He isn't in disguise now, the shoulders of his usual leather jacket reflecting the light.

"Sure, Boss, when you ask so nicely," I say.

I dip to dodge the face-level wooden beams. Gloria sits in the same folded metal chair but I can't see her very well.

"Why the hell is it so dark down here?" I ask. But then I see someone has put foil over the only window, a ground level square no more than a foot or two long. I point at the window. "Are we keeping out the alien transmissions or what?"

Brinkley doesn't humor me with a response. "Are you packed?"

"Just for a couple of days. Is that enough?" Already I'm thinking of the text I'll have to send Lane to let him know I'm leaving town and how undoubtedly grumpy he is going to be.

"Should be," he says. "If you are as charming as I *hope* you'll be."

I'm about to argue the depths of my charm when he tosses me a thick envelope that thuds against my chest. I peel back the tan flap to find a lot of cash and a license that isn't mine.

I hold the license up to the overhead light and read the name beneath my picture. "Who is Anna James?"

"You are," he says. "Until you get back. I don't want you leaving a paper trail or alerting anyone to your movement. So, *Anna*, be discreet as possible."

I dig into the envelope and find a check card and credit card also in Anna James's name.

"I also registered a car to Anna," he says. He tosses me the keys but they bounce off my chest and splatter on the floor.

"This isn't identity theft, right?" I pick the keys off the floor. "There isn't a poor Anna James somewhere who will discover I've run up her MasterCard, right?"

Brinkley only smiles.

"Um no," I say and hand him back the envelope. "I'm not destroying some girl's credit."

"Relax," Brinkley says and shoves the envelope

back at me. "You won't be ruining anyone's credit."

Gloria watches the exchange. "We're going to Ohio."

"What the hell is in Ohio?" I ask, distracted.

"Liza. She took I-76 out of Philadelphia and headed west. After it turned into I-70, she pulled off in a little town called Heath," Brinkley said. "She hasn't moved in a couple of days."

"Why? What is she doing there?"

"It doesn't matter what she is doing there," he says. "You have to find her. You're her sister-in-law. She married your brother a couple of weeks ago and then took off. Your brother begged you to bring her home. And even if she doesn't want to come, you just need to see her, make sure she is OK and find out what happened."

"Why did she marry him if she didn't want to?" I ask. "And why isn't my brother looking for her. Wait, my brother is 13. He can't get married."

Brinkley blinks at me. "This is Anna's story. Not yours."

"Oh," I say. "What's my brother's name?"

"Jesse," he says. "Jesse James."

"Is that your idea of a joke?" I ask.

"Andrew, then," he says. "*Andy*. Andy and Anna James."

"Oh God, we had those parents with the same letter name thing," I say. Immediately, I feel like a weirdo—*we*? "So wait, why isn't *Andy* looking for his own wife?"

"My things are already in the trunk," Gloria says. I take this to mean she's coming with me. "Where are you going to be?" I turn to Brinkley, giving up my campaign to understand why Andy is such a loser.

Gloria and Brinkley exchange a look.

"I have to go to Memphis and take care of some things," Brinkley says. He looks at his watch. "I need to go."

Gloria stands suddenly, sketchbook and pencils in hand.

I give her a once over. "Us too?"

She nods. I have one foot on the basement stairs when Brinkley grabs me by the elbow. "Be careful." His voice could have been mistaken for gentle in another life, if it wasn't so gravelly and drill sergeant-like. "*More* careful than last time. I won't be there to clean your prints off of anything and you have a record. *Remember* that."

"Oh shit, the Lovett job," I say.

"Yeah," he smirks. "I took care of the office. But I can't this time. So watch what you're doing."

"Good ol' B-dubs. Always looking out for me," I say and pull at his chin scruff, which he hates. I admit I do it just to see that annoyed look on his face.

But this time he doesn't pull away or swat my hand like he usually does. Instead, for a second, he just looks really freaking sad.

"What the hell is wrong with you?" I ask.

"Don't worry about me," he says, his expression hardening and all that gentleness disappears quicker than it came. "For once, I want you to worry about you."

Ally

I wake to the smell of bacon and eggs. Nikki's hair is adorably tousled as she stands in front of my frying pan, wearing just her boxers and a sports bra.

"Good morning." She leans in for a kiss as I come close to inspect what she's doing.

I can't remember the last time someone made me breakfast, and in my own kitchen no less. And *bacon*. Jesse is vegetarian. Frying up bacon would never happen.

Nikki hesitates when she sees my face. "Too much?"

"No."

"Because some people would panic at the sight of someone in their kitchen, dirtying their dishes."

"I'm okay," I say. I climb into a kitchen chair and raise the empty drink glass she put beside my place setting. I wave it around just a little. "Excusez-moi, garcon! Je voudrais du jus d'orange s'il vous plait."

Nikki grins and pulls a carton of orange juice from the fridge.

"Parlez-vous français?" I ask and steady my glass for her.

"No," she laughs. "But I understood 'juice orange' so I could guess. Do *you* speak French?"

"I took two years in college," I say. "But my pronunciation is terrible."

"I have to ask," Nikki says, transferring bacon from the pan to my plate. "Is there such a thing as a dog fairy?"

I arch an eyebrow.

"Because I swear that when we went to bed there was no dog. And now—" she points her spatula at the snuffling monster begging at her feet. Winston never looks so rapt and alert as he does at mealtimes. "—there's this."

"Oh!" I say. "Yeah, Jesse stopped by."

"Oh. Was that before or after we—"

"Before," I say.

Her shoulders relax. "Does he have a name? Or shall I just continue to call him Pug which is what I've been doing all morning."

"His name is Winston," I say. Winston cranes his neck my way and waddles over expectantly. I scratch him behind his ears. "Yes, that's your name."

"Are pugs usually that—big?" Nikki brings her plate to the table and sits down opposite me. I fill out my plate with the toast and eggs on the table.

"He might be a little spoiled," I say, opening the

butter. "But look at that face."

"I see it," she says. Then she looks up at me. "So why did Jesse bring him?"

I search her words for any tension, but find nothing. Either she is OK with Jesse or she's a very good actress. It is too soon to tell. "She's helping Gloria with a missing person case. They might be gone for a couple of days."

"A lot of people are going missing lately," Nikki says.

"About 2,300 are reported missing every day. About 661,000 a year," I say. "But most of them will be resolved. Last year there were only about 2000 unresolved cases."

"Is this statistical regurgitation supposed to comfort me?" Nikki asks. "Because it really isn't."

"Sorry." I shove some butter toast into my mouth. "I've got a thing for memorizing numbers."

"Good with numbers and French," she says. "What else? You went to college."

"For a little while. I was pre-law. I wanted to practice law with my brother. But I never finished."

"Why?" Nikki asks, folding her bacon and egg up in her toast and eating it like a sandwich. "You're definitely smart enough."

I blush. "Thanks. I dropped out when I found out Jesse was alive. I left school and moved down here to help her. I don't regret it."

At the same time our phones go off, vibrating against the table beside our plates.

"This can't be good," Nikki says. "Jeremiah says it is an emergency."

We dress quickly and make it to the safehouse in record time. As we pull up outside Nikki rakes a comb through her hair before pulling it up into a ponytail.

"We probably shouldn't mention. Not that I'm ashamed," she says. "But I don't want him to think we've lost focus."

Before I can say anything, she is already jogging toward the building and pulling open the big doors. But we haven't even reached the landing when we hear Jeremiah screaming at the top of his lungs.

I slow down as Nikki turns to give me a weary glance. When we open the door Parish sits where he always sits, in front of the monitors. But he isn't looking at the screens just now. His eyes are fixed on Jeremiah pacing the middle of the big room.

"What's happened?" I ask.

Parish makes a warning gesture as if to save me from something but he isn't quick enough.

"Do you see this?" Jeremiah yells at me. He takes a step aside and jabs a finger at the three black body bags lined up in the floor of the apartment.

"Jeremiah, what's going on?" Nikki asks.

"I sent a unit to pick up a child. *One child* we had

located in Athens."

Jeremiah's face shifts violently as he storms toward me.

"Don't," Parish says. He stands from his station and steps between me and Jeremiah.

Jeremiah is forced to switch direction and goes straight for the body bag. He rips the middle one open to reveal the corpse of a child, paler than white with blue lips. It's a little boy, no older than seven. His shirt is covered in blood with part of his skull missing. Nikki makes a sound beside me and I realize that low groaning I hear is me. I cover my mouth with my hand.

Jeremiah drops the dead child without ceremony, his little head cracking against the floor.

"You want to be merciful," he screams. "But they'll show us no mercy. None whatsoever!"

"Stop yelling at her," Nikki warns. "This isn't her fault."

"If you would have just talked to Jesse, this child could be alive now."

"*Could* be," Nikki adds. "Jesse isn't a catch-all."

"She's the best at what she does! And she's his weakness. We need her and this one," Jeremiah stabs a finger at Ally. "This one—"

"Jerry," Parish says. "Come on, man."

He tears open the second then third bag. He lifts them up for me to admire like deer kills in hunting season. "Look at them. Look at them."

I point my eyes in the general direction but I don't see much through the glimmer of tears. Only shining reflective light.

"This is what mercy gets you," he hisses. "This is what mercy looks like."

"That's enough," Nikki says. She grabs me by the arm and pulls me toward the door.

"You can't be half in!" Jeremiah yells before Nikki can get the door closed between us, blessedly locking us out into the hallway.

We stand in the bright white hallway outside the apartment. I can still hear Parish's and Jeremiah's angry exchange but not the specific words.

"Asshole," Nikki says. She clamps my shoulders. "Are you okay?"

I'm shaking. I'm blinking away the tears and trying to breathe. "The little boy. The way he *shook* him at me."

"We're leaving," she said.

"I need to tell him what I found out about the missing people," I say but I'm shaking. I'm shaking and I don't think I can look at Jeremiah again.

"What about them?" she asks. So I tell her what my search turned up and that Caldwell isn't taking people with NRD, but their replacements.

"I'll tell him," she says. "Get in the car and I'll be right back."

"He's going to kill her," I whisper, thinking of his captive.

"He's a hot-head but he'll get it under control."

"What do I do?" I ask.

You can't be half in. Do my attempts to protect Jesse make me "half-in"? If I really want to keep her safe do I—but how do I do that and keep her out of the way?

Nikki thinks I'm still talking about Jeremiah and the bodies. "You had nothing to do with that."

No, I didn't pull the trigger. But that doesn't mean I'm guilt free. Am I so focused on protecting Jesse that I'm getting others killed?

And if I am—am I okay with that?

The little boy's white face and pale lips says *no*. I'm not okay. But if it comes down to Jesse or a stranger—I don't know.

I don't know what I'm willing to do.

Jesse

I don't go see my boyfriend before we skip town because I know Lane will be so grumpy about all this. Instead I send him a text. Of course he doesn't respond. Even my cute heart and kiss-kiss emoticons do not move him.

It only takes a few hours to get to Heath, a small town in Ohio and apparently Liza's hangout. It seems this commercial strip is the big deal: a cluster of businesses, restaurants and stores crowding the four-lane highway.

We find a nice hotel in the middle of this main drag and pull off. I check us in because Gloria isn't great with people. They give us a room on the third floor, which we find after searching the wall-scuffed hallway the color of rotting fruit and slip my key card into C307.

The room is a standard double suite. Two beds, a single bath. A big window against the far wall with the curtains open to let in light. A TV sits on an average-looking stand across from the beds and a set of drawers for clothing beneath it. On the opposite side of the TV is a desk, complete with a couple of monogrammed pens and some paper.

Gloria puts her sketchbook on the desk, claiming it for herself. Only then does she toss her bag on the foot of the bed, closest to the door. "Home Sweet Home."

I crack a smile at her joke. It's good to encourage her. Not that I value social skills highly myself. For the most part, people are just weird and exhausting. But I think things would be easier for Gloria if she, you know, knew how to talk to *any*one.

"It's like we're roomies," I say. I curl into my bed careful not to touch the top cover too much. Ally has told me some horror stories about the top cover of hotel beds. Lots of bugs and body fluids.

Gloria opens her sketchbook, pausing over the pencil sketches before settling on a particular sketch. Turning the book toward me, she looks up. "You need to be here around 1:00PM."

I recognize Liza Miller from the earlier sketches, but the area surrounding her is unclear. It looks like a shopping center. The squat bundle of stores is oddly disharmonious though uniform in appearance: a hair salon, a sandwich shop, a coffee shop, electronic store and crafts store. Liza is on the sidewalk, pinned between the parking lot and shadowed cars and storefronts. She looks about ready to step into one of the stores, but it's unclear which one.

"Why 1:00PM?" I know better than to question whether or not it is today. Gloria has been exactly right on the day, a million times. But I know hours are difficult to pinpoint.

"The light," she says. "It's afternoon in these pictures."

"So what you're really saying is I should be there by noon, and be prepared to be there all damn day."

She shrugs.

"All right." I open my backpack and fish out fresh clothes and a toothbrush. "What will you be doing?"

"Drawing," she says. "I'm working on what's next."

"So what should I say?" I ask, turning my back to change my shirt. My jeans are okay. "I'm a zombie, you're a zombie. Let's hang."

Gloria grimaces. "Just don't use the zed word."

"Zed?"

"Have you seen the movie *Shaun of the Dead*?" she asks.

"Oh yeah," I say and realize she's making a joke. Two in one day! I'm so proud of her. "So nothing like 'I'm a zombie. You're a zombie! Zombie high five!'"

Gloria throws her coffee back like a shot of whiskey. Damn. "I don't know what you should say. Be charming. You're charming."

I laugh. "You're the only one who thinks so."

"Just do your best," she says.

"Okay, Mom," I say and close myself up in the bathroom.

It doesn't take me long to make myself presentable. I only wash my face, add deodorant and brush my hair. Add a bit of teeth scrubbing and I'm a brand new girl.

It isn't quite noon when I slip from the room. Gloria is already at the desk sketching in her wide-eyed creepy remote viewer stare.

It only takes me a few minutes to find the cluster of stores from Gloria's picture. It helps that Heath is tiny and everything is centered on this one strip. I park across from the storefront and look up at the trio: coffee shop, sandwich shop and hair salon. The crafts store and electronics store are a little farther back. I seriously doubt Liza wants to knit herself a scarf while on the run, so my guess is she will probably go into the electronics store or coffee shop. Given my problem with electronics, I really hope she just needs some java.

I see Liza.

She is short like me, with crazy curls and a pale complexion. In the cool autumn sun, she looks like she's just crawled out from under a rock and rejoined the living. Maybe it's her super dark hair that's doing nothing for her complexion. Who knows? I'm not a beauty consultant by any means.

Because I don't want to be creeper, I pretend to take a phone call. I laugh a lot. My imaginary friend is *hilarious.* After a particularly boisterous laugh, she glances up as she continues toward me on the sidewalk. I hold her gaze for a moment and laugh again. I'm still laughing when she enters the coffee shop.

I wait for a few minutes, until I see Liza take a seat by the large store front window with a coffee cup in her hand. Only then, once she is snuggled up with her drink and I'm certain she won't bolt, do I enter. I walk up to the counter, still on my phone with my imaginary friend. "Okay girl, I need some java. T-T-Y-L."

Then I hang up on "my friend."

"What will you have?" The barista has a little hook ring in his nose, enough to make me think of Ally. What would Ally do to convince this Liza girl to talk to me?

"A small mocha, please," I say. And then he asks for my name. "Je—anna."

"Janna?"

"Anna," I say. "Just Anna."

He scribbles my name on the side of a cup in black sharpie. As the machines whirl and click I try to think of the best way to approach Liza. But when the barista puts the coffee in my hand, I still don't have a solid plan.

Well, now or never.

I plop into the seat opposite her. "Hey, Liza. I'm Jesse."

The first look of panic crosses her face and I realize I've already killed Anna. What a short and sweet life she had. A car ride to tiny town in Ohio and a mocha. The End. But what will become of her brother and that crazy wife of his? Who knows?

I barrel on. "I'm not here to hurt you. I've got NRD too. And I know Caldwell is looking for you and you aren't safe. Gloria drew you dead—"

She bolts at the word *dead*.

"Awww, shit," I say, scrambling after her. "But I'm here to prevent that from happening!"

I drop my mocha, for which the barista yells at me, and run after her.

It's coming. The panic, the fear that if I don't stop her, she'll end up dead for sure. Not that I can replace her or anything if Caldwell showed up now, but I'm hoping I can still help. She's Caldwell's number 1 threat after all. And I know exactly how Caldwell handles his threats.

And then it happens. The electric fire rolls over my skin and *booms* out from me in a wave.

The shopping center stops. One moment it is alive and the next, *click*, like someone threw the switch, just like when I killed my house and everything went still and silent in a heartbeat.

A few people climb out of their cars, confused. The light at the intersection is dark and I'm pretty sure the reason the electronics guys have come out is because I've zapped them too.

I've never covered this much distance before. I'm not sure if I should be impressed or terrified. It has to be at least fifty feet. One man lifts his car hood to check something and a few others climb out of their cars, looking back at them with puzzled expressions.

The only good thing that happens is Liza slows down to a jog and then stops completely.

Only a heartbeat later she turns and runs at me. For a second I just watch her come. Just a simple *oh good, I won't have to run that far* crosses my mind. Then I realize she is trying to catch me.

I turn and run away.

"No wait. Wait!" she says.

I don't because my instinct is to run when being chased by someone with a crazy gleam in their eyes. Of course she catches me because I can't run to save my life.

She keeps pace beside me but doesn't try to grab me or anything. "Did you do this?"

She's gesturing at the remains of the parking lots, the stalled cars clotting the pavement, and the colorless streetlight waving ahead at the intersection.

"Yeah, sometimes I—It just happens."

She cuts me off. "You're one of the partis."

"Excuse me?"

But Liza doesn't care what I'm saying. She looks away from me and speaks to herself. The way I do sometimes with Gabriel. "If you're one of the partis then you aren't lying. He wouldn't work with you."

"Part piss?"

She isn't happy with my pronunciation. "The Par-*tiss*. Like, I can see through anything." She stands beside me with no fear now. Her cheeks are still a little flushed and her chest heaves with her elevated breathing.

"My clothes?"

"And your skin."

I strike a pose. "How are my bones? Am I getting enough calcium?"

"You've broken a lot."

"I'm a death replacement agent," I say. "I die a lot."

Sirens wail in the distance and she turns toward the sound. "We can't stay here."

She's right of course. And I know that if the others can't get their car to work, neither will I. Well, Anna is dead anyway. Might as well abandon her car.

"My hotel is close," I say. "We won't have to walk far."

Liza asks me *a lot* of questions as we walk A lot of questions about *me*: when did I first die? How? When did my powers show up? Why did they show up?

By the time we finally see Gloria's face, I'm foot sore and exhausted. My thighs are already starting to stiffen from chasing Liza. Our room is warm compared to the chill of the September afternoon. My bed in particular is soft and inviting in the lamp's soft glow, as Gloria has the shades pulled tight.

I quickly catch Gloria up on our meeting at the coffeehouse and the subsequent parking lot fiasco while Liza looks around our room. She is particularly interested in Gloria's sketches, the few she'd taped to the wall above the desk while I was gone. The second Gloria sees her looking, she takes them down and stuffs them back into her sketchbook protectively.

"Aren't you worried about housekeeping?" Liza asks. She's completely unfazed by the fact that some of those pictures were of *her*.

"We keep the Do Not Disturb sign on the door," I say.

"Smart," she says and takes a seat on the end of my bed, bouncing.

"Liza thinks I'm part piss."

Liza's ears turn red. "Par*tis*."

"A part of what?" Gloria asks. When I raise an eyebrow at her recognition of the word she adds. "*Partis* is latin for 'a part of'." She turns back to Liza. "What is she 'a part of'?"

Liza shrugs, eyeing that sketchbook again. But Gloria has no intention of letting the girl have it. Liza looks away as if to prove she doesn't care about the sketches.

"Do you think that's why we're on Caldwell's list?" I ask. "Because of our abilities?"

She leans forward. "Caldwell has a list that you've *seen*? How did you manage that?"

I don't want to mention Brinkley just yet. "Yeah, it's his death list, apparently. And you're number 1 and I'm number 2. We figured you saw something in Philadelphia and that's why you ran. We know about your handler."

She reddens in the cheeks to match her ears. "They found the body in the river."

"Sorry."

"I kept moving," she says. "I was taking my time, trying to throw them off my trail, you know?"

"Who?"

"The ones that killed my handler," she says.

The ones is pretty vague. "Yeah, but did you get a good look at them? Anything that can help us identify them?"

"It was dark."

Vague again.

"Why do you want to go to St. Louis?" Gloria asks. I don't point out that Liza never said St. Louis.

She pauses. "There's someone there that I want to meet."

Gloria's eyes narrow. "So you believe only certain

NRD-positives are *partis?*"

"Yep." She turns to me. "Do you know of any others with gifts?"

Gloria is the first to speak. "2% of the population has NRD. You're looking at 140 million potential *partis.*"

"But there's not really that many people with NRD," I chime in. "The international branches of the Church have done a good job of implementing upon-death head severance to prevent NRD in most developing countries. And with all the murders here—"

"It doesn't matter if there are a billion potential people," Liza says with an elated grin. "The few partis will gravitate toward each other like planets in a star's pull. We are meant to come together." She turns and flashes me a sugary smile. "Just like Jesse and me."

I open my mouth to tell Liza about Cindy and Rachel and Gloria grabs my wrist. Something she's never done. It scares me, jolting my heart.

"We can't escape Caldwell," Liza says. She looks crazy—her tone and wide eyes not helping. "None of the partis can escape each other. We'll all come together sooner or later."

"How do you know Caldwell is partis? Have you seen him do something?"

Gloria shoves me back. My elbow connects with the side of the TV and shivers with the electric shock of hitting one's funny bone on anything.

"*Owww.*" I yell in surprise.

Liza speaks to Gloria. "You see it, don't you?"

"What—?" I start. Not only does my arm hurt, but now I am being left out of the conversation. *Rude.*

"I'd hoped we'd get more time to talk," Liza says.

"We have plenty of time to talk," I say. "Everyone just needs to calm down."

Her grin is the kind of grin you'd give an idiot. She raises her fingers and Gloria jumps forward as if to grab the girl. But before Gloria can touch her, the snap comes.

Gloria stumbles, falls to her hands and knees. I scream, terrified.

"What did you do?" I scream. "What did you do?"

"This," she says. She brings her fingers together again.

Blackout.

Silence.

Like someone turned off the whole wide world.

When I wake up, I feel fine, which is better than the last few times I'd fallen into the hands of deranged nutbags. Better yet, I can see again.

"You've had an interesting life," Liza says. She sits

on the edge of the bed, flipping through Gloria's sketchbook. Gloria is tied to the desk chair to my left. Liza pulls a page from the back of Gloria's sketchbook and unfolds it for me to see. "Did this hurt?"

"Like hell," I say, barely glancing at the image of Eve straddling my chest, grotesquely sawing off my neck. I'm less concerned with an attack that happened a year ago, and more concerned about this attack. I'm tied with my arms pulled behind my back and knotted with something I can't quite recognize. A bed sheet maybe? It's uncomfortable, but doesn't bite my wrists like a rope or handcuffs would.

"*Obviously* you survived," she says. She squats in front of me and pulls at the T-shirt around my collar. "And I don't even see a scar." The moment her fingertips brush my throat, I yank my leg up between her legs and connected with her vag. She yelps and falls back against the opposite double bed laughing and groaning in turn.

"I should have known you'd fight. It's how the *partis* survive."

"I thought you just saw through things," I say. "What's with the snapping?"

Liza is holding her belly and laughing at me. "Did you think you were the only one?"

Did I? Well, no. I had suspicions about Rachel and Cindy. I've thought I was a freak ever since the shocky stuff started happening. And once it evolved into the pulse, I felt even weirder. Then this girl shows up and says she can see through stuff. That isn't weird. That's like Gloria. But the snap thing. The snap thing—

"You killed Jake," Gloria says. She never took her eyes off of Liza. I might be freaking out, but Gloria is still focused. Glad one of us is.

"Who?" I ask. And *why* did we switch topics?

"She's talking about my boyfriend," Liza says before Gloria can speak again. "Ex, actually."

"Why would you kill your boyfriend?"

"You have no idea what you are, do you?" she asks. "If you did, you wouldn't ask me such a stupid question."

"What am I?" I ask. I see small movements to my left and know Gloria is working on her restraint. The second she gets it free, we'll be in *much* better shape.

And she turns completely toward Gloria. Gloria quits moving. "I can see everything," Liza explains. "Not the future, like you. For me, everything is in real time."

Gloria watches her. Since I know Gloria was a badass squad leader with the military before she'd volunteered for NRD testing, I know she's probably thinking of a plan. And so I do my part to help.

I try for Liza's attention. "Jake was *partis*."

Liza smiles slowly. Something is happening. She

holds up her finger and I think she's about to snap again but it isn't a snap. It's *wait for it*.

"Do you feel that?" she asks.

When I don't immediately answer, the rumble grows. The whole hotel vibrates and a few pictures rattle then clink off the wall.

"You're doing that?" I ask.

"All of the partis are unique. Though from what I saw, you're a bit behind the rest of us. Your gift is pathetically underdeveloped. It's almost not worth killing you for."

"I'm a slow learner," I say, offended. Kill me, she wants to *kill* me.

"That is what your angel is for," she says. "Stupid. Where is he?"

My angel. *My* angel. Gabriel.

"You have an angel?" I ask. I'm in disbelief. I don't know why, I mean, Cindy saw Raphael, right? But Cindy's angel had tried to get her killed—at least that's what she said.

Liza bounces on the bed like a child. "But think about it. I'm saving you a lot of trouble. Do you really want to be the one who fights Caldwell? This way, I'll do it for you. After I collect more power of course. It would be about the only way to take him on. He's by far the most developed of us."

"Aren't you sweet," I say. It's important to remain nonplussed. Of course I am freaking out. I'm also trying to absorb everything she says. And I'm fairly certain she's just given me a vital piece of information about my father. Caldwell is one of the partis. He has a power.

"My power is pathetic," I say. "Why would you even want it?"

"It's pathetic now," she says. "But I'll change that."

My power is pretty pathetic compared to hers. And I am really surprised that I haven't freaked and exploded this hotel room yet. But the more I think about it, the more I realize I'm not really that terrified. This is problematic and a hassle, but I'm not fearing for my life. Not yet anyway.

A soft knock at the door, like a secret knock with certain pauses makes Liza smile bigger.

"Hold that thought," she says. But I can barely hold my lunch my heart is hammering so hard. *Gabriel.*

Liza moves to the side so a man can enter the room. He is Gloria's age, or a little younger. As worried as I am about a man coming into the room, I'm more terrified by Gloria's reaction.

She sits up straight. "Fuck."

"Hey Gogo," he says. It's a nice voice, like Morgan Freeman. "It's been awhile."

He's a black man a little darker than Gloria. He has short hair too, and nice looking cheekbones if you're into that sort of thing. But his eyes are sinister and he hasn't looked at me or Liza once. Clearly, he is here for Gloria.

"Say hello to my friend, Micah," Liza says. "He's going to keep Gloria company while you and I take a little walk."

"Um, *no*. I'm not leaving her here with him." I don't even have to think about this.

"Oh well, then just kill her," Liza says.

As if to illustrate this point, Micah with his massive whale fin hands grabbed each side of Gloria's neck. He seems to know exactly where to position his fingers. Gloria keeps perfectly still, her nostrils flared in fury. I don't know if this is instinct or years of military training.

"What? Wait!" I scream. I look at the man bent down into her face, his hands holding her whole throat. "Don't hurt her."

"If you don't come for a walk with me, then we'll just kill her now and ask you again."

"My legs are pretty stiff. A walk sounds nice," I say.

"Don't go," Gloria says.

"Are you worried?" Liza taunts.

"It isn't you—" Gloria begins but Micah tightens his hold, cutting off her words.

"She can't breathe," I yell. God, why won't

someone is this damn hotel hear me and come running? "You're choking her!"

"Micah," Liza warns. "We have a deal."

Micah's smile tightens but his hands relax. He still holds her face in his hands, almost like he will bend down and kiss her. Gloria doesn't hesitate to pick up right where she left off. "—she has to worry about."

Then she takes her eyes off of Micah long enough to give me a meaning glare. She's trying to tell me something. *It isn't you she has to worry about—?* God help me, I don't know what she means. But Micah doesn't look at me. In fact, it's pretty creepy the way he stoops and stares into Gloria's face without so much as a glance my way. If he isn't worried about me or what I'm doing, then he's confident I'm so screwed. Lovely.

Liza kneels in front of me and starts to undo my binds, which turns out to be a curtain tie-back. But before I am completely free she says, "You'll play nice or Micah will kill her. Do you understand?"

"Crystal."

"And if I am not back in 20 minutes," Liza says. "He will kill her."

She grins and because she is so young, so girlish— it is terrifying. The last of the cloth falls away. She offers to help me up but instead I help myself by pulling up on the side of the bed. I even take the liberty of *accidentally* stepping on her foot as hard as I can.

"We're going to have a little girl talk," Liza says, patting Gloria's cheek.

If I were Gloria I'd have bitten off her damn fingers, the snotty little shit. God I *want* to bite her, but it isn't an option. I have no idea how to use my powers on command and zapping the electronics in the room is hardly going to help us. And Liza will probably be quicker on the draw. All she has to do is snap.

"Micah tells me you two have plenty to catch up on while we're gone," Liza says. "Enjoy."

Liza holds the door open for me, exposing the hallway behind her. I would give anything for a cleaning lady to come by and see us; Gloria tied to the desk chair and a man looming over her. But no one comes—and I guess Liza knew that, didn't she? She could see through the walls after all.

I cast one last look at Gloria and she isn't looking at Micah. She is looking at me. *Don't go.* Her look pleads. *Don't go.*

"Good luck," I say. "I'll be rooting for you."

"And I for you," she says, face grave.

I don't know what kind of training this Micah has, but it is probably good training. After all, he knows Gloria and is somehow caught up in all this. And she's traveled in very few circles. But at least with Liza gone, maybe Gloria can use one of her tricks to escape. I have a feeling—call it a hunch—that Micah isn't partis himself. First of all because he is working with Liza. Secondly, he is *aging*.

Whatever happens, I hope Gloria wins—whatever battle comes after she breaks her binding. God, let her win.

"Just follow me and keep your mouth shut," Liza says. "If you make any move or try to alert anyone, I will snap my fingers and—"

I drop to a dramatic tone. "And my world shall be bathed in darkness!"

Liza smiles. "You're pretty funny."

I can't appreciate a compliment from a psychopath. "Does—did—Jake know about Micah?"

She snorts. "Jake didn't even put up a fight. He was all about *acceptance*. I'm hoping you are more of a challenge. I need my practice before taking on Caldwell."

He's my father, you know. God, I want to say it. I want to just throw it out there and see what she makes of it. But now that she's established herself as an enemy, she'll have to beat any more information out of me. And let me just say I am still pissed that I'd come all this way, thinking she was just another one of Caldwell's victims then turned out to be just another jerk bent on killing me.

"How do you know Micah?" I ask. Better believe

I'm sniffing for info.

"He's an AMP. He's been helping me search for the partis."

"Why?" I ask. "Why would he help you?"

"We both want to take down Caldwell," she says. "I can see the present and he can see the future. It's a mutual partnership."

An AMP like Gloria. An AMP who *knows* Gloria. There can't be many of those.

Gloria's voice pops up in my head. *It isn't you she has to worry about.*

But she wasn't talking about Micah. But who? Who else?

There is only one person I can think of—Caldwell.

Caldwell is here.

Ally

Nikki and I are lying in my bed. I've been crying about the dead boy for most of the day and she's doing her best to comfort me, but little can be said or done.

My phone vibrates impatiently on the bedside nightstand.

"Gloria?" I asked reading the caller ID. "What's up?"

"Please," she croaks an address into the phone. "*Please* come get me."

"What's happened?"

"Please hurry," Gloria insists. Silence stretches through the phone and I think she's hung up. But then she speaks again. "I think I need a doctor."

"Tell me where you are," I say. I take in all the information and when she is finished I say, "I'm on my way. Sit tight."

Nikki sits on the edge of my bed, slipping on her shoes and follows me into the living room. "What's going on?"

"Something has happened to Gloria and Jess. I have to go."

"I know you do," she says. "Do you want company?"

My heart lurches. "I'm not sure that's a good idea."

"Okay," she says, but I can tell she doesn't like this answer. She considers her next question carefully. "Where will you go?"

"Louisville."

"That's three hours away," she says. Then she arches as eyebrow when she sees me heft the fat pug from his bed where he was sleeping and grab my keys. "You're taking the dog?"

"I can't leave him," I say. "I don't know how long I'll be gone. Lock up when you leave, okay?"

I'm already halfway down the hallway hauling the pug when she calls down the hallway after me. "Call me if you get into trouble."

"Thanks!" I yell without looking back.

The drive is relatively quick, perhaps because I spend most of the trip in deep contemplation about all the horrible things that could have happened.

As I pull into the motel parking lot and park in the gravel lot outside a row of single-story red doors, I scan for *6*. It's in the middle of *4* and *8*, not *5* and *7*, this side of the building apparently designated to even numbers only. I leave Winston curled in a ball and snoring in the passenger seat.

I knock softly on the flaking red paint beneath the brass 6. "Gloria?"

I am about to say her name again when I hear the click of the deadbolt. The door cracks but I don't see her.

I put one hand against the door and start to push it open slowly. "Gloria?"

"Come in and shut the door," she says. "And do not scream when you see my face."

I take what she says seriously. Jess, not Gloria, is the one who exaggerates. If Gloria is warning me, this is bad.

I tuck my hair behind ears and take a deep breath. I enter the room.

I'm careful not to look at her until I close the door completely behind me. If I scream involuntarily, perhaps it will muffle the sound.

Only after the lock clicks into place, and several thunderous heartbeats, do I look up. My eyes canvas the double beds in hideous floral prints, the grimy lamps and cheap wall art.

Then I see her.

And a small scream does press against the soft flesh of my throat but I swallow it down and cover my mouth with my hand to help muffle the sound.

Gloria is covered in blood. It's drying, crusting around her eyes and mouth, crinkling because she moved that muscle beneath, blinked or frowned. Something. Her shirt is ripped on the shoulder like a large hand grabbed and tore at the fabric. Her face is swollen and purple on one side from repeated blows, I assume, as well as her busted lip. On her left cheek is a deep gash. That is where most of the blood has come from, what wet her shirt and jacket and made her look like she'd jumped in a giant bowl of strawberry syrup. But there is other damage I can't quite place, but I do notice. The strange angle of her arm. The way one shoulder hangs in its socket.

"Jesus Christ," I whisper. The tears welling in my eyes blur her face and I cannot see her. In a way, it is a blessing. I use this as an excuse to turn away and wipe my eyes. "Who did this to you?"

"Micah Delaney," she says. Her voice is strange. Either from the gash to her cheek, or she bit her tongue. "He is Caldwell's AMP. He's the one who maneuvered us into Martin's hands last year."

Delaney. Jeremiah has a Delaney on the team. I need to remember this name and tell him about it.

"Where is Jesse?" I ask.

"She's not dead, but—" Gloria looks up at me. "I'm sorry."

I steady myself against the door. *If he has not yet had the chance to, he will kill her.* Instead I say, "We need to get you to a doctor. You can tell me what happened on the way."

"Take me to Dr. York," she says.

"You know it's three hours back to Nashville," I say.

"It needs to be him," she replies.

"You're sure?" I ask and it is a stupid question.

"As long as I can stretch out in the back," she says. "I'll be OK."

"You are in luck because the front seat is taken," I say and I try to push Jesse out of my mind. I need to focus on helping Gloria. I can't let myself be blinded anymore. So I gather up Gloria, her shoes and her sketchbook and help her to the car. I give Winston a quick potty break and then help Gloria get situated in the back, giving her an emergency blanket from my trunk to cover herself. It isn't until the car is in drive and pointed toward the interstate that I ask my questions.

She tells me about Liza and Micah. About escaping and hitchhiking to Louisville before hiding in the hotel room.

"Micah has been manipulating the girl," Gloria says. "She doesn't know he is working for Caldwell."

"Do you think she killed Jesse?" I braced myself for the answer.

"No," Gloria says. "I think Caldwell took them both."

I feel something touch my shoulder and I look back to see Gloria offering me the sketchbook.

"Later," I tell her. "If you say Caldwell has them I believe you."

The last time Gloria showed me a picture of Jesse in trouble, it was a picture of her dying at the hands of Martin, another one of Caldwell's henchmen. I don't need to see what horrific fate Caldwell has planned for her this time. I don't think I can bear it.

"We can get her back," I say. But it doesn't come across as confident as I hoped.

"Yes," she says. "We have a chance."

Six impossible things before breakfast, Alice. My brother used to love to make comparisons between me and the mythical Alice in Wonderland, but these days, I'm really beginning to feel like I live in Wonderland. After all, my list of impossible tasks for today alone far exceeds six.

"Son of—," Dr. York says. His hands come out of his lab coat and clutch his hips. His blue eyes are narrow and assessing. "When they said you refused anyone else, I didn't imagine this was why."

Gloria doesn't reply. She looks like a little kid who just got into trouble—a bloody kid.

"Well I hope he— or she—looks worse," Dr.

York replies. He opens a drawer in the examination room and pulls out two latex gloves.

"He might still be unconscious," Gloria says. It's a delayed response, an attempt at the give-and-take of normal conversation, which admittedly Gloria isn't predisposed for.

This truth is further demonstrated by the fact she says nothing else for the ten minutes it takes Dr. York to examine her. He spends a considerable amount of time on her cheek and right shoulder. He examines the left forearm and then asks her to lie down and checks her abdomen.

"Are you pissing blood?" he asks.

"No."

I've worked with Dr. York enough to know he is setting us up for a rant, the kind he often lavishes on Jesse.

"How much damage?" I ask and I know he is secretly thrilled by this inquiry because I have given him the platform for his launch.

"A dislocated shoulder, a broken forearm and probably a rib or two. This cheek will require at least *eight* stitches and there is no telling if you'll have nerve damage though I suspect you got lucky there. Your facial muscles seem to still be working fine. I see no droop or loss of movement. It will scar. And you'll require plastic surgery if you ever hope to fix it entirely.

"I'm not vain," she says, and it is a flat, unfeeling voice.

"I need to put your shoulder back into place before I can turn you around and examine your kidneys and back for damage. And I'll need X-rays to confirm the fractures. Are you sure you don't want to tell me who caused this? It would be my *pleasure* to file charges."

Again she doesn't respond.

"I can keep a secret with the best of them," Dr. York continues, trying a new angle. "But someone is going to notice this and ask questions. You best prepare for that. Where's Jesse?"

We must have made faces. I know I flinched at the sound of Jesse's name and I can only imagine that Gloria too, provided some tell for the doctor to pick up on. I didn't see it myself because I looked away and focused on the cold white door with its sharp angles jutting from a thick doorframe.

His eyes widen. "Where is she?"

Gloria won't meet his gaze.

"We don't know," I finally say because Dr. York looks on the verge of real panic. "They were attacked and Jesse was taken."

Dr. York touches his chest and it's a gesture that I never want to see an elderly person do.

"Are you okay?" I ask.

"I'm fine," he says but all the color has gone out

of his face. When he looks up at me I can't tell if I'm seeing anger or fear. "I know you'll find her. And bring her back. We should contact someone."

"No," Gloria says and she looks him dead in the eye. "No."

Dr. York looks at his shoes. And there it is, the affection he has for her. She drives him crazy. I know because I've heard earful after earful on that score. Her crass tongue, her misanthropic, offhand way with people, her tendency for melodrama. But he cares about her.

He flashes me a tight smile and says. "Come with me, Ms. Jackson. Let's put you together so you can get back out there."

Gloria slips down off the examination table, clutching the back of the gown closed with her one good arm while the other hand hangs limp in her socket. She stops by the pile of her clothes and releases the gown long enough to hand me a cell phone, the one she retrieved from her house before I brought her here to the hospital.

"Call the first number," Gloria says and her voice is low as she glances at the open door to confirm the doctor has stepped out. "Tell him everything I told you."

And before I can ask her who I'm calling, she grabs the fold of her gown and disappears into the hallway.

I scroll through the phone's history and see the number. It's not a familiar number and it has no contact name associated with it because Gloria's contact address book is completely empty.

I hit send and for some reason my heart speeds up. On the second ring a man answers.

"You're late," the voice said. The unmistakably male voice that I know immediately, having heard it for years. "Talk to me."

"Brinkley?" I ask.

"Alice," he says and the irritation is gone. "What's happened?"

Jesse

It's hard to keep my mouth shut as we cross the lobby past three desk clerks. I search the neutral tones and stock furniture, and eye the guests checking in. A woman carries her bags toward the elevator while a couple sits on a couch looking at a map together. None of them look like they can do a damn thing to help me.

And unless he's invisible Caldwell isn't here. If invisibility turns out to be his special gift, I'm never showering or sleeping again.

Liza grabs me roughly under my arm, her fingers biting into my flesh. "Don't even think about doing something stupid."

Heat floods my face and I shrug her off of me. Even though she's killed someone, even though she thinks she's tough shit with her little powers, I couldn't care less. If Gloria saw Caldwell nearby and spent what was possibly one of her last breaths warning me, then he is my real problem.

Liza leads me to the edge of the parking lot, out

into a large field beside the hotel. The field isn't endless of course. Beyond it is a thin veil of trees revealing a neighborhood with quaint homes.

We are near the center of the grassy expanse when she stops walking.

"I'll tell you how this works," she says. "You have to use your power."

"Why?" I search the dark shadows of the trees at the edge of the field and my flesh crawls. Could he be in there? Crouching behind some bush or something? The parking lot is empty except for a myriad of parked cars or maybe he isn't here yet. After all, Gloria doesn't do exact times.

"It opens the channel," she says. "Are you listening?"

I quit looking around and humor her with a tight smile. "Channels open. Show my juju."

She kneels and pulls a knife out of her boot. Just great.

"I'm guessing you plan to scramble my brains with that after you use your power on me?" I ask.

"And you said you were a slow learner."

I give my best nonchalant shrug. I even smile. "I have my moments. Well, come on then. Let's be stupid and do this in broad daylight."

"This is not a joke," she says.

"I'm staring at a tiny girl with a dull pocket knife," I say. "I don't feel inclined to make the first move."

"Are you kidding?" Her knuckles go white as she twists the knife handle in her grip. The air around us smells like diesel and the cement of the parking lot. A fragrant breeze rustles the leaves in the trees. The hairs on my neck stand up.

He's watching. He's got to be watching. Stop, I tell myself. *Don't get hysterical.*

"If you could just have killed me you would have done it in the hotel room. But here you are waiting for me to do something. If I don't do it, you don't win," I say. "I'll just wait it out, thanks." *And I'll wait for him to show his face.*

"That's your logic?' She replies, indignant. "I didn't kill you in the room because he told me to wait. He wanted your friend and I wanted you. That was the deal."

The deal. Liza is too stupid to realize she isn't calling the shots. She didn't make a deal with Micah. That's like saying she made a deal with Caldwell's dog. Who do you think the pooch listens to?

"So why bring me out here? Why not just pull a double homicide in the room?" I ask. I keep checking my periphery for movements, a sign.

"He wanted to be alone with her. He said I should bring you outside."

"Then he wants us outside," I say. Why? *Why?* Because we are two sitting ducks in a field. I crouch, getting low to the ground, looking around me desperately. But I see no one.

"Get up. I won't fall for any stupid tricks."

"We should hide," I say. I look at the thick trees. I have a feeling about those trees. "I know you don't believe me, but I think this is a trap to catch us both." BOGO, man. Instead of listening like a calm, rational person. She screams like a banshee and runs at me.

I sweep my leg up and kick her in the leg at the right moment. She comes down. Then I do an aikido move, kotegaeshi, that bends the wrist to one side and I'm able to free the knife from her hand. But I don't stop here because Brinkley told me to always take my opponents weapons first and he included a great many things in the category of weapons. A hand is a weapon, a leg, if they are kickers—and for Liza, her fingers. I saw her do that terrifying snappy thing. And I know she can use it again if she wants.

I break the first two fingers on both her hands by twisting them back. I hear the *snap*, and her furious cry. Grabbing the knife and snapping her fingers only takes seconds.

"Stop *screaming*," I say. "And listen to me."

"You bitch," she says. "My fucking hands!"

She holds up the bent fingers already swelling to a grotesque size. Okay, I might have overdone it a bit.

"I couldn't have you snapping," I say. "Now *listen* to me."

"I can only snap with my right hand! With my

middle finger! You broke four fingers!"

"How was I supposed to know?" I say. "It's not like you explained the parameters of your snapping abilities."

"I'm going to kill you!" she screams and her face is so red it looks like it will explode.

Something hits me and cuts off my words. It's like an invisible wall pushing me down, knocking me back. My feet actually leave the ground for a moment before reconnecting hard, knocking the air out of my lungs as my shoulder blades carve a space for themselves in the dirt.

Liza is on her feet, a screaming bundle of rage. The ground shakes and I realize what is happening.

"No, no. This is what he wants. He wants you to show him what you can do," I scream but my voice doesn't carry over her own battle cry.

The ground rises, funnels up like an anthill growing from the earth. Liza's chest heaves with ragged breaths and she looks crazy with her wild hair and clenched fists. Isn't she worried about witnesses? Maybe she hasn't had her five minutes of fame, but *I* have and I hated the aftermath.

I don't stand from the crouching position I've resumed even though the anthill keeps growing. I can't decide what to do. If I run I will be exposed and Caldwell might take that opportunity to show himself and put the smack down on us. But I can't just sit here with Liza raising hell.

"I'm sorry I broke your fingers," I say. "But I need you to believe me. This is a trap."

A wall of dirt hits me from behind. A whirlwind of grass and clay hits me in the face and hair. I'm spitting up dirt furiously, about to be crushed under the weight of it. I'll suffocate.

All I can do it cover my face and feel the weight build.

Jesse.

The sound of falling dirt fades, softens and begins to sound more like wings. With my eyes covered, the brown becomes black and I can almost imagine the black feathers stretching around me blackening out the sky.

Let me in.

He's here, he's here and she won't listen.

Let me in, Jesse. Let me protect you. In my fear I forget what it means to be sane, that it means keeping the walls up and convincing yourself what you know is real, isn't *really* real. I told myself for a year that Gabriel wasn't real—that I was stressed and scared and I invented him. But now, I'm scared again. The fear is back.

I reach out for Gabriel, the way a person reaches out for a light switch in a dark room, fingers groping for something they can't see. I'm filled with that moment of panic when I can't find it, when nothing happens.

The dirt stops falling. The weight is heavy but not crushing. Coughing and spitting, I manage to pull myself out of the heaping mound of trembling earth. I turn toward Liza but she isn't there.

"Liza?" I say. I spit more dirt from my mouth. "Liza?"

Then I see her body lying motionless in the dirt. Without thinking, I jump up and run toward her. I go down on my knees beside her and seeing her like that, she looks like a kid.

Just a *kid*.

I roll her over in my hands and see something protruding from the side of her neck, like a miniature dart. I pluck it from the skin with my fingers. "What the hell is this?"

Jesse! Gabriel's scream makes my spine jerk. I suck air.

Something stings the side of my neck. A cold chill runs down my body, making me shiver and cringe. My fingers go to my neck with a fumbling urgency. I'm sure I was just bit by some weird bug until I feel it. Something large and *attached* to me. I pluck it from my neck and a small dart like the one in Liza's throat rolls to a stop in the middle of my cupped hand.

The world slows to a standstill. It blurs as if suddenly made of paint and a giant hand smears everything with one angry swipe. I try to stand but

I'm dizzy. The world is moving on a tilt.

Only a single dark shape, more of a shadowy blob than anything, moves toward me.

My knees give and I fall right into someone's arms.

"Gabriel?" I ask and wonder how my hallucination would be capable of catching me.

"No," the voice says. "Try again."

Ally

Brinkley agrees to meet me at the Dunkin Donuts off of 21st Avenue. Dr. York assures me that it will be a couple of hours before Gloria is stitched and braced and ready to go. No matter how much she protests, he will give her a heavy dose of meds and make her sleep for a few hours before discharging her. Sleep is the best medicine he says and having watched Jesse rehabilitate countless wounds in her own hibernation states, I must concur.

The parking lot is dark, with halos of white light casting circles upon the black cement. When I step from the car, I button my red coat immediately. My breath billows white in front of my face like puffs rising from a winter chimney. I hear his voice first, before ever seeing him.

"Why do you have Winston in your car?"

"It's been a long night," I say.

A dark shape hangs at the edge of the nearest white halo spotlighting an empty parking space. He doesn't want his face to be obvious in such a public place. I concede and cross the spotlight first.

"Where is she?" he asks.

I tell him everything Gloria told me to tell him. He's staring at his shoes like the way a little boy who is in trouble will stare down at his feet, head hung low.

When I stop talking, he lifts his head, throws it back like he would howl at the first rays of light cracking the horizon. Instead he releases a long exhale and his breath rolls up into the sky.

"Fuck," he says. A very precise but accurate assessment. "What I wouldn't give to still have that tracking node in her neck."

I'm not sorry he removed it. It was inserted for a different mission and it hadn't helped us one bit. Worse, it turned into this thing that Jesse played with. It was gross watching her shift it under the skin in her neck.

I release the anger I've been holding like a breath under water. "How could you be so stupid?"

He opens his mouth to speak and usually I'm very good about not interrupting. Unlike Jesse who prefers to get her point across before anyone has had a chance to speak.

"You sent her out-of-state to chase down a girl with NRD. *Surely* it occurred to you they might cross paths with Caldwell."

"But—"

I barreled on. "After what happened last year, you didn't hesitate to think that perhaps this was another trap? No, forget that. Of course it was a trap! Everything to do with Caldwell is trap. How could you be so predictable and reckless? How do you know Micah wasn't counting on Liza and Jesse convening in Ohio and him capitalizing on the two-for-one special!"

"I sent Gloria to protect her."

"Gloria almost died!" The neon orange OPEN sign flashes on and Brinkley takes a step deeper into the parking lot shadows. But dawn is almost here. Soon there won't be any shadows. "Where were *you*?"

"I had affairs to tend to in Memphis," he replies and I can tell he didn't mean to say this. "Unfortunately, it couldn't wait. I needed them to handle this alone."

"I hope those *affairs* were worth it," I hiss. "If Jesse dies it better be for a good reason."

He can't look at me. "I told Gloria to look for Caldwell."

My anger erupts. What began as a slow irritated boil, a collected heat around my face lashes out. The heat grows from warm to flaming. I'm seeing red. "I know it's incomprehensible to you, but Micah is the better AMP. There I said it and I'll keep saying it if it means we quit making stupid mistakes. We cannot just rush in because Gloria gives the clear anymore.

She *can* be wrong and she might be wrong again. I don't know what it is about this guy but he gets her every time."

Brinkley runs his hands through his hair and it is this small gesture more than anything that makes me realize he is real. This isn't some bizarre dream I'm having out of exhaustion or panic over Jesse. Brinkley is alive and standing before me, not just someone Jesse spoke about like a ghost. I was in on the secret that he'd faked his death, supposedly perishing in the basement though the rest of us survived. And though I'd known he was alive, this is the first time I've seen him.

He looks like shit, no longer the slightly plump guy I knew as Jesse's FBRD handler. He's lost at least 20 pounds, maybe more though it's always difficult to tell with men. He's quit shaving for sure. His dark features are further exaggerated by deep circles of exhaustion. He has more gray around his temples than I remember.

"You look terrible."

"You're more charming than I remember," he says. "Has Jesse worn off on you?"

"I am angry and I am tired."

"We need somewhere safe to talk," he says.

"Follow me." I climb into my car and back out of the parking spot. He climbs into his car and follows me.

I have a few reasons for bringing Brinkley to Jesse's versus back to my place. First, I don't know if Nikki is there. Secondly, it's the only other place I have a key for besides my own apartment and the office. We couldn't go to the office because it was too public and because Lane might be there. I was pretty sure Lane knew he was alive, but I knew he was unaware that Jesse had gone missing. Lane has a savior complex and is a guns-blazing kind of guy. He would probably be brash and irrational in his method of retrieving Jesse. If he could retrieve her at all. And I have zero interest in dealing with anyone's hysterical boyfriend right now.

Besides, I want to return Winston to his environment. Poor guy has had a long night.

But I didn't expect it to hurt to walk into Jesse's place without her. This is a surprise.

The house smells like her, something sweet, floral with a hint of citrus clean beneath. It's hard to describe her scent, but it is something like fresh laundry and jasmine until she started dating Lane. Now it's clean laundry and *boy*.

Brinkley insists on checking the house before we speak. I let him, doing my best to assure him that the broken glass will be repaired by Friday. I'm almost asleep on the couch when he finally joins me.

We set up at the kitchen table. Beneath the light of a Coleman lantern, Brinkley spreads his papers over the smooth table top. Isn't as much paper work as what Nikki and I have been working with, and nowhere near as orderly. Nikki and I have been working from crisp printouts kept pristine in organized folders. Brinkley's *notes* are a hodgepodge of scraps: gas receipts with scribbling on the back, motel stationary, half-sheets of ripped paper in a variety of ink colors. Very few sheets of paper look like they came from a computer at all—and even these have been folded so much that deep creases mar the pages.

I'm struck by how bizarrely quiet this place is without electricity or Jesse. I've long been aware she was a bit of a force. The way she moves about is loud and noticeable, but it's a noise I've grown accustomed to.

"I've put out a bulletin. If she appears anywhere public: video cameras, financial transactions, we'll know," Brinkley says.

"Good idea," I say. "Unless he's got her in a hole somewhere."

"We'll have to rely on Gloria for that," Brinkley says.

"But Micah—"

"Stop doubting her!" His voice is a sharp slap against my ear. It makes me shut up if nothing else. It takes me a moment to recover and he is already talking again. "Yes, Micah is working against us. *Yes,* he is the better AMP—technically." He shrugs his shoulders inside his leather jacket as if trying to relax a cramp. "But you can't lose faith in Gloria just because she got her teeth kicked in. She will never forgive herself if something happens to Jesse. Do not make her feel worse."

I fold my arms across my chest but I keep my mouth closed. I don't bother to remind him that Gloria's failings will not keep us alive. And I'm not being difficult. I love Gloria. But I think Brinkley is asking too much—of everyone.

"Gloria is amazing." Brinkley speaks with sincere admiration, raising his chin ever so slightly. "She is the most talented and dedicated individual I've had the privilege of working with. She will figure this out. As soon as she gets a hold of herself, of the situation, she will beat his ass. Just like she did today. Bet he didn't see that coming, did he?"

Good point.

"And *I choose* to believe in her and stand behind her in this until she finds her footing with this guy. We all have soft spots. And the strong overcome them. She'll beat him. I know she will."

My cheeks burn. "I hope so." And it is a sincere wish for Gloria—for all of us.

"Good," he says and pulls out a kitchen chair beside me.

But I have to speak my mind—at least one last

time. "What happens to Jesse when we all get killed?"

"What?" His brow furrows as he rests his weight on his forearms. I can't get over how James Dean he looks in this leather jacket.

"What if we die first, before Jesse?" I ask. "How is she supposed to carry on if Micah kills Gloria? If someone kills you, or me? Who will stand between her and Caldwell then?"

Brinkley looks so tired now with the pillows under his eyes. "I've made preparations, if anything happens to me. Have you done the same?"

"Me?" I'm surprised by the shift in conversation and in his tone.

"Let's start with why you're on Caldwell's list," he says. He pulls a piece of paper from the pile scattered across the table and slides it toward me. One of the few computer sheets deeply creased from folding. Sure enough, circled in red is my name: *Alice Gallagher.* I look from my name up to Brinkley's dark, assessing eyes.

I hold his curious gaze and try to decide how much he needs to know. It isn't out of some loyalty to Jeremiah and his group. I think it's because I'm still angry with Brinkley for using Jesse the way he did, with such little regard for her safety. Withholding information almost feels like a way to punish him.

"You know about the database that records the deaths, correct?" I begin. "It's also an online community where information can be shared on message boards and certain chat rooms."

"Don't tell me all you've been doing is—*chatting?*" Brinkley asks, and he sounds so suspicious.

At first, but look at me now.

"NecroNed runs a youth group for NRD-positives and young adults who aren't death replacers. VegZombie, she lives in New York, also runs a similar support group," I say. Brinkley still looks critical with furrowed brow. "The point is they aren't all death-replacement agents. Many of them are just involved in the NRD community. And being involved in the NRD community, they know things. Just like I know things. It's a good place to meet people in your own area with similar interests and goals." *It is how I met Jeremiah.*

Brinkley leans forward, catching my drift. "Like."

"Like I know Caldwell is up to something in the desert."

"What do you mean 'in the desert'?"

"Near Flagstaff, there have been reports of strange things happening in the desert at night, lights and explosions that make the ground vibrate even though no earthquakes have been reported."

"Sounds military," Brinkley says. I agreed. "What connects it to Caldwell for you?"

"A ten-year old girl, Molly, reported bizarre stuff happening in the Arizona desert and she identified

Caldwell." Of course, I don't give Brinkley her real name or care to elaborate.

"I've been sharing his picture around the site. Telling people to look out for him. I've also spread the word about suspicious replacements, encouraged people to bring more friends, assistants, whoever on the jobs to limit the possibility of an attack." All the things Jeremiah thinks are pointless, but I disagree. Search and rescue is important, but so it heading off the problem so that fewer people need to be rescued.

"It hasn't gone unnoticed," Brinkley says, motioning to Caldwell's black list, stabbing a thick finger at my name.

"Of course not."

But I wonder if that's the real reason Caldwell considers me a threat.

Jesse

When I wake my muscles are stiff. Not quite as bad as when I replace someone and come back to consciousness after too many hours of rigor mortis. It's more like that time Ally convinced me to go on a jog with her. What a dumb idea that was. I make little hissing noises with my teeth as I pull myself up in a sitting position from the cold floor. It's mostly my head that hurts. I feel sluggish like I do if I take cold medicine and then wake groggy the next morning.

And I'm thirsty as hell. My throat is so dry I don't think I can speak even if I wanted to.

I'm sitting on the floor of a large ballroom. The marbled floor is chilly with its polished stone. The soft rose-cream swirls are soothing. The walls are a beige color punctuated with austere white columns. Light streams through the windows in the ceiling letting me know that wherever I am, it's still daytime. Other than that I can't get a real sense of time or place. A strip of plastic flaps in a breeze like a wind-caught flag. I stare and stare but I can't make sense of the plastic, like something you would lay down before painting a room.

I pull myself to my feet and that lasts a whole minute. I hit my knees and dry cough back some nausea.

"It's the drug," a voice says. "The sedation darts take a while to wear off."

I'm terrified to look up from the super polished shoes I'm staring at. My heart is beating so hard that I think I might die.

"I feel your pain," Caldwell says in the same pleasant tone. The kind of voice you use when making polite conversation or offering someone a drink. "Did you know those are the same darts issued by the military to capture us when the public panicked? They rounded us up like cattle."

If you'd died a year later, they would have never taken you at all.

"Yes, but I didn't, did I? So they simply took me when my wife called to tell the police I'd come home. I walked all the way from the funeral home to find the police waiting for me. Did you never ask why I was buried in a sealed box? Did it ever occur to you that *nothing* was in that box? Of course, these are mighty big considerations for an eight year old."

Just look at him. Look at him. I press my hands against my dirty jeans and manage a deep breath. I can't bear to lift my head, but I do lift my eyes to meet his.

Caldwell looks exactly like his pictures. His eyes are the same color as mine and that alone is enough to make me look at the columns on the right. I count them and try to steady myself. There are six between the large wooden door and the opposite wall, with room for six more between them. It's a large room— and the reason why his voice echoes.

"You look good for an old man." My voice doesn't sound as steady as I would like. "What do you use? The blood of infants? Virgins? Infant virgins?"

Of all the things I could say to him, this is the best I could do.

"We both have secrets," he says. He offers me a hand but I don't take it. *I can't.*

"I already tried getting up," I say, and it feels like an apology, as if he deserves one. "I'm not one to repeat mistakes."

"Try again," he says.

I'm compelled to do exactly what he says and this time when I stand a small a wave of nausea rises but my rubber legs steady themselves, and so do my guts. Breathing helps. I just have to remember to keep breathing.

"See? I told you that you could do it." Here is his rehearsed smile. The one I've seen on television and newspapers. It's the leader of the Unified Church I'm looking at. The god awful man who is responsible for the genocide of thousands. *Tens of thousands* and he's only just gotten started. "I've had much practice with these things."

"Just kill me," I say. I try to be still except the dirt from Liza's attack is all over me—in my hair, my ears and down the back of my shirt. It itches horribly like a tag in the shirt. Feeling dirty is its own kind of torture.

"That would be rude," he says with another playful smile. "Surely before I died, we addressed rudeness."

A flash of Caldwell, wearing my father's blue mechanic's uniform erupts into my mind—a slightly younger man, wiping his hands on a ratty blue towel and stooping to eye-level of his daughter as he gently reprimands her. The vision is so vivid, so powerful, my knees almost buckle.

Don't let him in someone warns. Gabriel. And I think I see the dark darting of a bird—or something—high in the skylights, closing in.

"That isn't how I remember it. I have memories of you—him—but not like that. You put that into my head," I say.

Caldwell grins. It's the way I grin at Winston if I actually get him to sit or lay down for a biscuit—a bemused, patronizing kind of smile.

"Actually, it was Henry Chaplain's gift," he says. "Mental manipulation."

Then I remember Liza.

His grin widens into a menacing flash of teeth, like a fox seizing a rabbit. "I *may* have let Liza's handler observe the ritual between Henry and myself. And Micah *may* have dropped a bit of information here and there at my request."

"You read minds too," I say. "That's the second or third time you've done that to me."

Caldwell takes a step toward me and I take two steps back.

"Have you killed her already?" I say. I close my hands so they'll quit shaking and I raise my chin a little more. Baby steps, Jess. Baby steps. "That's the game here, right? Kill a zombie, win a prize."

He doesn't answer. He watches me with those eyes and it really is the worst part. If we didn't have that small similarity, it might be easier to see him only as Caldwell, the monster who kills people. But I only see those parts that remind me of before. The hazel eyes, the sun-kissed freckles and dark hair. His plastic surgery changed the other features, but not enough.

Not enough.

Caldwell blinks and looks away. "Your mind moves incredible fast. It's dizzying."

He wipes a small bit of water from the corner of his eyes as if he's held them open too long. It's the fake smile again. The rehearsed smile that's too quick to come and never stretches higher than the top lip.

"Liza is not dead," he says. "She seems less willing to challenge me than you."

"She thinks you are the worst of us," I say. And it is more than that. Caldwell exudes a sort of power—the way my skin crawls and everything in my body says *get away from him*. Like magnetics opposing each other.

Again he smiles. "You really want to know why she fears me?"

"I know—" I start to say but he doesn't let me finish.

"You know nothing about me!"

I take a step back, instinctively. Even this doesn't protect me. He pushes a million pictures into my head of women and men being tortured. Fists pounding on the edge of a water tank screaming, drowning. People pushed down onto their knees and the muzzle shoved against their skulls, brains spraying out the other side, drenching the next person in line. Shot for no logical reason. Sometimes in the head but not always. Some strapped down and electrocuted. Some injected with drugs, chemicals, hallucinogenics. Blood. Terror. Amputations. Experimental surgeries. Pain. Screaming. Women screaming for their children ripped from their arms and pushed into the back of trucks. Men being carved open while awake, guts spilling onto the floor in a splash of red.

I hit the floor, dropping hard. I can't make the

images stop. The images of The Reclamation. Being hunted like animals, running through the woods at night trying to keep ahead of the dogs chasing them. The things he saw. The things that happened to him—

"They kept me for *years* after the public release. They knew they could keep the few who had no families, no one to miss them. If only I'd been there for months. If *only*."

"Stop," I croak. I'm choking on my own spit. "Stop, please!"

The images do stop. As quickly as they came they're gone and I'm left with the high pitch buzzing of my own mind, like an ear that's heard too much— a headache forming behind my eyes. I put my face in my hands and take ragged breaths.

"Look at me."

I can't. I can't quit crying.

"Look at me," he demands.

I look up but I can't really see him through my bleary tears.

"Let me be clear," he says. Caldwell raises his hand as if to wave at someone behind me and makes a motion with his hand. The effect is immediate. A *billion* red dots appear on the floor between Caldwell and myself, then slide across the marble slowly up my dirt caked clothes.

He is regaining control of himself. "Unless you

want to be sedated again, I wouldn't try anything. Take it from me. It is harder to shake off the grogginess after the second or third dart, even with metabolisms as strong as ours."

"Why won't you just kill me?" I ask. I can't quit crying. They were just memories but I can smell the singed hair and taste the blood in the back of my throat. My arms are tender from needle punctures that didn't happen. My lungs burn from a drowning that didn't happen. Only my mind believes it did. "Just kill me!"

Because you want me dead, I know you do.

He opens his mouth to speak, and I cringe. Terrified he will push the images back into my mind again, I curl into myself, but the images don't come. Instead, a shrill feminine shriek echoes through the hall. Caldwell raises a hand and touches the ear bud I didn't see before. I've seen Brinkley wear one like this.

"You'll have to excuse me," he says with a haunting grin. "It seems she's finally been persuaded to challenge me."

"Why won't you just kill me?" I scream as he crosses to the big doors.

"Waste not, want not," he says, hand on the handle. Then he is gone.

I wait for several heartbeats. I count them out. Only then do I allow myself the thought I suppressed moments before. The image of Caldwell with his ear bud—a sign of weakness. Of limitation. He can't possibly hear all, see all, if he must rely on technology. He isn't God. At the very least, he has to be close enough. And with one weakness, I have to hope that he has more. And weakness means a possibility. And possibility means hope.

But hope is a dangerous thing.

Ally

Someone is banging on the door.

I must have slept hard because I wake up in the dark. The last thing I can recall is waiting for my tea to steep and sure enough it sits cold and forgotten on my side table. My heart is hammering as the pug tries to snuggle in closer, but I'm trying to get out of all my blankets. I even slept in my coat. Poor Winston must be desperate for a walk.

I come up on my toes to peer through the security hole on the front door and I'm not happy with who I see. Lane bursts in, taller than me by enough that he must bend down in order to clear the doorframe. It's one of the few things that amuse me about Lane and Jesse, the enormous difference in their heights. I often wonder if he ever feels like he is dating a child.

"Where is she?"

I feel like I'm still half asleep. "How did you get into the building?"

"*Where* is *she?*"

"Tell me how you got in the building," I insist.

I'm tired of people making demands.

"I followed a group of high college kids in. I could've gone home with them. They were baked out of their minds," he says. "Now tell me where she is."

"I don't know," I say.

When he leans his weight against the side of the couch I think of Jesse's kiss, that it happened right there, where he is standing, against the couch he is touching.

"Brinkley says she is still on assignment. That she is supposed to be with Gloria. But I just went to Gloria's to check on her goddam house and she is there— *without* Jesse."

It never occurred to me Gloria might ask Lane to check on her house. But it made sense that you'd send a boy to check on your house in a less than perfect neighborhood. A tall, semi-intimidating boy with enough weight to throw around. But I'm equally mad that Gloria was released from the hospital and no one told me.

Lane has no intention of stopping the train of words barreling though his mouth.

"I see a small light on and think someone is in there messing around, so I go in ready to beat the shit out of some punk kid or a junkie looking to pawn a TV and who do I find? Gloria. Gloria in the basement, drawing with the speed of a meth-head and her face is all beat up like someone took a sack of bricks to it. And most of her pictures are of Jesse. Gruesome shit. And I try to get her to stop and talk to me but she won't even come around—"

"What?" I come out of thoughts.

He shuts his mouth, surprised by my outburst.

"You tried to stop her?" I ask. "You tried to stop her and she wouldn't respond?"

"Yeah, but—"

"*Shit, shit.*" I yank my boots on without ceremony. Glad that I'm already dressed, I grab my keys and I'm out of my apartment in ten seconds flat. Lane catches up to me in the hallway, jogging after me.

"Where are you going?" he asks.

"Come with me," I say, and I don't hesitate. I just start down the stairs, rushing toward the doors, toward the parking lot. "Come with me!"

I tell him to come with me because if this gets ugly, and honestly I already know it will, I'll need his muscle. If Gloria was dead weight, I couldn't carry her out of the house by myself. But he could.

"Listen," he says, after buckling himself in. "I've been meaning to talk to you."

"Oh hell!" I exclaim, slapping a frustrated hand against the steering wheel.

"What?"

"I forgot to walk Winston," I say. "*Again.*"

We hit a pothole that I fail to swerve around and Lane pops up and hits his head on the ceiling. I can't stop myself from smiling.

"Do you really hate me that much?" he asks.

"I don't hate anyone. I don't have it in me," I say. "Unfortunately."

"I'm sorry."

"For what?" I demand. I hate it when people don't know what they're apologizing for.

The orange street lights fill then fade, fill then fade as I cut through the streets to Gloria's.

"For letting, Jesse die the other day," he says. "I don't want you to think I wanted her to do it for me. I really tried but for some reason it wasn't working."

"It happens."

"Not to Jesse," he says. "She can do it every time. No matter what."

My chest tightens at the sound of her name. Not just the name but the way *he* says it.

"Yeah, she's something else," I say and I mean the words to be sarcastic and almost funny but they come out tight and strained.

"I'm sorry I blamed you," he says. His pale eyes are round in the dark of the car as he looks across the seats at me, one hand bracing on the dashboard and the other on the ceiling above, just in case I hit another hole.

"I wasn't even there," I say, defensively.

"No, last year," he says. "I was so pissed that she chose to save you in the basement."

I look away from the road long enough to scowl at him. "What are you talking about?"

We hit another hole and Lane hits his head on the ceiling despite his efforts to brace himself. He grimaces. "Can you slow down?"

"No."

He adjusts his position, slouching down and bracing his legs against the dash. "In the attack, Jesse chose to save you."

"What's your point?" I ask. "If she'd chosen you or Brinkley, I'd be dead!"

"No," Lane groans. "I'm not saying I wish it were different. I'm glad that it worked out, but the fact is she didn't know I had NRD. So she chose you believing I'd probably die."

"You could've survived."

"I was stabbed in the chest!" he exclaims.

I take a deep breath and try to calm my nerves. I'm going to explode if I don't take this down a notch. *Hold on, Gloria.* "I still don't get your point."

"I'm just saying that it was hard watching her choose you. She left me for dead. We're all bleeding to death and the girl I love saves someone else. It was harsh."

My chest tightens and I don't think it's because I just whipped a 90 degree turn onto Harding Place. "It looks like she chose you from where I sit."

"Yeah, it's a matter of perspective, I guess. I just

wanted to say I was sorry for blaming you for that. I'm glad she chose you and that you aren't dead. You take good care of her. You're a great friend."

"Let's be clear," I say as I make the final turn into Gloria's neighborhood. "I think we both know that I don't want to be just her friend. And if you hadn't given her the damn ultimatum, I wouldn't be just her *friend*."

His mouth opens and closes. Finally the words have stopped coming out. Thank God.

"I'm glad that you don't despise me for *living*, but you'll just have to forgive me for not being more appreciative of your magnanimity."

The gravel spins under my tires as I slam on the brakes. Whatever Lane is about to say goes unheard because I'm already out of the car and running up the stairs to Gloria's dark house.

Jesse

Liza screams. I don't know what I can do, why I should even care to save her after what she did to me and Gloria, but I still have to try because no one deserves to have someone in their head like that. *No one.* I stumble toward the large door but I don't make it. A warning shot cracks open the great room.

"Stand down," a disembodied voice says. It's male and it is somewhere up near the ceiling. Only then do I remember the red beams of light and Caldwell's last threat.

No point in storming through the door for her then. They'll fire a bullet or sedation dart quicker than I can get through the heavy door and then I won't be of help to anyone, including myself. And who knows what horrors lie beyond the door itself. I have to be smart about this.

Liza screams again and it sounds as if someone is peeling the flesh off her bones. And maybe that is exactly what's happening.

My breathing starts to go again. It's always the first thing to go. I feel faint and stumble.

You must be calm. Gather strength. They are looking for weakness.

Gabriel's voice again and I start to feel him like a presence behind me but when I turn no one is there.

"He wants me to hear her screaming." My lip quivers and I hate myself for being so weak and pathetic.

A Gabriel-shaped shadow becomes a solid dark silhouette at the edge of a column, a thick line pulling away and forming. But it doesn't quite become alive. *I can help you, Jesse. I am here to keep you safe. You need only let me in.*

"I don't want anyone else inside my head," I say. Even though it's pretty clear my head is a total waste of time.

The screams come again, more agonizing. I have to get out of this room. Pulsing will get me squat. I'm pretty sure guns will still shoot even without laser pointers after all. And my luck I'd get shot and wake up somewhere worse than this creepy ass ballroom.

I shout up at the rafters. "I need to pee."

A pause.

"I'm going to pee on the floor if you don't tell me where the bathroom is," I yell. As long as I'm yelling I can't hear Liza dying in the other room.

Still no answer. So I do what I know I have to, prove I'm not bluffing. I undo the belt on my pants, yank them down as if I am about to squat. Of course,

I'm forced to show my bare ass before I get an answer.

"Stop! Do not urinate on the floor."

"Then tell me where to go." I try not to look super relieved. I don't even pull my pants up until a door on the side of the room opens.

A woman, as sleek and well-polished as Caldwell emerges with two armed guards. She has warm brown hair and glasses and looks more like a librarian than someone who should be escorted by guards. The closer she clicks those little black pumps toward me I realize she looks familiar. I've seen her somewhere. And it isn't until she stops in front of me and says, "Ms. Sullivan, if you would follow me please," that I realize I've seen her on TV behind Caldwell.

She's Caldwell's assistant. She is his Ally.

But according to the horrific memory Caldwell mind-raped me with, she was also in the detainment camps. I have a very strong visual of her arm being sawed off by a man in a surgeon's apron while she screams. Her eyes wide and rolling back in her head, it's clear she isn't under any kind of anesthesia. Worse she screamed for my father, her panicked bleating as clear in my mind as if I'd heard it myself: Eric! *Eric*!

But she has both arms here. And we aren't lizards. Either she had it reattached and it healed or Caldwell's memories are fabricated. They didn't feel fabricated.

"Can I see your arm?" I ask.

Her face flushes.

I hear a rustle of cloth up above me and know someone has moved up there.

"Stand down," she shouts. And I think she's screaming at me until she tilts her eyes upward. "I can handle a child."

She extends her left arm toward me as if she knows exactly what I was looking for and which arm to provide. And I do see it. A faint white scar, jagged and running around the entire circumference of her bicep.

They aren't fabricated. Those horrible things I saw happened. I've started to tear up again when she turns on those respectable pumps and motions for me to follow. I fall into step behind her and two guards fall into step behind me. I'm looking at the back of her neck as she walks away.

"Is he as big of an asshole when the two of you are alone?" I ask. "Or is that just his public persona?"

Something slams into my ribs. A sharp, jarring pain on my right side drops me to my knees in the long stretch of hallway.

The woman yells at the guard behind me. "His orders were clear."

The guard knows better than to do any whiny "she started it" or "but she's the one…" Instead he stands at attention.

She sighs. "Can you stand?"

I spit a mouthful of blood onto the floor and a questionable chunk of something solid onto the floor. "I think that's my tongue. There, that meaty bit."

"Eric did not want you harmed."

And it's that use of his first name that makes me look up at her. Her eyes are incredibly blue behind her glasses. Her sleek ponytail and the polish on her pretty nails are quite different than the image of her in my mind. The one being cut and carved like turkey while men in lab coats take notes. That woman was terrified, dirty and nearly broken.

"Why hasn't he killed you?" I ask. "He's killing the rest of us."

"Can you stand?" she asks again. An edge of impatience singes her words.

I try and manage it by relying heavily on the wall for support.

"Now," she says in a very schoolmarm voice. "Can you walk?"

I take one step and then another. Each time I bring my leg down, a sharp shooting pain makes my whole torso burn as if a knife is being slipped in between each of my ribs.

"Good," she says. "We will take it slow."

I don't know what I expected. Of course she has no sympathy for my broken ribs. She knows I'll heal. And as someone who has endured unbearable pain, she knows what our bodies can handle. But living with pain is different than just dying. Living with the pain is a whole lot harder.

It seems like forever before I make it to the bathroom. The bathroom is more like a closet with a toilet in it. It has no doors except the one where the woman and two guards stand.

"I will stand here while you go," she says. When I don't immediately move she grows impatient. "Go on."

I enter the bathroom and close the door behind me. What do I have? *Nothing.* A window in the high upper corner is the size of a small child. With much difficulty I climb up on the sink and manage to look outside of it, only to realize I am several stories from the ground. If I climb out, I'll likely break my neck and Caldwell will just collect me from the pavement below. Or he'll just go ahead and kill me while I'm unconscious. After all, compared to Liza, I don't have much of a power.

But what else do I have? Nothing.

I open the bathroom door and before they can speak, I slap the guard. Immediately, the other guard grabs my arms and shoves me against the wall. The shooting pain in my ribs makes my vision go spotty. It takes me a second to realize I'm the one screaming before I can bite back the agony and hit him with my other hand.

"That was for my ribs, asshole," I say. It isn't nearly as fierce as I'd have liked considering I'm whimpering, but it pisses him off.

"Do not injure. Only sedate," Caldwell's lady friend commands.

He will kill me. He will kill me. Come on, Jesse—isn't this enough to terrify you?

The one who hit me, pulls back the chamber on his gun and fishes out a dart by hand. I'm too close to shoot. He'll have to stab me with it.

I press against the cramped wall between the three of them. I feel squished. Claustrophobic.

Think of Liza. That will be you, Jesse. You'll wish you just had your arm sawed off a couple of times by the time Caldwell gets done with you. It'll be worse than—

Out of nowhere the image of my mother's barn burning pops into my mind.

The guard holding me twitches and goes down. Before the next guard can realize what's happening and get the dart ready, I put my hands on him and send him into convulsions. His eyes roll up in his head and I catch a whiff of sweat and burning hair. The woman isn't that stupid. She goes into the bathroom and shuts the door. No need for me to wonder where she got her self-preservation skills.

And I couldn't care less if she wants to save herself. Hell. I don't blame her. I climb over the mound of muscle and get the hell out of there. I can't move very fast because of my ribs, but I am moving.

Holding myself together literally, I limp the length of the hallway. I have an option of going right back toward the ballroom or left into a dark corridor that forks right at the end. I go left and embrace the approaching darkness.

Ally

*P*lease be okay. Just let her be okay.

The door is still unlocked from when Lane left in his rage. I tear through the house, straight to the basement where the dull light of a single overhead lamp dangles from a string, illuminating her collapsed body like a macabre stage finale, the hero displayed for the audience to mourn.

"Gloria?"

I barrel down the stairs and slip off the last step. I don't crack my head open but I bang my knees on the cool cement floor just beside her body. I roll her over and see the small stream of spit from the side of her mouth and the way her eyes are rolled up in her head.

"Shit, shit, shit." I place her head gently back down and I run up the stairs, pushing past Lane who has finally caught up.

In her bathroom, I pull open the medicine cabinet and find what I'm looking for. Two orange pill bottles and a syringe. There is also water from the tap in a glass and I carry these four items down the stairs with me. I take the few extra seconds here to pay attention to what I'm doing. A second slip with a huge needle and a glass in my hand is more dangerous—in addition to cracking my head open.

Lane is beside Gloria, giving her CPR.

"Move," I say. "That isn't what she needs."

I set the water and drugs down long enough to stretch her out on her back. When she is flat, I uncap the syringe with my teeth.

"Damn. That's a big needle—what are you doing?"

I lifted Gloria's T-shirt, exposing her breasts. Lane has enough decency to look away as I insert the long needle carefully as Dr. York showed me how to do it. More to the center than the left, to make sure I get the heart and not the lungs, and when I feel the soft resistance of the heart muscle tugging at the needle, I push my thumb down injecting the medicine. And as soon as it's administered, I slip the needle out quickly, hoping to get it away from Gloria before she jolts upright.

I barely miss her.

She comes up screaming, her mouth still foamy with spit.

"Shhh, shh," I say. Touching her arm lightly. She shrinks away from me as if my hand is on fire. I manage to get her to drink some of the water and I wipe her mouth. Then I give her the pills.

"You haven't been taking your meds, Gloria," I say. "You've *got* to take your meds, honey."

And holding the water glass while she swallows four large pills, two of each prescription, she looks like a bewildered child. She begins to shake violently, like someone suffering from hypothermia and I witness Lane do a surprisingly decent thing. He removes his jacket and throws it around her shoulders. I get her to sit all the way up and finish the water.

What they did to Gloria in the military was torture—mental and physical. Gloria is special now, talented, but I don't see her as the unstoppable machine, an all-seeing eye, like Brinkley does. Just look at her.

"I have to find her," Gloria says.

"Find who?" Lane says.

Gloria reaches up and grabs a fistful of drawings off her work bench. She offers me the crumpled drawings trembling in her grip. One hand goes over my mouth as if to hold in the horror and Lane snatches the pictures from me. But it's too late for me to *un*see them—the images of Jesse—

—somewhere in the continuum stretching between the present and the future—Jesse tortured to death, over and over and *over* again.

We call Brinkley using Gloria's phone. Lane is beyond furious by the time he shows up.

As soon as Brinkley steps into the Gloria's dank basement, it's as if the bell is rung. Brinkley and Lane are at each other's throats. I learn a lot more from this screaming match between them than I had expected. And I learn a great deal more from what *isn't* said: that Brinkley trusts Jesse's abilities more than he trusts the rest of us. And I get the distinct impression this has to do with the electric thing—and Regina's comments about the electronics in her husband's office all being dead come back to me. And there's her house to consider. And the bizarre situation with Gabriel that I've yet to process.

Worse, I can see how dreadfully tired Brinkley is. Taking a solo mission against the world is taking its toll on him.

They don't stop until Gloria speaks. "They were in Chicago, but he has moved her." She begins to cry, crumpling a sheet of paper in her hand. "She isn't *in* Chicago anymore."

I place a hand on her knee and pull the drawing away. I smooth the pencil sketch out and the soft graphite smears a bit under my moist palm, turning my hand silver.

This one is Jesse under a bed, in a room filling with gas. She is screaming, horrified. I have to look away, the world gone blurry with my own tears. "You don't know if it's happened yet."

Lane kicks Gloria's desk and the whole thing

rattles with his fury. "We have to go now. Pack up your sketches and let's go."

"We can't rush in," Brinkley says, grabbing Lane's arm and pulling him off the steps. "We have to be smart, tactical—"

Lane wrenches his arm away, knocking Brinkley back a pace before he shoves the picture at Brinkley. "That's gas like from the Holocaust chambers. You have military training. You know what that shit feels like in the lungs. We can't do nothing while she's being gassed, man."

Brinkley's head hangs and he takes a breath. His voice is smoother when he speaks again. "We aren't leaving her anywhere. But we can't just run in and get ourselves killed."

"So you'll let her suffer," Lane hisses.

"This is why I didn't tell you," Brinkley counters and his composure is gone again. It's the exhaustion talking. We are at the end of our wits. I'm running on fumes, emotionally. Gloria is running on drugs, and who knows what the hell these two are running on.

"You always think before you act and look where it's gotten her!"

"Stop," I say. I look up from the place on the ground where I crouch beside Gloria. "Please just stop. We have to take Gloria to see Dr. York. We have to *sleep*. We can't leave tonight, none of us can. Chicago is a big place and not-Chicago is even bigger.

Gloria can't draw maps with an X marks the spot. And Jesse is smart and resourceful. She'll be looking for an out, if there is one."

I know it's the truth, but it is easier to say than to accept. *We are a mess without you, Jess. Please come home safely.*

"I refuse to just sit here," Lane says and he storms up the stairs. Brinkley runs up after him.

I turn to Gloria, who looks completely and totally defeated, her shoulders slumped. Her eyes blood-shot and puffy. I see the fear, the terror and worse—the *disappointment*.

I place one hand on her shoulder. She doesn't shrink away this time. "Thank you, Gloria. For all that you did. We know more now than we knew hours ago and that means a lot. I know you'll find her."

She clasps one sweaty hand over mine, before covering her eyes with the other.

Jesse

This place is a maze. The corridors grow darker and darker with each footstep and I must have made half a dozen lefts and rights but I keep hitting dead-ends. I don't understand how it is so pitch black dark in here. Unlike in the great room where Caldwell left me, there are no windows in this ceiling and I smell sawdust. The sound of rustling plastic terrifies me and I freeze, listening for approaching footsteps.

It's hard to breathe through the pain in my ribs. Each inhale twists the invisible knife more deeply. I hit another dead-end and fall against it.

I'm never going to get out of here.

They're going to figure out where I went. They were just behind me. They'll find me and drag me back to Caldwell to await my execution.

I start to breathe heavy as the cold fingers of panic slide around my spine.

You've got to keep moving. Left, go on.

But left is where I came from.

Left, the voice says again and for a moment I

mistake the sound of flapping plastic for wings.

I tentatively walk forward unsure if I am hearing Gabriel or if Caldwell is inside my head. Then the building shakes. Tremors rattle the sawdust and the walls. And I realize I must be hearing Gabriel if Caldwell is still locked in battle. Surely he can't fight and mind-rape at the same time, right? Or maybe he is just that good of a multi-tasker. I hope Liza is putting up a good fight. *Keep him busy* I think, until I can get out of here.

A flood of shame washes over me.

Am I really going to leave her to die? Yes. Abandon Liza when she clearly needs to be saved? Yes. Can you save someone who doesn't want to be saved? No.

Nothing can be gained by going back, I know this. So why do I feel shitty, shuffling through the darkness desperately searching for a way to save myself? I swallow against the tightness in my throat but I don't stop.

The next hallway lightens with scaffolding high above me opening its mouth to let the light in. Then I hear something familiar—air, a cold draft. And cars, the whoosh of sleek metallic bodies in passing.

I touch this new wall and realize it's fabric, not plaster. My fingers search the heavy drapery, pulling it apart as a thicker draft wafts through. Then the curtain parts and I see—a huge *beautiful* EXIT sign, glowing red in the darkness.

I shove against the door and fall into bright light. The explosion of noise and light after that dark expanse of endless hallways is unbearable. The world blurs and shifts around me until the sound of a blaring horn brings back my focus. A yellow taxi whips around me and then several more cars swerve and blare their horns. I had stepped out into the middle of a busy street not realizing. I dash to the sidewalk opposite the building I just erupted from and steady myself against a brick wall.

I cradle my ribs and breathe as the world comes into view.

With a wide street between myself and the building I've just fallen out of, I am able to get a better view. It's a huge chapel, some old church squat in the middle of a huge city. It's a city identifiable by its packed streets, sky rise buildings and abundance of bumblebee-colored taxis. Most of the building is covered in flapping plastics and scaffolding with small signs posted on every few feet which read *Closed for Renovations*. I'm not surprised Caldwell has chosen a church as his fortress, but I can't be sure what city I'm in. It's cold here. Colder than I am used to, but the hair rising on my arms and the chill to my cheeks doesn't tell me anything specific. Lots of cities are bigger and colder than Nashville. I could be anywhere. I've never been to most of the north,

north-east cities so it could be any of them. But I've seen enough movies to know how this works.

I step up to the curb and start to wave for a taxi. One is just pulling over when I see the back door on the church open. The woman, Caldwell's companion and a couple of men muscle their way through the door. I duck into the cab and lay flat in the back seat unsure if they saw me.

"Where to?" he asks as if he doesn't notice me crouching bizarrely in the back.

And I have no idea what to tell him because I don't know where I am. And I don't have any money on me. My pockets are horribly, pitifully empty.

"I would like to go to—" I draw it out and try to buy time to think.

"Tell me where you want to go or get out."

I search the map and ID information on the back of the seat for a hint. *Where am I?*

The angry cabbie whirls and yells at me. "You're filthy. Street trash! Get out! Get out, street trash!"

"I'm not street trash," I wail. "I've just been— mugged, okay?"

Stuck to the back of the plastic divider hanging off his seat, I find what I'm looking for. The map is for Chicago. Chicago. Of course I'm in Chicago. The North American division for the Unified Church is in Chicago. I just didn't think Caldwell would bring me so close to home.

"I just want to go home," I continue. "Take me to Union station."

He gives me a credulous look.

"And we'll need to stop at my bank if you want to get paid," I add. "Please."

He eyes me for another minute then sighs. "I'll have to run the meter."

"Do what you got to do," I say. "Just get me the hell out of here."

And he does, but it's hard to get cash from the bank without ID. Despite the large open lobby and comforting music, the clean atmosphere and helpful teller, I feel a horribly exposed. I have to give them my password, my social security information and basically my life history. Apparently, covered in dirt makes people less interested in helping you.

So I make up a story. I've been mugged. I was dragged through the dirt and beat up when they took my wallet. Just give me some freaking money so I can get on the train and get the hell out of this godforsaken city. It isn't hard to say that last bit with sincerity.

Luckily, my bank has pictures of their clients on file that are usually printed on the front of our check cards. And because my face matches that picture, even caked in dirt, my life gets much easier.

My ribs are burning and throbbing like hell and the teller asks me three times if I am sure I'm all right.

I motion for her to fork over the cash and I limp out of the lobby.

I know trains don't go all the way to Nashville, but one can take me somewhere, *anywhere* that's not so close to Caldwell.

And once I get some distance between me and Caldwell I'll tell Brinkley where I am and he can pick me up. And I need to tell someone about Gloria. I hope she got away too.

Hassan, the nice cabbie who waits for me this whole time while I sort out my affairs, gets a $20 tip when I climb out of the cab at Union station.

I am on the steps of Union Station and a strange feeling overcomes me. I'm just about to turn when rough hands snatch me up. I go to scream but someone clamps a hand over my mouth. Then I see the flash of blue uniform. Cops. What? Why cops?

Someone shoves me onto the pavement and starts to cuff me.

And the people just watch. They just sidestep me. Even Hassan is quick to pull off the curb.

They drag me off the steps toward the dark alley running parallel to the train station. My shoes scrape against the cement as I struggle but it's hard to put up much of a fight with sharp jabs of fire burning my whole left side. They drop me on my feet in the shade of the dark alleyway but I can barely stand. I'm hurting so bad. I think struggling made it worse. I just want to lie down or something.

As the hands release me I look up to see Caldwell standing in the alleyway.

Caldwell with his right arm soaked in blood up to his rolled up sleeve. His left hand also has something dark crusted under the nails.

"Oh shit."

"You are an unappreciative guest," Caldwell says. "You left without saying thank you or even goodbye."

"Thank you. Goodbye," I say.

I start to back away but huge hands push me deeper into the alley. I turn to see it's actually four cops blocking my way out. When I turn back around Caldwell has a gun in his hand and he takes aim at my heart.

"Devon broke two of your ribs," he says. "I can see them from here."

If he can see it, then—"Liza is dead," I say.

The blood on his hands is proof.

"And your heart," he says with maniacal glee. "Your heart is beating so fast. Are you afraid?"

"No," I lie.

Instead, he raises the gun and points it right at me. If my heart wasn't pounding before, it sure as hell is now.

"We both know there is only one way to heal your ribs."

And before I even open my mouth to say

something sarcastic, or clever, or even to just be a jerk because this obviously crazy person has me at gun point, he pulls the trigger. And it is like someone punches me hard in the chest.

I've nowhere to go but down.

Ally

After dropping Gloria off at the hospital, I go home. Even though I just slept twelve hours, I'm exhausted again. Maybe I'm not eating right. Or exercising. Something. I have zero energy.

The dreams come quickly.

Jesse in a white cotton nightgown hanging past her feet, moving toward the barn at the edge of her parent's property. The barn itself is in flames, red-orange hands swirling and spinning in a Pentecostal ecstasy as they stretch up toward the star-filled sky. I'm behind Jesse, watching her walk away from me toward the barn. I'm screaming after her, but she doesn't turn. She just continues her slow, steady procession toward the fire as if the heat still calls to her like a Siren across the dark sea of the night.

Jesse falls to her knees in the field, not fifteen feet from the fire and starts screaming. Her howls shake my bones. Her hands wrap around her head as if drowning out some terrible sound I can't hear as I run and run toward her without ever gaining ground.

Then I see him—

—Caldwell emerging from the fire untouched, his pristine suit jacket smoking as he moves from the heat of the fire into the cold night. He doesn't see me. His gaze is fixed on Jesse crouching and wailing on the ground as he walks toward her.

I run harder and harder but I still can't get any closer. He will get to her before I will and I can't bear it.

And something is happening to Jesse—something that delights Caldwell to no end.

Her nightgown bulges in the back, rising up like a parachute behind her, filling like a balloon.

Jesse falls forward on her hands and knees screaming as if whatever invisible demon riding her back is causing her a great deal of pain. Her eyes are squeezed shut in the firelight as she clutches at the soil beneath her.

Then twin wings erupt through the stretched fabric of her nightgown. Her bare back is glimpsed only for a moment before the black feathers spill out behind her spreading and extending like a great eruption of tar. They settle and harden into the soft feathers. The wings themselves are twice as long as she is and blacker than the night above us.

Caldwell is clapping.

I've stopped running.

I'm standing in the field where we played as children, terrified to move a step closer. This is when

Jesse turns toward me, eyes rimmed with tears.

Her mouth moves, pleading but I don't hear her voice so much as sense it. *Help me.*

Before I can, Caldwell reaches down and grabs the top of her black wing and wrenches her back. He drags her into the fire screaming by those delicate wings, her arm outstretched toward me in a desperate plea.

I wake up drenched in a cold sweat. I've kicked my comforter into the floor and the chilly air from my open window ices the sweat on my skin. Winston is on the edge of the bed as far away from me as he can possibly get, watching me wearily. He cowers as if I've struck him in my sleep and maybe I did. I obviously thrashed enough to throw off the blanket.

I pull him to me and it isn't until I'm holding him that I realize I'm shaking all over. Not from the cold window which I yank shut in one violent thrust. I'm terrified.

Ally. Help me.

I leap from the bed and pull on my shoes.

Ten minutes later I'm outside the safe house, pausing just long enough beyond the entrance for an ambulance to whip past me heading toward the hospital. I'm only vaguely aware of the time, sometime after seven a.m. as I climb the stairs to our floor.

I burst into the apartment and the first thing I see

is Nikki sitting at the monitoring station. A smile begins to spread over her face until she gets a good look at me.

"What's wrong?" she asks.

"Where is Parish?" I don't wait for the answer. I storm across the room to the supply cabinet. I remove a electroshock weapon from the second shelf. I click it to see that it's charged and turn to face Nikki. She's standing at the station watching me as if partially worried she might be the one I'll target.

"He isn't a morning person. This is my shift," she says. Her eyes go to the electroshock weapon. "What do you need that for?"

I blaze past her to the room with the woman captive. Through the dark two-way glass I see her sleeping. Her head hangs forward, resting on her chest.

Nikki appears beside me.

"Can you be away from your post?" I say. I place a hand on the doorknob ready to turn it and enter the room when Nikki grabs me.

Her eyes are wide. "What's going on?"

I tell her about Jesse. I tell her about Gloria's pictures and about my dream and everything else that comes to mind and flows right out of my mouth as if a dam has broken inside me.

"I have to know where they would take her," I say. "I *have* to."

I go to yank the door open with both hands and Nikki presses on the door. "I'll go with you."

"You don't want to see me like this." *I* don't want to see me. The woman hears us rattling the door knob and is no longer sleeping. Her eyes are wide in anticipation and her mouth slightly open as she cranes her neck to stare at the door.

Nikki turns my chin so I have to look her in the eyes. "I'm not letting you go in there by yourself."

She releases her pressure on the door and I pull it wide.

I enter the room and look at the woman tied to the chair. Her forehead is slick with beads of sweat and her hair hangs loose around her head, heavy with a week's worth of oil and neglect.

"I'm going to be honest," I say, looking down into her eyes. "I've never tortured anyone before."

Her mouth is open as if she is unsure how to react to my blunt honesty.

"But the person I love most in the world was just taken by Caldwell."

"You're Alice Gallagher."

"Caldwell has her," I say, without stopping. I barely register Nikki slipping into the room and coming around behind me. If the woman hadn't looked away from me long enough to watch Nikki, I probably wouldn't have noticed at all. When she looks back to me, I make my move.

I show her the electroshock weapon before I click the button on. I let the blue-white electric lights *tattattattat* in front of her face, watching the static fire reflected in her eyes.

"I'll be clear," I say over the hissing, rapid fire click of the electroshock weapon. "I want to know where Jesse is and I'm willing to do some really terrible things to you to find out. I'll ask you a question and you'd better answer me. Do you understand?"

The woman hesitates and I put the electric fire to the exposed part of her neck. I watch her convulse in her seat before I must close my eyes, counting to three.

I click the electroshock weapon off.

"See how that worked? I asked a question and you didn't answer. If I ask you another question and you don't answer again, you know what will happen. Don't you?"

"Yes," she says. Her bottom lip quivers so I focus on her eyes instead. But even those are wide and hollow.

I can't do this.

"Do you know of any places in Chicago that they would take Jesse?"

She hesitates and I move the electroshock weapon toward her but I don't reach her neck before she speaks. "There is a cathedral on State Street. If she were in Chicago they would take her there. It's being renovated, so it keeps the people out."

Nikki goes very still in the corner and it is the sudden stillness that reminds me again she is in this room. That she is keeping her promise to stay beside me through this. And I don't realize how comforting her presence is until now.

I remember what Gloria said. *She was in Chicago but they've moved her.* "If they were to move her out of Chicago, but somewhere close to transport her without a big fuss, where would they take her?"

She opens her mouth then closes it in a stubborn clench. I put the electroshock weapon to her throat again and watch her convulse. My stomach turns. *1...2...3...*

"Where would they take her?"

The woman blinks back tears and spits at me. "She will get what she deserves."

I apply the electroshock weapon to her neck a third time, I feel Nikki come closer. She says my name.

My voice breaks. "Where *is* she?"

"The soulless are damned. Thou shall not suffer that bitch to live!" she hisses at me and I find myself putting the electricity to the exposed skin and really driving it into the side of her throat. Again and again as the flesh burns and the smell of it fills the little room.

Nikki is pulling at me, trying to get me to stop.

She manages to get the electroshock weapon away but it isn't enough. I'm overcome with the fear and anger from that horrible dream and I launch myself at the
woman. I hit her across the face once. Twice.

My ears ring with the violence of my own voice.

"Where is she? Tell me where she is! Tell me!"

"Abomination! Abomination!" she devolves into screaming it like a chant. Like a protective incantation that is meant to protect her.

I tear at her hair and scratch her face.

Nikki is trying to pull me off of the woman as my hands slide off her face, smearing her blood over the pale skin. Her nose. I've broken her nose and that is where the blood is coming from. My burning knuckles are slick with it.

Strong hands are pulling me away from the woman, out into the hallway. I'm crying and kicking at the air as I'm tossed into the hallway.

It is Jeremiah that puts me down in the hallway outside the interrogation room. "What the hell is going on here?"

But I can't bear to answer him. It isn't the anger in his voice that does me in. It's the concern, the hint of fear in his round eyes.

I crumple into Nikki's arms crying. And I let her tell him the story for me.

When she is finished Jeremiah says my name. When I don't look up he says it more firmly as if dealing with a petulant child. "Alice, *look* at me."

I meet his eyes, seeing only a blurry outline of a man until I blink back the tears.

"We will find her," he says. His voice is so soft, so kind I can't stand it. My chest contracts as if to protect myself. He reaches out and places one gentle hand on the top of my head. "We won't stop until we do."

Jesse

I'm naked.

And disoriented because one minute I was in the alleyway and now I'm naked in this tiny room on a tiny bed with a creepy-ass man in the corner watching me with a sadistic smile on his face. He has an absurd amount of muscle stretched under a black T-shirt. His beach bum hair is pulled back in a half-ponytail and his beefy fists are clasped behind his back. His pants are also black and baggy. His face is blank, expressionless except for that frightening hint of a smile.

The small twin-sized cot beneath me, white and squeaky with unoiled springs is tucked into the corner opposite the man. The last time I woke up on a cot, terrible things happened. I had a suck ass feeling that this would be even worse.

I press myself into the corner where the bed and wall meet and cover my body as much as possible. There are no pillows or sheets so I am forced to cover myself by strategically folding my arms and legs in front of my body. The wall is cold against my bare back, but it's more inviting than this staring weirdo. One small favor: the unbearable throb of my broken ribs has been replaced with the stiff hint of rigor mortis.

A loud voice comes from one of the speakers in the ceiling, a circular device that could be mistaken for a fancy showerhead. The voice is garbled and doesn't sound quite human. "Give her the clothes, Hanson."

Hanson removes a meaty fist from behind his back and holds out the clothes for me. When I won't move closer to take them the voice speaks again in a low warning.

"Hanson."

Hanson tosses the clothes toward me and I slowly, with one eye still on MmmBop there, pull on my clothes. They fit me because they are mine. Someone washed my clothes and all the dirt that Liza tried to bury me under is gone. The exception is my T-shirt ruined from a shot to the heart, has been replaced with a black one much too big for me. There is no graceful or dignified way to put my clothes on and Hanson shamelessly watches me angle and twist my body into the fabric.

"Is this your shirt? It looks like the one you have on."

He isn't humored, but I feel infinitely better now that most of my skin is covered. I do pause when I realize the underwear isn't mine either. But hell, I'd take a pair of underwear off a chimp right now, if it meant an extra layer.

I pull on Lane's coat and search the front for damage. They washed the dirt off but the quarter-sized smudge of blood on the left inside pocket is still there. And part of the zipper has been blasted away.

A hard knock comes at the door and somehow I know it is Caldwell. Maybe it's the knock itself that alerts me or this strange hum in my head.

"You can leave," Caldwell says. He passes beneath the staunch metal frame and enters the small room. Hanson doesn't so much as bat an eyelash, but Caldwell issues assurances all the same. "She cannot hurt me. God protects me."

I arch an eyebrow wondering if Caldwell really believes God favors him or if he is just so used to saying that religious propaganda in the presence of his followers that he just churns that shit out like butter.

Hanson favors me with a final unfriendly smile. If I have to translate, it is probably a look that says *hurt him and I will tear you limb from limb*. He holds this expression on his face until the heavy metal door closes between us and locks him out.

I pull myself up into a tighter ball, knees snug

against my chest, my back tucked back into the corner. It's more comfortable with a stretch of fabric between my skin and the wall. Caldwell sits on the edge of the bed despite the groaning protest of the springs.

"When you were a little girl—"

"Don't." I cut him off. I shove Caldwell's picture out of my mind. I don't know if it is a real memory of him or if he took it from my head and fed it back to me. I don't know what's real with this guy. "You're here to kill me. Let's not pretend."

"You're in such a hurry to die. What are you running from?"

I don't answer because his question has chilled me.

"And I thought this is what you wanted?" he asks. "Answers. A reunion with your father."

"*Don't* screw with me," I say. "Liza is dead. Now there's just me. We both know what you want to happen next."

"I do not want it actually," he says. He runs his palms along the front of his suit jacket. "I lack the motivation."

"You shot me at the train station," I say. "You seemed pretty motivated."

His jaw flexes and it makes me think of Lane when he's trying to control his anger.

"I shot you so you would heal," he says.

"Yes, why bother with the hassle of medical treatment? Is that how you stay looking so young?" I ask. "What do you do? Shoot yourself every time you stub a toe?"

A sinister smile stretches his lips. "Ribs take a long time to heal. And we don't have a lot of time."

That horrid gleam in his eye. *Eagerness*. He's as excited as a shark scenting blood. So why waste time? I don't understand. "Why heal me only to kill me?"

"But what about your questions?" he says and his face is a mask of seriousness. He even manages to mimic concern. "I thought you were dying for answers."

No, I'm dying for a new life. One where I can understand and put all this behind me. But that seems impossible from where I'm sitting. This has to be a game, some kind of new twisted game.

"For example," he begins as if he can't read my thoughts. And it wouldn't take a mind reader to know I'm suspicious anyway. "You want to know why I sent Martin to kill you."

He gives a small nod as if I've said something. "It was a mistake to send him. I didn't know what you were. Of course I had a protocol for that sort of situation. Should someone show a sign that the power was already present, the channel already active if you will, he was to simply bring that person to me. It was how we found Henry Chaplain, after all."

I hug my knees tighter against the wave of nausea.

It is too much to be this close to him. A warm buzz in my skull makes it hard to think. My thoughts feel damp and undefined. And my stomach twists as if I'm dizzy.

"So you see," he continues. "He would not have killed you. He would have brought you to me, had the FBRD not intercepted your body, of course."

His eyes narrow and I swear I can feel him in my head, the buzz intensifying.

"You want to know why I am killing so many people. Thousands upon thousands—and that's a modest estimate on your part, by the way. I've killed over 45,000."

My cheeks catch fire but I control my exhale. *Genocide.*

If Caldwell hears the disbelief and disgust in my head, he shows no sign. He pushes on. "I want to close the extra doors. By minimizing the channels, it controls the power flow."

It isn't hard to see where this is going. "You want to be the only one with power."

"Can't you feel the teeth he has in you?" Caldwell asks.

Who has his teeth in me?

"Gabriel," he whispers and a dark shifting shadow moves behind his eyes. "I can see his claws in your back."

This is another mind game. He probably only knows about Gabriel because he saw it in my head. If I am crazy delusional he'll see what I see.

"What do you think you are?" he asks.

"A girl with a neurological disorder, working for a system that exploits her disorder for profit," I say. "And perhaps a little insane."

"So scientific," he says. He turns his head and smiles, but his back is still straight and hands still folded in his lap. So prim and proper. Not a hint of the good ol' boy mechanic I knew and loved. "I *am* the angel now. There is no separation between the ego who knows himself as Eric and the power I possess. They are one and the same."

He slams into my mind. I'm reeling with the shock of the wave, so when he puts his hands on me and shoves me flat against the cot, I put up little resistance.

"What are you afraid of?" he asks me. And I don't know if he has spoken aloud or if the question is in my mind. He isn't shoving pictures into my head like he was before. He is opening me up, riffling through me with eager, hungry hands. If my mind was an orange, then he has torn open the thick rind protecting it. With greedy fingers he begins to pry off each sliver of delicate, juicy flesh. Pulling and sucking. Searching.

"Stop," I beg.

It's like slick palms against my skin. My memories are pulled up and examined one by one. Every private and personal thought his for the taking.

My mother. Her cotton dresses and white laces gloves, in a tiny church that smelled of old books. The tilt of her wide-brimmed Sunday hat. Her perfume, something like lilacs.

"Let go of me."

Caldwell throws these memories aside and digs deeper.

My little brother's birth. How my mother put him in my arms for the first time and called him Daniel. Danny, three-years-old, climbing into my bed because he didn't want to sleep alone. Me pulling him in and wrapping him tight and telling him stories.

"Stop," I beg. *What are you looking for?*

Ally, younger Ally, my best friend even in high school, promising to run away with me. She promised to take me away from all of this. Away from—me waiting all night with a bag packed under my bed, my ear straining to hear beyond my window for her voice or a tapping against the glass.

Then I wake the next morning to the sound of his voice in the kitchen, my bag still packed at my feet.

His voice.

I could almost feel Caldwell's excitement rise. *Who is he? Show me his face.*

"No," I whisper aloud. "*No.*"

These are my secrets. I don't want you to know. I don't want anyone to know.

The smell of burning flesh. The sounds of a man screaming and cursing me as flames lick his bones clean.

"Show me his face," Caldwell says.

"No," I scream. "Get out of my fucking head!"

I shove against his arms but Caldwell grabs ahold of me and shoves me down into the mattress again.

He shoves me down into the mattress and pins me on my stomach. I am suffocating in the pillow, in the smell of cotton and fabric softener. I am crying for my mother but she doesn't come. Why doesn't she come? A thousand nights and she never comes.

"No," I scream, trying to fight out of his grip.

"Show me his face," Caldwell commands. He is so much bigger than I am and he uses his weight to shove me deeper and deeper into the mattress, just as he forces himself deeper and deeper into my mind—as the springs groan and creak their protest.

He is turning me over, shoving my face into the mattress by the back of my neck. I can't breathe. I can't breathe. Mother—

Caldwell mimics the memory as I see it, and the motions are enough to fuel the fire. The terror. Despite my fury he rolls me onto my stomach, shoving my face into mattress and pins me there by the back of my neck. The springs crush my nose and I try to turn my head but I can't because he won't let go, won't even give me an inch.

I can't breathe. I can't breathe but he lifts my night gown anyway. He uses his disgusting fat fingers to yank aside my underwear and—Mom!—

But it can't be heard around the mattress and I haven't enough air to force out the sound.

"His face," Caldwell warns for the last time. He places a threatening hand on the back of my jeans. He slides the hand over my hip, reaching around for the button holding the barrier in place. He pops the button on the front and my hips feel the cold air brush against bare skin.

The face.

Caldwell pulls at my underwear, pulling them down over one hip.

His face melting in fire. Eyes boiling in their sockets. The moment I see it clear, can feel the fire against my face, Caldwell reaches around and his fingers brush the hair there.

The barn engulfed in flames, a man twisting and burning in agony while I do nothing to save him, nothing. As the sting of smoke clogs the back of my throat. The heat searing against my face. The whole world burning down around me. Eddie's burning hand clamps onto mine.

"I'm not holding you back anymore. Show me what you've got." Caldwell says with his mind or his mouth, I don't know. But as soon as he says it, I know it is true. Somehow he has been in my head, suppressing my ability to protect myself until the moment it would serve him best.

At this image of Eddie, the power rises and rolls

through me. I feel it lash out at him the way he must have made Liza lash out—and I know this is what he needs to kill me and take whatever it is he thinks I have left to give.

Go on, I tell him. *Take it all*.

Ally

Limbs quaking, I cross the downtown office carpet to the tall filing cabinet against the wall. This metal box holds all the records we are required to keep on our replacements for the FBRD should they ever come calling. But hidden in the mass is another file folder. It isn't under the appropriate letter. It's tucked away in the back, easily overlooked in the shadows of the drawer unless you know it is there.

I pull out the folder with trembling hands because I haven't stopped shaking since I left the safe house. I don't even bother to close the drawer as I sink into Jesse's desk chair.

The folder contains everything I've ever uncovered about Caldwell. His public image as well as tidbits gleaned through private investigation. I am determined to read this file fifty times if I have to. I can't just sit by and wait for Jesse to turn up dead.

But after looking through the photographs and the news clippings, the public records of properties purchased by the Church, it all begins to blur. It looks like a big pile of nothing. My fingers begin to move faster and faster, turning over each page as if expecting some key bit of information to fall from an invisible pocket. But nothing. I let out a frustrated scream, flipping page after page and I've devolved completely into crying when I hear someone say my name.

"Ally?"

My head snaps up from the strewn pages and it's Lane. He stands in the middle of the office, the door separating the comic book store and our work space stands open.

"Go away." I knock pages off the desk. "I'm busy."

He comes closer. "Are you okay?"

I spit my derision at him. "Do I look okay?"

I turn page after page but still find nothing of use. I knock the whole folder off the desk and it flies up in a cloud of white squares, warping and falling to the maroon carpet. I collapse on the desk and put my head on my hands.

A heavy warm hand comes to rest on my back. It doesn't make the mistake of giving me a patronizing pat or a *thatagirl*. It just rests, certain and steadfast on my left shoulder blade. I lift my head and find Lane crouching beside me, eye-level.

He needs a shave. And a weekend of good sleep to erase those deep purple bags under his eyes. But these are the reasons I forgive him. His eyes are wide and wet like mine. He opens his arms just a little—the subtlest of invitations and I accept. I fall out of the chair into his arms and he holds me.

He isn't stupid about it. He doesn't tell me it will be alright or sexualize it. He just holds me and lets me know that I'm not alone. I'm not the only one sick with fear for Jesse.

I am not sure the exact moment I start talking but once I do, I can't stop. I confess everything as if I am in the arms of a priest and not my best friend's boyfriend. My *ex's* boyfriend.

I tell him about our captive. I tell him how we've been working so hard to erase Caldwell from the face of the Earth because I know she will never be safe until he is dead, cut up in a million pieces and fed to the hogs just to be sure.

"I thought I could do this but I can't. I can't," I hear myself saying. He hasn't spoken once and I just keep talking. "I'll never be as ruthless as Caldwell and ruthless wins. It wins."

"There is nothing wrong with you," Lane says. He squeezes me tighter as if threatening me to contradict him.

"Jeremiah is right," I say. "I can't say I'll do anything to save her and then hold back. Look what happened! I should never have let her go."

"I sure as hell won't let Brinkley lead her by the leash anymore," Lane says. His chest vibrates with his anger.

"God," I say, feeling my mind circle back. "I should have questioned the hell out of the woman the second we got her. We should have found out whatever there was to find out before the shit hit the fan. Now look at us, scrambling like cockroaches when the light comes on."

Lane pulls back from me and I think he is ejecting me from his lap but he isn't. He grabs ahold of my face and forces me to look at him. "You did nothing wrong. You can't be blamed for the actions of a homicidal maniac."

I am looking into Lane's eyes and I remember who he is to Jesse. The comfort leaks away, leaving me cold. I stand and put distance between us.

"I'm sorry," Lane says. "I didn't mean anything by it."

I flash him a weak smile but I don't meet his eyes. "I know."

When I turn back and look at him, his head is hung low. He is the little boy in trouble again as he leans against the edge of Jesse's desk.

"I'm sorry that I've hurt you," he says.

I look up and meet his gaze.

"I know that it isn't easy for you to see us together," Lane says. "It wasn't easy for me when I knew she was seeing you."

My cheeks burn. I open my mouth to warn him,

tell him I have no interest in going down this road with him in the middle of all the other shit I'm dealing with, but he keeps going.

He must sense my unwillingness to have this conversation.

"Please, just hear me out," he pleads.

"I'd rather not," I say.

"I know but I don't know if we'll have another chance," he says. And without my permission he continues. "I know you hate that I gave her the ultimatum, but I love her."

He might as well have slapped me across the face, as much as the words sting.

"Ever since she chose to save you rather than me in the basement, I've wondered if I made a mistake."

"Please don't tell me you wish I was dead again."

He shakes his head. "No, but think about it. In moments like that, a person is pure instinct. She was watching the three of us die and had to decide who she couldn't live without. And it wasn't me. It wasn't *me*. And it's more than that," he says. "You love her too."

I can't hide my anger or my embarrassment of this conversation. "Of course I do."

"I thought you just wanted her. That she was just a friend with benefits," he says.

"Yes, because lesbians are incapable of loving, committed relationships. My love could never compare to what you give her, because I have to purchase my dick from the store."

He flinches. "That's not what I'm saying."

I shift my weight on the border of fury. "Then be clear."

He takes a breath. "I can tell you love her and I'm sorry I drove you apart."

My heart clenches. It burns just to breathe. "You're not as in control of this as you think you are. Jesse is a big girl. She is capable of doing whatever the hell she wants. You didn't drive us apart." *I did. By keeping secrets, by going off and joining Jeremiah and not telling her. Because she kept secrets, because somehow we got to this point by hiding from each other. She's going to die thinking things weren't good between us and that is my fault.*

"Stop trying to make this right," I say. "You have nothing to do with it."

Jesse

The hand relaxes on the back of my neck. He doesn't shove his fist into my skull or shoot me or whatever it is he needs to do to remove what he wants from me and close the door behind him.

Rough hands roll me over so that I am forced to face him. I take this first chance to yank my jeans up but I don't get them buttoned.

"That's it?" he says. He grabs me roughly by the arms. "That's it!"

He shakes me, lifting and slamming. Lifting and slamming me into the mattress.

Isn't that what you wanted? I can't speak aloud. He is still shaking me so hard that I feel as though my brain will dislodge.

"No," he says. He slaps me hard across the face once. And when that doesn't satisfy him, he does it a second time.

My ears ring. My body throbs and I can't focus on anything in the room.

He climbs off the bed and paces like a wild animal. He screams a long, frustrated roar.

I pull myself up to a sitting position and crawl back into the corner. He stops pacing and whirls on me. I can't hide the fact I'm shaking.

"The door is open," he says. He makes a jabbing motion with his hands for emphasis. His hair is disheveled, his shirt untucked and collar askew. And he couldn't care less. "And power is coming through."

He paces angrily back and forth, still gesturing wildly.

"The door is open and the power is coming through but he isn't there! He isn't there! But I *know* he is. I *know* it!"

At that he kicks the bed again and again. It rattles and shakes me, shivering beneath me like a cornered animal. I squeeze my eyes closed and wait for him to turn that fury on me. But he doesn't.

The strike never comes, the punch, the slap or the hair pulling. When I open my eyes he isn't even looking at me. He is staring at the floor with his hands on his hip.

"You haven't accepted him," he says. He is so furious spit is forming in the corners of his mouth. "That's *it*. We need to force you to come together. Every death separates you from your humanity, so— so if you won't embrace him willingly, we'll have to force you."

He turns and storms out of the room. The heavy door locks behind me.

My mind races, blurs with fear and confusion. What did he just say?

I know I asked him to kill me—because I wanted it to just be over and done.

But I don't want to die a hundred or more times in whatever creative ways Caldwell can think up.

What he did to me—what just happened—has left me feeling as cold and sick as anything that Eddie ever did to me even though he didn't actually touch me or violate me. I begin to cry. I can't help it and it's all I can do just to curl into a ball on the thin cot and weep. How will he do it? 100 shots to the heart? Maybe a good old beat-to-death? Fire? He knows my fears now. Maybe he will try to terrorize me at every chance so I'll lose my mind more quickly.

Something happens—

—a hissing sound, almost like turning on a water faucet. Except it isn't water pouring from the vents above my head into my little room. It's white gas, billowing down around me.

A gas chamber. This whole time I've been sitting in a gas chamber.

Shaking uncontrollably, my legs so wobbly I can barely stand, I slip under the bed. Underneath, I shove myself up into the corner and bury my face in

Lane's jacket. I take shallow breaths through the cotton fabric and try to focus on the scent of him.

Lane. Ally.

It stretches on forever and I contemplate whether it is better to suffocate myself with the jacket and close my lungs off to the gas before it can reach me, or just accept that it is coming.

I cry more.

I won't lie. I am terrified and that's what I do when I'm really, really scared. I cry. It isn't brave or charismatic, but it's what happens. And I'm screaming when the smoke reaches its bony white fingers under the bed for me.

As the darkness takes me, my lungs burn and I choke. I gag and try to push myself deeper into the corner away from the smoke burning my eyes and throat.

I hear his voice.

I'm here, Gabriel whispers through the darkness. *I've always been right here.*

Ally

A loud bang rattles my door and makes Winston bark and leap from my bed. I throw back the covers muttering. "What I wouldn't give for one night in my bed that isn't interrupted with a crisis."

I press my eye to the peep hole again, wondering who the hell was able to get into the building without being buzzed up. Cindy? But is isn't Cindy.

I open the door just a crack. "Jeremiah?"

Jeremiah stands there in a pristine white dress shirt beneath a sweater vest and in freshly pressed dress pants. Apparently he can keep his hair trimmed and clothes clean in times of need, unlike the rest of us who look more and more like hell as time wears on.

He steps through my doorway, widening it as he goes and I notice the roll of papers jutting from under his arm. I don't bother to ask how he got in. I've accepted that my locked entrance isn't so locked after all.

"What's happened?" I move back to give him room. "Where's Nikki?"

"I sent Parish on errands so she is at the monitoring station. You can thank her later."

"For what?" I pull a throw blanket down off the back of the couch and wrap myself up inside it. I'm not sure if it is because I'm a little chilly or because I feel uncomfortable in just boxers and a T-shirt in front of Jeremiah.

"I believe we have found Jesse."

My mouth falls open full of questions but he doesn't wait for me to recover. "Have you heard about the blackouts in Chicago?"

"No."

"No one else has either," he responds. "Except for those experiencing it. Delaney is the one that sent us the information and Nikki was the one who decrypted it."

Delaney. "There is an AMP working for Caldwell. Micah Delaney. Is he related to our Delaney?"

Jeremiah's eyes narrow. "Not that I'm aware of but I will find out."

I backtrack. "If Chicago blacked out, it would have been on the news."

"The blackouts haven't reached Chicago yet. They're originating outside of the city."

He pulls the papers from under his arms and makes liberal use of my coffee table. Because he is much bigger than me, he pushes my armchair back trying to fit into the small space between the coffee table and furniture.

The bunch of paper is actually a single large map rolled several times. "Why do you have a map?" It seems so old-fashioned.

"There isn't satellite in this area. We're having a hard time getting detailed images. It's just a small town in Illinois called Minooka."

"What do you mean?" I ask, still wrapped and lowering myself beside him. "Satellites can see everything."

He glances at me over the rim of his glasses. "No, not everything."

I look at where his thick finger points. It's a series of circles inside of each other. A small one surrounded by a larger, then a larger and a larger circle, like ripples frozen mid-quake on the surface of a pond. On the edge of each penciled circle is a time, ranging from four to six hours apart.

"The blackouts occur in timed intervals."

"Maybe the city is testing something?" I ask.

"No."

"What makes you think this is Jesse? In *Minooka*?"

His expression softens as he looks away from the map to meet my gaze. "Can you think of any reason why Jesse could be at the center of these blackouts?"

I think of Regina Lovett's accusation that Jesse

ruined her husband's office. I think of the number of
light bulbs I've replaced in her house in the past year
alone and the latest power outage caused by a serious
surge.

"Maybe."

He frowns. "Minooka has less than 12,000 people.
The surrounding areas are rural. The blast radius is
just now reaching the outskirts of Chicago. This
morning, power was lost to half of LaGrange. If it
continues to grow, people will notice. If people
notice, it will bring unwanted attention."

I tuck my hair behind my ears. "You think he'll
finish her off, if she starts to draw attention."

"So you do think she is causing this," he says.

I look away.

"Alice," Jeremiah says. "I know you haven't
worked with me for very long and I know you only
joined because you were looking for the tools and
means to protect Jesse. But you are going to have to
trust me. Or at least, trust that we want the same
thing."

"But we don't want the same thing, do we?" I ask.
"You want to throw her in front of Caldwell. I want
to keep her as far away from him as possible."

He sits back on his heels. "You aren't doing a
great job of that, are you?"

"That wasn't my fault!"

"I just think that if we collaborated with each

other we would be more effective and ultimately, Jesse would be safer," he says.

"Okay, tell me what you want with her. Tell me the real reason why you've been pushing so hard to recruit her. If you don't need her as a cure-all, then what do you want her for."

"It will take everything we have to defeat him," Jeremiah says. The lines around his mouth deepen and I notice the faint purple under his eyes for the first time. "And even that might not be enough."

My brow furrows. "But you seem so confident, so sure that it's only a matter of time before he's dead."

He gives me with a brief smile. "Have you never heard of the importance of morale?"

"But you do want her to fight," I say.

"I know you want to protect her," he says. His eyes soften, sympathetically. "I understand that, but I won't deny that we need her. I think he is like her. *Special.* Am I right?"

"What makes you think Caldwell is special?" I've barely accepted the possibility that Jesse is something else. I never considered the possibility that Caldwell is too.

Jeremiah removes his glasses and pinches his eyebrows. "Just this Saturday he gave a speech at 10:00 A.M. in New York. Then at 11:00 A.M. he had a breakfast in San Diego."

"The speech could have been recorded ahead of

time and there are the time zones."

"It wasn't recorded, which leaves us wondering how a man can give an hour long lecture in New York and then turn around and walk into Buca di Beppo in Mira Mesa. That's less than a minute from when he walked off the stage and into the restaurant, Alice. It was actually 8:00 A.M. there."

I don't know what to say. Caldwell is already scary as hell. I don't want to consider him with more at his disposal than an extremist fan base, trained killers, and a lot of money.

"We need her," Jeremiah says again. "It increases our odds of winning."

I consider this for several heartbeats. Caldwell marked Jesse as a target, not the other way around. And he will keep coming after her until one of them is dead. What if I cannot prevent it? Caldwell and Jesse. She *is* different. It's more than the NRD, it's the other things. Gabriel. What if all I can do is stay by her? Can I accept that?

Jeremiah senses my hesitation. "You can't be her human shield forever."

"As long as I'm breathing I will be," I reply, irritated.

"Do not be angry with me," he counters. "I don't want her to get hurt, but she is an integral part of this and *this* is bigger than just Jesse."

I want to test him, with something small. He's

been spying enough to know Jesse is different. What else does he know? "Caldwell is her father. Did you know that?"

His brow furrows. "No, I didn't and that is important information, which is just further proof we need to stop dividing our resources. We'll never win that way."

He's right. I know he is. Divided we won't get anywhere. It's better to pool our resources and present a united front to Caldwell. And if I'm going to protect her, I've got to be willing to go all in.

"I have some people you should meet," I say. "If we really are going to do this, then we need to put everything on the table. It should all be out in the open."

"I agree," he says, his palm still open and waiting.

"Come with me."

Brinkley is already at Gloria's when we arrive. I'm not surprised to find Gloria packing a small duffel bag, with clothes and toiletries spread across her bed. She has her sketchbook open on the floral quilt with several sheets jutting out from the neat square edge. I briefly touch her shoulder before returning to the kitchen.

Brinkley leans against the counter eating a fast food burger. The sound of ketchup splatters the plastic wrapper, the condiments escaping out the back as he bites into it. "She's been packing for an hour but she won't tell me where we are going."

I ignore this statement and move ahead as planned. "I want you to meet someone."

This is Jeremiah's cue to step from the dark hallway where he's been waiting silently into the lighted kitchen. When Brinkley sees Jeremiah he straightens his back and makes himself taller.

"Who the hell is this?" Brinkley says, but it's hardly a threat with ketchup on the side of his mouth.

"You asked me what I've been doing to piss Caldwell off enough to make his list," I say. I gesture toward Jeremiah. "*This* is what I've been doing."

"You've been doing this guy?" Brinkley asks. His tone is playful, joking, but there is something in his face I can't quite place. Relief? Curiosity? Expectation?

I blush. "Don't be idiotic. This is Jeremiah. He is leading a resistance against Caldwell. And I can see your face, Brinkley, so before you say anything insulting, let me warn you that it isn't a small operation. He has more connections than you do. Play nice."

Wiping ketchup from the corner of his lips, Brinkley flashes his best James Dean give-me-what-I-want-grin. "James T. Brinkley."

"Yes, I know," Jeremiah says, extending his hand.

"You were Jesse's handler and liaison for the FBRD, before she became a freelancer."

Another strange expression crosses Brinkley's face. He looks as if he has more to say, some retort to Jeremiah's assessment, but he says nothing. And when he catches me watching him, he forces a smile.

"So what is the plan?" he asks.

I tell Gloria and Brinkley about Minooka, Illinois. I have to raise my voice a bit to make sure it carries down the short stretch of hallway to Gloria, who continues to pack in the other room.

"We want to move immediately. It will be us four plus two others," I say.

Brinkley looks like he is about to object, but Jeremiah handles it nicely.

"Yes, Brinkley? What is it?" he asks the other man. He might as well say See? *I can play with others.*

"I have my own guns."

"Absolutely," Jeremiah says. "And we have our own equipment too."

Gloria comes into the kitchen with her duffel bag slung over her good shoulder and her sketchbook tucked under the bad, bandaged arm. I move to take it from her but she pulls back.

"Jeremiah, this is Gloria," I say.

Jeremiah smiles and it is a sweet and genuine smile. "It's a pleasure to meet you, Ms. Jackson. I'm very familiar with your work. You've done many great things."

Gloria doesn't quite know what to do with this gushing, so keeping one eye on Jeremiah she opens her sketchbook. She sorts through several pictures: most feature a vast field free of power lines, crops or without any signs of civilization. The primary object in the photo is a giant tree.

"I keep drawing this tree," she says.

"Between your drawings and Jeremiah's maps, I'm certain we will pinpoint her."

"Yes, it'll be so easy to find a tree," Brinkley says. He crumples up the remains of his wrapper and tosses it into Gloria's trash. "You can put your things in my trunk. It's a big trunk."

"You're assuming Jeremiah has less gear," I say. "And don't forget that we will have six people."

"I have a large SUV," Jeremiah offers. "It should be able to accommodate all of our gear and people."

Brinkley folds his arms over his chest but doesn't say anything.

"Caldwell has a benefit engagement this afternoon. Live and televised," Gloria says. "He cannot leave on a whim this evening. We should go now."

Jeremiah and I exchange a look. Caldwell's possible ability to leave on a whim is something we should probably discuss.

"What?" Brinkley demands.

"We'll talk about it in the car," I say. "Jeremiah, you can take my car to the safe house, get Nikki and load up. I'll ride with them to my place. I need to take Winston to a friend's while we're gone. Then we'll meet at the safe house.

"We do not want go up against him," Gloria whispers. Her fingers touch the edge of her sketchbook and her eyes gloss. "Not without Jesse."

I take Gloria's hand. "We'll get Jesse back first," I say. "Then we'll get Caldwell."

She nods and hefts her bag up higher on her good shoulder before looking at Jeremiah.

"Go on," I tell Jeremiah. "I'm waiting on someone."

Jeremiah leaves the three of us in the kitchen.

"Who are you waiting for?" Brinkley asks just after the sound of the screen door slams shut behind us. I don't answer.

Lane enters the kitchen moments later packed and ready.

"No," Brinkley says.

"He can handle himself."

"As well as you can."

"No more solo missions," I say, my anger rising. I know I'm red in the face. "Get this commando crap out of your head. It's done. We are all together now."

Brinkley gives me the death stare. Lane beams at me. I frankly don't care anymore. I'm tired of everyone, including myself, being so stupid and secretive.

I remember those sad blue eyes and pouty lips and try to see what Jesse sees. Try to see why she wants those arms around her. Why she loves his face, his voice? He smells good. I'll give him that. And he is symmetrical. But I still can't imagine her with him *forever*.

Usually I cannot so much as think of him without feeling the raw edge of anger, that burning irritation making me want to poke his eyes out. Usually just his presence agitates me and the sound of his voice grates on my nerves.

But the heat of my anger is gone. I don't like him exactly, but something has made me let go of the anger.

She chose you, he'd said. And I can't argue. She did save my life. For all the good it's done me.

"Don't die," I warn Lane. "I'm not dragging your dead body around."

Lane smiles. "Thank you for letting me in on this. It means a lot to me."

"We need the extra hands." I exhale slowly, releasing the tension in my chest. "And this might get you killed. So hold the applause until the end."

Jesse

If the gas killed me that was my 86th death. If it didn't, then I've only died 85 times, the last when Caldwell shot me through the heart. I can't be sure if I died in the gas or not, but I do know for certain that I'll die in this coffin.

And coffin is a fitting enough term for this wooden box. It isn't nearly as fancy as one of Kirk's coffins with satin lining and polished wood. This is just a wooden box, nailed together planks to seal out the dirt. And it is a bit bigger than a coffin. Because I am such a small person, I have at least a foot above and below my head. And the space between my face and the top of the box isn't enough for me to sit up, but it is enough for me to turn on my side and curl into a ball.

And that's what I do until the oxygen is gone and I'm gasping for air. Scared out of my mind, my body is forced to die this way. And again. And again. And *again*.

I quickly lose count. I try to scratch little tick marks in the soft part of the wood so I can count the rough grooves each time and know where I am, but it isn't a very accurate system. Sometimes the times between deaths are so quick I can't scratch a complete mark. Or I am too weak to scratch anything, becoming conscious only to realize I am wheezing for air.

But most of the time I am alive between deaths for the couple of hours it takes to deplete the air supply in my box. Someone must be opening the coffin and letting air in because the nails move. They jut down at new angles as if they have been pried up only to be shoved in again.

And dirt makes its way into the coffin.

Little granules stick to my tear-stained cheeks and dried lips. I try to keep calm despite my shaking, shivering and sore body—and the fact that I am laying in my own shit. Even the scent of fresh damp earth can't mask the stink in this chilly underground.

And all I can do is lie here. Talk about uncomfortable.

I talk to myself and try to explain the importance of not going crazy in a box underground. And the more I realize that is exactly what is happening, the more I bang on the wood, kicking and screaming and trying to claw my way out. Except I have to give this up too, once I realize I'm just depleting my oxygen faster by raving and sobbing.

Gabriel speaks to me in the darkness. *It doesn't have*

to be this way.

"Please, please," I beg. "Let me out of here."

I can do that for you, I can do anything for you. You just have to let me in, Jesse. Just let me in.

Ally

We turn off of I-55 onto a smaller Route 6 at Gloria's urging.

"I recognize this place," she says.

I don't know how. It looks like any other country road surrounded by flat farmland on all sides. Because it is almost October and harvesting season, the stalks of corn stand tall.

"Turn here," Gloria says and we maneuver the large SUV onto a still smaller unmarked road, with one side cornfield, the other side a dense tree line.

"Stop the car," she says. She pulls herself erect in the backseat, looking behind her and forward. "You need to park here. Now!"

Brinkley manages to maneuver the SUV to the shoulder but not completely. Suddenly the SUV turns off, coasts silently toward the ditch without power but still in drive, the ignition key still turned forward.

"Damn it," Brinkley says.

"What's happened?" Jeremiah asks calmly from the passenger seat. He has one hand, white-knuckled braced on the dash but otherwise, he's the picture of composure. I was surprised when he agreed to let Brinkley drive at Brinkley's insistence. And overall he's done a pretty good job of hiding his horror. But he isn't the only one who looks worried. Nikki is holding my hand tightly but she doesn't say anything. Lane is looking behind us as if he expects a car to rear-end us.

I appear to be the only one looking *forward*. "Brake!" I yell.

Brinkley slams on the brake and stops the car from coasting off of the road into the trees along the ditch.

He yanks the emergency brake up and eases his foot off the pedal slowly. The SUV remains poised at the lip of the ditch, tilting forward slightly but otherwise unmoving.

"We'll have to walk from here." Gloria flips through her sketchbook. She stops on a page. "It's almost a mile."

"That's consistent with the map," Jeremiah says from the front seat before opening his door and letting in a cool draft before he closes the door behind him and passes by our dark windows.

"What the hell is she doing out here?" I ask. "What did they do? Lock her in an outhouse?"

"She is in the ground," Gloria says, her face pinches in pain.

"They *buried* her?" Lane asks. He kicks his door

open and jumps down onto the street.

"Now I know why you brought the damn shovel," Brinkley grumbles to Gloria as they both climb out. "But she's not—I mean if she's pulsing, she's not really—" I hear a distant voice say and realize it is mine.

"No," Gloria says. "We still have time."

Everyone is out of the SUV but me and Nikki. Her hair is pulled up in a high ponytail and her clothes are all black. I flash a tentative smile and turn to climb out myself, but she grabs my arm and holds me back.

"You okay?" she asks. She leans toward me.

And to her credit it's a moment for intimacy, something sweet like a good luck kiss. Until the back hatch pops open and everyone is staring at us. Jeremiah and Brinkley lock eyes with us first and then Lane. Lane has almost an amused expression on his face.

"I'll be better when we find her," I say, and break my gaze with the others.

She releases me so I can slip out of the high seat onto the pavement. As everyone stands at the back of the SUV, retrieving what they think they need for the hike to find Jesse, I'd feel more self-conscious about the guns in clear view, if the road wasn't absolutely dead in all directions.

I slip my bright yellow backpack on over my red

coat. I'd packed more for Jesse than myself. Clothes and toiletries that she might want to freshen up with and snacks in case she is starving. Two bottles of water, a wash cloth and a blanket.

I admit, with the exception of a pocket knife, I left the survival stuff to the others.

I point at the huge gun in Brinkley's hand. "You can't just walk around with a rifle."

"A single-barreled shotgun you mean," he says. "And yes I can. This is deer country and it is hunting season. Here, take this."

He offers me a gun.

"I don't do guns," I say. So he offers the same gun to Lane who takes it. Jeremiah has his own and to my surprise, so does Nikki. From the way she loads it, it's clear she is no stranger to guns. Though I can't ever recall her using one on the other search and rescue missions we've completed in the last year.

"Do you mind?" she asks when she catches me staring.

"No," I say, face flushing. I look away. "I just didn't know."

Lane is watching us again and I think I see another hint of a smile on his face before Brinkley shoves a hideously orange cap onto my head.

"Wear this so we don't get shot," he says. "We need to hurry," Gloria says. "We won't find her in the dark."

I don't like the way Gloria stares through the trees. It makes my skin crawl. Then again, anything could do that, now that I have traded the warmth of the car for a chilly afternoon. The sun dips lower toward the horizon and I know we don't have much time.

We abandon the car and trek through the fallen leaves. It's almost impossible to do so quietly. Still, we take long steps through the darkening trees, careful not to drag our feet as we navigate the landscape. I strain my hearing over the crunch of leaves, for signs of danger.

When we break through the second clearing, I can hear water. We all stop, listening to it.

Gloria whispers. "I heard water in many of the drawings."

We only take a couple of steps before Brinkley throws his hand up. "Shhh, shhh."

No one moves, straining over the quiet to hear what Brinkley hears in the trees around us.

"There!" Gloria says and the sudden explosion of her voice makes me jump. Everyone's guns come up a little higher. Then I see what Gloria is pointing at. The tree. A monstrous oak, its branches spread wide like stretching arms, and grasping hands. "She's right *there*."

I have a horrible feeling Micah has set another trap just before Gloria takes off across the field. I reach to grab her and stop her from rushing out into the open but my fingers slip off the back of her jacket.

"Jackson, hold!" Brinkley shouts.

Jeremiah and Nikki both aim their guns but I don't see anything.

"What is it?" I whisper to Nikki, just as Gloria stops.

Then she goes down.

I'm about to run and Brinkley grabs me, forces me down. I hit the dirt with an *umph*, little particles of dry grass and leaves entering my mouth in my surprised inhale. Then I realize it isn't Brinkley covering me, it is Lane.

"Did she get shot?" My voice is a pitiful excuse for a whisper. "What's happening?"

Jeremiah pushes the intercom pinned to his shoulder, much like a police walkie-talkie, and whispers. "Hostiles in trees." If the person says anything in response, it's directly into Jeremiah's earpiece. I didn't ask who he was talking to, Parish maybe or someone like him, monitoring us from a remote location.

Brinkley starts to crawl toward Gloria and Lane and I imitate his elbow crawl toward her collapsed body.

Nikki and Jeremiah hang back. When we reach Gloria, it takes both Lane and I to roll her over from this awkward position while Brinkley keeps his gun pointed into the woods.

The first thing I do is check for a pulse, looking for a wound or blood. But there is no wound, only a small dart protruding from the side of her neck perched between my fingers and her carotid artery. I pull at the tiny object and Gloria's skin puckers.

"What is this?" I ask. I hold the dart up to Brinkley between two fingers. He looks but only for a second before focusing on the trees again, searching them for movement. "A sedative. Military grade."

"Why would they sedate us if they want us dead?" I ask. "Apart from torture, maybe?"

"They didn't want *her* dead but I'm not willing to bet they feel the same way about me," Brinkley says. "I'd say their last message was pretty clear." And they did nearly stab him to death, so he has a point.

Brinkley quits searching the trees and lays flat on the ground by me and Lane. "They can only have two options once they see we won't get up and expose ourselves."

Lane slaps Gloria lightly on the cheeks to wake her until I grab his hand.

"I'm listening," I say because Brinkley still hasn't completed his thought. And listening isn't all I am doing. I'm also looking for signs of movement. Nikki and Jeremiah are crouched low, still covered by the tree-line.

Brinkley gets to the point. "They can wait until Caldwell comes. Or they can rush us."

"Do you have a plan either way?" Lane asks.

"If they rush us, they will have to show themselves. If they show themselves, it will come down to guns and hand-to-hand."

"I'm no Sylvester Stallone," Lane says.

"But if they wait, we'll have to do something," Brinkley says. "Before we run out of time."

"The dart was in the right side of her neck," I say. "So the shooter must be on that side, in those trees."

"I don't think Caldwell would guard her with just *one* person. We have trees on all sides, so we have to assume shooters are on all sides. Mr. Right just shot first."

"So what is the plan again?" Lane asks.

"I have a way to draw them out," he says. "But it puts you both in a dangerous position."

"Danger, ha! I laugh in the face of danger ha, ha, ha!" I laugh out loud.

Brinkley grins. "Psychological warfare."

"*Lion King*, actually," I say.

He grins wider and hands me his gun. When I start to object he shoves it into my hands hard, scraping my half-open knuckles against the cold metal. "Just hold on to it for a minute. Keep your eyes open and if you see anything, point and shoot."

I don't look at Brinkley, keeping my focus instead

on the trees, until he stops rolling around in the field and motions for his shotgun. I give it back as he hands me a gas mask and a small pistol.

"Put this on," he says.

"What was all that—?" Lane asks. "You looked like a damn gymnast."

"I threw a tear gas canister. Put on the masks!"

Lane is already pulling his mask down over his face. I do the same as I turn back to look at Nikki and Jeremiah.

"What about Jeremiah and Nikki?" I jab a finger behind us. "You forgot about them!"

"What are those?" Lane asks pointing at the cylinders Brinkley pulls from his backpack.

"More tear gas canisters," he says. "I'm going to throw one in each direction and draw them out. Have the gun up and ready. When I say *run*, you take off toward Jesse's tree. Don't stop for anything."

"But what about Jeremiah and Nikki?" My voice echoes in my mask. "And what about Gloria?"

"She'll be safe here," he says. He puts a mask over Gloria's face, checking the nozzle for the sound of her breath. "If they wanted her dead they would've shot her, not sedated her."

"And what about them!" I gesture to Nikki and Jeremiah again.

"They'll have to protect themselves," Brinkley says. "You're the one that said they could."

"You're a jerk," I say. When I look back Nikki and Jeremiah have disappeared. They must have realized what Brinkley was doing and fell back. "Why didn't you give them masks?"

"I don't have any more."

"This is not how you work in groups!" I yell. "And this gas will probably kill the trees!"

"Fucking hippy liberals," Brinkley grumbles. "We can come back and plant 50 trees and nurse the baby squirrels back to health if you want, but if we don't get Jesse out of the ground *now* before Caldwell or full dark gets here, we won't even be alive enough to do that."

Point taken.

"Ready. In 3….2…."

My heart is hammering in my throat, making it hard to breathe and swallow and I feel like I'm suffocating in the mask. I feel Lane's hand tighten on my backpack.

"…1…*Go!*"

Lane yanks me up and I'm running.

Jesse

I can no longer tell the difference between reality and my dreams. Part of me understands I am in a box, underground, in some sort of panic-induced trance. The other part of me believes I am seventeen, suicidal and reliving the last few hours of my life.

When I get home from school that day, on the last day of my life, I barricade my bedroom door. I pull my desk and chair over to block the door. I pile on my books, possessions, everything with weight, on top of the desk. My mother comes to the door at dinner time and I tell her I have a headache and just want to sleep.

Underneath the bed is a small wooden box. It was my paternal grandmother's jewelry box. When she died my dad took the box and then he gave it to me for Christmas when I was eight. It was the last present he gave me.

Inside the box is a bottle of my mother's antidepressants. *25mg QTY: 100.*

The cold light of winter filters through my

curtains, the single oak behind it gnarled and bare. The grass dead and yellow beneath the white sky. I listen to my mother in the kitchen, the clang of pots and pans as my brother's baby voice chatter harmonized with the smell of something meaty. I think *I won't remember her voice. Danny's laugh. I'll be dead and won't remember anything.*

I'm half right.

I watch the old oak through the window as the white day gives way to the red of sunset. My room grows dark but I don't turn on the light. Instead, I pull the darkness around me like a blanket and take my first pill. I lose count at 18, feeding them one after the other down my throat and chasing them with a sip of alcohol that burns my nose and stings my throat.

My father loved a good rum and Coke.

When I'd found an old bottle of booze in the back of the pantry shortly after turning twelve, I'd put it under my bed, inside an empty Hello Kitty suitcase. It's what I used to wash each pill down. One after another until my limbs grew too heavy to lift. I still held the jewelry box as I crawled into the bed and leaned my hot forehead against the cold glass of the window pane.

The door rattles. The desk bucks and a pile of soft back books slide off the surface and hit the floor. Another push and the desk rocks back again.

Taking the alcohol with me, I slide open the

bedroom window.

It's hard to get the latch to give with thick fingers and only one hand. The desk behind me inches back, further and further. A crack then a sliver. Then enough for a foot, a hand, and elbow.

The window gives and I crawl through. I hit the dirt on my hands and knees. The bottle rolls and spills but I pick it up. The impact against the cold earth jars me but I can't feel much. I push through thick sludge with my limbs mostly numb from the cold. My legs and arms aren't working at full capacity as I pull myself and the bottle up. My shoulder bumps and slides over the grooved paneling of the back of our house as I stumble forward. I hear him behind me, hissing from the window but I keep moving. Step after step until the edge of the house gives way and I stumble again.

The barn's soft motion light comes on. It isn't even a real barn for animals or something like that. My dad erected it as a place to keep his cars and a place to work on his cars when his friends needed an oil change or a belt replaced. Somewhere he could do the work without charging his boss's price.

And somehow I make it there and fall into the golden strands of hay still clutching my father's favorite drink. The cars are gone and the hay is only here to mask the scent of oil Eddie hates so much.

My whole body is heavy with the gravity of one

thousand suns and softens into the mound of hay.

Until I feel the hands on me. Until he is turning me over and trying to shove his fingers down my throat.

"No," I groan. I don't want to be brought back. Especially not to him.

I turn and hurl into the hay and he pulls me up by the hair but I can't stand. I am on my knees, nearly unconscious, and he is fooling with his pants.

No.

I turn the bottle of booze over and wet the hay with it. And then—

No—Gabriel interrupts my dream memory. He walks into the dream barn in his beautiful black suit, black wings unfurling behind him in all of their glory. Those eyes, jaguar green behind his fallen black hair, hold me entranced. He moves around the slow motion of Eddie burning, screaming, his mouth open in horror but no sound coming out save Gabriel's voice.

You must remember it the way it happened.

Gabriel forces me back. Back to my bedroom counting the branches of the oak tree.

For each oak limb I take a pill and a sip of booze.

I am almost asleep when the door bucks and bulges. It is the sound of the books hitting the floor that sends me out the window.

In the barn, he covers my mouth with his sweaty

palm. The stink of him: the sweat and tobacco on his breath makes my stomach turn.

He pushes me down onto the hay.

He shoves his fingers down my throat and I am forced to turn my head and puke. Again and again.

"—do you hear me?" he says.

He shoves his fat fingers down my throat again. And I bite him. Hard until I feel the blood from those bloated knuckles hit the back of my throat.

"No." I spat the blood onto the dirty barn floor.

He jumps back and shakes his bleeding hand. "You little bitch."

The world is still spinning and I know I've taken too many pills to be saved no matter how many times this fat, stinking pervert forces me to throw up. He might believe he's gotten them out of me, but my body tells me otherwise. Or maybe he doesn't know about the pills at all—only the rum.

He undoes the belt on his work pants and yanks the leather from its loops. "What did you say?"

"No." My word slurs but it felt good to say it, to get the word out without a wad of mattress suffocating me. To hear it echo, full-bodied in the air. "No. No. *No*—"

Something connected with the side of my head. The pain is too sharp to be the flat sting of a leather strap. It isn't until I see the buckle trail through the dirt that I realize which end connected.

"The answer is still no." I gag. My body wants to puke up the pills and alcohol as much as Eddie wants me to.

I am dry heaving when he slams my back flat against the barn floor. My bare feet land in the soft hay just as all the breath goes out of me.

Remember me, Jesse. Remember what it felt like.

"No," I whisper in the darkness of my coffin.

I will protect you.

"I burned the barn with a match."

No, Gabriel insists. *Remember me.*

Eddie's hands yank at my jeans, pausing only long enough to give me a hard slap across the face when I fight back. The stench of him and the barn choke me as much as his thick hand. The rafters above blur in and out of focus.

Let me in Jesse.

"I can't," I cry, rubbing my hand over the rough wood of the box.

My fear consumes me in this living burial. It rolls me like a wave over and over as I brace against it.

Then it is as if the bottom of the coffin is a trap door opened and I am falling. Down and down into a cold dark and just like the night in the burning barn when I saw—

But Gabriel won't give up on me. *What do you see?*

An impossibly beautiful man with bright, inhumanly green eyes. They blaze like torchlight in his skull as his black wings extend out on either side of him. Crow's wings in flight, so beautiful, gliding toward me. I am fighting Eddie and losing. Fighting until this beautiful man says—

I am your strength.

And I—

Open your arms and I will catch you, Jesse.

Lying on the barn floor beneath Eddie I stretch open my arms and Gabriel takes me. He fills me with a coursing power, a vibrating electric fire like the soft warmth of a sunny day, starting in my chest and then fills me to the brim.

"No," I whisper. I look Eddie in the eye, his red rimmed, unfocused eyes. "No more."

The flame ignites. Not by a match or spark, but from me. *I* ignite. And Eddie's shirt is caught and blazes up as if wet with gasoline. He jumps back screaming and wailing and trips over my extended leg into the soft hay pile, which erupts as if firebombed.

Gabriel's strength is enough to help me stand and walk as if my body isn't dying at all. As if the bottle of alcohol and bottle of pills, the last inheritance from my living parents, haven't carried me over Death's doorway. I watch flames unfurl around him, eating the hay and the wall behind it. Then it takes the rafters one by one—so quickly—as thick black smoke rolling through like storm clouds across the plains before tearing open the roof and revealing a starlit sky.

But I am not in the barn anymore. I am in this God awful coffin with Gabriel's power rolling through me and I feel like I will burst. My skin wants to stretch in all directions, crawling with the power.

But I can still see him.

Him—dream Gabriel or real Gabriel, I don't know because the memory and the waking nightmare have become one or were always one—he walks past the enflamed man and comes toward me. He takes a slow step then another. A drumming sound begins deep in my chest. It fills my head up and gets louder and louder. Each pulse in time with his approaching step. But as the planks from the barn ceiling fall and come crashing down on me, I fall with them. I fall through the black side of twilight. And Gabriel dives from the burning barn into the depths to catch me. His wings stretch out on either side of him as his ivory fingers reach toward me.

But I am falling so fast. A great rushing wind tearing at my hair and face.

I don't want to die, I tell him. I don't know how my voice can carry through such a dark place. And I don't know when the bottom of this fathomless cavern might come, when my back might finally connect with cold, unforgiving stone.

I reach toward him and our fingers brush. *Don't let me die.*

He grabs ahold of my wrist and pulls me into his arms. Those black feathers smell like rain come to quench the fire. He envelops me in softness and holds me against his cold chest, soothing the blaze of the fire against my face.

Please, I whisper again. *If I die—*

I will never let that happen. Gabriel brings his lips to mine and breathes life into me once more.

Ally

Brinkley lets out a battle cry and hurls an open
tear gas canister into the trees. Then the sound of
another canister cutting through foliage, whipping
through branches. And another.

Immediately the gunfire starts. Just as Lane and I
fall into the shadow of the oak, I see someone
stumble out of the woods. Brinkley, on one knee in
the field, shoots him in the chest. A burst of blood
blooms red through the bad guy's shirt and he goes
down.

Lane's heavy arm prevents me from rising too
high off the ground.

Brinkley is down on one knee, crouching low and
picking off the guys who emerge from the smoking
trees. Coughing, hacking their lungs up. But Brinkley
doesn't see the one stumbling up from behind him.
The one gagging, but trying to steady his weapon on
the back of Brinkley's head at the same. I raise my
gun and shoot.

I miss him of course. I've never fired a gun in my life. But it gets Brinkley's attention and he turns and finishes the guy himself. Then Brinkley returns the favor and fires three shots into the tree limbs above us. I'm crouching, hands over my head. Little splinters rain off the tree, hitting my coat like soft, sporadic rain. Then I heard Brinkley's shots change direction and the splinters stop.

Two bodies hit the ground beside me in a sickening thump. Lane swears and pulls me back away from the two men who were presumably guarding Jesse from the branches above.

"You okay?" Lane asks.

I'm shaking. "Yeah. Yeah, I'm okay."

The gunfire is dying down around us. When it is silent for several heartbeats, the smoke filling the field and trees, I raise my head and call out. "Brinkley? Nikki? Jeremiah?"

No answer.

The smoke thickens, bringing with it an eerie silence. A dark shadow emerges from the white smoke, lumbering like a strange hunchback creature. I stand slowly, pushing myself out of Lane's arms. Lane raises his gun and watches the solitary figure approach.

It isn't until I hear a string of explicative vocabulary that I'm certain it's Brinkley. And the hump on his back is Gloria.

"Where are Nikki and Jeremiah?" I brush off my knees and adjust my hideous orange cap and gas mask. I try to count the bodies. I want to say six. I think I see six but the gas is thick. "Please tell me you didn't accidentally shoot them."

"I didn't," he says, his voice is muffled by the gas mask, like mine, but he is clearly offended.

"How do you know?" I ask.

"I checked the bodies. They probably fell back when they saw the gas."

"Because they didn't have masks!"

"You're the one that brought extra people!" Brinkley counters. "It isn't my fault. They said they had their own equipment."

"Go look for them," I say. "While Lane and I dig up Jesse."

Brinkley grabs me as I turn to rush across the field. "No. If they are as resourceful as you say they are, they can handle this. We'll regroup once the gas dissipates."

I'm angry. I can't believe how inconsiderate Brinkley is with his lone wolf act. He could get people killed. We needed to work *together*. That was the *plan*.

"How will we know the exact spot where she is buried?" Lane asks. He's inspecting the ground, sweeping a foot over the dirt.

"The earth should be disturbed." I help search the ground around us as the white gas begins disappearing through the trees like phantom fingers.

I'm hoping this means Jeremiah and Nikki will reappear.

"Keep your mask on," Brinkley says, pulling his own shield down.

"There," Lane points at a square patch of dirt on the ground. It's slightly darker and looks unsettled.

He starts to dig at one end of the grave. I choose the other, using my hands to scoop away the lightly packed earth.

I try not to think about the fact that I'm digging *into* a grave, the creepiness of it. I focus on Jess. *It's Jesse in there. It's Jesse in there.* Not somebody's corpse. Just Jess. And I have to get her out.

We dig faster against the dying light, and the monsters that might come with the darkness.

The shovel hits something hard. I plunge my fingers in beside the spade and wood catches my fingers.

"Back up," Brinkley says

Once I am clear of the hole, I notice the knees of my jeans are stained green-brown, and my jacket is covered in clumps of sticky grave dirt. I search the clearing, the evaporating white smoke of a misty dusk but I still don't see Jeremiah or Nikki. *Please be okay.* I'm half-convinced they were shot down while retreating and Brinkley just doesn't want to tell me.

Gloria stirs against the tree where we propped her, but her eyes remain closed.

Brinkley wedges the head of the spade into the corner of the box working it back and forth.

The wood creaks, protests as the nails are pulled out, like lips pulled back, exposing long, sharp teeth.

My hot breath on my face is unbearable, so I jump into the grave, safely below the gas circulating above and pull off my gas mask. The smell coming from the makeshift coffin is terrible.

When Jesse dies, her body expels all that is in its bowels. It's not the most dignified aspect of the replacement process, but it happens nonetheless. But by the look of it, Jesse had been sitting in her piss soaked jeans for a long while.

My vision blurs, making it hard to focus on any more details of her there. Her stiff body framed by the wooden box, framed again by the walls of dirt on each side. I'm crying. And my voice cracks behind my mask as I yell at Brinkley.

"Get her out of there," I say.

"I need your help," he says. "Both of you."

They climb into the ground and grab her feet. I gag again, dropping her leg and hurling against one of the dirt walls of the grave. I place a hand against the cold earth to steady myself. Brinkley is saying my name, impatient.

I pull my sweater up to cover my mouth and lift Jesse's legs. Lane carefully drags himself out of the hole with Jesse in tow, holding her up by lacing his arm under hers. Still holding her legs I help him heft the rest of her out. Then Brinkley reaches into the hole and pulls me up. The smoke has dissipated and both men pull of their masks.

"Turn around," I say. "Both of you, while I clean her up."

Brinkley hands me the backpack before turning around. Lane turns his back also but the expression on his face as he sees Jesse is heartbreaking. And it is hard to see her this way. Not just sad, but hard. I want to kill someone for what they've done.

I pull clean clothes, underwear, a wash cloth and a bottle of water from the bag. I pull off her pants, underwear and toss them back into the grave. I wet the washcloth and do my best to wipe her down. I'm glad I packed a second bottle, because it takes both to clean her up. I don't know what I'll do if she wakes up dehydrated. She'll just have to tough it out. If I were her and I had to choose between a serious thirst and a shit-caked ass, I'd suffer the thirst.

She's warm still and not stiff, so it's easier to manipulate her limbs into the clothing. As I edge the denim fabric up on each hip, I feel a pulse in her abdomen artery. I press my fingers to her neck to confirm. *Yes.* Her heart is beating. It is the fast, panicked pulse of someone afraid.

Don't be afraid. It's just me, baby. Just me.

"I'm done," I say. They turn around.

"The farther we get from the grave the better," Brinkley says.

"We can't drive out of here," I say. "The car is shot."

"We'll have to walk the three or four miles into town and get help," Lane says.

"Just walking would take us an hour. Dragging Jesse and Gloria will take longer," Brinkley says.

"It's the best plan we've got," I say. "We have to keep moving."

Brinkley carries Gloria across his back like a fallen comrade and Lane and I carry Jesse. But it is harder than it sounds and we aren't getting very far. Our only hope is to head back toward the SUV and town and hope we run across Jeremiah and Nikki. My back aches, sore from hefting Jesse through the woods. Then I feel the press of her hand against the back of my neck.

"Help me sit her down," I tell Lane.

"What's wrong?" Brinkley asks.

"She's breathing," I tell them. Her eyes are still closed but she is breathing. Her chest rises and falls in a slow steady rhythm. "She's waking up."

I kneel and take her hand into mine. "Jess, baby? Can you hear me?"

She squeezes my hand. My relief is immeasurable.

"We're here," Lane says. He takes her other hand.

The grip on my hand tightens and her mouth opens, sucking a deep gasping breath of air.

Her eyes fly open. She leaps to her feet, knocking us both back, surprised.

"What the hell?" Brinkley swears and tries to maneuver Gloria off his shoulders. But he's too slow and we are too stunned. Jesse tears right past us and bolts back the way we came.

"Not that way!" I scream after her as I watch her run back toward the danger. "Jesse, wait!"

But she doesn't seem to hear me. She is running as if her life depends on it.

Jesse

I can feel Ally. Ally pulsing, almost coursing through me. But how? And how is she here? I can't bear to stop and find out. If I don't keep running, I might explode. So I keep pushing, tearing through the corn. I'm aware of the shouting behind me but I can't stop. Gabriel's power is making my skin crawl like fire ants have built a colony under my flesh. In my blind panic, legs pumping, it takes me a minute to realize that the barn, the coffin, it is all behind me. All of it a dream—except for Gabriel.

And I feel someone else—not Ally. It is not unlike feeling the blood pounding in my own skull. A present pulse tuned to my own frequency somehow and I turn toward it.

I erupt into a clearing and see the house. It looms over the corn with its large white face and dark eyes reflecting the dying light. I could keep running, I could. But something about the child's pulse—and it is a child, I realize, from the feel of it—calls to me. So I slow down. I enter the house feeling the sensation of the child pulling me toward it. Not just a child. Men, women—people I know. Somehow.

It is hard to move slowly when I feel like I'm going ten directions at once. I lick my lips and swallow. I shake my hands to release tension. I do it all again—but it isn't helping.

My fingers trail over the flaking yellow wallpaper, brush cold door knobs and chipped wooden door frames of the hallway between the front door and kitchen as I try to steady and ground myself.

The kitchen is cold and hollow, the counters stained and dusty. The refrigerator unplugged is pulled away from the wall. The basement door is already open a crack so I listen for movement before opening the door wider and stepping inside toward that pulse. I don't hear anyone. The steps creak as I descend into the darkness, each foot scraping against the wood as it reaches blindly for the next ledge. It smells like damp rags and earth. And there is a chill that's settled into the concrete walls.

I reach up above and pull the string tickling the top of my head.

Dozens of bodies lie in rows. It seems so strange to see them stretched out on the basement floor. It isn't the sort of place to find dozens of sleeping people. And their breath is the only sound filling the dark space.

The one that calls to me, the little pulse echoing

my own rhythm, is lying in the floor between a man and woman. I lift her from the cold floor and realize who it is. Julia Lovett. She is soft and warm in my arms but heavy dead weight.

"I don't understand," I whisper. "Why are you here?"

Gabriel appears. I can feel him inside me yet I can also see him like a hologram projected from my chest.

He stands tall beside me with his wings tucked away. His suit is immaculate as usual with the exception of a few stray down feathers clinging to the dark sleeves. His hair is shaggy and shoulder length, falling into his beautiful green eyes.

I can't look away from his face. "Who are they?"

He wants more power.

"Then why take them?" I ask. "They aren't doorways. I thought only the partis whatevers are doorways."

Can't you feel him? The power inside me swells and I almost drop the child in my arms. I do hit the ground, a jarring pains shooting through me when my knees connect with the cement.

"No, no more," I beg and still manage to hold the child.

But he doesn't cut off the power. He dials it up higher. I cry out and clutch Julia tighter. Tears stream down my face. It is almost like seeing something beautiful or moving and crying from the sight of it. It isn't pain or sadness. Intensity. It is simply intensity.

Quit fighting me, Gabriel commands.

"You're hurting me," I whimper. "Please stop. *Please.*"

He dials it back a notch and a small clarity comes. I open my eyes and focus on the people nightmaring on the basement floor. I can only really fixate on the colors of their clothes—a blue sweater. A green coat. Until more details, rather impressions come from the roll of power. It's as if the power is probing the bodies like insect feelers, then giving me the data.

"He is trying to *make* a door to my power," I say. I glimpse the soft green flames burning inside them. Not quite the red of the living, nor the blue of NRD. The soft green of near death that remains for a person once they've been saved. And a few flames *feel* familiar. Like I know them somehow. But as I search each face I become more certain they are strangers, all except the child in my arms. So the others? "But not just my power."

He will terminate them once he realizes he cannot gain power this way.

"We can't leave them here," I say. After my lovely time with Caldwell, I could just imagine what he had in mind for these poor people. And they didn't do anything to deserve this. All they wanted was more time. And so do I.

He can feel you.

It isn't much of a warning, but at least Gabriel manages to say something before the pressure changes. Someone strong tugs hard. It's as if the rope around the power inside me is yanked hard.

Caldwell.

He is a cold northern wind blowing across the desert. Gabriel stiffens and Caldwell's threatening hold lessens. The tension is released in the line and I know that somehow Gabriel has done something to protect us from Caldwell. Or was it me? I'm losing my ability to distinguish between the two.

"He'll come find me now that he knows I'm out of the box," I realize.

Yes.

I push myself to my feet and climb the stairs quickly back to the kitchen, still clutching the sleeping child. But I freeze when I hear a sound above me. Someone upstairs is moving in an unseen room.

I don't so much as breathe as I strain to hear.

"We have to hurry," I whisper, watching the ceiling. And Julia stirs in my arms. "We're almost out of time."

Ally

My heart hammers wildly. I'm huffing white pillars of smoke out of my mouth as I tear through the woods after her. Jesse is not an athletic girl. I go to the gym more in a week that she does in six months but she is flying through these woods. It isn't natural, the speed she is maintaining and yet I'm watching her grow smaller and smaller in front of me. Lane is beside me, trying to keep pace and he has a small lead on me because of his longer legs, but he can't catch her any more than I can.

I marvel over the fact that Jesse can move at all so soon after a death. I've watched her moan and whine for days and days after a replacement leaves her stiff and grumpy. And here she is scaling fallen trees and branches like a monkey in its natural habitat.

"Jesse, stop!" I say. I'm desperate for her to slow down. The distance between us terrifies me especially after we break through the clearing, past her grave into the opposite trees, the ones we knew to be full of Caldwell's henchman. But she doesn't stop here. It isn't the grave she came back for. It is something else in the woods.

My side burns. I can't keep the pace I'm using to follow her. And at this pace she is gaining more and more ground.

"Jesse, please!" I call out. I don't know who might hear us on this side of the clearings. I'm still waiting for Jeremiah and Nikki to pop up or for one of us to trip over their bodies. In the woods it is so much darker. The last traces of sun are unable to penetrate the uppermost branches.

Then she disappears. I can't see her at all.

"Jesse!"

"Damn, do you see her?" Lane asks. His breath is as panicked as mine.

"No."

I run harder and harder but she isn't there. Then I see the break in the trees, the light suggesting a clearing or at least a break in the woods of some kind. I slow just a tad as I emerge, taking a precautionary look around, but it's just an open field lined with corn. Thick high stalks of it. Then I hear the sound of the stalks swaying and I look up. A few yards ahead, something is knocking them down.

Jesse.

"Where did she go?" he asks me.

"Shhhh," I say. I motion for him to be still and quiet. Thank God he listens.

I take a sharp left toward the sound of breaking stalks. This is terrifying, being in a cornfield as dusk runs its icy fingers over the earth's collarbone. I don't look anywhere but straight ahead, because the sound of corn rustling is making me sick with fear. I half believe that if I look to the left or right of me I will see some unimaginable horror in the corn, leaping toward me.

When the corn ends suddenly, giving itself over to a grassy front yard, it is like coming up for air. I stop long enough to clutch the side of my burning ribs. It's a large white farm house in the middle of nowhere. God, this is a horror movie waiting to happen.

But then I see Jess, climbing the steps of the porch and entering the house. A house I am certain she's never entered in her life.

"Jesse!" I hunker low, looking left and right but I don't see anyone. Lane mimics my movements.

He must feel as exposed as I do. "Why the hell did she go into that house?"

"I don't know." And am I really going to enter a strange house in the middle of nowhere just as night falls? *Really?*

I make Lane go first and he pushes the front door open carefully and the groaning creak is hideous. Straight ahead is a door leading to a kitchen. I know it's the kitchen because I can see the white sink illuminated beneath the window. To the right is a staircase leading up. On the left is an open archway leading to a room. It looks a bit like a living room or study: furniture and books. A fireplace that looks cold and unused, coated in a dusting of gray soot and ash. Ruins from years of neglect.

I place one foot on the step to ascend the stairs, thinking I hear movement up there when a cold hand grabs my wrist. I open my mouth to scream my head off but the cold hand releases my wrist and clamps itself over my mouth.

Jesse.

It's Jesse covering my mouth. I want to throw my arms around her. Squeeze the living shit out of her and maybe even cover her face with kisses—to hell with Lane. But I can't because she is holding a child.

"Jesse," Lane whispers. He is just as visibly relieved as I am.

"Don't go up there," she says. And she takes a step away from me, urging me away from the stairs by giving me room to step away. I don't like the looks she gives the ceiling above our head. "It's not Caldwell but someone is hiding up there."

Jesse holds a little girl. And not just any girl. Regina's little girl. I need no other evidence to know this is Caldwell's place in one way or another.

"How did Julia get here?" I ask.

Jesse offers me the little girl and I take her. She is heavy in my arms and I expect her to stir or wake but she doesn't. I use a gentle finger to pull open her eyelid and realize she isn't sleeping. But she is too warm to be dead and little soft breaths puff from her nose. She is drugged to unconsciousness. Maybe on the same sedative Gloria is on.

"Caldwell's been capturing people who've been replaced and he's trying to use them to——" Jesse begins. "——to make their replacers 'wake up' or to access their power somehow. But he's about to realize he can't, and when he does, he'll kill them."

I think of the list Nikki and I poured over searching for a connection.

"There are more downstairs," she says.

"More people?" Lane asks and the second her arms are free he pulls Jesse to him. Normally, I can't bear it. But it's an awkward embrace with Jesse's face pinched in annoyance. And that makes it bearable.

Jesse pulls away from him and motions for us to follow her. Lane brings up the rear, still holding the gun Brinkley gave him ages ago and I'm behind Jesse holding Julia.

There is a basement door inside the kitchen, just past where the hallway and kitchen meet. She opens the old, chipped door and enters. I want to stop her. Scream for her to, but floorboards above my head creak and I don't dare. Someone is in this house and here we are creeping around. What the *hell*? I want to get out of this house, not descend into its bowels.

Jesse pulls me into the dark, then Lane and closes the door behind us. For a moment we are in pitch black darkness with only rickety shallow steps beneath our feet. I'm terrified I'll fall with Julia in my arms, but then the light flares to life and I realize Jesse isn't beside me as I thought she was. She'd silently slipped down the stairs and pulled the rope chain before I'd realized she'd even moved.

At the base of the stairs I gasp, and hug Regina's little girl closer to me.

I don't count them all. They lay in rows, arranged, uniform. The fact that nothing else is in the basement tells me that furniture, old boxes, the things that collect in a basement in a normal house were removed to make room for these bodies or they never existed because this is a ghost house, some kind of phantom illusion. The two small windows at ground level on the far concrete wall are covered with aluminum foil, blocking out all light.

"Are they alive?" Lane whispers.

The anger boils inside me. "We don't have a car. And we'll need vans or something to move this many people."

Jeremiah should really be here. Where the hell is he? I was going to kill Brinkley.

"What did you mean he is looking for a way to get to 'people like you'?" Lane asks her.

She doesn't answer. And I have a feeling this is

connected to the *special* traits Jeremiah was worried about but I just can't deal with that right now. One problem at a time.

"One by one," I say. "We'll have to carry them out and hide them in the cornfield. That way if Caldwell comes he won't be able to find them, for a while at least. Then we will call for help."

"Who will we call?" Jesse asks.

"I know people who can help."

Nikki. Jeremiah. And if they are dead then Parish will know what to do. We just have to get somewhere with some cell reception.

Lane kneels beside a body. I recognize him as one of Jesse's replacements. Frank, I believe. A construction worker. Jesse watches me though the dark of the poorly lit basement. It isn't the horrible animal eyes I saw earlier. It's just Jesse. Yet—

Then she breaks her intense gaze. "He will be here before we can move them all."

"Who? Caldwell?" Lane asks. Jess nods.

Lane hefts Frank from the ground and starts to carry him out of the basement. With Julia Lovett sleeping innocently in my arms, her moist breath warming my neck, I follow him.

I cast one last look at the swelling darkness, and listen to the vibrations of their unified breath. We are almost out of the basement when someone opens the door.

All three of us freeze, panicked by grey light from the kitchen. But I recognize the face.

"Oh thank God," I say and squeeze the unconscious child in my arms. I ignore the burn in my arms and heft her higher.

"Brinkley," I whisper. "Where is Gloria?"

"Here," a meek voice says. Another shadow peeks around the edge of the kitchen door and relief washes over me.

"The drug wore off?" Lane asks.

Brinkley grunts. "Thank God. I couldn't have carried her another step."

"How did you find us?" Lane asks. He steps into the light, still holding the large man. He's strong. I'll give him that.

"I saw you go in," Gloria says. And she doesn't mean with her own two eyes.

"You weren't out for very long," Lane says. "Shitty sedative."

"How long?" Jesse asks.

"I'm not sure," Brinkley looks at me and Lane for confirmation. "Less than an hour."

Jesse's brow furrows in concentration. "He couldn't have moved me from Heath to Chicago in an hour. Either he kept sedating me or he can move with people."

"What are you talking about?" Lane asks.

She shakes her head. "Never mind."

"You're just in time to carry some bodies," I say.

Jesse takes the lead, cutting a path through the high corn. We move adjacent from the front door, left at a diagonal. In the middle, Jesse lies a child down then turns and heads back to the house alone. Brinkley, Lane, and Gloria do the same for the ones they are carrying. Gloria struggles with her bad shoulder but I don't chastise her. If someone had cut one of my arms off I'd still be trying to haul Julia out of here. I could hardly chastise her this once for pushing herself.

I hesitate. "It's chilly out here. We can't just lay them in the dirt."

"We just need time for the sedation to wear off. Then they can walk on their own," Lane says. "This is the best plan that we have."

I can't argue. So I lay Julia down beside the woman Jesse carried and straighten her little jacket. I button it around her and pull up her knee socks, making sure her little legs are covered at least. Then I follow the others back into the house.

It's harder than it sounds, carrying unconscious bodies up stairs. I heave, and more than once I am *certain* that whoever is upstairs must hear us. "He" must hear feet slapping at the steps, *kalump, kalump,* as we struggle (some of us more than others) to drag the people to safety.

An explosion rocks the house. I scream. I don't

mean to, but I scream. I'm terrified. I rush into the house and see Gloria and Brinkley coming out of its mouth and entering the corn with one body between them. I rush into the house and find a second body abandoned on the floor. Someone must have dropped her and ran when the explosion rocked and I drag this woman out into the corn myself.

"Where is Jesse?"

"Upstairs," Brinkley groans as he lowers his person to the ground and then helps get the woman off my shoulders. Thirty. We only saved about thirty, give or take, if I missed one or miscounted. That means at least ten bodies are still in the basement.

"Upstairs?" I run toward the house. I hear Brinkley swear and tear through the corn after me, saying my name. But I still reach the house first.

"Jesse? Jesse!" I scream her name. No need to be stealthy now.

But she doesn't answer.

The house is burning and she does not answer. I watch paralyzed, the black smoke funneling into the sky.

Jesse

I don't want to die.

I accept that I saw it as my only way out once upon a time and even in all the death replacements in the years that followed, I was still running. But now—

Now I feel my desire to live even more strongly than I did the night I managed to kill Eddie.

I don't want to die.

I won't let that happen Gabriel assures me but that doesn't make me feel any better about taking the stairs one at a time up toward the sound of feet pacing in the upstairs rooms.

Every time I bring my foot down the wood creaks and my heart speeds up, pounding. Why does this house have to be so freaking old?

I'm so shaky and jittery with the power I stop and lean against the fading wallpaper.

Can you pull out or something? I ask him in my head. I feel so jittery and shaky. My hands tremble in a soft *tap pat tap* against the wall supporting me. *I do not want to go all Rachel and carve myself up okay? I need you to manage this somehow. Gradual increases. Anything. I just feel like I could rip my eyes out if it meant relief.*

The power decreases. Not as much as I'd like. My skin is still unbearably itchy and burns and I feel like I might piss myself, dancing that fine line between extreme need and loss of control, but at least I can think. At least I don't feel like I should run through a solid wall and brain myself.

My shoes scrape the top step in a last shaky lift. A decaying rug runs the length of the hallway toward a door at the end. It once must have been a beautiful vibrant red but it's now more of a rust color. Just beyond its dull frayed tassels, the door is cracked. Through the crack I glimpse a man pacing back and forth. His shadow moving along the wall, large and looming behind him.

I take another shaking step toward him and then another.

"Who's there?" he demands. It isn't a man's voice. And I think this is the only reason I can bear to proceed.

I reach out and press my fingertips against the chipped white wood. Splinters pull at my fingertips as I push more and more weight against the wood door. With my palm flat against the scratchy surface, I force the crack to widen. A slow groaning creak announces me.

He's just a kid.

He can't be older than sixteen with his dark hair and eyes. He wears the same black fatigues as all of Caldwell's men, but he is so scrawny the clothing hangs loosely around his slumped shoulders. There is something sunken about his face. He's got the look of someone who is sick and has been for a long time.

When he sees me those huge brown eyes double to the size of tea cup saucers.

"Hi." I even manage a little smile.

"Not you," he says.

I hold my hands up in a sign of peace. "I'm not here to hurt you."

And if he'd wanted to hurt me he wouldn't have called out to me when I was in the hallway. He would have waited to jump me or something. He's just a kid. A scared kid.

The boy's lip begins to quiver. His shoulders slump even more. When the boy coughs again I notice the deep puffy pockets under his eyes.

"Are you sick?" I ask. I ease into the room. It is a bedroom, disheveled and lived in. Take out boxes are piled over the dresser and overflow from the small wastebasket in the corner. The bed is rumpled and slept in. A small bag with clothes protruding from partially closed zippers tells me he's been staying in this room for a while.

"Yes I'm sick," he says and it's with such hatred and derision, as if he thinks it's my fault. My mind still struggles to focus against the power rolling me over and over like a wave.

"You look really sick," I tell him. I let my concern show. "Do you need something?"

Caldwell appears behind the boy. *Snap* and there he is. It's as if I blinked and in that instance he positioned himself between the boy and the window behind him. His pristine appearance doesn't fit the decay of the room, not in his soft gray suit and red tie. He should be on television, not in a dilapidated farm house in the middle of nowhere.

Another voice breaks into my head, not Gabriel's.

Caldwell won't save you if you let her go. He promised to heal you but he won't if you fail him.

"You can't heal the sick," I say aloud. I look right at him because I want the boy to turn around and see him too. "No replacement can."

"Shut up!" the boy screams. He pulls a gun from beneath a rumpled pillow on the bed and points it at me. "Get out of my head you devil!"

She wants to hurt you, the other voice warns.

"No I don't," I argue. "Turn around."

It's a trick. She wants you to look behind you so she can get the gun the moment you turn your back.

Now I understand. It is Caldwell's voice. And those words are the lies he's feeding to the boy.

But why project them into my head too? Why let me hear?

She is one of them and she is here to kill you.

"No," I say argue. "That's a lie."

The boy's eyes are like glass marbles, reflective and hollow. Caldwell has him. How many people can Caldwell enter like this? Control, confuse and manipulate? One? Ten? A hundred? How many minds twisted under the weight of lies and false promises of salvation? The boy doesn't even hear me.

The boy lifts the gun from my chest higher, right between my eyes.

This is a kill shot. Even for me.

I don't have time to react. I don't have time to realize I can't break the spell Caldwell has on the boy. And he knows it—the sick smile on his face tells me so. One instant my brains are about to be all over the peeling wall paper and then—

Gabriel waits for nothing.

He throws the door wide and the voltage erupts through my body. I'm screaming from the pain of it. It's not the sort of pain you feel if injured. More like the way a tooth aches from an exposed nerve—times a thousand. Raw, sensory overload.

I squeeze my eyes shut against the shivers of agony raking my spine and I hit the ground on my hands and knees. I'm screaming and screaming but it isn't helping.

"Gabriel, please!"

You are stronger than you think.

I don't feel strong. The live wires inside me are burning me alive and I don't know what is happening except that it is Gabriel's doing, not Caldwell or the boy. I have no idea where those two are or what I must look like to them in my agony.

Then it stops. Just as suddenly as the flood of burning pain overtook me, it's gone. The connection between Gabriel and I goes slack and I collapse completely to the floor whimpering. I shake and shiver. Blinking back water as if a great wind has just blown through me.

Gabriel tries to get my attention. *Get up.*

But I don't believe I can move. The fetal position in the only position I can manage just now. It takes several long moments before I can focus on the old, peeling wallpaper. A certain hiss and crackling is strange. And the heat. I feel heat coming from somewhere.

When I open my eyes the whole side of the house is gone.

Gone.

It's as if the boy turned into The Hulk and jumped through the window taking Caldwell and the rest of the wall with him. Boards and planks hang from all angles, broken and jagged like teeth. Outside I can see the trees through the curling smoke fuming from the room and the haze of heat escaping.

The bed and walls are on fire. And in none of it

do I see the boy or Caldwell.

I desperately search the flames until I start choking on the smoke. Oh my God, I did this. I did this.

Get out, Gabriel warns.

"But the kid!"

Get out!

I hold onto the doorframe and pull myself up, stumbling into the hallway hacking and wheezing. It isn't until I'm down the stairs and out the front door that I dare to draw my first breaths of clean air, great big lung fulls. Tears sting the corners of my eyes and my throat feels as if I've jabbed a hot poker down it.

"Ally?" I ask him. I left her in the basement with the others. I have to go back.

Alive.

I turn toward the corn. The stalks sway gently as if whispering my name. The heat from the house wafts against my back and blows my hair into my face. The last light of day has been replaced with thick shadows.

Jesse. It isn't the corn calling me down off the steps. *Jesse I've waited so long for this.*

Caldwell's pale face emerges, first a phantom before his dark limbs take shape. And Gabriel doesn't wait for him to pull any tricks. He fills me, pushing like a hand into a glove. And I have only a moment to feel Ally and the others behind me before Gabriel takes me completely.

No. I can't let him throw a firebomb with her so close. *No!*

You are capable of so much more than you think, Gabriel pleads. *You must trust me.*

Caldwell drags the burned body of the boy beside him and it is enough to make me collapse.

Only Gabriel's power holds me up on my feet as more and more of them emerge from the shadows.

Caldwell's men with their guns raised at us.

I can feel Ally so close now but I don't look back. I can't afford to take my eyes off of Caldwell for an instant. Not now that I am the only one standing between him and the people I love.

OK, I tell Gabriel. *I trust you.*

Ally

The house is engulfed in flames. Bits of wood are collapsing, smoldering and the rest is gone. I feel the heat rolling against my back as Lane and I scramble away from the steps. But as I turn away from the porch I see Jesse.

I start to rush toward her but Brinkley grabs the back of my coat.

"No, no, wait," he whispers. "Look."

Then I see them. The black shadows moving in the corn. The corn itself sways back and forth as the sharks cut closer to us.

Then I see him. Caldwell emerging from the corn, dragging beside him a dead body by the hair. At first all I can see is him, my mind absorbing and reconciling the many faces I have in my mind of this man: Caldwell, the TV personality. Caldwell as Jesse's father. Caldwell as Eric Sullivan, who I saw only in photographs, which Jesse lovingly showed me when we were children. All of it coming together in one very real moment as I first lay eyes on the man.

Then I see the dead body.

A dead body. But it isn't someone we know. A flush of shame burns my cheeks at the relief I feel. Men are emerging from the corn around him. Maybe three or four dozen—or more—I can't tell. I can only see their black shapes separating from the stalks, menacing shadows slinking towards us. They don't shoot us. Or sedate us. For now they are just watching. Guns raised, they wait.

"He was supposed to guard this house," Caldwell drawls. He releases the dead body and steps over it. "But he was afraid to confront you. *Afraid*, hiding upstairs like a cowering dog."

I look at the man. At his dead eyes.

"I only gave him two jobs. Sedate," Caldwell says. "And annihilate any unwanted guests. It was hardly too much to ask for, now was it?"

Where is Gloria? Nikki? Jeremiah? And where the hell did these men come from? There are no cars here. No sign of transportation. How will we get away? Because that is what I want to do. Take Jesse and run.

"You look well, Alice," Caldwell says. His grin stops me cold. "It must be the physical exertion. It adds color to your cheeks. And what were you doing to exhaust yourself so thoroughly?"

"He can read your mind," Jesse says. Her shoulders are taut, tense. I don't know what she is waiting for. But something subtle is changing around her. As strange as it sounds, I swear I can feel it.

Lane stiffens beside me.

"Oh, there isn't a clever thought in your head," Caldwell says to Lane. "It's Alice here that interests me. What have you been doing with yourself these days, my dear?"

I don't gratify him with an answer. And I can't hold his gaze. Even though he is several feet away from me, I can feel the pull. The magnetism. It is a snake's gaze. The snake that lures the mouse into its mouth with the slight sway of its body. I know better.

"You are a smart, *smart* girl," he says. "If only you hadn't caused me so much grief I'd have liked to get to know you better."

Something happens. Jesse makes the smallest of movements. Then I see the pale purple shimmer.

Caldwell must see it too because he lifts his hands and I think he is going to touch her. I step forward again, ready to run at him, to do anything to keep him from touching her but Brinkley twists his fist around my coat more firmly.

"Look," Lane whispers.

Caldwell runs his fingers over something iridescent. Like water, it ripples and glides.

His grin widens as he presses harder, his fingers flattening as if pressed against a hard surface. He can't penetrate it, whatever it is, and when he realizes this he laughs with pure abandon as if delighted.

"You do not disappoint," Caldwell says to Jesse.

And if it wasn't for the wide, maniacal smile on his face, making him look hungry and desperate, this could be mistaken for fatherly praise. "Oh what I could do with your gifts."

Again Caldwell's hand slides admiringly over the barrier, the force field, a *magnetic* field. The one I saw between her and the tree during Julia's replacement. The reason for her 100% record.

Caldwell murmurs to Jesse, speaking low like a lover. "I will have what I want from you. One way or another."

The hell you will, I think. And I hope he can hear me.

Jesse doesn't answer. She is only holding his gaze, but I can see in the blazing firelight of the house behind us.

He moves.

It must be a trick of the light because one minute, Caldwell is standing on the other side of Jesse's barrier, then the next he is in front of me. *Right* in front of me. I hadn't even seen him move. Like New York to San Diego in a single bound.

Caldwell reaches to snatch me by the throat or strike me. Brinkley and Lane both come forward to stop him. But everyone stops because the same violet shimmer ripples over me protecting me from Caldwell.

"What the hell?" Brinkley marvels. Lane looks like he wants to say something too, his mouth open but speechless.

Caldwell throws his head back and the maniacal laughter erupting from his throat is enough to make my hairs stand on end. "That is amazing!"

Caldwell tries to push his fingers through the barrier surrounding me, to grab hold of me and though his fingers are dangerously close they don't reach me. It doesn't give. Instead his arms quiver, flexing with his efforts.

"You've replaced Alice, haven't you?" He turns his animated expression toward Jesse but she still won't give him the satisfaction of speaking. "You've tainted her field by replacing her and that is how you control it," he says, running vampire pale fingers over the barrier surrounding me, like trailing his hand through warm water. "Because it is her field I feel, not yours. You've just made it solid with your own power."

"Get away from her," Jesse says.

Her warm breath rolls like smoke from between her lips and collides with the chilly night. The house is still burning and I'm thinking of the remaining bodies, if we could still run in and save them. But even from this distance I can feel the heat of the flames and my throat burns from the thick smoke.

And then there is Jesse—I can't leave her.

"There's always another way," Caldwell says. And he turns on Lane.

Shots fire. Jesse screams, a piercing shriek of terror.

Brinkley jumps from the porch and sort of rolls but it isn't as smooth as it would have been in the movies. Lane just falls off of the porch, shot. As Jesse runs toward Lane, I see the purple wall around me fade.

I'm not shielded from Caldwell anymore though I am dangerously close to him. The second I realize this, I turn and run.

Caldwell catches my movement and grabs the back of my coat and a bit of my hair because of how long it is. He has a death grip on me when gunfire cuts close. It isn't Caldwell's gunfire.

I look up to see Nikki and Jeremiah with reinforcements. My relief is immeasurable.

Caldwell takes a step back and is gone. Just gone as if he never stood there at all.

Nikki wraps her arms around me but I don't let her hold on to me. I'm turning wildly to make sure Caldwell doesn't reappear.

"Did you get Jesse?" Jeremiah asks. Flames dance in his glasses as he looks at the engulfed house.

"Yes and I think we found the people from your list," I tell him. "We moved them to the field. You'll need to order transport. And there are still about ten more inside. They don't have NRD. But I don't think you can go back inside for them."

"I can," Nikki says.

I grab ahold of her.

She grins and gives me a deep kiss. "I told you you'd like me."

She disappears before I could say more.

"Did you see Caldwell disappear?" I ask

"New York to San Diego," he says. He presses his earbud. Whatever he heard makes him run into the house after Nikki. Gunfire erupts in the corn all around us. Caldwell's men and Jeremiah's men clash but I don't see Caldwell. Jesse is still bent over Lane crying, but he isn't shot in the head. I am about to check on them when I hear crying, the soft, frightened whimpering of a child. And I still don't know where Caldwell or Gloria or Brinkley is.

I run through the dark to the place where I laid Julia down.

I cut two more rights around tall stalks and I see her in the firelight filtered through the corn. Julia is awake, sitting up with her face on her knees as she rocks herself back and forth. I lift her from the dirt and whisper gently into her ears.

"It's okay, baby. Hush, hush. You're okay."

"Mommy," she whimpers.

"I'll take you home to your mommy, okay? Don't cry."

She cries harder. "They're dead!"

"No, they're just sleeping," I say, but everyone smells terrible. I am not surprised she would mistake them for dead.

"I want to go home. I want my Mommy."

"Look at me," I say. I push hair away from her eyes and see her face is grubby and snotty and little strands are stuck to her wet cheeks. "Do you recognize me?"

She sniffs. "You came to my birthday party."

I nod and smile. "Yes, I came to your party. So that means I know where you live, right?"

"We had cake."

"We did, yes." Part of the house collapses and I worry about Nikki. *Please get out of there.* I hold her tighter and she wraps her little fists around my neck. "So you believe me when I say I can take you home, right?"

Caldwell steps out of the corn in front of us. I turn to run but he is behind me. It's like a bad dream. A hallucination. I put Julia down on her feet and step in front of her. I don't want her near him. I push Julia farther away, but she clings to the back of my legs. I'm pinned. Because I can't move an inch further without touching Caldwell. And I can't take a step back or I will fall on Julia and knock us both down.

Caldwell strikes me. He hits me hard across the face and the night erupts with stars. I am knocked off my feet and Julia topples to the dirt behind me. She is frantic and her cries reach the hysterical volume that only a child can achieve.

Caldwell turns just for a moment as if to strike her and I grab him. I grab his arms and turn his back toward me. He grabs my shirt in one hand and he punches me. The stars above whirl and slide. The fire coming from the house swirls too, and coupled with the starlight, I feel like I am on a carnival ride, one of the topsy turvy ones that sling you this way then that, reducing the crisp night sky to nothing more than an impressionistic painting, a colorful smear. I close my eyes.

When you protect her, you're protecting Chaos and Destruction. Caldwell's voice slithers through my mind, slimy and cold. *You don't know what she is, Alice. You have no idea what she will do to this world.*

He hits me with a flood of images. So hard, so overpowering that I sink to my knees, only to have him hold me up. Images of Jesse as a devil, feral, destroying the world. An image of a man, a beautiful winged man blowing a horn is superimposed over burning cities, dead bodies. So much death. So much destruction.

"Keep your stock images to yourself," I say. "I know you're a liar and I know Jesse would never do those things."

"You don't know what she is," he says. "Or what

she's capable of."

"She's not a monster," I say. *I would never let her become a monster.*

"I know." He grabs my throat with both hands and squeezes.

Jesse

It takes an eternity for Lane to fall off of the porch to the ground below. Another eternity before I can force my legs to move toward him. I'm already running before I realize that horrible sound is my own scream. Lane is already on the ground when I reach him. The ground is cold and damp as I inch my hands under his neck and cradle his head.

"No, no, no," I whine.

Lane coughs blood, spitting it all over his chin. I wipe it away with a thumb but it only smears dark red like war paint across his rough stubble.

Ally screams and I look up to see Caldwell grab her by the back of her coat.

Gabriel, do something!

But he doesn't have to. People appear out of nowhere, guns blazing and Caldwell runs like the bastard he is.

"Jess," Lane whispers. He is twining his hand in mine. "I'm so glad you're okay, baby."

"Shut up, stupid. You've got a *hole* in your throat," I say. I look at the wound in his neck where the bullet tore open his carotid. So much blood. I press my hands against it but it isn't working. He's going to bleed out and die. He'll die.

He'll live.

"Shut up!" I yell at Gabriel.

Gunfire erupts around us. Momentarily bursts of light spark in the night as the good guy reinforcements chase Caldwell deeper into the corn. Gabriel shields me, standing between me and the others, wings spread wide. And by proxy he protects Lane from a few stray bullets. The purple shimmering around me, tightening in a warm glow. But there is little point in protecting Lane from bullets now.

I kiss Lane's cheeks, his forehead. He gurgles and I don't know if that was supposed to be a laugh or if he is simply choking on his own blood.

"Quit trying to talk," I tell him.

Ally screams.

My head snaps up and I look through the corn toward the sound. Sparks of gunfire can be seen deep in the corn, in the rows that aren't illuminated by the burning house. But her scream didn't come from that direction. It came from the left.

He has her, Gabriel warns.

Then I hear the hysterical screams of a child.

I look down into Lane's face and press a hand to his cooling forehead. His eyes are so big. So desperate.

"Don't go," he says.

He'll live. She will not.

I kiss his lips and taste sweat and blood.

"Please," he gurgles. He grabs at me as if to hold me close. "Stay with me."

"You'll live," I tell him. "I promise. You'll be okay." *Assuming no one runs over here and cuts off your head or blows out your brains while you're all vulnerable,* I thought. But I had the good sense not to say this.

I pull my hand from his and he is surprisingly strong considering he must have lost most of his blood at this point.

"Don't be afraid," I say over the sound of gunfire. "When you wake up I'll be there."

He doesn't care. He reaches for me anyway, vainly trying to sit up but managing only to lift his head. The wound in his neck opens wider and bleeds more.

The child screams again and I can hear her cries in between the lulls of shouting, gunfire and chaos.

"I'm sorry," I tell Lane and then I run to find Ally.

I can feel the pulse of her long before I see her. That distant drumming that harmonizes with my own. And I can even feel Julia's smaller, separate beat. I cut through a row of corn, silken stalks slapping at my cheeks and realize I'm at the edge between the trees and the corn. A figure crouches beneath me. A gun raised and pointing at me before I can even react.

"Go on," Gloria says.

"But you've been shot," I say. I look at her face, damp with sweat despite the cold air. The wound in her gut bleeds and bleeds. There's a dead body beside her, face down in the dirt but I can't really see him in the dark of the trees.

"You're dying." And I could sense it.

"Go *on*," she says. The red of her blood shines like slick oil on the back of her hand and fingers. She points me in the right direction but I stumble into a tree. "Go on or you'll have to bury her too."

Don't let her die, I command to Gabriel as if he has power over these things. *Don't you dare let Gloria die.*

He says nothing.

The air is heavy with the scent of ash and gunpowder. It's like the scent of fireworks after all the explosions have ended—but more metallic.

I turn a corner and I see them.

He is choking Ally. Then he hits her in the face twice, her head rocking back.

Julia clings to her legs and screams. He could kill her with any one of his gifts. He could mind fuck her into oblivion but he chooses his fists. Why? *Why?*

Then it occurs to me he could be doing both.

I slam my fist into his jaw. I hit him twice more and see the wild fire blaze in his eyes as he tastes his own pain. No one has dealt him physical pain in a long time and I can tell. The shock and surprise. The fury.

Protect her, I tell Gabriel and he does. He reaches out for Ally's drumbeat and strikes that cord. He envelops her, wings out, protecting her and the child.

It is all the distraction Caldwell needs to regain his focus.

He hits me and I hit the dirt. Something in my shoulder snaps with the force of his blow. Dirt is blown up in my tumble and gets into my eyes. I cough as another blow connects with my ribs and I feel the explosion of pain. My ears are ringing, blocking out the gunfire, the girl's crying and Caldwell's own heaving breathing—leaving me with only a high-pitched whine.

Then I think the mind rape will come. The snap, or earthquake, but Ally puts herself between us. She can barely move, but she won't let him get close. But then another blow rocks me and for a moment the world goes black.

"Jesse? Jesse!" Ally yells. I hit the ground, scraping my hands on the little rocks in the soil.

He snapped and the world went dark. But it didn't work on Ally. And I recover sooner than he intended by the look of confusion on his face. The power is new to him. Lucky for us.

Then everything changes.

I see the gun first. Held by a disembodied hand, the muzzle is pressed firmly against Caldwell's temple. Brinkley in his leather jacket like a debonair James

Dean come to save the day. Brinkley fires a shot without hesitating.

But Caldwell disappears.

When I see his face again it is only for an instant as he turns those eyes on me.

It isn't the eyes, it's the hands that matter. The two white hands that close around Brinkley's neck and twist before he has a chance to change the direction of his gun.

It's as if someone has yanked out my engine. I sputter and come to a complete stop. I jump forward but Caldwell is gone. I turn around and around but he doesn't reappear.

I turn and see Ally kneeling beside Brinkley. Julia weeping and holding onto her coat tails. Ally puts her face in her hands and that is all the answer I need.

Brinkley is dead. Dead. The man that pulled me from the wreck of my old life and gave me a job. A purpose. The man who tried to prepare me for all of this.

Dead, *dead*. The man who stood beside me, protected me even after the danger grew. The man who'd rather desert his job, his loyalty to his brothers-in-arms than to leave me at the mercy of Caldwell.

"No," I say. I kneel beside him and I put my hands on his neck, at the weird angle where the flesh bulges from a displaced vertebrae. "*No*."

"You can't replace him," Ally says. "He's gone."

"I can," I say again as if saying it over and over will bring him back.

"Jesse," she warns. She pulls me away from the body up to my feet. She shakes me.

"I can save him," I say and fall to my knees again. "I save everyone."

I can save him. *Gabriel, save him.*

Gabriel stands over me with those brilliant green eyes, his shaggy hair fallen into his face.

I search the rows for Caldwell but he hasn't come back.

"I'm still here!" I scream into the night. "Don't you want me? You wanted a fight, well I'm right here you, coward!"

"Jesse," Ally shakes me again, pulling me up. "We can't stay here."

"Come on!" I scream. I scream until my throat burns and head pounds. "I'm right fucking here!"

But Caldwell doesn't come back.

Ally

Jesse is hysterical that Caldwell got away. It takes strength I don't have just to drag her back toward the others. At the line where the trees and cornrows meet, a group of people congregate.

Gloria is on the ground with someone patching up her stomach. Jeremiah stands beside her. And as soon as I see him I realize the gunfire has stopped. How I could have missed the eerie silence I don't know but now men are simply walking the corn rows, dressed in black mission gear. Two men lift a dead body and carry him out of sight. Another stoops to pick up a discarded shell.

Jeremiah sees me first. "Caldwell?"

"New York to San Diego," I say, feeling cold and stiff as I approach the little group.

Jeremiah's jaw clenches then relaxes. "We have Lane safe and ready for transport and we recovered 48 innocent people. That counts for something."

"Does it?" Jesse asks. But I don't think anyone hears her but me.

"We all knew this would be a long battle," Jeremiah says.

For the first time, I see the body in the grass, hidden in the tree's shadow. "Who is that?"

"Micah Delaney," Gloria says. As soon as Gloria sees me she swears. "Your face—"

"Don't tell me. I don't want to know," I say. I nod toward the body again. "This is good news. He's been the root of our trouble since this began with Caldwell."

"We are safer," Gloria admits, hissing as the medic digs deeper into her wound. "But not good news."

"Were you close?" Jeremiah asks. His voice is full of compassion.

"A long time ago," she says. But she doesn't need to. The way she fingers the hair beside the gunshot wound in his head says everything. It's tender, undeterred.

A silence falls on us until Jeremiah takes a step forward and gingerly turns my face in the firelight. "Your nose is broken and this cut by your eye looks bad." It was probably my nose ring that scratched my eye when Caldwell ripped it out.

The medic moves as if he plans to come to my rescue.

I raise a hand. "I can wait. I want someone to look at Jesse. Good luck getting her to sit still."

Kory M. Shrum

Nikki appears at Jeremiah's call. I'm relieved to see her, unharmed. "It's done. The transport will move them to the Chicago base. We have six vans to use. I designated one for the bodies."

"Two," Jeremiah interjects. "We will have to use two vans for the bodies."

"We don't have the space," Nikki argues.

"We will have to make space," he says. "We can't pile Caldwell's dead on top of our own. Our people will see it as disrespectful—we have to make room."

"Just leave their dead," I say.

"And the evidence of our having killed them?" Jeremiah asks. "We can't."

When I speak Nikki realizes I'm here. She comes around Jeremiah. Her mouth hangs open in shock then closes into a clench. "Your face!"

"I wish everyone would stop saying that," I say and wonder just how bad my face really looks. It certainly burns like hell.

"Who did this?" Nikki asks.

"Why does that matter?" I ask.

"Because I want to know who to kill." Her words sound like a joke, but her face holds no humor.

I laugh and it sounds cynical even to me. "Get in line."

"Caldwell?" she asks, clearly surprised. "Why would he go after you himself?"

"To get to me," Jesse says, still pacing like a caged

animal. And she isn't giving Nikki a friendly look. She turns toward the night and screams into the cold, black air. "And it's fucking working!"

Nikki reaches out to touch me and something happens. The area around my body hardens, the shield back in place. Nikki is surprised and confused. And it takes me a minute to realize what's happening.

"Jesse," I say.

"I'm not doing anything," she says with an arched eyebrow, but she's stopped pacing, her mouth open a little in surprise.

The shield doesn't disappear until Nikki lowers her hand, clearly irritated. She turns back to Jeremiah. "Four vans to move 48 people. Then we're just going to have to pile them in."

"Put them in sitting positions," Jeremiah instructs. He's been strangely quiet and observant this entire time. His face is *too* emotionless for what he's just seen. I want to know what he's thinking, what assessments he is making about Jesse.

"You'll get people into each van," he says.

"No, you have to let me," Jesse says. I took my eyes off of Jesse for two seconds and now she is arguing with Gloria, kneeling in front of her.

"You were shot twice," Jesse says.

I come closer so I see the second wound. A small, oozing hole in Gloria's right shoulder.

"Don't be so stubborn. Let me help you," Jesse

says.

"You don't know that," Gloria says. "With what they did to me, I—"

"What are you talking about?" I ask.

Jesse looks up at me from where she crouches. "She thinks I can't replace her because of the magnetite in her brain. But she's an *idiot* if she thinks I'm just going to watch her die without even freaking trying."

"You can't replace someone with NRD and I suspect you can't replace me either," Gloria says.

"You're dying," Jesse argues. "I can feel it. You're bleeding to death."

I try to cover Julia's ears from all the swearing, but I'm certain it's pointless by now. But the child seems unresponsive, sucking her thumb with a glazed expression on her face. I won't be surprised if Julia is diagnosed with shock.

"You don't know that," Jesse counters, then turns on the medic, one of Jeremiah's, a short man with stiff dark hair and big biceps, examining Gloria's shoulder with gloved fingers.

The medic frowns at Gloria. "You have lost a lot of blood."

"I will still need medical attention, even if you replace me," Gloria says.

"We will ensure you receive medical care," Jeremiah says. "And we have transport coming."

Nikki's face lights as if remembering something. "Stetson is fixing the SUV so we can drive it back. But I don't know how we will get to it. We can't ride in transport. They are more than full."

The medic rips a piece of gauze tape, then looks up at us. "You can take my car, sir."

"Thank you," Jeremiah says. "You're a good man, Nate."

"What about the fire crews, the media, the police?" Gloria asks. Jesse dabs the sweat off her forehead with a piece of dressing the medic gives her.

One of Jeremiah's men tries for his attention. "You need to get out of here before they show up. Our local guys can talk, but we need your face off camera, boss."

"We don't need much more time," Jeremiah says. I catch Nikki looking at me, at my ruined face, before she looks away. Something warm is flowing into my eyes, and it's sticky. I have a good idea that it's blood, so I keep Julia close so she can't see my face. It is probably the stuff of nightmares for a kid like her.

Jeremiah reaches for the little girl and I pull back.

"No," I tell him. "I want to take her myself."

Jeremiah relents when another helper whose name I don't know runs up to him with a walkie talkie. "Depp needs to talk to you."

Nikki looks down at Jesse. "We loaded your boyfriend into transport. Do you want to ride with him?"

Jesse doesn't even respond to her.

"Go on," Gloria says.

"Not without you," Jesse says. And her eyes gleam with tears. "I can't."

Gloria's face pinches in a spasm of pain as she turns her head to look at me. "Brinkley?"

"He's dead." My chest tightens. "Caldwell."

"I'm going to kill him," Jesse says. "I'm going to make him *so* sorry."

Jeremiah cocks his head listening to something on the com. Then he meets my eyes. "We need to get into the transport now. All of us."

The medic and Jeremiah help Gloria up and Jesse stays close, unwilling to leave her side.

I turn away from the burning house and the wilting cornstalks, curling against the heat. I turn away from the dead bodies of Caldwell's soldiers and Jeremiah's own causalities. With a child in my arms, I turn and hobble through the darkness away from the sounds of sirens and the bright, blazing sky.

Jesse

"**I**'m going to kill him," I say. "I'm going to fucking kill him."

I have admit I'm starting to sound a bit like a broken record even to myself, but who is here to tell me shut up? Only Gabriel. And one of the benefits of having your own delusion is he can't complain much. He's as stuck with me as I am with him.

"He is very powerful," Gabriel says. He is stretched long on my bed, his wings tucked away, suit still impeccable. His shiny shoes are on my duvet, which would normally piss me off, if I didn't know they were fake feet or whatever.

"Then we will have to do it sooner rather than later," I say. "As soon as possible before he sucks up anymore super powers."

A soft knock comes at my door and I know who it is by the heavy irregular way the fist connects with the door.

"Yo," I say, as Lane eases it open slowly.

"Can I come in?" he asks, hesitating in the doorway.

"Don't be stupid," I say. I'm trying for casual but my heart is beating too hard. Not from my "down with Caldwell!" speech but because this is the first time I've seen Lane since Brinkley's real funeral, and he doesn't look happy to see me.

He comes into the room and closes the door. He looks good in his button up ocean blue shirt, his hair a little wet from the shower. I like the scruff he's growing and I'm about to say something inappropriate about rug burns when I see his face.

"Somebody die?" I ask.

"It's not that bad."

"Just kind of bad?" I ask, sinking onto the edge of my bed. Gabriel tucks his legs in and fades into the background. He doesn't disappear. The days of Gabriel disappearing are over I'm afraid. I've known it since I woke up from the coffin. I might have been able to forget him for years, and fight him off for another, but now—now that's over. At least, he's been doing this super polite fading thing when I talk to other people. I can still feel him, but he sort of smudges into my peripheral vision.

"Just yank the Band-Aid off," I say because Lane is taking too long. "I don't do slow pain."

He exhales and looks up to meet my eyes. "We need to take a break."

"You're breaking up with me?" I ask. My chest tightens and my throat feels like I stuffed a bunch of marshmallows down there. "Why? Because I let you die?"

"No." He runs his hands through his hair. "Well, sort of."

"Caldwell was beating the hell out of Al, if I didn't go—" I am pacing the floor again. I appear to have a hard time sitting still these days.

"No," he says, throwing his hand up to stop me. "No, I know. It's not about Ally."

"What the hell then? Am I supposed to stop everything I'm doing every time you die? Because people with NRD die *all* the time, dude. Get used to it."

"It's not that," he says, slipping his hands into his pockets.

"Then spit it out," I say. "Caldwell is still alive. I don't have telepathy skills."

"I am not sure I love you."

I take a step back.

"Let me explain," he adds, quickly.

"Uh, okay. Please explain in excruciating detail your reasons for not loving me."

His brow furrows. "It's not like that. Shit. Just let me talk okay?"

I throw my hands up again and gesture for him to continue.

"I respect you and I admire you," he says, which is the most bizarre direction I've ever heard a guy take off in for a breakup, but whatever. "But I don't think I love you the way Ally loves you."

"No one loves someone the same way, that's the stupidest idea," I say.

He takes his hands from his black slacks and holds them up in front me. "Let me finish."

"Go on then," I say.

"Ally has this really selfless love for you. She'll accept anything you throw at her. She'll stay by you and fight for you and if you give her shit, she'll just forgive you."

"You're making me sound bad."

"What I'm saying is," he presses on. "I'm mad at you for the dying thing. The first time when you chose to save Ally instead of me, it really hurt. And then again in Illinois, I was there all over again, even though I knew I would wake up and be fine."

"I don't get your point."

"My point is I wasn't scared for you!" he says. "In both those instances, as I was dying I was *mad* at you. I was jealous. I should've been scared for you. I should have been terrified that I was going to wake up and you would be *dead*."

I just stare at him for a long time unsure of what to say.

"If I was really in love with you, that's what I should have been feeling, but it wasn't. It's not what Ally would have felt."

"Stop comparing yourself to her. You're different people."

"I forced your hand last year for selfish reasons. And I'm breaking up with you now in hopes of fixing that."

"What about what I want?" I ask. "What if I find selfish dicks really hot? Like super attractive?"

His smile tightens and flattens out. "I tell you I don't think I love you and you aren't crying. You aren't heartbroken. Brinkley is—was—right. If I'm not 100% on your team then I'm a risk to your safety."

"What do you mean? Brinkley is dead. He can't say anything."

Lane shakes his head. "It doesn't matter." He comes closer and forces me to look up into his face. He wipes away a tear from the corner of my eye.

I shrug him away. "If you want to dump me, fine. But don't baby me afterward. I don't need your pity."

"No, you don't."

"Then why are you still here!" I say.

"I just want a break, Jess. It's not like I want to stop seeing you," he says. He slides his hands back into his pockets.

"You can't have both!" I say. "You can't dump me and want to see me."

"We just need time to think," he says. "And if we come together again, naturally, when we are both ready—"

"Come together—" I say, laughing, but it's malicious and snide. "What is this? A Beatles song?"

Lane backs toward the door and I almost stop him. I start moving forward without meaning to but stop myself. There's no way I'm begging him for anything.

"I'll call you," he says.

"Don't bother!" I yell at the door the moment after he shuts it. I feel stupid. I wish I could've come up with something better to say.

I hear a small scratching at the door and open it. Winston sits there in all his chubby glory. When I open the door wide enough he waddles into the room and takes the little doggie stairs up into my bed. Gabriel is solid again and the dog seems to sniff the air around him suspiciously, but sees nothing before curling into a ball on the fluffy duvet.

"What the hell was that about?" I ask Gabriel. "Can you believe that crap?"

"He's afraid Caldwell will use him to hurt you."

"That's stupid," I say. "The stupidest thing I've ever heard."

But I'm already thinking about that last motorcycle ride we took to watch the sunset. How beautiful it was and how totally naïve I'd been. I couldn't simply forget what was happening by running off with Lane. I was in this mess. It would follow me no matter where I went or who I dated.

By the time I sink down onto the bed beside Winston I'm crying, whole-heartedly. Gabriel opens his wings on either side and draws me into his arms.

"Do not be afraid," he says, softly into my ear before planting a warm kiss on my right cheek. "I am right here. I will be everything that you need."

Ally

I'm watching Jesse lounge on the back porch singing breakup songs at the top of her lungs when the doorbell rings. I open the door to find Gloria, manila envelope in hand and her arm in a black sling.

"Come in," I say and step out of the way.

"I can't stay. I have to get to the airport," she says.

"Where are you going?" I ask. But she doesn't answer me. Instead she gives me the envelope. "What's this?"

"Brinkley wanted me to give it to you," she says. "You're supposed to decide how much Jesse should know."

"Why?" I ask, peeling back the flap to see what is inside.

"She's unstable and it will only get worse."

"You said Gabriel was real," I say. "And we can't ignore her abilities. I don't know about you but I am inclined to believe after what I have seen."

"She will try to go after Caldwell," Gloria says and her brow furrows. "She isn't ready."

I find a letter, keys and a notebook inside the envelope, one of those black and white composition notebooks we used in elementary school. I look up at Gloria with questioning eyes.

"Read the letter," she says.

I peel back the topmost flap of the pristine white envelope and slip out the single sheet of paper. I know Brinkley's handwriting and my chest swells a little at his scratchy script.

"Alice—" I begin, reading the top.

"Just to yourself," Gloria says. "I don't need to know what it says."

Alice—

I asked Gloria to keep an eye on us. Be careful what you wish for, right? When she told me my own death day just a month after we got out of that godforsaken basement last year, it wasn't that I expected to live long. I'm a cynical old bastard and I always prepare for the worst.

But I can't say I wasn't surprised.

I want you to know I made preparations for Jesse. I talked to the few people I trust. Really trust—and I told them I was going to die and that when I did, Gloria would come to them with their own letters and requests. Everyone I asked has a good reason to fight, that's for damn sure. But I know people can be cowardly—so I am not sure how much help is on the way. I trust Gloria to make sure the information makes it right into their hands. But I only know one who will come for sure.

If I'm wrong and no one steps up, I want you to know that I trust you too. You've always had Jesse's interests at heart and I think that's the real thing that scares Caldwell. Not this sleuthing crap.

Don't let her forget who she is.

She's a good kid and the minute she forgets that, we've lost.

It's a hell of a hard thing to ask, but I know you're the best person for the job.

If you want to continue working with Jeremiah, know a couple of things—yeah I know, digging is unethical. Save your lectures for the living, kid.

Jeremiah has the money and connections that he has from his filthy rich wife, Tamara. From what I can tell, she gives him anything he asks for, which is fine and dandy until you realize she is a billionaire because her father built Develacor, the pharmaceutical company. Also, a problem if you know that Caldwell has invested a lot in Develacor, before and after Tamara replaced her father as CEO. I'm not saying Jeremiah is dirty. I'm just saying you need to question who offers you help and ask why they are so damn interested in helping. Everyone has their own agenda. That's rule #1.

You're smart. And I know you can be ruthless when it comes to Jesse. And it will be ruthless.

In the meantime, keep her head on. Keep yours on too. Read this journal and know there's more if you want it, just ask G for the rest. And the keys are to a deposit box in your name. G knows where. But with knowledge comes a hell of a burden. If you can get through the first journal and if you still want to know more—it's your choice.

I wish you both luck, kid. I'm sorry this was my stop but I've done all I can to make sure you receive help along the way.

I hope to God it's enough.

Brinkley

I turn the letter over though I know nothing is on the back. Only then do I fold it up and put it, the journal, and the keys back in the envelope.

I speak to Gloria who has patiently waited this whole time. Maybe making sure people read the letters is part of Brinkley's last request. "So you're flying off to deliver letters, I assume."

"Jeremiah offered me a job," Gloria says, adjusting her arm in the sling. Only a small shimmer of pain crossed her face.

"Are you going to take it?" I ask.

"It was a very good offer," she says. "And it would allow me to stay close."

"This is getting very dangerous," I say. "You took care of the AMP—"

"Micah," she says, correcting me.

"Micah," I agree. "If you want out of all this, now is a good time."

Gloria smiles and because it's a genuine smile, it is gorgeous. "Did Brinkley tell you how we met?"

"No," I say, amused. Amused as I can be anyway with allegations laid against Jeremiah and the journal heavy in my hand.

"I'll tell you sometime," she says, moving away from the house toward her new yellow Jeep. "But let's just say there's a reason we go way back. I'm no runner."

"Be careful," I call out, waving to her until she is safe in her car.

I slip the envelope into my bag by the front door. It isn't that I don't want Jesse to see it. I just want to look through it before I show it to her to better prepare myself for her reaction—whatever reaction that might be.

I check on Jesse who is lounging in her patio chair

with a snoozing Winston between her legs, her empty root beer mug beside her on the glass table. Her words fall away just as I appear.

"Gabriel?" I ask.

She sighs. "Is it weird? It's got to be weird for you."

"No," I say and place a hand on her knee. "You've always been pretty weird."

She smiles a sweet, genuine smile. "Yeah, I guess that's true."

"Though I could do without all this terrible breakup music," I say, reaching across her to turn down the volume. "The neighbors are sick of 'You'll Think Of Me' at this point."

"May I remind you that I was dumped yesterday? I'm *processing*," she says, thrusting her chin out. "I'm *releasing*. It's healthy."

"Lane is an immature idiot," I say. "I don't believe for a second that this was some magnanimous gesture."

"Who knows what he's thinking," Jesse says and lets out another deep sigh. "But you know what's great for sad people like me?"

"What?" I ask, but I'm already smiling. I know her too well not to see where this is going.

"Sex. Really hot lesbian *sex*." She bats her eyes at me and I feel something inside me soften.

"Jess—"

"Wifed up already," Jesse says. "That's my luck of course."

"I'm not your rebound."

"No, you're my best friend," she says. "Which is why the sex would be so good."

"If I didn't have a girlfriend."

"She's your girlfriend?" Jesse asks, brow furrowing.

"Not officially," I say.

Her face brightens. "So we could have sex—theoretically."

"Nikki and I could have sex *theoretically* if someone would quit cockblocking me." I'm getting angry again.

"I've never heard you say the word cockblock before. How crude," she says, but she's smiling. "And I don't know *what* you're talking about."

"Oh, I'm sure you don't."

Jesse turns toward someone I can't see. Gabriel I'm sure, who must be leaning against the deck banister, judging by her gaze. She smiles suddenly as if he's said something funny.

"Yeah, I can't control my shield. You can't blame me for your bedroom problems."

I'm about to argue that when a text buzzes on my phone.

Jeremiah: *All is good at Olivet's. Jesse can return whenever she likes.*

I forgot he was going to see Kirk today. In

exchange for rescuing her daughter and relocating them both safely, Regina helped us to flush out the person responsible for the brick threat. He was arrested and Regina spoke to the remainder of the congregation, urging them to leave Jesse alone. I'm not sure if they listened, or just getting rid of the harasser did the trick, but things have been quieter.

Jeremiah also fixed all of Jesse's electrical problems and the glass. In fact, he replaced all her glass with bulletproof glass and installed a state of the art security system. There are even motion sensors in every room.

"Jeremiah?" Jesse asks.

"Yeah," I say. "Kirk's place has been secured. You can go back anytime you like."

Jesse smiles. "Take that bitches! Nashville is mine!"

I can't help but smile.

"Can I have another root beer?" She asks, cuddling up to me.

I gently shove her off, playfully, but not before her ponytail brushes my cheek and I warm, soften.

No, I say. *You're not someone's rebound.*

"Don't push your luck. Just because you were tortured doesn't mean I'll let you torture me." I scoop up the empty mug.

"I would never." She grins. "Unless you asked me to."

In the kitchen I place the used mug in the dishwasher and take out a fresh mug from the freezer. Before I can find the bottle opener for the root beer, the security panel by the door gives a chirp. I look up and see the motion sensor blinking for Jesse's bedroom.

I rush to the back door to find Jesse out of her seat, talking to air again.

I throw the door open.

"Gabriel says Caldwell is in the house," she says.

"Should we call someone?" I ask. But already the shield around me is shimmering in the sunlight.

"He's gone?" Jesse asks the banister. "Are you sure?"

I look over my shoulder at the security panel and sure enough. It's no longer flashing red. All lights are green.

"We have to go look," I say. "Or if it is a bomb, we should have someone else go look."

"It's not a bomb," Jesse says.

"Are you sure?" I ask.

"Well, Gabriel is."

It takes me a moment to consider whether or not that is good enough for me.

Jesse and I—and I assume Gabriel—creep quietly through the house. Jesse brings Winston which I think is ridiculous given the circumstances until she explains there is no way she is leaving him alone with

Caldwell popping in and out of her house as he pleases.

"If he takes my dog I will *really* kill him," she says.

Jesse throws open the bedroom door and it slams against the wall behind it. "Whoops."

No one is inside.

"Are you sure? What if he's invisible?"

I don't respond because I know she isn't talking to me.

"He's not here?" I ask.

"Gabriel doesn't think so."

Then I see it. On the end of Jesse's bed is an envelope. At first I panic, thinking it's Brinkley's envelope.

The idea that Caldwell popped into the house, took it, emptied it and left it tauntingly at the end of Jesse's bed.

But when I get close I realize this envelope is bigger with different dimensions and much lighter. Jesse snatches it from my hands and opens it, shaking the contents out onto the bed.

Photographs. About a dozen photographs of me and Jesse. Jesse alone. Me alone. Jesse sleeping in her bed at night. Me sleeping in my bed with Nikki. I feel shaky.

"Why show us these?" I ask.

"He's threatening us," Jesse says. "He wants us to think nowhere is safe. That he can get as close as he wants to us and we'll never know it."

"He could just pop up behind me right now and kill me if he really wanted to," I say. I think of Brinkley, of the last moment I saw him alive. "Why pictures? Why the manipulation? He's messing with us."

Jesse puts her arms around me. She is so incredibly warm, but I'm still shaking.

"He's definitely a sick dude but it's more than that," she says.

Jesse lets go of me and lifts a photograph from the bed. She turns it over and shows me the message I missed at first glance. *Still closer than you think.*

"He threw the brick?" I ask.

"No, the writing is different," she says.

"I don't understand," I say. "Is he threatening you?"

She turns toward the empty air. Then nods. "Yeah, he's making me an offer."

"Why would he do that?" I ask but my heart is pounding with fear. It feels right. The message. The way he has held himself back. He could kill us at any moment. He could kill me now. But he hasn't— which means he has a reason not to. "Why?"

Jesse looks at me over the rim of the photograph, her grin sinister. "Because he can't do it without me."

ACKNOWLEDGMENTS

I would like to gratefully acknowledge my first readers, Kathrine Pendleton, Angela Roquet, Katharine Tighe, Sharon Stogner, G.R. Shelley, Carmela Gillette, Victoria Solomon, and Mandi Hooley Kaufmann—and others whom I've surely forgotten. (Sorry!) You guys were indispensable. All mistakes are my own.

Many thanks to family, friends, bloggers, and Twitter-ers who showed love for Dying for a Living and no less enthusiasm for this sequel. In particular, Kriss Morton, Rebecca Poole, Elizabeth Poole, Leslie Church, Shelly Burrows, and A.B. Shepherd—but there were many more. You rock my socks!

Thanks to John K. Addis for his help with the cover and author photo.

Thanks to The Four Horsemen of the Bookocalypse, my critique group, who continue to challenge and improve my writing every day. Let's ride!

And thank you Kimberly Benedicto. As if your laughter and patience weren't enough—*here you are, standing there, loving me/Whether or not you should/So somewhere in my youth or childhood/I must have done something good.*

ABOUT THE AUTHOR

Kory M. Shrum lives in Michigan with her partner Kim and a ferocious guard pug, Josephine. To learn more, connect with her on Facebook, Twitter, or her website: www.korymshrum.com

And if you like her work, she asks that you please support her by reviewing it, wherever possible.

Made in the USA
San Bernardino, CA
11 May 2016